HOSPITAL OF SECRETS

Dr. Keith Berrington found Nurse Charlotte Arrowsmith stumbling about in the darkness near the woods which belonged to her family. What had happened to her? Why were the neighbours gossiping? Dr. Berrington tries to help Charlotte, and soon realises he has fallen in love with her. But for Charlotte there was much heartache before she found happiness.

QUENNA TILBURY

HOSPITAL OF SECRETS

Complete and Unabridged

LINFORD
Leicester

First published 1971 by
Robert Hale Ltd., London

First Large Print Edition
published 1984

British Library CIP Data

Tilbury, Quenna
Hospital of secrets.—Large print ed.—(Linford romance library)
Rn: Emily Kathleen Walker
I. Title
823′.914[F] PR6073.A/

ISBN 0-7089-6022-7

Published by
F. A. Thorpe (Publishing) Ltd.
Anstey, Leicestershire
Printed and Bound in Great Britain

1

DR. KEITH BERRINGTON slowed down as he approached the spot where the best view of Rolborough could be had. He often drove up here after a long spell of duty, to look out through the break in the trees to where the land fell in a sharp precipice to reveal below a scene of incredible beauty. There were the stacks of the old factories like pale mauve fingers in this uncertain light of evening, their bursts of ugly black smoke gone for the time being, leaving the sky a washed out pink with little streaks of grey. A windy day tomorrow—so Lenny Quexford said—but old Granfer Trippick had taken him up sharply on it and pointed out that the weather in these hills couldn't be judged on the same merits as the weather in other parts of the country. Special, this district was, old Granfer Trippick always said.

Keith smiled to himself as he pictured his

patients. Those two wouldn't ever leave the hospital, and he sometimes thought they knew it. Lenny, a thin little man from the boiler section of one of these very factories which looked so innocent in the evening light, and old Granfer Trippick a night watchman further in the town. There was the town, all silvery of roof in the last rays of the sun, and there on the slope of the hill was the hospital. Never, Keith thought, looking keenly at it, did it stop looking sinister. A great grey hulking mass of buildings that would have been better as a prison.

He had thought that before, often, and he amazed himself to have such an unreasonable thought. Of course the hospital had a gaunt look; its appearance was a mark of the time when it had been built. It had the solidity of a Victorian railway station, and about as much beauty! But it had been modernized up to a point inside, and it did its work efficiently in this district where there was always a formidable waiting list and casualty figures which made the flesh creep at times. Only that morning there had been casualties from the caves beyond Carbey Hill, as a change from the usual pot-holing incidents. There had been a very odd explosion in an innocent-looking building where an old firm ran a quiet business in toy-making. A lorry out of control had run down St. Peter's Hill into the one Tudor building left in the town, and crushed it, bringing down part of the department store next door. And the boy who had been missing for four days had been brought in from the lake beyond Valentine's Cross.

Keith shook himself. It was time to go, if this place didn't cheer him up! He took one last look across the sleeping town to where the river could be seen, a silver sheet peeping slyly between the hills. Now the sky was losing its soft greyish pink and becoming uniformly grey. The trees whispered like voices as he started up the car again, and gently nosed his way round the bend in this quiet road, away from that edge where there had been enough incidents in the past, and downhill through dense packed woodland.

He was loathe to return to the town.

There was nothing to return for really. He had no social life these days. He supposed he was still missing Rosemary. It was on this stretch of road, driving down this hill, gently, slowly, drinking in the beauty of the evening, that she had said to him, "Let's not go on, Keith. It's not for us." So reasonably, so quietly. She was right, too. They had steadily been slipping apart, ever since Verrall had come to the hospital, and Rosemary had been honest enough to admit it. She had always seemed such a quiet girl, but she hadn't wanted to stay in Rolborough all her life. "I want to see the lovely places of the world, Keith, and you just want to stay here and keep up with this treadmill of yours, trying to heal all the sick, trying to put the world to rights. I can't do it! I can't!"

He pulled up again, in a layby. Now everything was dark, very dark, because dense woodland hemmed him in on both sides. He lit a cigarette with a hand that was shaking. He really mustn't come to this place any more. You couldn't keep on thinking of someone who had gone out of your life so reasonably, so quietly. You couldn't keep on tearing yourself apart because there was only yourself, and a life you had chosen, and you couldn't find anyone to share that life with you because it was so—what? Deadly? Grim? Non-sensical?

He threw the cigarette away after a few puffs, and it made an arc of light and lay burning in the tricksy little breeze, making now a brilliant red glowing spot, now a dullish red, as the breeze fed it and left it.

Suddenly there was a rustling in the trees and something came crashing through the undergrowth, seemed to mount the wire fence and toppled over, out on to the road. Near enough to his headlamps to look like a dark blue bundle, a large dark blue bundle with blurs of white . . .

He wrenched open the door, shot out of the car and hurried across to look. The bundle seemed to shake itself all over, and rose, swaying a little, and it resolved itself into a nurse in dark uniform that was uncomfortably familiar. She was from his own hospital.

"Good grief, what on earth are you doing

here, in this lonely place, by yourself, at this time of night? It's almost pitch dark!" he exploded, and turned her round, right into the headlamps' glare. "Why, it's . . . Nurse Arrowsmith, isn't it?"

"Oh, Dr. Berrington, I'm so glad it's you!" she said, and flopped against him.

He held her firmly, supporting her, and then suddenly she straightened up, laughing a little in embarrassed fashion. "Oh, what an awful thing to happen! I heard your car—I didn't know it was yours, I mean—I just ran to the fence, hoping to catch it before it went—"

"Can you walk? Then back to the car with you and take a nip of something I have in a flask—you're in a terrible state! I must get you back to Matron at once."

"No! No, it's nothing like that!" she gasped. "I just stayed out too long and then it was so quickly dark and . . . No, that story won't do, will it?"

She obediently took a sip of the flask and choked over the spirit, but she seemed less shaky now.

"No, I'm afraid it won't," he said

quietly. "Just what did happen in the woods there? You seemed terrified, the way you threw yourself over that fence!"

"I was," she admitted. She looked up into his craggy face; such a familiar face at the hospital, above his white coat. She knew it to be tanned because he was always out and about in the countryside all on his own, in all weathers, and she knew that those eyes, now such dark pools in the gloom of the car, were a brilliant blue, keen, but reassuring. Not a handsome face, but a very strong one, from its high brow, its large lean nose which somehow assumed an importance that other men's noses didn't, and the strong determined chin. He walked with importance, too, as though he were someone quite special but rarely remembered it—casually important. Now he was just a man in a turtle-necked sweater and a jacket, who presented the known, as against the unknown out there, and she wanted to lean against him, hard, and to be told by him that it was all right, and that this nightmare would soon end.

But of course that was wishful thinking.

The nightmare would never end, she believed, and anyway, Dr. Berrington—kindly as he might be to everyone in the hospital—couldn't be expected to feel anything special about one not very tall and not at all a handsome, second-year nurse who had been found tonight in such very odd circumstances. "Do you mind very much if we go away from this place?" she said urgently. "I feel as if eyes are watching me everywhere."

He nodded and drove on, slowly, and while he drove, she talked. "I had a message asking me to go to that neck of the woods," she said, choosing her words with care. "I went because it was light then, only the person who was to meet me didn't turn up, and it grew dark. You know how it slowly gets dark, and then when you're thinking, you suddenly come to yourself and realize how the time has flown."

He agreed, with reservations, but he kept quiet and let her talk.

"Well, I decided I couldn't wait any longer, so I started to go back to the road, only—well, this seems so stupid now but at the time it wasn't stupid, only scary—I got the idea that someone was following me and I somehow missed the way back to Gate Lane."

"Gate Lane. That will be where the bus stop is."

"That's right! At last I got out to where your car was, but by then I was sure I could hear running footsteps behind me, but I was equally sure it wasn't the person I'd gone there to meet."

"This person was—who?" he asked. He had to ask it.

She said collectedly, "My cousin. Derek Ferndale. It's our land, but I expect you know that. It still belongs to Ferndale House, though I can't think for how much longer. My uncle has been on the point of selling a lot of the land for ages, I believe, only there was some sort of complication and it didn't go through."

Now he remembered. The Ferndales had been friends of Rosemary. Friends of Verrall's, too. Merely because of that, a coolness against the Ferndales arose in him, that he was never quite able to lose, but for the moment he was silent. So silent that Charlotte Arrowsmith glanced nervously at him.

"I know you'll want to report this to Matron, but I wish you wouldn't. It's so important that I—oh, this is so difficult. You see, there's some trouble. I don't know what it is. I had hoped to find out tonight, only Derek didn't come."

"Might I ask, Nurse, why you can't call at Ferndale House in a civilized fashion, if these people are relatives of yours?"

She didn't miss the frigid note in his voice, but she dismissed it as normal. After all, as RMO it was his job to be concerned with the nurses. Well, concerned with their health, anyway, and if one of them got into a scrape in a wood after dark and had a breakdown or something, Matron would not mince her words to Dr. Berrington if she discovered he had known about it!

"Derek," she said desperately, "particularly didn't want Uncle George to know that he was going to tell me, well, what he had come to tell me."

"And you say Derek is your cousin."

"Yes, that's right." She didn't sound too happy about that, either. "I can't think what can have happened to him! When he says he'll meet me, he does!"

He had nothing to offer to that. She said desperately, "It's not a very convincing story, I know, but it's the truth. I wish you'd forget all about it. I promise I won't go to the woods again after dark. It was pretty silly."

"Then what will you do? I confess I'm rather in a fog with your explanation, but if you found it necessary to go there this time, why not another time? And who was it who scared you? A tramp? Your cousin playing tricks?"

That annoyed her. "No, Derek wouldn't play tricks on me! Goodness, he's the kindest person! Besides, he was too worried to play tricks! No, it might have been one of the lads from Ewbrook St. Peter. They're not supposed to go in our woods, but as we can't afford to keep all the boundaries in repair, it's difficult, and they don't do any harm out of reason—it's just courting."

The RMO's freezing silence didn't

encourage any more confidences on that score, so she plunged onwards, "And I couldn't possibly go to the house because I don't live there any more. I—well, it's all rather difficult, but the fact is that Uncle George married again and his second wife didn't think I ought to go and be a nurse. Or if I did want that sort of career, I ought to have gone to a big teaching hospital in London, and not the local one where the stable-boy's father is a patient, and the housemaid's sister is a ward maid. She's . . . sensitive about things like that, Uncle George's second wife!"

"Really!" Dr. Berrington said coldly. Charlotte couldn't know that he was thinking that this was the woman who had been such a particular friend of Rosemary and her mother. He just couldn't believe it.

"She's quite nice really," Charlotte offered. "I expect it's me that's all wrong. I'm a rebel. I usually prefer to go through the back way and have tea with the housekeeper rather than with Isabel. Well, the housekeeper's motherly. She gives me advice sometimes. I doubt if Isabel could—

she's not the advising sort, really." She glanced at his austere profile. "It's very kind of you, more than kind of you, sir, to give me this lift, and to—well, to not say you'd go to Matron is spite of everything—"

"I haven't decided about that yet," he said gruffly. "What I want from you, nurse, is an absolute promise not to go in those woods, or anywhere like it, after dark. Bless me, what's wrong with your cousin meeting you in Rolborough for a coffee or something, if you can't bear to go decently up to the house to speak to him?"

"I don't know," she confessed, and for a moment she sounded worried again. "Oh, well, I expect he'll telephone me to explain. Would you be kind enough to drop me in Duke Street instead of going right up to the Nurses' Home, and then—"

"Certainly not," he said frigidly. "Having extracted you from one situation which I didn't care for, I shall take particular care in seeing you go into the door of the Nurses' Home—or else I shall go to Matron."

Before the justice of that argument,

Charlotte had nothing to say. She thanked him civilly for the lift again when he pulled up outside the Nurses' Home, and shot out of his car and up the path as if the man (or whoever it was) in the woods, was still after her.

Dr. Berrington thoughtfully put his car away. But he was by no means convinced that he ought not to go to Matron. Something in that girl's voice when she begged him not to do so, bothered him. Something about the cousin.

Rosemary had said something about him. That was it! Now he knew why he didn't like any of that business. He sat down in his lonely room in Residents, and tried not to think about Rosemary, but to concentrate on Nurse Arrowsmith instead. He knew her perhaps better than the other nurses of her year because she was that sort of young woman. He had first become aware of her in her first week at the hospital. She had been the only Lamb on arrival to get lost, and that, she explained, when he had found her in the Residents' Car Park and taken her back, was simply because she was a local girl and felt she knew the hospital well enough to take a short cut.

His lips twitched as he recalled her as she had been then; a very vigorous young woman, so different from his lovely Rosemary, who had had soft blonde hair and quiet grey eyes. Charlotte Arrowsmith had black hair, strong short black hair that curled tightly at the ends, and waved all over and was not the sort of hair that a cap could be kept on securely for very long at a stretch. Her dark brown eyes were very expressive, he recalled, and they had been very indignant on that occasion because she had been so cocksure of herself and had been caught out.

On the second occasion, she must have had a briefing as to who he was. She had flushed red to the roots of her hair, and her eyes had been distinctly reproachful, as if she had felt it was his fault, to have been lurking about at a time when she could well have done with solitude in which to find her own way out of a tangle.

A tangle! Charlotte had always been in tangles, and it had seemed inevitable that he should be on hand to get her out of them, such as the night the boiler had burst, and she had been in the basement, using the way under the path. lab. to get into the Nurses' Home after hours. She had been out in the grounds, he recalled, the night of the big gale when those elms had come down and crushed the new shed that had been the cause of so much dissention among the outside staff. They had fought for a new one for months, years almost, and the first day it was erected, it was doomed. Charlotte had been out then, he recalled, and had managed to slip inside undetected, in the excitement of the fallen trees.

She had seemed to have a charmed life, and he shouldn't really have been surprised to find that she was the one who had come hurtling out of that wood tonight. But he hadn't been able to say so. If he had, and put it on a friendly basis by recalling her past scrapes, she might have relaxed and told him all about her troubles. But he couldn't do that, because there had been a long silence between them. He had ostentatiously avoided Charlotte, without quite realizing why. Now he wondered whether it hadn't been because he had lost Rosemary, and Rosemary had always expressed a cool manner towards Charlotte, and his half amused, half parental interest in a turbulent junior nurse. Now he asked himself, amazed that he hadn't seen it before, whether Rosemary had decided that because of that interest of his in Charlotte, they had better split up? Perhaps it wasn't so much because of Verrall after all!

He considered the matter, but finally decided that it couldn't have been that. No, Rosemary was already friendly with Verrall, and when he had gone to London, she had broken off with Keith, quietly, tidily, with dignity, too. No, it just must have been Verrall, and not Charlotte, the root cause.

Briefly he let the anguish of losing Rosemary wash over him, and when he came up out of it, he took time to think with some surprise, that it was a little strange he had never realized that Charlotte Arrowsmith was related to the Ferndales. Not that she talked about herself or her background.

Her impudent nose uptilting, her eyes sparking anger or dancing with fun, as the mood took her, she seemed to be wrapped up in her life at the hospital. She had such a lot of friends, and even authority looked half kindly on her scrapes because she was so good on the wards, and so much loved by the patients.

And now she'd got herself into some scrape with this young cousin of hers. He wondered what Derek Ferndale was like. He vaguely remembered George Ferndale as a man who seemed to have been welded into the saddle, he rode so naturally and well; a florid man who, when not in the saddle, was to be found in the Kings Arms at Ewbrook St. Peter. Not the type of man Keith Berrington cared about.

Charlotte was at that moment listening to her two best friends echoing those sentiments. Sylvia Ramley said, "My father wouldn't let me go to the dance at Ferndale House because of the way your uncle carries on," and Linda Keeble, whose home was in the Midlands and who knew very little of the district, could say with confidence, "I saw him, that day we walked through Ewbrook St. Peter on the way to Ogmarsh, and honestly, his eyes were the most blood-shot I'd ever seen in my life! He ought to be in here, if you ask me, Charlotte!"

"That isn't the point! Never mind my Uncle George's drinking habits. It's what else he's been up to that worries me. I mean, Derek isn't the sort to have secrets. He would normally have come on the telephone to tell me outright what was wrong, not sent me a note asking me to go to the woods! I can't get over that!"

"Look at his note again—it might have been someone else playing a joke on you," Sylvia advised. She hadn't liked the enterprise at all and had wanted to go with Charlotte.

Charlotte went to her bag and after a lot of rummaging found the note. It was typewritten.

"That doesn't help!" Sylvia said scornfully. "Might have been anyone!"

"No," Charlotte said. "It's typed on the old machine in the office at Ferndale House. I know it, because the 's' drops a bit. If you haven't enough ready cash to mend the roof of the stables, you're not likely to throw it about, having one of the letters of the typewriter re-set."

"Well, I think you should tell your cousin Derek to ring you up in future or you'll be in the muck," Linda said bluntly. "And another thing, all right, it was providential that one of the doctors had to be sitting there in his car at the time, but what I want to know is, how come it was the RMO and what was he doing there?"

Sylvia put in swiftly, "That's easy. They say he was jilted in that lane. I've heard a lot of people say he moons about the place a lot when he's feeling low. That sickly-looking staff-nurse—what was her name? Oh, yes, got it! Deane! Rosemary Deane! She chucked the RMO and went off with the gynae man of the time, What's His-Name? Oscar Verrall; There's a sinister name for a nice girl to take on for life. Rather her than me!"

"Oh, yes, Rosemary Deane. I'd forgotten all about her," Charlotte said, turning away. "Something Derek said about her once. Can't remember. Oh, I wish the silly clot hadn't made that appointment in the woods. What made me agree to go there? I shall tell him a few things next time I see him!" she said wrathfully.

But she didn't, because the next time she saw him, he was in no position to have anything said to him. He lay, sheet-white, in the end cubicle of Casualty. Charlotte had been sent for, and her heart had been drum-drumming with an unusual sense of disaster as she hurried down. She had only just realized that the man in the end bed on her ward, with the stomach wound that wouldn't heal, was not just any Yates, but Yates the father of Tom Yates, the stable boy at Ferndale House, and that had jolted her quite a bit.

Now, going into the end cubicle, because she couldn't see Sister Casualty anywhere, she saw Derek, and Bob Culver, the Casualty Officer, bending over him looking anxious, and Dr. Berrington, who as RMO had just admitted Derek. He was looking more grave than usual. Harris, the senior nurse, flicked her a look of sympathy, which was by no means usual, either. Harris usually had nothing but scorn for Charlotte's set, and Charlotte in particular.

"Derek!" she whispered. "What happened to him?"

Her legs felt shaky, and there was a roaring in her ears. Someone's strong hands (Dr. Berrington's?) grasped her by the elbows, and someone pushed a chair behind her knees and she found her head thrust down between them, and through the roaring in her ears, someone said Derek had been found shot, at the place where she had stumbled out of the woods last night.

2

AT the end of that dreadful day, Charlotte went to her two friends like a homing pigeon. They were waiting to hear all about it, with ill-concealed impatience, having been fed by so many stories on the grapevine, all different, that they were now consumed with curiosity about the real truth of the matter. "Who shot him?"

"I don't know!" Charlotte said, with what was for her a most peculiar helpless manner.

"Didn't he say?" Sylvia demanded. She was on the main ward, and the private wards down the corridor were outside even her best fabrications. She had tried to get in to see him but had failed. Nevertheless, a fleeting glance at the very sick Derek being brought down from theatre was enough to fill her with excitement and anticipation. "He's so gorgeous!"

"My cousin Derek? Don't be silly," Charlotte said, with the forthright manner of a first cousin who has been brought up with a young man as a brother. Derek had no more charms for her than her own brother could have had, had she had one. "But poor boy, he didn't deserve that. It's so queer!"

"What is? What *happened*?"

"If you mean, what happened to me, after I'd been sent for to Casualty, just about *everything*! You've no idea! I had to tell the story to the police and the press and my Uncle George and to Matron, and you'll never believe this but the RMO wouldn't say a word! Not a word! He didn't tell Matron he knew about last night and he just stared at me as if he'd never seen me before! How about that?"

"That's queer," Sylvia allowed. "But what happened? I mean, what's the outcome? What are the police going to do?"

"Nothing. Begin at the beginning," Charlotte muttered to herself. "Sit down, both of you, and ask me questions if you want to, because I'm in such a muddle and there's something I wanted to hang on to, in my mind, only so many people have been pestering me that it's slipped."

"Well, first of all, when you were sent to Casualty," Linda prompted, curling up on Sylvia's bed.

Charlotte pressed her fingers to her eyeballs. "Ugh! That was quite horrid. I just stared and stared. I've never seen our Derek look all white and knocked out before. He's a very coloured young man—usually red and brown, out of doors colours, you know, and he's usually spitting mad about something or worked up some way or other. Even when he laughs he goes red in the face. But he wasn't doing anything. Just lying there, the colour of white marble, you know?"

"Like dead," Linda said tactlessly, and received a huge kick from Sylvia. "Well, you know what I mean! Eyes closed and all that. Didn't he open them or say *anything*?"

"No, not then. Sister Casualty talked to me. I nearly fainted. I could have kicked myself, but it was the shock. It was the last thing I expected."

"And then?"

"Well, this is the odd part. He was whipped off up to theatre and I naturally thought it was a .38 bullet because most of the people at home have got that size. I don't know why. Only it wasn't—but first of all, Bob Culver (isn't he sweet?) leaned over and said to me, 'Lotta, don't say anything!' and the RMO gave him a look of loathing. Honestly! Then he turned it on to me. And I could have dropped with shock because he's always been so nice and kind to me."

Sylvia's eyes met Linda's. They had been talking about this before Charlotte returned. Linda said, "Why does the Casualty Officer call you Lotta?"

"They do at home, you know," Charlotte said, rather impatiently, forgetting that Linda, who was not a local girl, wouldn't know that. "Bob's been a guest at Ferndale House in the past. Not as a friend of Derek's so much as that his sister used to be friends with Isabel. That's my Uncle George's second wife."

Sylvia noted that the usually good-humoured Charlotte was makin[illegible] weather of having to explain all th[illegible] to Linda. Charlotte had dark [illegible] under her eyes, too. She had taken a beating. Sylvia wondered whether she was as casual about her cousin Derek as she pretended.

"Didn't the RMO say anything about last night, just to you, I mean, when the others weren't near?" Sylvia asked. It was the thing she wanted to know most.

"No, but first of all, I had to tell the police about it, and they asked some quite peculiar questions, I don't mind telling you. Things like who was likely to be in the woods at that time who had the right to be there. What do you make of that?"

Sylvia and Linda exchanged looks again but shook their heads, so Charlotte continued, "And all the time I wanted to know how Derek was getting on, but I had to go and repeat it all again to the press (and I didn't tell them much, you can bet!) and to Matron and to Sister Tut and Sir Ralph stopped me—can you imagine?—and said he knew Derek and it was a pity he hadn't one any more about making up his mind to come here to study. Honestly, I never knew my cousin Derek had ever thought of going into medicine!"

It wasn't all. Charlotte was keeping something back, they could see. It wasn't like Charlotte. Sylvia said awkwardly, "Yes, but did Matron seem to know anything about last night?"

"That's the odd thing about it. She didn't, and to judge by the way the RMO was looking so frostily at me, I was sure he would have gone back on his word and told her. The thing is, I didn't tell the police about it and I didn't tell them why Derek had asked me to meet him. I pretended I didn't know why he wanted to have such a secret rendezvous. Have I done wrong, do you suppose?"

Linda said, bluntly, "Of course you have, you mutt! Now you'll never be able to say why you went to meet him, no matter what comes out."

"I somehow don't think it will matter," Charlotte said, in a queer hushed voice. "Because my Uncle George turned up, sober and decently dressed, for once. He'd been sent for, and he seemed to think Derek wouldn't 'do' and he said that as if it was something shady Derek had done and as he might not recover, no one, but no one, was to know anything about anything."

She choked on the last words, and looked blankly at the other two, as if it was now beyond her reasoning. "Derek never did a shady thing in his life," she whispered.

Sylvia went down the passage and came back with a flask of hot tea that someone had made, and one of their neighbours brought a packet of sweet biscuits and an apple apiece, and another one brought chocolate. Each one stayed to ask what had been going on, delivered her offering, and also her bit of gossip she had picked up. The gossip was wild and wonderful. Derek was held to have been selling secrets to a foreign power, having an affaire with an actress whose husband was liable to be trigger happy when jealous, and up to the ears in debt. All these stories were delivered with convincing details.

"Who could have started them?" Charlotte could only gasp. "It isn't like Derek at all! He was worried about something that was going on at home!"

"The thing is, is he going to 'do', Charlotte?"

"I don't know," she said hopelessly. She wandered over to the window. "Isn't it funny? The day's gone, and all I've done is to keep seeing people and telling the same story over and over, and it doesn't mean anything any more, because I know he must have gone to the woods to meet me, just as he arranged, and I know he wasn't there. I searched, everywhere. I know those woods. And I know it wasn't Derek coming after me. Was he shot already then? No, he couldn't have been, or else I'd have heard it. Well, I don't know. Yes, he must have been. It must have happened well before I got there. Then why didn't I fall over him? And whoever it was who was coming after me, must have shot him, but why leave it so long? He must have seen me waiting because it wasn't dark then! And why didn't I see Derek lying somewhere? If that boy from the village who found him could have seen Derek, why couldn't I?"

She was talking to herself. Sylvia moved restively. "Eat some chocolate and have a drink. We're all on in ten minutes, unless you've been excused, Charlotte?"

"What? No—No, I haven't. Matron said it would give me something to think about, keep my mind off it. Anyway, she's hoping Derek will say something to me the minute he comes round. It wasn't one of our bullets—it was an Army pistol, not one of ours at all, so who could have done it?"

Sylvia thought, she isn't mentioning the RMO any more than she has to. Linda, who never kept her thoughts to herself because she couldn't, blurted out, "You know why the RMO looked at you with such loathing, don't you?"

Charlotte looked surprised. Sylvia said, "Shut up, Linda!" so Linda didn't say what she meant, but went scarlet and shot out of the room.

"Don't take any notice of her. She's heard some more rumours," Sylvia said hastily. "She means well. She likes you an awful lot, but she just can't keep her tongue still."

Charlotte nodded absently. She ate a little, drank a little, changed her apron and tidied herself, and went down to the wards again. Sylvia went with her. They were on the same ward. Linda, who was in the women's section, had gone on ahead.

It was a visiting afternoon. As they pinned back the doors for the stream of men and women to come in, Charlotte thought of her uncle and the way he had looked at her. Absently she saw familiar faces in the crowd, without actively identifying them. One or two of the servants from Ferndale House, one or two people from local shops, and a girl with an over-made-up face and very blonde hair and such startling clothes that everyone was looking at her, a fact that seemed to please her very much. Tom Yates, out of the Ferndale stables, even let out a soft wolf whistle as she went by. Charlotte watched her. She stopped at Granfer Trippick's side. So this, then, was his darling grand-daughter Jill. Poor old man!

As Charlotte went down the ward to collect food and flowers the visitors had brought, the old man called her over. Bristling with pride, he said, "There you are, nurse! My little pet! Isn't she everything I told you she was, isn't she, isn't she, eh? It fair makes me proud to see her come on the ward."

Jill said, "Oh, Granddad, don't be soppy!" and batted her false eye lashes very quickly and glanced at Charlotte. Charlotte looked at the old man and nodded her head, vigorously.

"Everything," she agreed, because that way she didn't have to echo the different points he had made about his granddaughter from time to time. Charlotte privately thought, with a sense of shock, that without all that make-up, Jill Trippick would be just a pallid washed-out, pinch-faced little girl from the back streets of Rolborough, with nothing at all to recommend her.

Granfer Trippick went on, his claw-like old hands closing over the young plump white one with its painted nails, "She's just like her mother, she is. (My daugher, my Susan.) Aye, she was a pretty one, she was. All the boys were after her. But she chose a chap her own age, not like little Jill. Eh, love? A chap your own age is best, you know," he said anxiously, transferring his attention to his grand-daughter.

For an instant the smile slipped on her young face, and anger lit her eyes; sharp, mean anger. She didn't like her grandfather to tell her that in front of the nurse.

Charlotte said brightly, "I'll just put these flowers in water for you. Aren't they lovely? And you are not to worry—I'm sure Jill knows what she's doing, and wouldn't make you unhappy for worlds!"

Jill seemed undecided whether to look gratified or merely mulish, and finally it was a queer mixture of the two emotions on the face she turned to Charlotte.

It was queer, Charlotte felt, going down that ward now. Yates, who had previously been, in her mind, just Bed 14, the recovering duodenal ulcer, was not the father of Tom, the boy who had held her horse for her since the big roan had been bought and given them so much trouble. And beside the bed of the recovering broken hip was Mrs. Overton, the comfortable person who had sold wools and embroidery silks to the nurses since Charlotte had first come to the hospital—occasionally turning round to talk to Brenda Newey, the second housemaid at Ferndale House, who now appeared to be the sister-in-law of Bed No. 4 who had come in from a car smash with multiple injuries but who was the most cheerful man on the ward. His lorry had been a write-off and he had lost his job because he had been drinking, but he had been a pleasure to look after.

And now the intensely personal had crept in. Isabel had been right, of course. Charlotte should have gone to a hospital in London. But Isabel had that way of saying things to upset Charlotte. It had been out of the question to do what Isabel had wanted. In any case, it was doubtful if her Uncle George would have agreed to Charlotte going to London to live and work while she was under age. Charlotte had never been quite sure of the reason for this. It had something to do with Derek, and there were times when Charlotte felt that her uncle believed that she and Derek were going to make a match of it. Such a ludicrous idea as that, floored Charlotte. They had racketed around together, she and Derek, since they had been in their prams almost, and people like that never teamed up together.

On the way back with the vase of flowers for Granfer Trippick, Mrs. Overton plucked at Charlotte's apron and said, "It's all right, duck, about that grey wool you was asking for. I got it—it come in this morning! I'd have brought it if I hadn't of forgotten, me head being so thick nowadays!"

Charlotte thanked her, and then the multiple injuries man knocked his jug of water all over himself and Charlotte had to put screens round and change him.

Brenda Newey sat by the man in the next bed until Charlotte had finished. "It's ever so funny, me seeing you doing all that clearing up and me sitting here quite the lady," she giggled.

"Ah, well, that's the way it is," Charlotte said briskly. And felt she could cheerfully have wrung Brenda's neck. Brenda was only at Ferndale House by courtesy of old Aunt Elizabeth Ferndale, whose money kept them going. Everyone else among their friends and neighbours had had to cut down drastically on indoor staff, clinging on to the outdoor people as by necessity.

When Charlotte left the ward again, all the gifts had been disposed of, and all the flowers put in water. There was the dank smell of flowers, the sharp tang of raw fruit, the acrid odour of an orange being consumed nearby. The staccato notes of one high voice among the visitors' rumbling tones, and the rustle of paper—a typical visiting day with its noises and its impressions. But it was different somehow, in a way that Charlotte couldn't define and somehow didn't like. There was a sinister sensation, and it heightened when she saw the man looking at her.

He was just a man; not too well dressed, not too anything, really. The sort of man one wouldn't recognize again, he was so ordinary. And yet the look he bent upon Charlotte was no ordinary look.

She said, "What do you want? Visitors are in there—it's almost over, anyway, the visiting hour."

"It's all right," he said, in a purring voice she loathed. "I just came out for a spell," he said vaguely, and turned in to the ward again.

She watched him, and he went and sat by No. 3, who never had visitors. Yet the chair was by the side of the bed, so someone must have been there, and although No. 3, had his eyes closed and his head phones on, that may only have been while his visitor was out of the ward. Charlotte had half a mind to go across and speak to No. 3, perhaps find out who this visitor was, and why his appearance had so far been so tardy. But nothing came of her good intention, because a girl was hovering about in the passage, so Charlotte went back and spoke to her.

She looked a nice quiet girl, rather upset. A visitor, a first-time visitor. Charlotte was always sorry for the people the first time they came here. They didn't know what to expect and the stark white cleanness and sterile tidiness of the place intimidated them, until the first visit was over.

She went over to the girl. "Who did you want to see?" she asked kindly.

"A friend of mine. He was shot in the woods," the girl said anxiously. "His name is Ferndale. Derek Ferndale."

There was no permission for anyone to see Derek, except close relatives. Derek's father had been, but even Charlotte herself hadn't been allowed to see him, so Charlotte took the girl to see the ward sister. She said her name was Fay Iverbury and her pathetic dark eyes behind the brown-framed spectacles lit as Sister St. John took her into her office. That was the last Charlotte saw of her that day.

The visiting hour was almost over, and when the bell went there would be a stampede. Charlotte went to see if the juniors had got the bread and butter all ready and the urn of tea made. One junior unfailingly put too much tea in, and the other made fawn coloured water and cried over it. It was no different today. Charlotte spoke sharply to the one and comforted the other as always, and speeded them on their way with the tea round. Mr. Overton was looking rather spent, as he always did after his visitors had gone. Brenda Newey's brother-in-law was looking eagerly, bright eyes inquisitive, raking Charlotte as she passed. It was odd, since he usually talked so much, doing his daily stint cheering up everyone else. And Yates stared, too, with an odd calculating look that was frankly unsettling.

Charlotte came at last to No. 3. "You had a visitor today, then!" she said, smiling. "Feel brighter now?"

He smiled uncertainly, put off his headphones and invited her to repeat what she had just said.

Charlotte obligingly repeated it. He looked oddly at her, and said quite clearly, "I didn't have a visitor, nurse. You know I never have any visitors!" and he looked rather reproachful, as if he suspected her of teasing him about his lonely state.

"I'm sorry," she said, at once. "I understood—but yes, he came and sat down beside you here! Here's the chair!"

"He? I wondered what that chair was doing there, nurse, but I assure you, no one has been to visit me!"

The man next to him was too ill to take much notice of anything, but the older man in the far bed said, leaning over, "Came and sat right beside you! Saw him myself! Wondered what was going on. Thought he might be a probation officer or something—you know, doing his good deed for the day. Well, I know *you* never have no one come, don't I?"

"Did he say anything, Mr. Clark?" Charlotte asked him, but the older man said, "Not a thing. Just sets, that's why I think to meself, it's just someone doing his good deed. Anyway, *he* didn't give no one a chance to talk to him," he said, pointing in good-natured derision at No. 3. "Got his eyes shut, a-listening to that highbrow stuff he always listens to!"

"But it's impossible!" Charlotte said blankly. "You both mean a man came and sat by you, and you don't know who he was, or why he had come? He just came in, sat by you, and went, without speaking?"

"No, I'm not," No. 3 said firmly. "I'm not saying a thing, on account of it was such a dreary programme I was listening to with me eyes shut, that I dozed off. Lot of clacking old hens in the ward, anyway. Give me the headache they do, so I always drop off if I can, and having my headphones on tips the wink to people (well, *most* people) that they're not welcome!"

"So you didn't even know you had a visitor all the time!"

"No, now wait a bit, nurse," his neighbour put in anxiously. "Let's get it right. He went down the ward first, looking as if he was lost—couldn't find the one he wanted. Then he went to No. 14, and said a few things, and then he pushed off and spoke to No. 22, and come on here afterwards."

"He should have told me what he wanted!" Charlotte fumed. This was the one thing the ward sister didn't like. "I found him outside, wandering about and I asked him what he wanted but all he would say was that he came out for some fresh air."

"Cheeky!" Mr. Clark's neighbour observed. But beyond that he had no more interest. He got on with his tea.

Charlotte began to go down the ward to No. 14, when she suddenly recollected who he was, and changed her mind. Yesterday she might have gone and asked him a question, pleasantly, casually. Today, however, she had no mind to, for today he was the father of Tom Yates, who worked in the stables at home.

In desperation Charlotte spoke to Sylvia about it. It was amazing what conversations they could hold, passing each other with bowls of hot water or when pushing the trolley for doing double backs. The cryptic remarks they threw at each other during the making of a patient's bed defied any patient to know what they were talking about. In this way Charlotte put it to Sylvia that there had been someone in the ward who had had no business to be there, unless he had called to see Yates.

Sylvia had seen the man. "I honestly

thought he knew who he wanted, the way he looked at her," Sylvia said with a grin, and it didn't take much of mental gymnastics to realize that Sylvia was referring to Granfer Trippick's colourful granddaughter.

"Don't let You-know-who hear you say that," Charlotte warned abstractedly, and let her attention wander to the two juniors who were standing over the old man himself, both of them looking rather puzzled.

Sylvia followed her glance and said in resignation: "Oh, no, they're at it again! Wouldn't you think they could manage to get something right for just once?" and she went briskly down the ward to them. Before she returned to resume the conversation, Charlotte had been called away by Sister St. John, to go into her office. She looked worried.

"Nurse, there has been something rather odd happening," and she didn't seem to know how to resume for the moment. "That girl you brought to me."

"Yes, Sister?"

"Tell me again about her. Every little

thing you can think of. Where you first saw her."

Charlotte wrinkled her brow and tried to remember. "She was looking lost and rather upset, I thought. She said she wanted to see a friend of hers who had been shot in the woods. Well, there was only my cousin who fitted that description. Oh, yes, and she said his name, and it was my cousin. She said quite clearly, 'Derek Ferndale'. And she gave her own name without hesitation, as Fay Iverbury."

"I see. You're sure she said just that and nothing else?"

"Yes, Sister, quite sure. That's why I brought her to you because I knew he still wasn't allowed visitors outside the family."

"Up till then, no. You haven't been allowed to see him yourself yet, have you?" Sister St. John said, looking shrewdly at Charlotte. "I think perhaps it might be of use if you were to go and sit by him, and have a word with him when he opens his eyes. He says things quite lucidly sometimes, and then he slips away. He might say something which you can make something of."

"She did . . . visit him, Sister?" Charlotte was surprised.

"Well, yes, because of two things. She said she was to have married him last week but something happened to prevent it."

"Marry him!" Charlotte ejaculated.

"Yes. Is that news to you? Well, the other thing was that your cousin had been muttering something that sounded like 'Fay' in his delirium."

Charlotte's astonishment was unfeigned. "He *did*?"

"Yes, and yet when he saw her," Sister began, but didn't finish that. "Well, go and see him for yourself, and tell me what your impression is. You must know him better than anyone else, I think!"

Charlotte went with her to Derek's room and released the nurse who was sitting by him. It was clear that Sister St. John wasn't going to be very far away, although after taking Charlotte up to the bedside and finding Derek's eyes were open, and saying gently, "Mr. Ferndale, here is your cousin to see you," she did back away to the door. But Charlotte knew she hadn't gone. She was standing just behind the screen.

Derek looked up at Charlotte with hot feverish eyes.

"Lotta?" he murmured at last, though the recognition seemed to be only fleeting.

"Hello, Derek," she murmured and held on to his hand.

He moved his head restlessly, but when he felt her hand close over his, he turned suddenly to her, and his eyes were clear and comprehending. "Why didn't you meet me in the woods?"

She hadn't expected that. It took her off balance. She absently pushed his tangled hair back off his forehead while she thought that one over. How could she explain to him, here and now, that she had waited until it grew dark and that someone had pursued her and scared her badly, and that she had finally run, tumbling over the boundary of the woods, almost into the arms of Dr. Berrington? There wasn't time for all that explanation now, and anyway, Derek might not be ready to face the thought of that painful event in the woods. To worry him unduly would be disastrous.

Besides, what had happened to him? Who had shot him? Who, Charlotte asked herself frantically, had come after her like that, chasing her so relentlessly that she had been almost numb with terror by the time she had sighted Dr. Berrington's car?

An answer wasn't necessary, however. Derek had closed his eyes again and his hand had gone slack. Charlotte waited for Sister to reappear and carry her off again, but she didn't. It was so quiet in there. Derek's hair lay tumbled on the pillow. Wild, curly on top, too short at the back and sides; very Derek-ish, just that little bit different from anyone else, and he looked so vulnerable somehow. Such a little boy.

But he wasn't, Charlotte reminded herself sharply. He was a man; older than herself by a good three years. Old enough to intrigue and make secret meetings in the wood, old enough to get himself shot at by a baleful enemy, old enough to have arranged a secret marriage with that girl, that Fay Iverbury!

Derek opened his eyes again. "Got to see Fay," he muttered. "Fay, Fay—that's the name! Fay! Where is she? Find her, Charlotte. Must see her."

Charlotte opened her mouth to murmur encouragingly that Fay had already been to see him, when he said, quite incomprehensibly, "Who is she? Do you know, Lotta? Do you know anyone called Fay?"

He's wandering, Charlotte thought, with a little flutter of apprehension. Sister moved out from behind the screen. Listening to every word, hanging on the conversation, gathering scraps to help them. Charlotte willed herself not to look behind her, so that Derek shouldn't see that Sister was still there. At the moment his burning eyes were on Charlotte's own, as if trying to pierce the veil and look into her mind for the answer to that riddle.

Charlotte said steadily, "I don't know her, Derek, but I thought you did. Fay Iverbury, isn't her name?"

"Who *is* she?" he asked again.

"Someone you like? Rather a lot?" she suggested.

"No. No. Don't know her." He strove to think, so she patted his hand and said, "Don't bother now. I'll come and see you again, shall I?"

"No! Don't go!" It wasn't like his voice at all, it was so faint and panic-filled.

She said, "All right, I'll stay a little longer. But don't you really remember her? She came in here—such a pretty little thing. Great dark eyes. Very unhappy about you." To help remind him, Charlotte added, "Dressed in red."

"Her?" He tried to concentrate. "What are we talking about *her* for? Who let her in? *I* don't know her! She upset me. She kept asking me . . . things . . ." Sweat stood out on his brow. Charlotte hastily wiped it, and stood up to go, but still Sister St. John wasn't signalling to her. Charlotte could now see the RMO just behind her. They both wanted her to stay.

She sighed, and settled herself again in the chair, and tried to look relaxed, but she wanted to weep. It was so strange to see Derek lying like this, so ill and helpless. He was the vigorous one, the one who scorned sickness and weakness in any form. She took his hand again, squeezing it comfortingly, in her own two, and said softly, "Don't worry, Derek. Darling, when weren't you able to manage a pretty girl, for goodness sake!" and she laughed softly.

His eyes again burned into hers, but he wasn't really listening or thinking about that girl now. "Things about Uncle George," he muttered. "She said things about him."

Uncle George. Yes, it had been about him that Derek had in the first place wanted to see Charlotte herself in the woods. Impulsively she leaned over him.

"I know, old chap, but then you wanted to tell me about Uncle George, too. When you're feeling better, I shall want you to tell me what you called me to the woods for. I did wait for you, but you didn't turn up, you know."

"I didn't? Where was I, then?" He rolled his head from side to side, impatient that he couldn't remember. "Lotta, Uncle George—something bad's happening at home!" he managed.

He wanted to tell her, so much, so she sat very still, inviting him by her silence, to talk.

"He's . . . being blackmailed . . . do you understand?" he whispered fiercely. "I overheard something," he added.

He lay there panting with the effort, imploring her with his eyes to say something, but she couldn't. She sat stunned. That there was something very odd going on at Ferndale House, she was prepared to admit, but this sort of thing? She couldn't believe it. Uncle George was not the ideal neighbour, and he was no one's friend; he drank too much, he was rude and overbearing, he used people as he willed, and you couldn't rely on him to be in the same mood twice running. There were people who said he loved horses better than people, and he drank too much, and ran into debt and had to be baled out by old Aunt Elizabeth but . . . was any of this cause for blackmail?

"It can't be!" Charlotte murmured.

"It is so. I heard something," Derek said again.

"But what?" she asked blankly. "For

heaven's sake what could you have heard to make you think such a thing?"

Derek's thoughts were wandering again. He could only roll his head from side to side, and feverishly pluck the sheet.

"Well, never mind now," Charlotte whispered.

She was more shaken than she realized. What *was* going on at Ferndale House? Uncle George and his sudden quick rages that turned him purple in the face; Isabel with her queer secret little smiles, as if she knew that something was going on and no one could do a thing about it; rich Aunt Elizabeth, who was financially carrying them all on her shoulders, and scorned them all, Charlotte believed—every one of them; Miriam, George's step-sister, with her unpredictable moods and her sudden swooping visits to Ferndale House which upset everyone. Where, among those people, lay the answer? And how could Charlotte get it, to relieve Derek's mind and give him a chance to recover?

Derek appeared to be fast sinking back into that twilight sleep that had claimed him for so many hours since the accident, when suddenly he jerked his eyes open again and asked clearly, so that the two at the door couldn't help hearing, the thing that was worrying him most: "That girl who came in here—Lotta, who *is* she?"

3

SISTER ST. JOHN questioned Charlotte so closely about that conversation with Derek, that Charlotte left her at last with her head reeling. The RMO had been in Sister's Office with them, and under his close scrutiny of her, Charlotte had felt unaccountably shaken.

All the young nurses were just a little afraid of him, and yet at times he could be so kind and understanding. Now those keen eyes of his were distinctly chilling. He thought she was up to no good, she told herself. But then why shouldn't he think that? He, and he alone, knew about her visit to the woods that night.

Unfortunately Sister St. John had heard enough of Derek's conversation to want to know about that, and Charlotte hadn't known how to answer, so she had contented herself with saying: "He had sent a message for me to meet him on our own land, Sister, so I went, but he wasn't there. I'm afraid that as a family we are not very united, and it would have been less peaceful if I'd gone up to the house in the normal way. He knew that, and he didn't want to make any more trouble. I know he's worried about something but I never did find out what it was."

"And this young woman who persuaded me to let her visit him—are you sure you have no idea who she is—in relation to your cousin and his health and peace of mind, that is!" but to that Charlotte could only shake her head.

Sister St. John turned to the RMO, clearly indicating that it was his turn to do some questioning. But he found it distinctly hampering that she should stay there, because Charlotte, he was sure, had the key to the mystery and probably couldn't betray it. Certainly not in front of Sister St. John, not without admitting the scene that had taken place between the RMO and Charlotte, at the woods in the darkness. Sister St. John wouldn't care for that story at all!

He said mildly, "Could you cast your

mind back a year or two, nurse, in case this has its roots in an earlier period? It would be a great help if you could, for it seems to me that this young woman is put out because he doesn't remember who she is, and he is equally put out about something which he apparently feels you should be well aware of."

It wasn't quite what he had wanted to say, but he could find no other way of putting it without demanding to talk to Charlotte alone. Sister St. John wasn't going to leave them to talk this out between them, either. She was much too intrigued to go away just at present.

Charlotte answered carefully, "I haven't seen my cousin all that much in the last year or two, since he has been away from home, and I have been living in the Nurses' Home, you understand. I couldn't really say who his friends are, or how many new friends he has made out of the district." And with that, they had to be content.

Charlotte was allowed to go, with instructions not to go too far away, but to her there was only one thing to do now. If Uncle

George's activities were worrying Derek, then clearly Charlotte must approach Uncle George about it. Much as she loathed the idea, that seemed to be the one sensible way out.

She telephoned to Ferndale House to make sure he would be in, and of course got Isabel on the telephone. Charlotte smothered her irritation and asked in a reasonable voice if she could speak to Uncle George.

Isabel asked at once: "What about?"

Charlotte hesitated. If she said the ward sister had asked for information, Isabel would offer to give it. If she told Isabel the RMO wanted some information, Isabel would still insist on getting it to pass it on to the RMO herself. Isabel was like that.

While Charlotte was thinking over what she should say, another voice near at Isabel's hand asked coldly, "Who is it?" Miriam's voice. So Miriam was at home again! That posed a problem Charlotte would have liked more time to think over.

Isabel said sharply, forgetting to cover the receiver, "Something concerning me, dear, not you!" Isabel always called Miriam "dear" in that tone.

Miriam said clearly, "Well, I don't advise you to take any more calls for my brother George. He doesn't appreciate your zeal, and he'll be back at two himself, anyway."

Whether it was intended to give information to the person at the other end of the line, or merely to irritate Isabel, Charlotte didn't know, but it did give her the information she needed. Uncle George would be returning at two.

Isabel said sharply, "He's only your stepbrother, dear, but he happens to be my husband and—"

Charlotte quietly replaced the receiver, leaving them to fight out an old bone of contention, and decided to go back to Ferndale House and wait about the grounds in order to intercept her uncle on his return.

George Ferndale was not in a good mood. He rode back on that frisky bay mare he had recently bought. He was too heavy a mount, and she tried every day to throw him, unsuccessfully. He looked angry as he dismounted, and eyed Charlotte in her hospital uniform, with misgivings. "Oh? What is it, then? Derek worse?"

"I wanted to talk to you, Uncle, alone if I could!" she said quickly. "No, he isn't worse, but it does concern him. I did telephone first, but Isabel wanted to help me and she can't!"

"Why can't she?" drawled Isabel's voice, behind her. Isabel stood there, a mocking smile on her thin lips. This was Isabel's worst trait, this wanting to be in on everything; her inquisitive nose had earned her more dislike in the family than anything else about her.

Charlotte said evenly, determined to keep patient with her, "Because it concerns the time before you even knew us, Isabel. That's all! And it's in Derek's interest that I must have the information."

"Before my time, eh?" Isabel said sharply. "Well, then, we'd better all go in to my sitting-room and discuss it, because I'm pretty sure I ought to know about it."

She turned to lead the way, but George

Ferndale hesitated. "What's it about?" he snapped, in an undertone that wasn't intended for the ears of his second wife at all.

Charlotte, on inspiration, murmured experimentally, "Fay Iverbury?" and was rewarded by her uncle's puce complexion changing colour. Unwittingly she had scored a mark on a subject she wouldn't have dreamed of touching, if she could have talked to her uncle reasonably and quietly.

He didn't like shock tactics from anyone, but he said, "All right. Let's walk," and he threw the reins to the stableman who had hurried out on hearing his return.

He led Charlotte up to Upper Old Meadow, where, she suspected, he felt reasonably safe from Isabel's snooping. She could hardly get close to them without him knowing, with the breadth of what was now barren land all around them. They stood at last, leaning on the last good stretch of boundary fencing, while George Ferndale considered his niece.

"Do you really know someone called Fay Iverbury, or is it just a name you came across and you're using it to get out of me what you want to know?"

Charlotte shook her head. "A girl came to the hospital by that name and she was allowed to see Derek because of what she told the ward sister, only—and this is the odd part—he keeps saying he wants to see Fay Iverbury but he doesn't seem to know who that girl was who came."

"What a lot of rot!" her uncle said.

"Well, there it is. He's getting awfully worked up because he keeps asking to see Fay Iverbury and when they tell him she's been to see him he keeps saying he doesn't know who that girl is."

"What did she look like?" George Ferndale demanded.

"Small, pretty, somehow pathetic, with soft dark hair and big dark eyes," Charlotte offered.

He snorted. "Well, I can tell you straight out, that that isn't what Fay Iverbury looks like at all! It seems to me you've cooked up that story to get me alone to ask something else. What is it now?"

"It's true, all of it, uncle."

"Well, if it is, what made them let her see him, seeing that the rule was made that no one outside the family could? In fact, I thought I was the only one, as his next of kin, who'd been allowed in."

"That was true, until that girl came, and she said (so I heard) that she and Derek had planned to marry some days ago, only it had fallen through for some reason."

That really surprised her uncle. He stared at Charlotte for a minute, then let out a snort of laugher. "What a lot of poppycock! As if—listen here, my girl, you must know as well as I do, that Derek wouldn't consider marrying some strange young woman! There is, after all, Great-Aunt Elizabeth to consider! No, you just go back to your hospital and forget it."

"But I can't, Uncle! Don't you see? Derek gets so upset because he says he must see this Fay Iverbury! Why does he? How well do you know her? Do you know why the thought of her upsets him?"

Her uncle was obviously very angry. "It's a long story," he said at last, "and one I don't really propose to give to my niece.

What I want to know is, how did young Derek get hold of this girl's name? Can you tell me that?"

"No, I just don't know," she said frankly. "I wish I did. We all wish we did. He's very worried about something. Sometimes I think he's worried about home. About you!" She asked it on a note of a question, wondering all the time whether she had done right. He turned a darker shade of puce but didn't answer, so it was difficult for her to decide.

"Are you in any trouble, Uncle? Are you sure I couldn't help you if you were to tell me?" she ventured.

"Damme, girl, how should *you* be able to help me if I can't help myself?" he shouted.

She shook her head. "I don't know. I just wondered whether an outside view on it might unwittingly help. Besides, it's Derek I'm thinking of, and he *is* worried about something that's going on at home here."

He considered her, rather sharply, she thought. "Don't mind, Uncle, my asking," she pleaded. "It doesn't matter to me what you do, but if I did happen to know someone who could be of use to you, help or advise you, you know I'd be only too glad to—" She broke off, quailing a little before his look of intense dislike.

"If you really want to help," he said at last, "there's a way you can. Oh, don't look so eager! It's really quite simple. Keep away from Derek!"

She frowned, genuinely puzzled. "Keep away from him? But how can I? He's on my ward!"

"I don't mean now, and you know it! And don't think I've been taken in by all this nonsense about him being just a cousin that you couldn't think of in that way! It's a very fine front, my girl, but I can see you'd jump at him, if you had half a chance. Well, don't! Never did approve of an alliance between cousins and I approve even less of you two getting hitched up. Just leave Derek alone!"

She felt as if her uncle had struck her in the face. There had never been any love lost between them, but up till now she had kept out of his way. She hadn't realized how much he disliked her.

"I just don't understand you," she said helplessly. "It's family—just a family feeling—to help if one can. That's all! As to Derek, we've always been close friends but nothing more. Nothing at all. There never was anything further from my mind," she finished miserably.

She watched him go. He hadn't even stayed long enough to catch the last words, but had started striding off away over his lands as if he bore them and everything else a deep personal grudge. Everyone came beneath his withering glance—even one of the men who came up to him to speak, and was brushed off as if he were a mere fly. The man stood staring after George Ferndale as if he thought his employer had gone mad.

Something must be wrong, very wrong, for even her uncle to behave like that, Charlotte thought. He hated her, even more now, for having come across the name of that girl, of whom he seemed to know a lot, but had told Charlotte nothing. He hated her, too, it seemed, because of her closeness to Derek. But it was true what she had said; there was no question of being in love with him. Their closeness, so it seemed to Charlotte, was more of a brother and sister being deep friends. Whenever either had problems they took it to the other. It had always been so. Both were orphans, both had looked to George Ferndale as a father, and had been deeply disappointed. And now George Ferndale wanted to separate them, it seemed.

Why, in heaven's name, why?

Feeling distinctly chilled, Charlotte made her way back. Her shoes had suffered, walking over that field. Her uncle had had riding boots on. Nothing could do much worse to his appearance—he had been mud-splattered anyway. Charlotte had to go back to the hospital, and if she weren't careful she wouldn't have time to clean up before going on the wards. Her second pair of plain shoes were at the repairers.

Sighing, she started to run. Isabel watched her streaking towards the drive. From her vantage point at the topmost window, Isabel shared her husband's dislike of Charlotte and glared at Charlotte with satisfaction. She couldn't have said what it was about Charlotte that she disliked so much, for Charlotte rarely bothered about clothes or make-up or going out to parties or borrowing money—all the things Isabel understood most and were the most dear to her heart. Perhaps it was the fact that men (most men, but, not, it seemed, George!) were drawn to Charlotte. Men, children, animals. Even that savage beast of a new mare of George's, never openly threatened Charlotte, though it had recently made a show of rearing at Isabel only yesterday. And Charlotte had no taste for riding, even! It just wasn't fair, Isabel thought. Nor was it fair that Charlotte had the deep devotion of Derek.

Moreover, the old aunt Elizabeth liked Charlotte. She had kept her liking well hidden until that last letter, and then it had shown through plainly, though the old lady undoubtedly hadn't realized it and wouldn't have let it show if she had. With a family like the Ferndales one didn't show favouritism if one wanted peaceful days. Aunt Elizabeth had seen fit to remark that there was only one real person among them, only one who could be trusted, and that was young Charlotte. And why, Aunt Elizabeth had demanded, didn't she hear any mention of her in the family's touchingly devoted letters? She would, she said, *like* to hear how young Charlotte did, at that hospital of hers.

Isabel went and made a telephone call, smarting all the time about Charlotte. But the person she called wasn't in, and that didn't please her, either. It was not the first time she had telephoned him and wondered where he was, that his telephone kept ringing and ringing.

Restless, she wandered about, thinking of Charlotte and wondering why she had been running. She would have wanted the next bus back to the hospital, of course, and George would have been too bad-tempered to offer her a lift. Well, it might be fun to offer a lift to Charlotte herself, and perhaps to get some idea of what she and George had been talking about.

She caught Charlotte up on the Rolbrough Road. Charlotte didn't know it, but her bus had gone by ten minutes early. Isabel had a great deal of pleasure in telling her she had lost that bus, and of seeing how much it meant to Charlotte to be back late at the hospital.

"I'll take you back, if you like," she said softly.

"Will you?" Charlotte asked, jumping at the offer without questioning it. "Thanks a lot!"

"I will—if you tell me what George said to you," Isabel bargained.

Charlotte was in no mood to be trifled with. "All right," she agreed, and got into the car. There wasn't much she could tell about Uncle George, anyway, and after she had said it all (except the bit about herself and Derek) which she couldn't for worlds have admitted to Isabel, she glanced at her uncle's second wife and said bluntly, "I suppose he's in debt again. Is that it?"

"Now why would you want to know?" Isabel purred.

"So that I can go to Derek and tell him to stop being a silly clot and worrying about his uncle because it's the same old thing,"

Charlotte said frankly.

"Oh! Doesn't Derek think the trouble is the same mixture as before?" Isabel said slowly, looking ahead all the time.

"I really don't know. None of us do, do we? He's not in a fit state to tell us. But he's certainly worried about something. Do *you* know who Fay Iverbury is?"

"Darling, what makes you think I'd tell you if I did?" Isabel drawled. "You are the last person in whom I would confide!"

Charlotte was very angry. "That's not fair! I've told you all I know!"

"In exchange for a lift back to the hospital, and here we are," Isabel said. "And if you want my candid opinion, I'd keep out of it if I were you. Derek will be all right. He always lands on his feet. There's nothing you could do to help him, anyway!"

Charlotte got out and stood staring sombrely at Isabel. "If you want my candid opinion," she said slowly, "I think you should try to find out what my Uncle George's problem is. After all, you're his wife! And it could be that he's worried about you. Well, there can't be any harm in my pointing out, surely, that my Aunt Elizabeth may not always be wanting to spend her money on baling the Ferndales out of trouble."

Isabel smiled, and it wasn't a very friendly smile. "I hope you are merely taking a stab at my dress bills. Anyway, you are wrong, aren't you? Aunt Elizabeth will always be wanting to keep the Ferndales baled out, because of a thing she calls 'the proud family name' and because she's made of money anyway and hasn't anyone else to spend it on. And I have it on good authority, anyway, that my dress bills are the least of the objections she raises."

After that shot, Isabel made a brilliant exit by flashing up the street, right across the nose of the RMO's car. It was a good thing he was in the habit of driving carefully, otherwise Isabel would have sliced the bonnet off his lordly black saloon. He was livid. Charlotte wished the earth would open and swallow her up.

He got out of his car. "Was that a friend of yours?" he asked. Icicles dripped from each word, and he didn't have to say any more. Scarlet-cheeked, Charlotte nodded.

"Actually my Uncle George's second wife. She—she doesn't always look when she drives off and she was rather cross with me."

"I see. Well, you'd better tell her, the next time you see her, that if she doesn't want to be on the inside of this hospital, she had just better learn to look before she drives off."

Charlotte escaped. She wasn't far off being late, in spite of the lift Isabel had given her, and it wasn't with any great pleasure that she faced her friends, who seemed to live at the windows when anything interesting was happening.

"Lumme, we nearly didn't have an RMO just then!" Linda burst out, her eyes crinkling with laughter. "Was that a friend of yours, Charlotte?"

"It was Isabel, my Uncle George's wife," she said shortly. "And in case you're worried about it, I may assure you that the RMO wasn't in a social mood. He was livid about a near accident, and ticked me off—

as if it was my fault!"

Linda was in a leg-pulling mood and couldn't leave well alone. "Isn't it funny?" she said dreamily, studying the ceiling. "The RMO's supposed to be girl-shy since he was jilted, but whenever I see him or hear of him, he always seems to be hellbent on getting close to Charlotte here. Well, I mean to say, even the grapevine's got it."

"Got what?" Charlotte asked, dangerously.

Linda, started now, pretended not to notice Charlotte's mood. "Everyone's saying he was mooning about the lane by the woods and brought Charlotte back in his car to the hospital. Me, I always believed my Grannie's old saying, about once bitten, twice shy, only the RMO doesn't seem to know that one, or else he wouldn't fall over backwards to be with someone as accident-prone as our Charlotte here!"

4

CHARLOTTE had never been one to mind a bit of leg-pulling. Sylvia, busy getting into her clean uniform, and in danger of being late as usual, wasn't looking, but mechanically listening for the snort of laughter that usually came from Charlotte. This time Charlotte didn't laugh. Sylvia looked up at her, saw the look on her face and wondered.

"Never mind that!" she broke in, impatiently. "Something's come up, Charlotte, about your cousin Derek. I shall have to tell you quickly—I'm late. Well, we all are, I know. But the fact is, your Derek's been shouting for you again. No, hold hard—no use rushing over! He's under sedation again. It seems to be this Fay person who is worrying him. Have you been out somewhere to find out who she is?"

Charlotte abandoned her momentary anger against Linda for making a joke of the

RMO. It had bothered her. She wanted to know why she minded, but there wasn't time to think about it now, but, she promised herself, she must think about it later. It made her uneasy.

She said to Sylvia, "Yes, I have. I don't know why I thought I could, you know, but before I went, it seemed to be the thing to ask my Uncle George outright for the answer I wanted. He certainly seemed a bit shaken when I mentioned the name of Fay Iverbury to him but he didn't tell me a single thing! What on earth can I do next, to find out what's bothering Derek? What would *you* do?"

Sylvia paused, taken aback. She had no way of advising. Her background was against a flat in a London suburb, with the local park as the only bit of open space. "Do you have things like gamekeepers any more?" she asked at last.

Charlotte, busily cleaning her mudded shoes, said bitterly, "We do, indeed!"

Sylvia continued, "I was just wondering if (you being you) you could talk to their womenfolk, persuade them to think back if anything was seen that day, little insignificant things they wouldn't have thought of mentioning before, but which might be quite important. Well, yes, I know the police questioned them at first, but I was thinking of the sort of things they might not think worth mentioning to the police, but they'd talk about, woman to woman."

"Like what?"

"Like being in the woods for silly reasons like cutting branches of greenery when you're too skimped to buy flowers from a shop. Or taking junior for a walk to find the sort of coloured toadstools he'd heard about in the telly story for tots, when elves come out of them and have thrilling adventures. Well, can you *see* a woman admitting to that sort of jaunt to the police? But if she did take such a walk, or going to pick nuts (or whatever they pick because they taste nicer got fresh and growing) she'd discuss it with another woman, and maybe what she saw that struck her as a bit odd but not worth mentioning to officials. See?"

Charlotte was ready now, and paused. "Yes, I do see," she mused.

"And," Sylvia went on, putting the last pin into her cap without much hope of its holding it there for long, "like how that kid from the village just happened to be at that spot in the woods when he found your cousin lying there shot. I've never understood how that got explained away."

Charlotte stared. "That's funny, why didn't I think of that at the time?"

"Think of what?" Linda, unabashed, broke in. "What are you both talking about?"

"The boy who found my cousin," Charlotte said, going first out of the room and waiting for the others to follow. "I *know* how he came to be in the woods, don't I, though come to think of it, he didn't tell the police this. They were all playing a version of that silly game. (Cops and Robbers) only they were fed-up with my uncle for getting tough about it and threatening them, so they changed it, and they were planning to stalk the gamekeepers instead. I thought it was rather funny at the time, only of course they wouldn't dare tell anyone about it. They'd get into awful trouble."

"So there were several kids in the wood that day!" Sylvia mused.

"At least a dozen and they must have seen anything that was to be seen. Brian Banks, wasn't it, who discovered Derek?"

"Yes, the kid who was allowed in to visit his mother when we thought she wasn't going to 'do'."

Brian Banks. Small and skinny, ginger of hair and pale blue of eyes; a carroty weazel, her uncle had said scornfully about him. Yet he struck Charlotte, the next afternoon, as being a very bright boy.

He was doing errands for his mother's next door neighbour and earning a few coppers, and he had contracted to clean shoes at one house and clean out the hen houses at another. He had a little list of jobs and was striking them through as he did them.

"How many have you got left, Brian?" Charlotte smiled.

"Ten, miss, and if I don't get 'em done on time through talking to you, I shall lose five bob."

"What are you saving it for specially?"

"Me Mum's birthday, see?"

"Could you consider talking to me as a job, because I want to know some things that only you can tell me; things to help my cousin Derek who is ill in hospital. You remember him, don't you?"

Derek was, Charlotte remembered, instrumental in speaking for the hut the Cubs used. Uncle George had wanted to sell the land it was on, and hadn't cared if the Cubs had nowhere else to hold their meetings. Derek had found them another site. Brian creased his face up into a wide grin. "Yes, I remember him, miss. We all like him. Still, it'd put me back an awful lot. Gotta go."

She grabbed him as he made to streak off. "Not more than ten minutes, surely, and if you answer me properly it will be worth five shillings to me. Wouldn't that compensate you?"

"Five bob, miss, for answering a few questions? All right, done!" he said recklessly.

He was sorry soon after. Charlotte walked him to the small stone bridge over the stream, which was just inside her uncle's boundary and they could be reasonably quiet, and she started with some energy and directness: "The day you found my cousin lying in the woods, how many others were with you, or anywhere in the woods playing that special game?"

The colour slowly drained from his face. "You're going to tell on us," he accused her hotly.

"No. I'd only do that if you'd done any damage. Did you?"

He shook his head fiercely. "Not much we never—your uncle he's so peppery, we just went for a bit of a lark to tease Joiner, that's all. He's daft."

"My uncle thinks Mr. Joiner is a very good gamekeeper, so you had better be careful," Charlotte said, but her lips were twitching. "How many of you were there?"

He reckoned swiftly. "About ten of us."

"Could you give me the names and addresses of your pals?"

"Here, what for?" He was suspicious and unwilling to co-operate now.

"I ought to have explained from the first. I want to ask each one of you a set of questions: exactly the same questions. Like a game, really, because none of you must compare notes. I want you all to tell me first the answers, before you let each other know. Get me?"

"Yes, I know that game. But what sort of questions?"

"What you saw in the woods at certain points. Things you might not think worth mentioning, but which might mean something to me."

He didn't understand, of course. "We're going to get into trouble, aren't we? We never pinched nothing, not much, only a berry or two, or a nut, like."

She sighed. She would have to take him into her confidence, and she didn't want to, because it just might be against her own people. But she must, if she wanted help from the children.

"Look, Brian, there's something very mysterious happening in our woods and I want to know what it is."

This he understood and brightened at once. "Oh, why didn't you say so at first? We could send out a search party, me and the gang. We're good at it!"

"But you'd be seen and get into trouble," she said quickly. "Or one of you might get caught in the traps, or something. No, my way is best, I'm sure. Just answer my questions and if I don't get the answers I think I ought to get, then we'll consider your way with the gang."

"All right," he said, resigned. "What do you want to know?"

She put five shillings on the top of the post, to let him feast his eyes on it, and she said, "This game you were playing in the woods that day—am I right in thinking that all of you kept an eye on the sun or listened for the church clock striking, and marked a plan where you were at certain times?"

"That's right, miss." His suspicions deepened. Grown-ups weren't usually so interested in his activities with his friends. "It's all right, miss—I mean, it wasn't wrong. I couldn't have been, because the plans we used were a bit like the ones in a game the Cub Mistress taught us. You know, using a bit of carbon paper to get two copies. The maps had to be all alike."

"I am not trying to trick you," Charlotte said slowly and earnestly. "I just want to make sure I've got it right. If you've all been taught how to duplicate your maps of the woods, then we shall know they're all alike. And what I want is fresh maps made out, and people marked on them. Where these people were at certain times which I shall give you."

"What people?" he muttered.

"Well, it's my own business, but actually, our outdoor staff. You know them all, don't you? It's so they won't be getting into trouble for being where they shouldn't be, so you will be helping them, you see? And it has to be secret. Our secret, yours and the gang's, and mine."

That last sentence won him over. Interest flared in his young face. "Cor, miss, I like that! It's a right-down detective game!" But he wouldn't agree to his friends having to answer the questions alone. "Let's get together, miss, because they can't do nothing if I'm not there to see it's all in order." Also he said he wanted his cub-mistress in on it. "She'll make the copies better 'n us, miss, them maps. Besides, she'll want to, on account of us learning to map-read."

Charlotte eyed him with dismay. "But I can't take her in, because she'll tell her mother, and her mother will tell all the customers in her shop, and all my family's secrets will be all over the place."

Young Brian was a realist. He said hardily, "Well, they will, anyway, miss, if we find out, won't they? They would be out, them secrets of yours, if we didn't do this game for you, on account of Sid what's the new undergardener up at Ferndale House being married to our cub-mistress's sister."

That was news to Charlotte, and clinched the matter. The most important thing here, it seemed, was to encourage the boy's need to keep in touch with his cub-mistress, so Charlotte reluctantly agreed, and the last she saw of him was scurrying into a small house near his own home, where he was due to scrub a floor for sixpence.

She walked back all round her uncle's land, thinking. What did she hope to find out, for heaven's sake? Where people had been at, say, five minutes before she had run out of the woods? No, it would have been dark then and the children all home. Better make it at five minutes before the children went home. But Brian himself must have been in the woods after dark, and he must have had a light, to enable him to stumble over Derek and to recognize him and to fetch help to the right spot. She hadn't properly thought about that, and it raised new issues.

She forced herself to go through the neck of the woods where Derek had been found, and then to follow her own path, as near as she could remember it, to the boundary where she had found the RMO sitting in his car.

As she reached the boundary, she saw he was there now, in the same place, sitting in his car, only this time he was staring into the gloom of the woods, and when he saw Charlotte come running out, he appeared to be far from pleased.

He opened his door and came out to meet her. "You! Haven't you had enough of the terrors in those woods?" he exploded.

"It's daylight, sir," she said mildly.

"And I was only trying to find out something, any small thing, which might help my cousin Derek. He *is* in such a way!"

He nodded, and his anger abated, but he still stared at her, frowning, as if something puzzled him. "I know how you feel. I suppose that was what really drove me here. To sit and see the place, and to think what could have happened. Did you find out anything?"

She shook her head, helplessly.

"Have you had any tea? Well, it's teatime, so come and have some with me, will you, and let's talk about this. I don't like your cousin's condition, I confess it, and there's something going on which is worrying him inordinately."

He held the car door open for her to get in, and even when he had shut her door, he hesitated before walking round to his own. She watched him stand there, frowning into the dense woodland, as if by so staring, he could force out the person who had shot Derek, and to make him say why.

When he did start up the car at last, it was towards Tamworth that he drove. A pleasant country town with nice places to sit and dream away an afternoon in a tea-shop window, or dance in a hotel with a man you liked specially. Charlotte, for perhaps the first time since she had come to the hospital, found herself thinking of being in one's nicest clothes, looking pretty and smelling of exotic perfume, with a man like the RMO beside you. The RMO always looked elegant, no matter what he was wearing. He managed to look aloof, too, from the countryfolk, and the people of Rolborough who filed into Casualty. Aloof, yet queerly deeply a part of them when he came to understanding their needs.

Angrily she started talking, about anything, anything at all, because she was so distressed to find herself thinking about a man in much the same way as Isabel did, and Miriam, and other nurses at the hospital. Romance, indeed!

He let her talk for a while, and then he said sharply, "Don't! You're babbling, and it isn't like you. What are you afraid I shall find out?"

She reddened slowly, deeply embarrassed, until it occurred to her that he wasn't thinking at all about the way she felt about him, but rather that she might be hiding some secret she had discovered in the woods that day.

She covered her hot face with her hands. "Oh, it's all such a mess," she said, in despair. "I've been in those woods, trying to bribe a small Cub to take his gang of friends and play a map-reading game, marking times and spying on the staff at Ferndale House."

"You've done wha-at?"

"It sounds despicable, doesn't it, put like that? But I didn't mean it to be. It's my only hope, to find out who shot my cousin Derek. To find out what was bothering him, still is bothering him. I've never seen such a strong, hearty, happy young man go to pieces in such a short time."

"I'll agree with you there!" Keith Berrington said shortly. "Is this wise, this step you've taken?"

"Probably not, but as Brian Banks pointed out to me, if the village doesn't get wind of what's going on through him and his friends, they'll find out some other way. Scandal is the breath of life to Ewbrook St. Peter."

"Don't I know it!" Keith Berrington muttered, bitterly.

She watched him thoughtfully and remembered the broken engagement and of how people had talked. Not a new story but horrid to the two people more concerned.

But although she waited, he didn't offer to tell her of what he had meant. She said, making fork tracings on the tablecloth, and not attempting to eat the creamy pastries he had ordered for her, "Something upset my cousin very deeply, and I'd be a fool to think it was just what he told me it might be."

"And what was that?"

She shrugged. "He thinks my Uncle George is in deep trouble, and then he was afraid (or too ill) to say any more. I'm well aware that my Uncle George is usually in debt, but then we have a rich great-aunt who keeps baling him out, so it really shouldn't be all that trouble to him. I know it sounds rather dreadful but we at home are used to it. No, I would have thought it was some very bad trouble, but I just can't think what it can be!"

"Tell me again about your family. There is the Uncle George and his second wife Isabel," the RMO mused.

She looked rather surprised. "Did I tell you that?"

He looked rather nettled. "No, to be honest I had a—friend, who knew Isabel's sister," he admitted.

"Oh. Then my family are friends of friends of yours."

"No, don't have any finer feelings on that score," he hastened to assure her. "I never knew much about the connection, and —well, it's all over now. I'm never likely to run across your family. I merely asked because your cousin mentioned a name, in one of his lucid moments. Miriam—would it be?"

"Oh, her!" Charlotte didn't sound very pleased. "Perhaps, though he never had much to do with her. She's the step-sister of my Uncle George. They don't get on well. What did Derek say about her?"

"It was hard to be really sure. I had the impression that he was worried about letting this Miriam know about—whatever it is that he knows and we don't. Does that suggest anything to you?"

"No, to be frank, it doesn't. She's not in his age group; she hasn't a single thing in common with Derek, and besides, she's recently met someone whom we hope she'll marry." Her lips twitched. "Well, we hope it will make her more human." She spread her hands. "I'm being rather horrid, you'll think, but, well, Miriam is rising forty and a hard rider. In fact, horseflesh is the only interest she had, so if she can meet a man with the same interests, to like her, well, wouldn't that be nice?" and the dimple he remembered, appeared in her left cheek again; the dimple when she was caught out and knew it.

"I do agree, without even knowing the lady," he said, and laughed. "But how does she fit into the anxiety vortex of your unfortunate cousin?"

"I don't know, I just can't think," Charlotte fretted. She thought of Warren

Jeakings who was interested in Miriam. Just as weather-beaten as she herself was, and just as found of horsey things, and apparently not short of cash. What could Miriam have done to fit in with Derek's worries? "This girl who said she was going to marry Derek—it just can't be true! Derek and I have been very close. He would have told me. I can't believe it. But . . . he said he didn't know her, and he asked me who she was, and he was fretful about her. He couldn't be suffering from general amnesia, could he?"

"I think not. He remembers other things, but nothing that will help us, it seems."

"Money. It's the only thing that has ever bothered my family. The lack of it, that is. We need money to repair Ferndale House and money to repair the fences; money to put the stables in order, and to buy more horses. Oh, but what's new about that? Derek wouldn't ask me to meet him in the woods to talk about that. No one would shoot Derek in order to stop him from talking to me about the need for money."

He looked up sharply at her as she spoke. "What is it, Dr. Berrington?" she asked.

"Nothing. I was just thinking." He was remembering something Rosemary had said, about George Ferndale, and the old aunt. Something he felt sure was relative, but he couldn't capture the thought. "This old aunt of yours, is she going to leave all her money to your uncle, or some other member of the family? Such an apparently small thing might well create trouble. Had you thought of that?"

"No," she said, frowning, "but it does make me wonder what she would do if one of the family started a scandal. She can tolerate debts and drinking and gambling, but infidelity is a thing that has made her come near to having a seizure in the past when it affected her friends—what it would do to her if it was in the family, I can't think."

"Has it given you food for thought?" he asked, watching her. "I must get to the root of the trouble if your cousin is to recover, you know."

Her own eyes were deeply distressed as

she looked up at that. "You don't think Derek will 'do'," she said softly.

"I'm not going so far as that, but I do feel that you know more than you have said."

She shook her head. "It isn't that so much as the feeling I get on my ward. It's so queer, but so many of the people there are connected with us at home. Apart from my cousin, there is the father of one of the stableboys and there is the brother-in-law of one of the maids, and some of the visitors are from the estate. It's . . . too close, if something like a scandal were to crop up out of this affair of Derek's. I couldn't do much to hide it from the world, with so many familiar pairs of ears listening, so many familiar pairs of eyes watching. And Miriam's friend—"

"Don't tell me he's connected with the hospital in some way?"

"Warren Jeakings? Oh, no, hardly! I was only going to say that although the turf is his one hunting ground, his background, one might say, he does come from a very good family. It isn't his fault that he was a younger brother."

"Warren Jeakings," Dr. Barrington mused. "That's odd. I've heard the name, recently. Oh, well, perhaps not. Are you going to stop worrying about all this, and to keep away from those woods? Or are you going over to help the Cubs?"

"I shall keep well out of their way until they have something to report," Charlotte said firmly. "It isn't very much to shout about, is it, having to find out what one's family secret is, through the little boys of the neighbourhood?"

"But when it concerns a young man's life and health, it is, of course, rather different. It is the end and not the means that counts."

It comforted her, on the way back to the hospital, and although Dr. Berrington said no more about it, she felt he would be there ready to help her.

Whenever she went back on the ward now, Charlotte felt that eyes were following her wherever she went. It was not a medical ward but there were some very sick men in it, but those who were mending took a lively interest in everything, and not the least in the Ferndale family and the nurse from Ferndale House.

The most popular man on the ward was Tom Yates' father. He had plenty to say about what went on at Ferndale House. To believe that he only saw life from the stables, because his son Tom worked in that part, was a fallacy, Charlotte saw, with a little prick of apprehension. While she was hurrying up the ward with bowls of hot water for the evening washings, she caught the words, "And our Tom's sweet on the girl who went to be a temporary help in the kitchen, and what she didn't hear about that family wasn't no one's business."

He didn't seem to think that Charlotte had ears like anyone else, nor did he appear to be troubled with the thought that the indignant Sylvia, or even the juniors, would bother to listen and repeat bits of his conversation to Charlotte later. Charlotte vaguely remembered the girl who had helped for a time in the kitchen. She had resembled a little the Cub Brian Banks, but was not so prepossessing. With a shock it came to Charlotte that that girl must have been a cousin of Brian Banks. Well, it couldn't be helped. The whole village must know a great deal about the family already, but it wasn't nice to hear people hazarding guesses as to why Isabel went to London so often, when she could have got her hair done in Ogmarsh like everyone else, or bought her clothes in the big expensive shops in Tamworth.

On another occasion Charlotte heard Tom Yates' father say clearly to his neighbour, "I'm not saying the second Mrs. Ferndale has got a *friend* either in London or anywhere else. I hold no brief for her, but then neither do I hold any brief for that husband of hers, who is a Right One, to my way of thinking, anyway, what with his drinking and his gambling and his debts. All I'm saying is, I'm glad my lad *is* a lad and not a girl, because I wouldn't want any girl of mine to work in *that* house, that I wouldn't!"

Sylvia said, in passing Charlotte, "I can't let this go on. If you won't tick him off for gossiping about your family, then I'm going to! I think it's disgraceful!"

"No, don't. Don't say a word", Charlotte said quickly. "I suppose I ought to stop him, but it won't help. He'll talk if he wants to, and anyway, if I say anything, he'll only save it up to say when I'm not here. I'd rather hear what he's saying."

Sylvia shrugged and left it at that. The men had nothing else to do but gossip, until the newspaper round in the morning. True, there was the radio, but most of the men preferred to talk. Only No. 3 lived for his radio programmes, but then he was a quiet man who didn't talk much anyway. And speculation was rife about the mysterious visitor he had had that day.

"Who could it be, that's what I want to know! I mean, they ought to find out who everyone wants to see, before they let 'em in, that's what I reckon!"

"You couldn't do that, not without a Pass or some such thing, and that'd take all the visiting time, clearing 'em."

"Well, I'd feel better about it, that I would. I mean, lying there helpless, you don't know what'd happen, because the nurses take themselves off for the visiting hour. Haven't you ever noticed? I want to know where they get to!"

"They have to eat like us, they tell me," his neighbour chuckled. "You can't blame 'em, can you? They'd be daft if they didn't get off, once we're all set with our people here. No, but seriously, what *could* happen, here in the hospital, with staff all round us!"

Charlotte, who had been busy with a helpless patient three beds away, couldn't resist pausing for a moment to try and hear what was said in answer to that one.

Tom's father said, surprisingly, "What could happen? Plenty! I was reading in the paper only yesterday that a witness in that case about the night watchman being killed (you know the one!) was in hospital and someone come in, in amongst the visitors, and sat down quiet and well behaved with decent clothes on, and put his paper bag of fruit on the locker like everyone else, and no one the wiser—he even looked like an anxious relative! And all he has to do is to lean forward and stick something in the chap in bed, and there he was—dead! The visitor ups and goes out all quiet like, and no one took any notice! How about that?"

That story went the rounds of the ward, in spite of Tom's father being told not to circulate such stuff. But it *was* a thought, as Charlotte and her friends had to agree later.

"It's just seeing what you expect to see," Linda said, her eyes dancing with excitement. "Like that postman who delivered letters to every house in the street, and knocked with a parcel at the last one, and when the door was opened, well! He came out of the gate and no one was surprised to see a postman leave the house, but what he hadn't done in that last house!"

"What?" Sylvia couldn't resist asking.

"Never mind that," Charlotte broke in. "Are you two aware of the amount of gossip that's going the rounds, about my family? What have I done to deserve it? They stare at me, no matter what I'm doing! Haven't you two noticed?"

"Yes, and that reminds me," Sylvia said. "I meant to tell you before. It's that Yates. He was telling the others that his boy, when he hasn't much to do, stands at the corner of the stables and trains powerful opera glasses on the house and sees what's going on inside! Don't you think you ought to warn your Uncle George? I mean, that boy can't be such an asset that they couldn't afford to throw him out—they ought to if he really does things like that."

"What on earth does he hope to see?" Charlotte said blankly.

"They were saying that he reported to his father some very odd visitors to the house. Shady characters from the race track. That sort of thing!"

"Well, what business is it of theirs?" Charlotte said wrathfully. "Oh, it's no good my telling my Uncle George—he won't listen to a thing I say. They'll just have to get on with it. Though I suppose he'll blame me when he finds out how much gossip about him there is on the ward."

It was dark when the nurses came off the day shift. The bigger hospitals were working the block hour system, so that no one worked through the useful hours of the day, but came on earlier and got off early, or came on late and went proportionately later. So long as you worked your full eight hours, it was argued, the system was fine, but somehow the General Hospital at Rolborough had never accepted that a new idea could possibly be a good one. As it was, Charlotte went off duty at eight that night, when it was dark and the shops all shut, the buses put back to their slack time schedule of one an hour (which she had just missed) and the whole world drearily damp and humid, she thought dejectedly.

As she stood on the pavement looking around her, wondering if there was the slightest hope of getting her uncle on the telephone without Isabel or Miriam knowing, shrill young voices hailed her, and a group of Cubs on bicycles squealed to a halt. Brian Banks came tumbling towards her.

"Talk about coincidence, miss, and here you are, all nice and ready for us outside! Me and my pals have been arguing about how to get you and I say that we can ask a porter and they say they'd just send us off."

"Brian, what are you and your friends doing in Rolborough after dark? Do your people know about this?"

"It's all right, miss, our Cub Mistress is here somewhere. We've got to meet her and the others. We got five minutes so we just thought we'd come over to the hospital. Here it is."

He thrust a bundle of papers into her hand, tied up with a bit of string. "Cor, we had a whale of a time getting all these bits jotted down, and it don't half make you think what goes on in them woods!" he said, enthusiastically.

The others all talked at once, but presently Charlotte reduced them to law and order. "Where *is* your Cub Mistress? I'd rather like to speak to her," she said.

Their faces fell. "Well, we didn't tell her we were coming to the hospital to try and see you because she said we had to telephone in the day-time to make an appointment. And we'll get into awful trouble, cos we said we were just going to ride about Rolborough—Miss, I don't suppose we could take a peek at the ambulances while we're here, could we?"

Charlotte looked regretfully down into

their eager trusting young faces. "If it had been a quiet night, I'd have loved to take you over and let you peep, boys, but it so happens that there's a flap on in Casualty. See all those lights on over there? That's Casualty."

They looked and were thrilled to see an ambulance go in at top speed, its light flicking on the roof, its raucous notes sounding. "Is it a three-star?" Brian asked knowledgably.

"No, my lad, it isn't, or I wouldn't be standing chatting with you," she said briskly. "But they're busy enough!"

All the same, it wasn't easy to persuade them to go back to where they had left their Cub Mistress. Charlotte was aching to see the facts they had gathered.

When she did manage to return to her room and spread out the maps on her bed in unexpected solitude, Linda and Sylvia having vanished somewhere, Charlotte couldn't believe her eyes at the information the boys had collected. She felt a little shiver of apprehension that so many people—grown-ups and children—had access to discover every move the family at Ferndale House made at any hour of the day or night, it seemed. It didn't worry her much that people should know the exact hour of the day that Isabel ceremoniously watered her exotic plants, nor the hour set religiously by for Mrs. Endon to go to her still-room or Miriam to retire to gloat over and polish her prized collection of horse-brasses and examine her hunting prints. But what did bother Charlotte was what the inmates of Ferndale House, their staff and others, had been up to in the woods at that hour of that regrettable day when Derek had been found shot.

5

AT last Charlotte decided she had better try to telephone her uncle, but the call boxes in the Home were all being used, so she went out to the call box in the road outside.

With her cloak held round her because the night was chilly, she waited outside of yet another occupied call box and thought it a bad omen that she couldn't manage to speak to her Uncle George. Somewhere, something was happening that she herself should have been aware of, but had somehow missed.

She thought of Isabel—hostile, extravagant, hating every other woman in sight. Why had Isabel married Uncle George? She must have known that he hadn't much money. He wasn't a bit attractive, he was years older than Isabel, and they hadn't, so far as Charlotte could see, a thing in common. Not like George's step-sister Miriam, who at least shared with George a love of the countryside and horses, racing, and everything allied to horses. Isabel, George, Miriam, Derek—what was going on which concerned them all, hidden behind a protective wall which the neighbourhood was whittling away inch by inch while Charlotte was still prevented from getting a glimpse of their secret?

The girl in the box showed no signs of finishing her call so Charlotte, in desperation, decided to slip into the hospital and use one of the call boxes in the main hall.

Keith Berrington was just coming out as she reached the main door. He looked so tired.

"Hello, where are you off to?" he frowned. "I was just wondering if there was half a chance of contacting you!"

Here was the very person to discuss these maps with, she thought, and she told him briefly what she had been trying to do. "But I don't suppose my Uncle George would listen, even if I were lucky enough to contact him. He'd probably tell me I'd imagined gossip on the ward."

"Then he would have me to contend with, because I've heard it, too," he said crisply. "I'd like to discuss that with you. I've got an hour. Do you want the car, or are you hankering for fresh air, like me?"

She said, "I'd love a walk," so he just started walking, with a bare nod of the head. He looked as if bed would be more appropriate for him, she thought critically. But it would have been hot in Casualty. He probably would feel better out in the cold night air. So she told him about the Cubs and the way they had got their maps and notes to her.

"I don't know what to think about it, Dr. Berrington, but now so many people will know what we do. No one, among the outside staff, was in the place he ought to have been in, on that afternoon when Derek was shot, and it doesn't seem to me possible that he could have been there in that place without me hearing or seeing something . . . unless in the dark I had wandered away in the other direction and then doubled back. I'm not very good in the dark and I haven't much sense of direction, but why didn't I hear the shot? That's what I keep asking myself."

"Come to think of it, why didn't I hear it? I'd been sitting there quietly in the car, with the engine off, for some time," he mused. "No traffic to speak of, in that lane, at that time of night, to confuse the issue. Start again, will you, and try and describe what the Cubs saw. Or better still, shall we try and find a coffee place open, and sit down quietly and study the things?"

She agreed with him, whatever he wanted, he sounded so spent. But she needn't have worried about the place he had in mind. He knew Rolborough like the back of his hand, and he went unerringly to a little place in a quiet back street, a place that was reasonably clean, and he amused her by buying fish and chips for them both, served on plates with a blue and gold band round the edge, and hot sweet tea in plastic mugs.

At that hour they had the place to themselves, with the exception of one man in a corner; a big burly man eating quantities of veal and ham pie and chips, with no thought of anyone else. Together, in comparative peace, Keith Berrington and Charlotte studied the maps.

They were grubby, dog-eared, and written up in a variety of boyish handwriting and block capitals, but they were surprisingly correct in their detail. She said so. "It's really an exercise for the Cub Mistress, you know. She's keen on this sort of thing."

He nodded, and went over them with her. Here at an improbable spot where the stream raced over an unexpected precipice and made itself into an impromptu waterfall, Brenda Newey was said to have been standing for half an hour, looking "as worried as our Mum when our Dad don't turn up with his pay packet".

"Brenda Newey is one of the indoor staff and shouldn't have been anywhere else but in the library dusting at that particular time," Charlotte said. "She also visited the hospital. Her brother-in-law, you know."

Again the RMO nodded. Charlotte said, "I can't think who the blonde girl can be, or whether they got enthusiastic and put in that she was frightened, out of sheer exuberance. Oh, this account says she was watching two other people," Charlotte said, turning over another map.

On someone else's map the comment had been that the blonde had been watching Isabel and a man, and someone else had entered on his map that Mrs. Ferndale had come out in a temper and started ticking off one of the gamekeepers.

"So we have a maid outside looking worried when she had no business to be outside at all, and a blonde of unknown origin watching your uncle's second wife and a gamekeeper. Not very edifying, is it?"

"It wouldn't be, if the woods were public, but they are supposed to be private property and there are plenty of trespass boards up, even if the boundaries are broken down in places," Charlotte pointed out. "And this enterprising boy finds he saw our housekeeper, without a hat and coat, looking all around her. Now that I find really astonishing, for never have I seen Mrs. Endon out of the house, unless it's in the herb garden, or departing on her half day in all her very best. Or, of course, on Sunday evening, bound for church. She's a creature of habit, and I have heard her say many a time that she wouldn't be cajoled into going in those woods for all the world! She distrusts the woods. I think she must be the only one who applauded my uncle when he first started threatening to sell the woodland to developers."

That impressed Keith Berrington, she could see. "And this account mentions two big boys," he mused, "also looking frightened behind them as they ran." But being the RMO he felt it necessary to dampen any spurt of enthusiasm. "H'm, probably being chased by game keepers."

Charlotte wasn't going to lose even his temporary interest like that. "Except," she pointed out, "that they were all congregated at this end of the woods, talking—a thing the gamekeepers shouldn't have been doing at all!"

"Yes, I agree that taking the thing as a whole and putting it all together, something odd must have been thought to be going on, even if it wasn't. And then we have our patient babbling about someone called Fay Iverbury and there is also the very queer business of a young woman wanting to get to him insisting that he had promised to marry her. How does that strike you?" he asked, looking up at Charlotte suddenly. "Personally that part savoured as a practical joke."

"A joke?" she asked sharply.

"Yes. A bit of nonsense on your cousin's part, proposing to some little girl at some time in the recent past, and it happens to be recoiling on his head now. Nothing to do with our present problems, I mean."

Charlotte flushed angrily. She didn't like that at all. "If you knew my cousin Derek really well, you wouldn't think that. He just wouldn't do that sort of thing to any girl."

"Convince me. Tell me about the young man. He's my patient and I can't find out a thing about him. What he does, what he's like, what he likes about anything. People seem to be cagey about him. You tell me!"

She needed no second invitation, if only to present Derek in a most favourable light to the RMO Keith Berrington noticed it, and wondered a little.

"He's fun to be with," she said, "but not the sort to have acquired a young woman who comes and insists she was to have married him, because he was so definite in saying he didn't know who she was. I mean, if Derek had promised to marry someone, he wouldn't slide out of it like that. Not for anything. He wouldn't fail to recognize her, nor would he pretend to. And he doesn't ever drink enough to propose marriage to someone without remembering it afterwards, so don't think he does!" she finished vehemently, because she noticed the raised eyebrows of Keith Berrington and took exception to it.

"Have some more tea, and cool down," he advised quietly. "I'm not really suggesting anything about your cousin. I just want to know why there are people who would get in and bother him if he wasn't being specialled."

"I wish I knew," Charlotte muttered. "Frankly that girl worries me more than anything Derek told me. I don't think I can get worked up about peril for Uncle George, because he's the last sort of person to care about what might happen to him. He's a hard rider and a hard drinker, and he'd knock a man down without blinking. They tell a story of how he had been drinking all evening, after the races. He'd lost heavily and said there was another race the next day to make it up on (and he did, incidentally) but when he was leaving the town, three rough fellows attacked him and pulled him off his horse. He tackled the lot of them and remounted victorious. Why, *why* is Derek worried about *him*?"

"I take your point. And the rich old aunt that everyone talks about—how does your Uncle George regard her? How does he stand, regarding her, if I may ask?" Dr. Berrington murmured.

"Oh, well, there it is. Aunt Elizabeth has all the money and everyone knows it. If any one of the family run into debt, the creditors just shrug, send in their bills and wait till they trickle through to Aunt Elizabeth's solicitors who settle them after a struggle, but they do settle in the end. She always says she doesn't mind debts; it's scandal she couldn't tolerate. She would just wash her hands, financially and otherwise, of any member of the family who made a scandal."

He looked sharply at her. "Have you got that right?" he said quietly. "Are you sure you don't mean that she'd wash her hands of the lot of you?"

"Does it matter?" Charlotte asked tiredly.

"Well, yes, I think so. In that case, if someone was on the point of starting a scandal, then the others would automatically start to get worried, including my patient, because of his own prospects in the future."

Charlotte considered the point, allowed it had its uses, but finally rejected it. "No, I don't think I ever heard that she'd cut the lot of us off. She's very fond of her family, although we are far from perfect. And that being the case, I can't see Derek going out of his way to solicit my help to keep Uncle George from being cut out of the Will. There isn't any love lost there, you know." She thought about it and finally pronounced, "In fact, I can't see any one in our family minding if someone else was cut out. We're not horrid, just realistic. What one loses, another gains by."

"How very shocking!" he said, with a smile. It was a small smile, but it helped. It did light his face up and seemed to lift the exhaustion from his shoulders.

She pushed the theme a little further to amuse him. "We *are* shocking, at least, everyone says so," she grinned. "Didn't you know?"

"I know *you* are shocking," he said, in an odd intimate tone that surprised her. "When I remember all the scrapes you have been in, and managed to wriggle yourself out of most of them, unaided . . ." He broke off, rather confused. She was embarrassed too. He had never had that intimate tone in his voice before.

She pulled herself together. "Yes, and I shall be in big trouble now, if I don't go back to the hospital. Look at the time!"

He got up at once, and in doing so, spilled the maps all over the seat and the floor. They gathered them together, knocking their heads together in the process. He helped her to her feet, and stood there, holding her hands still. "Charlotte Arrowsmith, I have to thank you for what you are doing to me. Do you know what that is?"

She shook her head, her face still hot and confused.

"You're giving me a responsibility again, someone to look after. I've had no one since . . . well, since Nurse Deane decided that we weren't really suited to each other. But you will know about that, of course! Perhaps I'm not the sort of man to make a good husband, but it's quite clear to me that I need someone to worry about, and it seems I've found someone. Am I right?"

She didn't know what to say, so she pulled her hands away and gathered the papers together, and murmured, "If you really feel that the burden of an accident-prone second-year nurse to disturb your quiet life is what you want, sir, you seem to have got it! But I warn you, it won't be comfortable."

"That's for me to judge. And when not on duty, no more 'sir'."

"What shall I say, then?"

"What's wrong with my name? Don't you like it?"

She did, but she remembered too vividly hearing the others talk about Rosemary Deane, then a staff nurse, drooling to her cronies about "dear Keith". It was much too recent, and it had spoilt the name for Charlotte. "KB," she decided. "Will that do if I call you KB? It suits you!"

That seemed to amuse him. "No one's ever called me that before," he said, and in his heart he was glad that she wasn't going to call him Keith. He could hear Rosemary softly purring the name. Rosemary had had a soft touch for everything, and whatever she had done or liked, had remained exclusively hers.

His smile vanished, thinking of Rosemary. He carried Charlotte's untidy mass of maps and notes with him back to the car. Charlotte, not quite reaching his chin, scurried along by his side, working out the time, too preoccupied to notice that his smile had gone, and he had retreated somewhere with it.

"That hour went quickly!" he said suddenly. "I shall have to hurry, too," so the intimacy fled entirely. But when he reached the hospital, he said suddenly, "Dinner with me tomorrow night, Charlotte? I shall have had some more thoughts on the subject by then!"

"All right, KB," she said quickly, but somehow the way he had invited her had put the thing in perspective for all time, she thought, as she got out of the car. He was to be a friend, just a good friend, no more no less. She went to her room in an oddly disappointed frame of mind and couldn't think why.

The next afternoon, however, something happened to put all Charlotte's doubts out of her mind and spring her high to an elevation that made her eyes like stars when she went to meet the RMO. Derek had a visitor.

At this stage, he was allowed permitted visitors at any time and the girl who had said she was Fay Iverbury appeared again.

She asked rather timidly if she could see him again if she promised faithfully not to say anything to him. "I know he was upset last time and I've realized why, but I won't let the same thing happen again," she said earnestly.

"What do you mean—what did happen?" Charlotte asked quickly. "You can tell me—besides being the nurse on duty today, I'm his cousin."

"Oh!" That seemed to make the girl more unhappy. She said, "Oh, dear, I hadn't realized that. I seem to remember someone said so when I was here before. Oh, perhaps I'd better go."

"No, no, for goodness' sake don't do that, not before we clear all this mystery up," Charlotte said briskly. "I'll speak to Sister when she comes up to her office again. She won't be long. But meantime, let's clear up one thing: you're *not* called Fay Iverbury, are you?"

The girl looked scared through her unattractive spectacles. "No, I just said that to make him see me. I didn't think he would otherwise. I knew he wanted to see Fay, though, so I said I was Fay, just to get into his room."

Charlotte said, trying to hide her excitement, "And who is Fay Iverbury?"

"She's the person I work for. She owns the King's Head."

Charlotte felt shocked and looked shocked. The handsome big blonde woman who owned that particular pub was Fay Iverbury? And what, for goodness sake, had she to do with Derek? Why, now he was so ill, did he keep clamouring to see her? She said blankly, "And you? What is *your* name, then?"

"Me? Oh, I'm Patsy. Patsy Wakeman, that is. I serve there."

"Oh, I see," Charlotte murmured, her head reeling. "But I don't begin to understand—why did you want to see my cousin so badly? You must know how ill he is? And why, why in the world tell us that you'd both been going to be married?"

"Well, it's true!" Patsy returned, with some spirit. "It was all arranged, though I don't know whether he meant to carry it out. He must have, come to think of it, because he was playing up for his aunt's money and he heard that his aunt wouldn't leave him anything if he didn't marry and settle down."

Charlotte was angry. "Now that can't be true! He didn't even recognize you!"

"But that's what I'm trying to tell you—I thought of it when I left here. I kept wondering and wondering why he treated me like a stranger, and then I looked in a shop window and saw that I'd got my glasses on! I forgot to take them off. I don't suppose he'd ever seen me with them on before—of course he wouldn't recognise me. They make me look so different—look!" and she whipped off the offending glasses as she spoke.

They did make a difference; all the difference in the world. Without them, Patsy was softly pretty, in a way to make men feel tender and protective, Charlotte saw. Just the sort of girl, she supposed helplessly, to appeal to her cousin Derek. "But he can't have known you very well, not to know about them!"

"Oh, I don't know," Patsy objected. "I naturally don't wear them for work, and I don't put them on when I'm out—well, on familiar ground I can manage. But I'd never been to the hospital before, so I wore them to read all the directions so I wouldn't waste time getting lost, and I suppose I forgot all about them."

Charlotte digested that. Sister still hadn't returned and she didn't know what to do. She still wasn't convinced that it would be the right thing to let this girl in to see her cousin again, remembering the last time and how upset he was. She said reflectively, "So you're planning to marry my cousin because you think he's going to be rich!"

The girl coloured painfully. "Oh, no, that's not the way it is at all, though I knew you'd think that! Derek wanted it that way but I—I guess I'm silly over him. Not that it matters now. But I've always been, ever since I first saw him. And I just wanted to see him, the once, and try and make him remember me so he won't keep on being upset about some stranger bursting in—that's what he kept saying last time I was here, and I can't bear it," she choked.

Sister appeared at the end of the corridor. Charlotte left the girl and went to meet

Sister to tell her what had happened. Sister took Charlotte into her office, to talk in peace. She was shrewd and understanding, but she did so like to take her time over things. Charlotte fretted over the time she had left the girl waiting, and she wasn't entirely surprised when a junior burst in and said that a visitor had got into Mr. Ferndale's room.

Sister rose wrathfully. "Who let anyone in?" she demanded, but Charlotte said quickly, "It'll be that girl, Sister. I expect she decided not to wait for permission. I'm sorry."

The junior capped things by saying, "It is a girl, Sister—the one who was here with glasses, who upset Mr. Ferndale. Only she took them off beside the bed and he shouted out something that sounded like "Patsy!" and—I'm afraid she's kissing him."

6

THE best that Ogmarsh could offer was a smallish family hotel. Charlotte went out dressed for that, and found that Keith Berrington drove her into Tamworth to the Royal, where Charlotte's plain little dark blue wool dress didn't do much for her. But she didn't usually worry about clothes so long as she was neat and not hopelessly out of fashion, and it made her uneasy that she cared so much about how she looked, for this man who obviously saw her only as a rather tiresome second-year nurse that for some reason he felt responsibility for. There was a young woman near her with piled hair and long earrings, wearing a long sleeved, backless creation that never saw its beginning in Tamworth, and even the elderly lady at the next table looked crushingly elegant in a dark green gown that dully glittered every time the light caught it.

And Keith Berrington looked absolutely right for this place, too. Charlotte could have kicked him for not warning her.

He didn't seem to notice, either. He listened avidly to her story of Derek's visitor, but only after he had given a great deal of attention to the menu and the wine list.

"So your cousin Derek really did mean to marry that girl," he said at last, speculatively looking at Charlotte. "Do you mind?"

"No, why should I?" she said, colour slowly staining her cheeks. But it wasn't entirely true. She did mind. She had wanted Derek to do better than that. How would that girl cope with Ferndale House, if and when the old aunt left Derek all her money? In her heart, Charlotte was convinced that that was what would happen. Aunt Elizabeth was no fool, and if Uncle George really thought he'd inherit, he hadn't assessed his elderly relative correctly. All that money, and a little wife like Patsy Wakeman who, if Charlotte read her right, would want no more than a little house on that new estate outside Ogmarsh, and a little car, and Derek in a bowler hat and striped trousers boarding the eight fifteen every morning, with everyone else's husband. Poor Derek, couldn't he *see*?

Keith Berrington remarked, "I'm glad you don't mind. I had an idea it would be rather like this. Well, so now we have a formidable list of questions still unanswered, if what you tell me your cousin was able to offer after his visitor had gone, amounts to no more than this."

"He was too dizzy with happiness to think much about it," Charlotte admitted, with a small smile.

Keith's eyebrows went up, and his lips twitched. "This I must see. Well, we now have (according to your very juvenile detective friends) a blonde girl looking scared in the woods, a housemaid from Ferndale House who shouldn't have been out at that time, with a man we haven't accounted for. We don't know what your very circumspect housekeeper was doing in the woods, either, do we? Didn't your cousin bother about that? Oh, well, no, I suppose someone had the sense to sedate him after the excitement of his lady friend's visit."

"Yes, but I talked to him just before I came out and he didn't seem to be really interested in all this any more. Only about . . . Fay Iverbury. And he wouldn't say how he heard that he was to get in touch with her. He just kept saying, over and over, 'I must see Fay!'"

He thought about it. "And you say your uncle obviously knew the woman and wouldn't say who or what she was, in all this business?"

She flushed. "My Uncle was quite startled at the mention of her name but now we know she's the owner of that pub, it probably only means he owes her a lot of money. Even my friends in the nursing staff seem to know about my Uncle George's drinking habits."

"And your cousin is still anxious about what is threatening his uncle?"

"Yes, he still keeps saying that he thinks my uncle is being blackmailed. In fact, he did tell me how he came across that information." She searched in her bag for a piece of paper torn from a notebook. "I wrote it down. He heard my uncle on the telephone, and Uncle George said to someone, 'Pay it off at once? You must be mad! I can't raise that much!' Well, it's obvious, isn't it? He *is* being pressed by someone for money."

"But not necessarily blackmailed," the RMO pointed out, with eyebrows raised again. "Your cousin must have heard something else, although that in itself doesn't sound too good. Tell me, why did he want you to know especially? Are you in the habit of fixing things for your family?"

Charlotte said slowly, "Derek always did come to me when he was bothered about something," and because this sounded so wistful even in her own ears, and she was afraid he would think she cared specially about Derek that way, she said quickly, "I expect, of course, it's because I'm full of good ideas and a lot of energy for putting them into practice. My old aunt calls me one of the *do-ers* of the world. I'm not sure that was a compliment. Are you?"

"I think it was," he said quietly. "But on the face of it, I don't see what else you can do here. It is odd, I agree, but if your cousin is settled about that young woman and he recovers satisfactorily, and doesn't want proceedings taken, I doubt if you need fear anything further. Until someone is found who was seen to shoot your cousin, or the weapon is discovered, I don't see that much *can* be done."

"But I can't let things go, not now I've got all this information," Charlotte objected. "I know for sure that Derek was right, and not just getting worked up over nothing. Anyone can see from these facts that something very wrong is going on at Ferndale House, and Derek will come back to it, I'm sure. He isn't one to let his own happiness side-track him from doing his duty by the family."

"Oh, heavens," the RMO said faintly.

"But you don't have to worry about us," she said quickly. "You've done all you could, and if Derek (I mean, *when* Derek) recovers, you can forget all about us."

"Do you think that is what I shall want to do?" he asked.

She fidgeted under that close look. "Oh,

I don't know. I know you indicated that it gave you something to do—"

"Is that all I gave you to understand?" He looked shocked. "I thought I mentioned something much more important."

"Being friends with me," she said swiftly. "I know you did and I'm grateful, but I must have been a sore trial to you in the past, and I've been thinking about it lately, and I don't want you to feel responsible for me and my family. I know you said it would be interesting (or something like that) but I can't believe it. You'll meet someone else like that staff nurse—"

She broke off, wishing she could wind the clock back to the point before she started this extremely tactless conversation. She felt out of place, a nuisance to him, but she didn't have to make things worse by saying that sort of thing, did she?

He considered the point gravely, turning his wine glass so that the liquid caught the light and gleamed like a jewel. "Did you know her, Charlotte?"

"Who? Rosemary Deane? Yes, a little. She was terrifically efficient and pretty and cool and self-confident and—oh, all the things I'm not and never will be."

"Yes," he said, glancing at her.

"Whenever anyone talks about being a staff nurse and getting medals and being considered the tops, it's always Rosemary Deane they think of and mention—those who knew her, that is. And the little new ones who don't know her, get told about her."

She refrained from adding that people called her the "Iceberg" and that they considered the cool efficient consultant who had won her deserved all he got. But then no one really liked Oscar Verrall, either—not for himself. For his work, yes, but how could you like a man who had retreated so long ago behind a cast-iron exterior? A man so dedicated to his work that he forgot to be a man ever?

"You're very kind about her," Keith said unexpectedly. "Perhaps you didn't know her well enough to feel anything else about her. And yet I don't know—I remember particularly one embarrassing scrape of yours, when Rosemary was on your ward. I remember seeing the way she looked at you—"

Now Charlotte really coloured. "Well, I must have been an awful brat," she said defensively.

"You don't have to be so nice about Rosemary Deane," he told her gently. "We parted most logically. She was right, of course. I wasn't the right person for her. I have no ambition, you see. I just want to stay here, in this part of the world . . ."

He broke off, looking into the middle distance.

It was all very well, Charlotte thought, trying to pretend he didn't care about Rosemary. But there he was, sitting there with his mind winging away from Tamworth, to London no doubt, where Rosemary would be setting up a smart flat to meet all the right people for her Oscar's sake; people who could be of use to him. Rosemary would, of course, know all the right people, and the right things to say. The right things to wear, too.

The navy dress reproached Charlotte. She looked down at it, and wondered why, for the first time, that she hadn't cared more about clothes and make-up. Probably because these were the things Isabel cared most about, and that was enough to put anyone off.

"What do you want to do with your life, Charlotte?" he asked suddenly.

"Oh, I don't know! Nurse," she said, confused. No one had asked her that question directly before. Even among her friends, no one had gone so far as to face the distant future; the present was grim enough. "It's pretty feeble, isn't it, not having a special 'thing', except, perhaps, that I thought I'd like to work among malnutrition cases. That would mean going to Africa, I suppose, and I'm not really clear in my mind if it's Africa I want most, or the diseases. I expect it's all mixed up—I want it all. You see," she said in a burst of confidence, "no one really needs me here. Not desperately, I mean. It must be nice to be really desperately needed."

She looked up and found his eyes on her, with a look she hadn't seen there before. She couldn't place it but decided that it might just be that she had stumbled on the thing he was most interested in.

He nodded thoughtfully, and said, "Of course, you've two of three more years yet. You might change your mind and settle for your midder and then drift into District Nursing." And because it struck her that he was just making conversation and still thinking with regret about Rosemary Deane, Charlotte said, "Yes, I might, at that. No use looking too far ahead."

"There are other people who desperately need help, of course, nearer home," he added, still not looking at her, and when she didn't answer that, he continued, half to himself, "I remember Rosemary said it was no use looking too far ahead, and then suddenly one day she knew what she wanted—London, smart consulting rooms, or a sanatorium in Switzerland. Either, she said, would be a challenge. It would appear that the back streets of Rolborough were not a challenge."

The back streets of Rolborough. Of course! Now Charlotte saw what he was getting at. She said, "You think that my malnutrition diseases might well be here? You'd better not let the local authorities hear you say that! Very proud of their baby clinics!"

"I could take you to a lot of families who haven't apparently heard of the baby clinics, or perhaps for one reason or another have and can't or won't attend," he said softly.

And then he started talking about them, and Charlotte listened so enthralled to Keith Berrington on his pet hobby-horse that she forgot her unsuitable dress and the elegant women around her, she forgot Rosemary Deane, everything in fact but Keith Berrington talking about the subject nearest his heart. She divined, too, that it was seldom he did talk like this, to anyone. She didn't stop to question why it should be her he was talking to; she just listened, afraid to miss a single word. This might not happen again.

He took her arm when they left. Friends, he had said, hadn't he? He looked quietly satisfied. Yes, he's found someone to unload his theories on, about the poor of

Rolborough. Was that what she wanted? She was shocked to suddenly glimpse just what she did want of him. She wanted to share his life, working for the poor of Rolborough, with the satisfaction of knowing that he belonged to her; not to just listen to his theories about his work and to know that his heart and mind were still in the keeping of that other girl!

Charlotte's panacea for woes of any kind was work. She threw herself into it, and took on extra duties, so that she had less time to think. Derek began to mend quickly now that he had his Patsy there. He talked to Charlotte while she made his bed and washed him. "Do you like her? Fancy me not knowing her with those hideous glasses on! Isn't she pretty? Charlotte, is it going to be all right with the family, do you think? Lotta—you must help Patsy when she marries me. Don't let Isabel get at her, will you?"

"You're really going to marry her, Derek?" Charlotte asked carefully, and when his glistening smile wavered a little at her tone, she added quickly, "You will let

Aunt Elizabeth see her first, though, won't you?"

"Good grief, why? Patsy's marrying me, not Aunt Elizabeth!"

"But it would be a courtesy, Derek," Charlotte pleaded uneasily. It didn't take much more than such an omission for Aunt Elizabeth to touchily decide it was a grave slight to her, and if Derek was hankering for a legacy, no matter what size, he must surely have some sense about it, and show courtesy even if he didn't feel it. She tried to put this to him but he wouldn't listen.

"You don't understand, Lotta—it's to be a bedside wedding!" he stunned her by saying. "I've asked Sister about it this morning! Well, good heavens, they say I shall be in here some time and how shall I have any peace of mind not knowing what's happening to Patsy?"

"She can surely look after herself for a few more weeks, Derek," Charlotte protested. "She's done so all along!"

He shook his head, impatient again. "You don't understand! Of course she's done so all along but now it's different—it's this business of Uncle George's! She'll get caught up with that, and there's this Fay Iverbury. I must see her! Why doesn't she come?"

"Why do you have to see her?" Charlotte asked him.

"Because she knows about Uncle George, I feel it in my bones, but she just laughs and tells me not to be a silly boy. She knows, Lotta, and I must find out! I'm sure it affects me but I don't know how!"

"If I were you, I'd let Uncle George stew in his own debts. It'll bring him to his own senses much more quickly than if you interfere!" Charlotte said robustly. "Besides, you asked me to do what I could and I'm having a go, though I must say I didn't get very far with Uncle George. He looked livid and as good as told me to mind my own business! He looked as if the sound of Fay's name had given him quite a turn so I suppose he owes her plenty!"

Derek shook his head. "No, I don't think it's as simple as that. Sometimes I think Patsy knows something about it but that she's too scared to say. Sometimes I get the impression that quite a lot of people are concerned and she's terrified of the lot of them. She's afraid about me being in here so long. How long do you think I shall be here, Lotta?"

"Well, you were suffering from exposure as well, when you were brought in, Derek," Charlotte told him frankly. "Otherwise a healthy chap like you wouldn't have been in such a pickle. What sort of nursing abilities has your little Patsy got, or is she helpless?"

He was so indignant. "Of course she isn't helpless! She had to nurse her old grannie for ages before she died. No, that's what worries me," he said, turning his head fretfully from side to side, in a new way that wasn't like him at all but was tied up with his condition since he had come here. It worried Charlotte, who had the nagging anxiety that he would never be fit and strong again as he had used to be. "I think Patsy's personally scared about something. I think they think so here, too, or else why would they agree to a bedside wedding? I'm told that isn't usual," and he looked directly at her.

"I believe if you can cook up a good enough reason it can be laid on any time," Charlotte said, trying to sound more serene than she felt. "I suppose you'll have a posh ceremony to clinch it when you get out of here."

Derek brushed that aside as of no importance. What worried him was plain. "*If* I get out of here," he fretted. "That's what worries me. And if I don't, what will become of Patsy? You'll take care of her, Charlotte, won't you?"

"Don't be silly, Derek, of course you'll be all right. Just as you always were. Only, do be sensible—at least write to Aunt Elizabeth about it. All you have to do is let her *know*—she's old and feels that people want her money, not her. Let her see that you care for her approval of Patsy!"

"That's good advice, I must say!" Derek snorted, with something of the old vigorous manner she knew so well. "And what sort of position shall I be in if she writes back and says she doesn't like it at all? Have you thought of that, old girl?"

It was a thought that Charlotte couldn't

put aside lightly and he knew it. Living as they all did under the shadow of that rich old woman's pleasure, they were apt to bend their existences to suit her, and it wasn't right, Charlotte told herself fiercely.

She looked almost enviously at the visitors that afternoon. They didn't belong to a county family. Their lives were their own. Mrs. Overton was happy so long as trade was fairly good in her little wool shop. Brenda Newey, like most local girls, pretended she didn't care for service but it suited her, until she got married, and that would probably be to a young man in a good factory job in Ogmarsh. Even old Granfer Trippick's Jill had no worries—she was apprenticed to a hairdresser in Ogmarsh, and hoped to go on to a larger town, so the old man had confided to Charlotte. They were all of them free as air. Charlotte briefly envied them.

It was during the visiting hour that she became aware of the gossip again. It struck a chill deep into her, because it was all about her family.

She heard it first of all when she was

bending over the bed of the patient beside Mrs. Overton's husband. A new young man who had been receiving medical treatment for his ulcer but now had to be operated on. He was very much distressed, and while Charlotte was reassuring him and his young wife, about the routine of the operation, she distinctly heard Mrs. Overton say, "That housekeeper is not like that! Time and again she's been in my shop for knitting wool and always cheerful and nothing in the world to complain about. But this time I knew something was wrong. Real white she looked. Said she'd leave today if she could find another place like it—the things that were going on in that house—" but there she broke off, for her husband had noticed Charlotte bending over the next bed, and squeezed his wife's hand in warning.

Charlotte went down the ward worriedly. Mrs. Endon was the last person to say such a thing to an outsider, and Mrs. Endon had been in the woods, hadn't she—a thing that was as much out of character with the housekeeper at Ferndale House, as if the woman had taken to standing on her head.

Lenny Quexford had a new visitor, one Charlotte hadn't seen before. Lenny was listening avidly to the man, who looked a decent little man, rather like a clerk in an office. In fact, Charlotte suddenly thought, pulling up and looking round at him—now she came to think of it, he looked just like one of the male clerks in the solicitors' office, the family's solicitors. But why should one of their solicitor's clerks come and visit Lenny Quexford, who hadn't a shilling in the world beyond his sick pay and unemployment benefit? She shrugged and walked on again, scolding herself for being so jittery. Granfer Trippick called her over, and she forgot about Lenny.

Granfer took her hand in his gnarled old one. "Nurse, dear, I'm so worried about my Jill!" He usually began like that nowadays, so the significance of the conversation passed over Charlotte's head, worried as she was over Derek. "She went early today, on account of not wanting to answer my questions, I suspect. I'm an old man and it seems to me that she ought not to be doing what she's doing. You tell me, lass!"

"What *is* she doing?" Charlotte smiled. She was privately of the opinion that Jill Trippick could very well look after herself. She concentrated on the thought of Derek and whether that infection he had would be eradicated completely or whether he would be like young Smithers who had been in and out of the hospital for years for something similar. Derek wouldn't be able to ride again, and without the county horse trials and the local hunt, what would he do? Go to the city, like men in the village? A city office?

He might well have to, anyway, if he upset Aunt Elizabeth, she reflected with uneasiness. Derek wasn't too young to have to commute to a City job. They had just thought of him as young at home because Aunt Elizabeth was obligingly keeping him at university, but Derek was only fooling away his life, wasn't he? And how would a wife like Patsy fit into that?

Granfer Trippick gave Charlotte's hand a shake, seeing her attention wander. "And he's old enough to be her father, and it's not right!" he said, anxiously. "You'd think Ferndale House'd be far enough away from Ogmarsh."

Charlotte's thoughts bounced back with an uneasy jerk. Who had the old man been talking about, for goodness sake? "Oh, I shouldn't worry," she said mechanically, but the old man wouldn't have that.

"I do worry!" he said. "Oh, I'm not blaming you, nurse. Why should your people worry about the inside lives of the folk they employ? They're not employing game-keepers for the likes of my grand-daughter to go out with, but this one's not the one I'd have chosen for my girl."

Now Charlotte began to understand. It would be Mears, she supposed. A florid, big swaggering fellow who drank, so it was said, and who had a bit of a reputation in the village, with the girls. Well, Jill must know what she was doing!

"What does her mother say?" That was always a safe one.

"She don't get on with her mother," the old man said. "She don't live at home with her mother any more. Got a room in a girl friend's house. I don't like it, but there, it's near her work, which her home is not, seeing as it's here in this town."

This town. Rolborough. Charlotte tried to pin her thoughts on to some little back street where Jill Trippick lived but all she could see were the mean streets that meant so much to the RMO.

She did what she could to comfort Granfer Trippick, but on the way back to the ward kitchen, she was caught by Lenny Quexford again. His visitor had gone. He said, "Nurse, you still live at home, don't you?"

Charlotte, who chatted easily about most things to the patients, was inclined to be guarded about this question, ever since the trouble started. She said warily, "Why, Lenny?"

"I'm not being nosey, Nurse. Just a bit worried, like. My visitor just now, he said a thing that worried me. Do you still live at home, nurse?"

"Yes, I do, but what's it got to do with your visitor, Lenny?"

"Well, he seemed to know so much about

your people. I've known him all my life. His folks used to live next door to mine, only they moved to a bit better district, and it was good of him to come and visit me, only, see everyone's talking about your family, and I didn't take much notice, only when he starts, too—"

Charlotte felt a lot easier. So that was who the man was—a respectable one-time neighbour. How wrong you could be! Thinking he looked like a clerk in the solicitor's office! She said, kindly, "Well, it's the only hospital everyone local has to go to, and everyone's bound to be interested in each other. You must know that Yates has a son in our stables, and that one of the maids at home visits your pal across the way who tried to have an argument with his lorry. So you see? And there's my own cousin in a side ward—"

"Yes, nurse," Lenny said doubtfully, but he was far from happy.

"Now what *is* it?" she said, very kindly.

"I dunno, nurse. I'm an old hand here. Been in and out for years and I'm in proper now. But never before has there been this atmosphere—secrets. I don't like it. Whispers all the time. Don't you feel it, nurse?"

She did, but she couldn't say so to a patient—she'd send up his temperature. "Oh, come on, Lenny, you've been reading too many books out of the hospital library. Or else it's that thriller serial when you put your headphones on at night—I've seen you! Frightening the wits out of yourself!"

He grinned, but couldn't resist adding, "That don't make this a regular hospital of secrets, though, nurse!"

She went off laughing at him. The visitors sprang to their feet when their bell went, and there was the shuffling of their exit, and the clearing up afterwards. But Lenny's remark couldn't be shifted. *Hospital of Secrets*. What an odd thing for such a sensible little man to be caught saying!

And it didn't help when Sylvia caught her coming out of the kitchen, pushing a trolley of tea-things. "I say, is there someone at your place called Warren Jeakings?"

"Yes, there is—at least, one of my family knows someone of that name. He's a friend of my Uncle George's step-sister Miriam. But how could you have heard it, Syl?"

Sylvia looked fierce. "I heard that little brute Tom Yates telling his father about it and he wasn't bothering to lower his voice, either. All the people around were pretending not to be listening, but you know how it is when you can hear an account of someone having the father and mother of all rows!"

"The—*what?*" Charlotte had to laugh. "Oh, no, now I've heard everything! Now such a thing isn't possible! Jeakings is a hail-fellow-well-met-type—I doubt if he'd quarrel with anyone. It just isn't his way. And besides, Miriam wouldn't quarrel with *him*! She hopes to marry him and she isn't really young enough any more to let a decent catch go, poor old Miriam. Besides, she doesn't quarrel either, really. Let's off a stinging remark if she feels like it, but anything so lowbred as a row—no! Definitely not!"

"Well," Sylvia said, one eye on the purposeful approach of the temporary staff nurse, who seemed to feel it was her duty to chase up the second-years but to leave the juniors to their own unfortunate devices, "before I vanish, I just tell you for what it's worth—that horrible little Tom Yates was spinning a yarn about being in the stables and listening in to this row and thoroughly enjoying it! And from what I heard, it certainly was a row, and I don't think he's capable of making that sort of story up."

Charlotte's hands were shaking as she handed out cups and poured tea. What was happening to everything? Miriam in a vulgar brawl, down in the stables, where presumably that lad had had his big ears flapping? No, surely not!

She glanced across at Tom Yates' father, and he was looking across at Charlotte, speculatively, enjoying his own thoughts. The trouble was, he knew what the row (if there had been one!) was about, and that would seem the key to the whole thing. All Charlotte's thoughts clamoured that this might well hinge on what was happening at home, which worried Derek so much. But for heaven's sake, what could happen?

As she asked each patient how many slices, and cut cake for those who wanted it, she thought of Miriam; cool, well-bred Miriam, whose fine tailoring and magnificent posture made up amply for her lack of good looks. A fine horse-woman, a good business woman, who had, in her quiet way, made a lot of money from her antiques. One—perhaps the only one, apart from Charlotte herself—who hadn't always been pestering the old aunt for money. No, the more she thought of it, the more Charlotte was convinced that that story wasn't right—Miriam wouldn't quarrel with Warren Jeakings.

What would Miriam do, though, she asked herself, if she had discovered that Warren Jeakings was perhaps interested in some little village girl, like, perhaps, Granfer Trippick's Jill? Only that was absurd, wasn't it? Jill was going around with flash Albert Mears, that new gamekeeper her Uncle George hadn't cared about from the start.

But Miriam *was* at Ferndale House, and the chances were that she had been in the stables with Warren Jeakings, because they rode together regularly every day. And

Tom Yates would hardly tell a story publicly, using names, if it hadn't been true up to a point.

Charlotte couldn't bear it. She knew she had to go and telephone Miriam, not to ask her outright, of course—one didn't approach Miriam like that. But she might be able to assess from Miriam's tone, if anything was wrong. Or it might be worth while to even tell Miriam what she had heard on the ward, even if Miriam played up for Tom Yates to be sacked. He wasn't all that good at his work, and he was a little menace with that long tongue of his.

In her tea-break, Charlotte went to the switchboard and asked to telephone Ferndale House. She looked so worried that the porter on duty asked her if all went well at home.

She glanced sharply at him, but before he could say anything else, another call came through. He said he'd put her through in the end booth, but presently he called her. "Nurse, do you know where the RMO is? I can't find him!"

"He's about somewhere. I've not long

seen him," Charlotte said, and tried to remember where. The porter got her home on the telephone and she spent a fruitless five minutes trying to persuade Isabel to admit that Miriam was about.

"Darling Charlotte," Isabel purred, "you are always telephoning and wanting to speak to someone in a very secretive manner and it won't do, you know!"

"Isabel, there's nothing secret about my telephone calls," Charlotte said wearily. "Now may I speak to Miriam? I haven't got long!"

"No, darling Charlotte, you may not. This is now my home and you can tell me anything and I will pass it on."

Charlotte tried to tamp down her sheer frustration, but it wasn't possible. This was how it had been when she had wanted to speak to her uncle. This was how it was when Derek had arranged to meet her in the woods. Charlotte knew that if she tried to reason with Isabel she would finish up by quarrelling with her so she said shortly, "Never mind!" and hung up.

The porter was still phoning around to

find the RMO. He called to Charlotte.

"Look, nurse, how would it be if you were to speak to this party—a friend of the RMO? She wants to arrange to meet him and I thought that you—" He didn't finish but looked apologetic. Charlotte eyed him thoughtfully, but it was no use taking the point up with him. He had probably seen her out with the RMO in his car and thought they were all friends together. She nodded and said she'd do her best and went back into the telephone booth.

But the minute she picked up the receiver, she wished she hadn't. The caller was Rosemary Deane.

7

ROSEMARY DEANE had a soft voice, and a brevity that was deceptive. The men all liked her, unreservedly, but not many of the nurses cared about her. She was the sort of staff nurse who looked frail and clinging but who was rigidly efficient under that soft manner, and the nurses were never really sure that her kindness was sincere. She never did a thing without reason, Charlotte had heard many an older nurse say, and the younger ones were always suspicious that Rosemary might be secretly taking a "dig" at them beneath that soft gentle tone.

Charlotte remembered all that now, when Rosemary said softly, "Oh! Nurse Charlotte Arrowsmith! That's odd! I wonder how it is that the porter thinks *you* might be able to give Dr. Berrington a message?"

"Perhaps because I might see him on my

ward in ten minutes time when I go back on duty," Charlotte said crisply, "but if I can't help you, I'll turn you over to the Casualty Officer if you like!"

"Oh, no, you'll do, my dear," Rosemary said softly. "I don't suppose people have got it wrong when they say you're in his car more often than not. So next time you find yourself there, ask him to meet me at The Copper Kettle tomorrow at four thirty, will you?"

"Goodness, you could have entrusted that message to the porter, couldn't you?" Charlotte said, puzzled.

"Not entirely. I also wanted to ask you about something else," Rosemary purred. "Do you happen to know a man called Rory Utting?"

"Rory Utting? No, I can't say I do. Is he an old patient—why should you think I would know him?"

"No, he isn't an old patient. His interest is horses, and I believe you still have a few at Ferndale House."

"Then you should contact my Uncle George, not me! I don't even live there any more," Charlotte said with distaste. "Why don't you telephone there?"

"I have," Rosemary said softly, "and I only get dear Isabel on the telephone. Now I like Isabel as much as most women, but she's my sister's friend, not mine, and when I want her husband for a word or two, I don't care to be blocked by her. I thought you might have better luck."

Charlotte almost but quite warmed to her, simply because she suffered from Isabel. "I don't have any better luck—I've just tried," she said.

"Oh? You want Rory Utting too? I wonder why, now!"

"Oh, Nurse Deane, don't be silly—of course I don't want Rory Utting! I don't even know him. You do, remember? No, I wanted to speak to someone else in my family but Isabel wouldn't let me."

"Why don't you go over to Ferndale House in person?"

"Because Isabel would see me come and be at the door to meet me," Charlotte said in exasperation.

"Someone's got to take a message to Rory

Utting," Rosemary said. "I can't reach him, and your cousin Derek will be in even more trouble if someone doesn't."

"Derek! Now listen, if you know anything about what's worrying my cousin Derek, the RMO will be terribly glad! Do you?"

"Well, I want to talk to Dr. Berrington, don't I?" Rosemary said gently. "Don't forget, The Copper Kettle tomorrow," and most aggravatingly she rang off.

Charlotte was fuming. Who on earth was Rory Utting? She still had a few minutes of her tea-break, so she thumbed through the telephone directory, but no such name was there. She wondered if it was the name they had given to something. The whole thing was such a stupid mystery. It might even be a horse. Charlotte remembered an old joke of her uncle's about a Mr. Montmorency which had turned out to be a racehorse they had all thought would win and when it had come in last her uncle had been in a foul temper for days, and the last canvas in the gallery vanished. Aunt Elizabeth had been terribly angry then, too, Charlotte remembered, and had said roundly that rather than sell the family portraits, why hadn't they come to her to buy them? At least they wouldn't have had to leave Ferndale walls.

There was not time to think of anything else. She was due back on the ward, and she had had no tea. If Sister knew she would have a great deal to say about it. Nurses, she averred, couldn't work if they didn't eat regularly; little and often. Aunt Elizabeth was a stickler for regular food, too.

The thought of Aunt Elizabeth nagged at Charlotte during the rest of her time on duty. There was Derek, getting married tomorrow and not even having told her he had thought of it. Charlotte doubted, now it came to the point, whether anyone had acquainted Aunt Elizabeth of Derek's accident—if she found out, the old lady wouldn't be at all pleased about that! And there was Uncle George's trouble. Whatever it was, Aunt Elizabeth would want to know. She would find out sooner or later—she had an uncanny nose for trouble and she was always more angry if she thought she had deliberately been kept in the dark.

Considering it had been a visitors' afternoon, her patients weren't very happy, Charlotte could see. She spoke to Granfer Trippick. "Why don't you stop worrying about young Jill? I assure you, young girls of her age can very well take care of themselves nowadays!"

The old man's answer surprised her. "You only see 'em in this hospital, nurse, love. All protected, you young gals are. What with Home Sister a-watching over the hours you come in at night and Sister Tutor a-seeing of you not getting hold of the wrong ideas. Oh, I know all about that! I've heard enough to set me thinking, in all the months I've been in this hospital, and if I'd had my way, my Jill would have been in here as a nurse! There! What do you think of that?"

Charlotte mentally shuddered at the thought, but she didn't let the old man see that. Instead, she said, "Well, I don't know. We don't all like the same kind of job and I would say that your Jill was very happy and suitably settled as a hairdressing apprentice."

"Ah, yes, maybe," he fretted. "But it's the freedom she gets! Too much of it! And the girls she mixes with and the life she leads, living in lodgings. And all that muck she puts on her face and the clothes she wears—thinks of nothing else! All her money goes on them things! And her hair—it's not really that colour, you know," he confided. Dropping his voice, he said, earnestly. "She dyes it! What do you say about that?"

Charlotte laughed and patted his hand. "Lots of people do that nowadays, you know. Some people wear wigs, too."

He was very shocked. She wished she hadn't said it. "I don't think your Jill will wear a wig, so don't worry."

"No, but she makes her hair all blue sometimes. I wish she wouldn't—it was such a pretty colour when she was a little nipper. Like honey, thick honey, it was. Do you dye your hair, nurse, if I may make so bold as to ask?"

The shades of Ferndale House hanging

over her, she thought ruefully. "You may ask and I will tell you—I do not! In fact, my friends tell me I don't think enough about hair and make-up and clothes."

"You're all right, lass!" he said earnestly. "Don't you change! If it's the men you're thinking about, I can tell you there's one fine chap who wouldn't have you change, *I* know!"

She looked startled, so he amplified, with a chuckle, "That nice Dr. Berrington! Ah, that surprised you, didn't it? I've seen the way he looks at you, lass!"

Charlotte took her hand away. "Yes, well," she said hastily, "that's a lot of nonsense and you know it, you bad old man, and what is more, I shall have to be moving, or I'll have Sister after me."

"No, wait nurse—there's this favour I wanted to ask you, about my Jill," he pleaded. "I'll only keep you a minute—I wondered: would you talk to her? Would you? Go to her hair shop where she works and tell her from me—well, you'll know how to put it. She'll listen to you. Will you?"

"What do you want me to tell her?" Charlotte murmured, distressed. This was what came of allowing the patients to tell you all about their private troubles. She didn't want to have anything to do with the truculent Jill. But he was such a dear old man and if she could only make him easy for a *little*. "What is it that you think I can achieve by it?"

"I want you to tell her, seeing as your folks employ the chap, to keep away from that Albert Mears, that game keeper who comes in here to see Yates. Too old for my Jill, that Mears is. Old enough to be her father, and he's not a good man!"

He was very much upset at the mere thought of Mears and his Jill, so Charlotte said hastily, "Well, I'll try. I have to go into Ogmarsh very shortly. I'll try, but don't hope for too much! Even if I tell her, I doubt if she'll take any notice of me, you know!"

"She will! I'm sure she will! Thinks a lot of the folks at Ferndale House, my Jill does," the old man said.

Later that afternoon Charlotte saw the

RMO going up the stairs. As she herself was returning from an errand for Sister, she ran up after him, calling to him.

He turned, and his formal "Yes, nurse, what can I do for you?" was belied by the nice, warm crinkly sort of smile he turned on her.

She hesitated, drinking in that smile, then she sharply called herself to order for poaching. He still belonged to that Rosemary Deane and anyone would be a fool for thinking otherwise. That seemed confirmed when she said, "I have a message for you, sir. A personal message, over the phone, from Miss Deane—Miss Rosemary Deane."

His face changed at once and he came down on a level with her. "Well?" he said, and all feeling was wiped out of his voice.

"The porter couldn't find you anywhere and I happened to be near so he asked me to speak to her. She wants you to meet her tomorrow at The Copper Kettle, for something urgent."

"What time, for heaven's sake? I'm not off tomorrow!" he said, in an exasperated tone, but when Charlotte told him the appointed time, he said he'd manage it somehow.

Yes, she told herself as she hurried back to her ward, he'd manage it somehow. He can pretend to be exasperated and whatever he likes, but that message has made his day. He'll be there!

An old patient had once said to Charlotte, "I pray my dear, that you'll be one of the favoured ones, and never know heartache. That face of yours tells me you've never had it. I trust you never will." In those days, on the women's section, it seemed to Charlotte that almost all of them had known it, but it was true: it hadn't touched her. Now she knew that she, too, had been touched by that dreadful thing. There was a cold lump where her heart ought to be, and she couldn't tear away from her mind the picture of his face as he had smiled at her, and then the smile had died, and all his thoughts had been caught up with just the mentioning of that other girl's name—that girl who hadn't wanted him, who had chosen someone else instead.

She rushed about her duties, and took on some that should have been done by the two juniors as well. It had been a long time since Charlotte had scrubbed macks but she scrubbed them at the same time as she tried to scrub out of her thoughts the aching yearning for Keith Berrington. She couldn't have said when it had first implanted itself there inside her; she only knew that it was a little like toothache, growing and growing, and that it would never leave her.

Her set smile didn't deceive the men, but by common consent they didn't ask her if she had headache or had had a strip torn off by Sister (a favourite description for the worst kind of malady on that ward) but they looked sympathetic and that hurt Charlotte more than if they had pretended not to notice. So she rushed about so that none of them should have the chance to ask her quietly and personally at the bedside, what was wrong.

If she thought that making herself physically tired might help, she was wrong. It didn't help a bit, and when Sister looked sharply at her and surprised her by sending her off duty fifteen minutes earlier than usual, she didn't know what to do.

Sylvia and Linda were both dated for that evening, so when Bob Culver, the Casualty Officer, passed Charlotte and asked her to take pity on him for three hours, she recklessly agreed to do so.

He seemed surprised. He had asked her before and always been politely but very nicely refused. He snapped up his advantage while it was still good.

He was a nice fellow, but rather giddy when out for the evening. Charlotte knew what it would be like, because of what the others had said; snatched food between dancing, and the dancing was the gyrations of the moment, not the formal waltzing and fox-trotting that Aunt Elizabeth gave grudging approval to. Charlotte impatiently decided that she had thought enough about Aunt Elizabeth that day and tried to throw herself into having fun with Bob.

But the lights hurt her eyes and she began to feel deadly tired. Bob let her sit down for longer than his restless feet usually allowed, and looked searchingly at her.

"What made you come with me?" he asked gently at last. "Had a row with the RMO?"

She threw her head up. "Goodness, has the gossip on my ward reached Casualty as well?" she exploded.

"No. I just use my eyes. He seems to sense when you come through Casualty. You look as if you're trying not to look in the direction where he is. It's as simple as that."

Charlotte looked agonised. "Oh, no! It can't be so obvious, on my part, that is! But on his part—no, you're mistaken!"

"Rot," Bob said robustly. "You must see the way he smiles at you. Can you honestly say he's ever smiled at anyone else like that? And people still chuckle over the way he used to get you out of trouble when you were a junior. He never sorted out any other junior, to my knowledge!"

"That," Charlotte said crisply, "was in the days when he was engaged to Staff Nurse Deane, so he could afford to be kind to someone else!"

"Honey, you really do need to be untangled, if there is such a word! You've got it all wrong, I do assure you. No RMO if he's got any sense, gets involved with any young nurse, certainly not through kindness. I'll own he's always been a law unto himself, but there are some shrewd persons who beg to offer their opinion that his tender helping of your troublous early career was more than enough to show the Deane Iceberg where she stood, so she looked for other fields to conquer. But yes, don't look so shocked, I was one who contributed that idea myself!"

"Then why did you ask me out with you this evening?" she said, in a muffled voice.

"Oh, that was mechanical, I suppose, because I've always liked you and you did look so wretched. And I know what it's like to be all alone and wretched. I did want you to come!"

"And I came, and I'll tell you why I came. Because although I'm soppy over the RMO he isn't soppy over me, and I had that rammed home to me when I saw his face, at the thought of meeting his dear Rosemary again tomorrow."

"Wha-at?" Bob Culver was more than startled. "How do you know he's meeting her?"

"Because she gave me the message for him over the telephone and I passed it on to him. He forgot all about everything and everyone from that moment, I assure you!"

"And I assure you that you are the world's biggest idiot for passing on that message, love! Why did you do it?"

"Why not? She would have phoned him again, I suppose, and told him that she had asked me to tell him. How would that have made me look?"

"Well, what do you know! I suppose she's had a row with poor old Verrall."

"What's this Oscar Verrall like, really like? I only know him as an extremely chilly individual with a big sense of his own importance."

Bob grinned. "Honey, I couldn't improve on that description, and it's also my poor opinion that he only offered for dear Rosemary because she belonged to the RMO. No love lost between Verrall and the RMO ever. I only wish the chap had married her before they had a row, so she wouldn't have come back and harassed poor old Berrington. I like him. He deserves something better than the Frigid Deane!"

"How do you know she's frigid?" Charlotte asked unthinkingly. She found Bob shaking with silent laughter at her.

"Darling girl, what a question! How would I know except that I tried to kiss her once, and I still feel the icy wind when I think of it! Oh, don't worry—I won't try to kiss you. I like you too much. But girls like Rosemary are rather a challenge. You know, we chaps do rather hanker to have it noised around that we alone were responsible for melting the iceberg. Silly lot, aren't we?"

Charlotte was honestly distressed to think that the girl the RMO still cherished in his thoughts should be spoken of like this by every man in the hospital. To have her name bandied about as a sort of joke, seemed all wrong, since she had been Keith Berrington's choice.

As if reading her thoughts, Bob said, "Of course, poor old Keith Berrington always did have his head in the clouds. He probably regards her as an angel, and takes her coolness as proof of that. To get her into a clinch would be to sully her pure white robes. (Sorry, that was unpardonable of me!) Well, Charlotte, since we have somehow got ourselves into a quiet little corner for a heart-to-heart chat, why don't we discuss something really interesting, and which I confess is tearing me apart with curiosity. The gossip, love, sweeping through Casualty from the upper wards like a breath of titillating fresh air; just what is going on at Ferndale House?"

8

OGMARSH was not Charlotte's favourite place in which to spend precious leave, but she had promised the old man and she was determined to do her best to see Jill and to make some impression on her.

On the bus journey to Ogmarsh, she framed opening sentences, and heard in her mind, the way Jill would answer, and it was all rather discouraging. And intruding into Jill's imaginary conversation was the conversation with Bob Culver last night. It wasn't nice to feel that he knew how she had let herself fall in love with the RMO. "Unrequited love" might be an old-fashioned phrase and one to call up ribald laughter among the juniors when they got out old-fasioned books from the town's public library, but when it was applied to one's self the word unrequited was not funny, only rather appropriate and singularly chilling in its sound.

What Bob knew about the gossip was disturbing, too. How could people be hearing such things about the Ferndales? It might, of course, be true that one of the Cubs had come into Casualty with a thorn deep in his foot, which had belied the Cub Mistress's earnest attempts at First Aid, and that Bob himself had encouraged the boy to talk, to take his mind off what had been a rather tricky business. It just might be so. But Charlotte couldn't help feeling that Fate was very much against her, to let such a thing happen. One couldn't even write it off as coincidence: this was the hospital for the whole district. They all came here, and everyone knew the Ferndales, and if something interested them about the Ferndale family it wasn't likely that they wouldn't remember that there was a nurse related to the Ferndale family. In fact, the Cub might well have mentioned Charlotte's own part in that afternoon's detection in the woods, when they had pushed their skill at mapping a stage further. Bob had had an amused twinkle in his eye when he had reported what that Cub had said, and Charlotte had had no doubt that Bob's report had been selective.

It was no use being annoyed about it now. Even if the Cub hadn't talked, there was no doubt that the gossip on the ward would trickle down through Casualty. One of the ward maids could have brought it, or one of the porters. The hospital grapevine was very efficient.

Charlotte dragged her thoughts back to Jill, and to her apparent interest in Albert Mears. At the back of Charlotte's mind was the teasing memory that Mears had been a married man. No wonder Granfer Trippick was worried!

In the end, Charlotte wasn't really ready to talk to Jill when she arrived in the High Street, because the preliminary asking of permission for a young apprentice to come out and talk hadn't after all been necessary. Charlotte almost bumped into Jill herself coming out of the cakeshop next door, laden with bags of sticky buns and fancies to have with their cup of tea. Jill recognized Charlotte and looked put out for a moment, then she pretended she hadn't recognized her.

"Jill! I was coming to see you!"

"What about? I saw my grandfather yesterday and he was all right then!"

"My dear, your grandfather isn't worse, only very worried about you," Charlotte said hastily.

"So?" Jill pouted.

"Look, can we go somewhere quiet and talk?"

"No, we can't, because I've got to get back and I'm not allowed to talk to people in working time. And I haven't got time after the shop closes on account of I'm making myself a dress and I don't get much time to borrow the girl's machine upstairs."

"Then I must talk to you now, because it's really urgent," Charlotte insisted. "Your grandfather mustn't be worried and I promised him I'd speak to you—"

"What about? He didn't say anything to me when I was there yesterday! What's he asking the nurses to talk to me for?"

"He didn't mention your friendship with Albert Mears?"

That did get a reaction. Jill flushed then whitened. "What if he did? How does it concern you?" she said.

"Mears is in my family's employ, and I believe it was said he's a married man."

"Well, he isn't, and what if he is working for Ferndale House? He can be friends with who he likes, off duty, can't he—and anyway, if anyone's going to speak to me, then it had better be Mr. George Ferndale."

"I think you'd be sorry if it were my uncle speaking to you or Mears," Charlotte said evenly. "He wouldn't be as calm as I am, for a start."

Jill bridled. "Well, I don't want anyone to talk to me, thank you very much! I go out with who I like and I can take care of myself and if Albert doesn't mind anything, then I don't, and I'll thank you not to stop me from getting back to my work any longer!"

She marched right past Charlotte into the shop, with an audible sniff. The shop door banged unnecessarily behind her.

Charlotte was filled with a sense of failure and also of injustice. There was no need for the girl to treat her like that, and no need for

Granfer Trippick to ask Charlotte to do such an impossible task—as he must have known it would be.

Charlotte stared in the window of the next shop unseeingly, trying to master her emotions. It was the person at the back of the window who caught Charlotte's eye. She was beckoning her.

Charlotte went to the door. It was a cake-shop. Not like the one that Jill had been in to buy her sticky buns, but a window with a sedate Copper Kettle in the centre, and a silver tray of home made pastries beside it, as the sole decoration. Charlotte only realized that it was the place where Keith would be taking tea with Rosemary when she had got to the now open door and the person in the lilac nylon overall waited for her.

"It's Dr. Berrington—at that table at the back. He saw you standing at the window looking in and he asked me to tell you he'd be glad if you'd join him at his table."

"But he has a guest already," Charlotte protested. She didn't want to see Rosemary with him. She didn't want to have to speak to Rosemary again anyway, not after that telephone conversation.

"No, nurse, she sent a note that she couldn't come, so I believe," the woman said. So Charlotte followed her into the quiet, almost empty cool gloom of the exterior, where it smelt of home made cakes and coffee and polished tables and where copper and pewter pots and plates glistened on the oaken walls and hung from beams across the ceiling.

Keith Berrington was on his feet, holding out a chair for her. Charlotte, shaking a little at the thought of this unexpected meeting with him, felt she could do with a cup of tea, and sank gratefully into her chair.

"For such a happy person, you looked singularly out of sorts with the world when you looked in at the window, so I thought I must try and do something about it," he remarked. "Trippick's grand-daughter brushed you up the wrong way? I saw you talking to her when I came in."

Charlotte nodded and managed a rueful smile. "The poor old man was so worried about her and seemed to have convinced himself that I'd be clever enough to wean her away from one of our gamekeepers, but all I got for my pains was a good deal of rudeness and smart retorts. I wish I hadn't tried now."

"Never mind, I'm glad you tried. At least, I'm glad you told old Trippick you'd try. I don't want him worried for his remaining time with us."

"Hasn't he got . . . long?" she murmured. She liked the old man. He and Lenny Quexford had been on the ward so long that they would leave a hole when they went that wouldn't be filled very quickly.

He shook his head. "Stop looking sick, Charlotte. You know the rules—don't get involved emotionally with the patients!"

She nodded. "I know, but it's easier said than done with some people, isn't it? What about you, Dr. Berrington? I'm sorry about the message I gave you, but she was so insistent—I thought she'd be very angry if I didn't convince you that it was urgent for you to come."

"Don't worry," he said briefly. "It isn't

the first time this has happened. I shouldn't have come, if you hadn't looked so anxious about it. If I'd spoken to her on the telephone I certainly wouldn't have come. She's just a little bit spoilt, you know."

He smiled that specially nice smile again. Charlotte wanted it to go on for always, and then told herself sharply not to be a fool. Common sense told her that this man would always be specially nice to some people, but probably after his experience with Rosemary Deane he would never get emotionally involved with any woman again. He was essentially a very shy man and easily hurt, she thought.

"I'm sorry, but I did want you to see her. I suppose I shouldn't have, but she talked to me about something else and she wouldn't give me any answers. So I thought if you talked to her and found out—" She broke off, colouring. It really was a cheek on her part, she supposed.

"Perhaps you'd better tell me exactly what she did say."

"She asked me if I knew someone called Rory Utting," Charlotte said, genuinely puzzled, and repeated word for word the curious conversation she had had with Rosemary Deane over the telephone. "I'm afraid I had a fellow feeling for her when she confessed to being unable to get past Isabel to speak to my Uncle George. It really is too tiresome the way Isabel won't let anyone speak privately with anyone else in the family unless she hears about it first."

"I had heard before that she was like that," he agreed. "But this business of your cousin Derek, we really ought to get that cleared up somehow, and time's going on and nothing happens!" He frowned. "And now, for some reason, Rosemary decided against talking to me about it."

"It's all rather queer, isn't it?" Charlotte agreed. "I sometimes wonder when it all started."

"So far as I'm concerned, it started when you hurtled out of the wood, practically in my arms," he smiled.

She shook her head, a little impatiently. "No, it began before that. Derek began to behave oddly, looking worried and not really listening when anyone talked to him.

I met him once or twice in the town and I noticed he was changed."

Keith Berrington got out a notebook and a stylo and said briskly, "We'll write it down as you think of it. Point 1, then, shall be the change in your otherwise amiable cousin Derek. Yes, what happened next?"

"It's not easy to say exactly. Uncle George was always testy, sometimes the worse for drink; perhaps just about then he was a little more so in every way."

"Point 2, then—Uncle George also showing signs of strain. How did Isabel react to all this?"

"I suppose I might say that she got even more inquisitive, to the point of coming out to be with us, the day I went to see Uncle George. She was going to insist on staying with us until I said what I'd come to say, only he told her to go in the house, and he walked me right up on to High Meadow, where no one could possibly hear what we were saying."

"Which was?" Keith murmured, looking at the page ready to note down anything else of interest.

"I asked him (and I shall never know why, except that perhaps I had a feeling that if I was dramatic enough I'd shake him into answering my question about what was wrong with his affairs) I asked him if the name Fay Iverbury meant anything to him."

"Oh, yes, and as I remember it, he looked rather shaken."

Charlotte agreed, remembering that uncomfortable visit. "Miriam was there that day, though I never discovered why."

"That was unusual?"

"Well, yes, it was rather. She doesn't live at home. She's got her own place, though she uses the Ferndale horses. She's only interested in horses and the horse brasses she collects, and some rather valuable hunting prints. She's only keen on Warren Jeakings, I suppose, because he likes the same things."

"Warren Jeakings—I know that name, surely!" he murmured, but he gave it up. "No, can't place it." He looked at Charlotte. "There are times when I believe your cousin Derek knows perfectly well who shot him (or guesses) but I can't persuade him to talk about it. It *is* an important thing, you know. It would lead us, I'm sure, to what was worrying him, and although you don't believe your uncle is being blackmailed, I'm not so sure. After all, the rest of the family couldn't afford to have such a thing going on, could they?"

"He doesn't seem to be really guilty," Charlotte mused. "He wouldn't scare easily, and he'd deal with any blackmailer with the only way he knows—with his crop. He's terrific in a fight when the drink's in him."

"And when it isn't?" Keith smiled.

Charlotte shook her head in a bothered way. "You think, with Derek, that this hinges solely on my Uncle George but I'm not so sure. Whatever it is, it reaches out everywhere. The housemaid, Brenda Newey—what was she doing in the woods, looking scared, that day? She isn't the sort who'd risk tearing her nylons—she likes dressing up and going out in men's cars, not scrabbling about in the woods. And

Mrs. Endon! That I can't get over, and it must have been a pretty big reason to take her out into the woods! I told you about her!"

Keith was inclined to dismiss the housekeeper. "She probably followed the housemaid to see what she was up to—and the maid was probably meeting someone there that she wouldn't like to be seen meeting in the open, in a town for instance."

"That might be all very well in someone else's woods which might be private, but you know our woods aren't private at all! Bless us, they were crawling with Cubs that day!" She bit her lip, very vexed that something about her own home should elude her like this. "And who on earth is this Rory Utting?"

"And who was the man who sat beside No. 3? We never did find out about that, did we?"

"No, but I could have, I suppose. Well, he did go and talk to Tom Yates' father, but of course, I couldn't ask him, as his son is in our stables," Charlotte said worriedly. "The gossip!"

"Perhaps I will," Keith said thoughtfully. "Do we know who visited Lenny Quexford?"

"One of the male clerks in our solicitor's office," Charlotte said reluctantly. "Not from any business reason, it appears, but simply because his family used to live next door to Lenny. After he'd gone, Lenny started to ask questions about my family. It isn't like him. And he said the gossip that was going around rather scared him. He called it the *Hospital of Secrets*. To be so dramatic not like Lenny Quexford, is it? If I didn't know him better, I'd think he was scared, too, and that was since seeing that solicitor's clerk."

"And you doubt that his story was true—the neighbourly visit, Charlotte?"

"I doubt everything," she sighed. "If only I could expect an answer when I ask Uncle George if he's got trouble. I did ask him and he as good as invited me to mind my own business. And you know, come to think of it, Isabel has a rather guilty manner sometimes. I wonder if they know about this girl of Derek's and that it's worrying them? I can't think Aunt Elizabeth would approve of it, you know. She's always said she wouldn't tolerate a scandal, and perhaps she'd regard Patsy Wakeman marrying Derek as a scandal. After all, we don't know much about her, except that she works in the King's Head."

"But if that were so, it would be so private and connected only with your family, that it would hardly reach out to other people, and it certainly wouldn't scare people to go in the woods!" he objected. "Charlotte, don't be tempted to go into those woods yourself again, will you? Not alone!"

She smiled, a little surprised. Was this another façet of his self-imposed guardianship of her safety? She said, "All right!" and she said it a little too easily, too casually, for his peace of mind.

"I mean it, Charlotte!" he insisted, so she said it again.

"Charlotte, if Rosemary rings up again, find me, or ask her to call me again later. Don't take any messages."

She frowned, so he said quickly, "It

really is over, you know, and I don't want her to question you about your family either. They may be her friends but that doesn't mean she has any right to question you."

"You look cross all of a sudden," Charlotte smiled.

"Perhaps I am, about that," he agreed.

A little glow stole over her. Just for a moment she could pretend she came first with him, even before the soft-voiced Rosemary, who had once claimed his heart and who now had a chilly-mannered consultant dancing to her tune. Then the effect was all spoilt by the manageress coming to his table and saying, "I'm sorry, Dr. Berrington, to have to interrupt you, but there's a telephone call for you. No, not from the hospital—from the young lady who was to meet you here earlier," and Keith Berrington got up at once, excusing himself to Charlotte and went to the telephone.

That Rosemary! She had had him on a string once and she still had, for all his fine talk, Charlotte thought angrily. She was shocked at the resentment that flared in her. But it wasn't any use. People said that he had taken such a header for Rosemary that whatever she did, he would still go running when she beckoned, and didn't this prove it?

He had left the notebook carelessly on the table, open, at a point where he had entered private details about her family and their mysterious problem. It meant that much to him. She closed it, angrily, then decided she wouldn't stay. He would be in no mood to talk to her when he came back from the telephone. She got up and walked out.

The street was still full of people. She and Keith had talked about so much in such a little while, she was surprised to find that the shopping crowds were still filling the High Street, and that the road was still packed with traffic. One old-fashioned car, surprisingly chauffeur-driven in this district of owner-drivers, took her eye. It looked so much like Aunt Elizabeth's old-fashioned limousine, and the chauffeur looked so much like the old aunt's man, that Charlotte's heart beat faster. Now she, too, was beginning to feel intimidated about the old aunt!

Well, she wouldn't be, she thought impatiently. She stopped to look in a shop, when a boy touched her arm. "The gentleman, miss, he's calling you! Down there, at the bottom of the alley he went! Quick!"

Automatically Charlotte followed the boy's direction. In her thoughts, "the gentleman" could only be Dr. Berrington. Hazily she thought he might have a casualty down there and want help. On other occasions she had seen him strip off his coat and deal with a casualty—she had watched him deal himself with a schoolboy who had fallen in the canal and on another occasion he had stopped an artery while waiting for the ambulance. She ran.

Behind her, someone called, "Miss Charlotte, come back!" or she thought someone called that. But that was silly. Who would call her that? No one had, since old Aunt Elizabeth's chauffeur had last had occasion to speak to her, and that was so long ago. As the shadow loomed up before her, and she felt the sickening blow on the back of her head, she was hazily thinking that Aunt Elizabeth and her man were still very much on her mind. So much so that, as she sank down in a huddle with the darkness closing over her, her last conscious thought was that, improbable as the High Street, Ogmarsh was, for her old aunt to be driving through in her dignified limousine with her man at the wheel, somehow it had really happened and they were really there.

9

CHARLOTTE had never before been in the hospital's sick bay. By the nature of things, Keith Berrington, as RMO, attended to her, and she wasn't surprised to find his manner stiff and cold. She remembered the way she had run out on him while he was on the telephone. He would, of course, be offended. He didn't like it either, when she said, among her first few questions, "Did you pick up the note-book with all those private details in about my family?"

His face had set a little more coldly, and he had said frigidly, "Of course! Did you think I would leave it carelessly about? How came it that you went out and left it there for anyone to look at? You might have waited, Charlotte!"

Sixes and sevens, and it was all her fault. She closed her eyes and waited for the thudding in her head to ease up, but when she opened her eyes again he had gone, leaving Sister to make her comfortable and see that she kept still and quiet.

Sister said rather grimly, "What a way to speak to the RMO and him so upset about you, too! I've never seen him so upset about anyone since he was engaged to be married, and here you can't even speak civilly to him."

Really, Charlotte thought, how mixed up can anyone get? It was the RMO who wasn't being civil when she had asked him a perfectly reasonable set of questions.

Why shouldn't she want to know what had happened to her and why shouldn't she want to know about the safety of a notebook that concerned her family?

But that was as nothing compared with the shock of waking later to find Aunt Elizabeth sitting by her bedside.

Elizabeth Ferndale was elaborately made-up to look a lot younger than she really was. Her clothes were expensively plain and couturier made, and she wore a few pieces of madly expensive jewellery with devastating effect. Sister was comically over-respectful to Aunt Elizabeth when tea was brought.

Charlotte, wondering if she herself were wandering, waited for the older person to speak first, and when Aunt Elizabeth did, Charlotte knew she wasn't wandering. "Well, girl, when I take the trouble to come over especially to see you and not your graceless family, why do you dive down an alley and lead my chauffeur a precious dance, and get yourself knocked out?"

"Oh, is that what happened?" Charlotte said faintly. "Why? I mean, why would anyone want to knock me out?"

"I don't know! What I want to know is, just what *is* going on, Charlotte? Why wasn't I told that Derek was in this hospital? And who is that frightful young woman in the impossible clothes, who insists that he is going to marry her?"

"Oh, that'll be Patsy Wakeman," Charlotte said. "I did advise him to tell you about it but I think he felt so ill he didn't want to do anything at all about anything. I was going to telephone you—I had meant to that afternoon only I saw someone to please a dying patient, and then the RMO insisted on talking to me and—"

"—and you walked out leaving him to look for you instead of waiting at the table until he returned!"

"Did he tell you that?"

"He did! A fine, upright sort of man like that, and you lead him a pretty dance and generally behave as a lady should not! Don't you want him, girl?"

Aunt Elizabeth, Charlotte thought, with a tinge of humour, still didn't know that the virtue of "being a lady" was practically forgotten, and that one did not join in an unseemly battle for a man whose heart was still belonging to the first girl-friend, even though she had long ago abandoned it. Aunt Elizabeth just wouldn't understand.

"I don't know," Charlotte said, at last, "and he doesn't want me, so it doesn't matter. Whatever impression he gave you, he just wants someone to fuss over and feel responsible for. Darling Aunt Elizabeth," she said quickly, as the older woman seemed about to protest, "he said so, in as many words. I think he'll be a confirmed bachelor now."

Aunt Elizabeth sat back and folded her lips, remembered her make-up and the anti-wrinkle cream she was depending on, and relaxed her once-beautiful mouth, but her eyes were disapproving. "I hope you're not going to be frivolous, girl!"

"No, Aunt, that isn't me, and you know it, I think," Charlotte said tiredly. "Dr. Berrington keeps going back to that girl. She used to be my staff-nurse. To be honest, I don't like her. I suppose it was pride that made me walk out of that tea-shop. If I can't wean him away from the memory of her, then I don't want to compromise with a lukewarm friendship."

Aunt Elizabeth understood that sentiment and approved. "But why go down that dreadful little alley and get knocked out?"

"That puzzles me, why I should be attacked," Charlotte confessed. "As to why I went down there, a boy ran up to me and said that Dr. Berrington wanted me—no, that isn't right. He said something about the gentleman wanting me and I at once thought Dr. Berrington had been called out to the back of the tea-shop for an accident. Well, that thought leapt to my mind and I didn't stop to think."

"H'm." Aunt Elizabeth eyed Charlotte thoughtfully. "You're sick and silly over him and it won't do, you know! You'll finish up like me—old and lonely and probably rich and then what will you do?"

"Not rich, darling aunt," Charlotte said sincerely, because she liked the older woman's blunt speech and ways. "Not rich, but if I ever got enough money to do it, I'd so much like to do what I told him the other day, and he wouldn't believe me. I suppose I've always wanted a life in the tropics, and not really thought of it until recently. He said the malnutrition cases were here in this town, if I'd only let him show me." She frowned. "But I think he'd rather show his staff nurse."

"He being Dr. Berrington? Never mind him! Suppose you had money—would you put it to good use, or would you frivol it away?"

"Oh, I don't know what I'd do with money," Charlotte said, a little impatiently. "I only know what I'd like to do if and when I qualify. I suppose it's possible to join a missionary team or something—people do go out there all the time and not necessarily with a lot of money. I wouldn't want to stay here, once I was free and qualified, to get away. I don't see that a lot of money would really help. Anyway, I'd never have any. I never have had a bean to bless myself with," she smiled.

The thought that Aunt Elizabeth's money was being talked about, never occurred to her, because that had always been earmarked for either Uncle George or Derek, whichever one happened to be highest in Aunt Elizabeth's good books at the time her life ended.

Aunt Elizabeth nodded and remarked, "That's as you are thinking now, but supposing Dr. Berrington proposed to you and you married him? I imagine the dream of working in the tropics would then fade, unless he shared it?"

Charlotte shook her aching head. "No,

his dream is here, in Rolborough. That, I imagine, is how his romance came unstuck. His staff nurse wanted the bright lights—London or Switzerland."

"She would, from what I've heard of her! Well, girl, he is in love with you if ever I saw a man in love, so you'd better think about it."

Charlotte frowned and made the effort to get this straight. "No, Aunt, not in love with me—interested in me. He always has been. I've amused and intrigued him somehow (I can't think how) even when he was engaged to be married. He got me out of all my scrapes—well most of them, and the others I got myself out of, and amused him so much that his staff nurse got very angry indeed. In fact, it may have started the quarrel which ended that affair. But it doesn't make him in love with me." And as Aunt Elizabeth kept shaking her head, Charlotte said on a more intense note, "Well, if it is, then it isn't the kind of love I want from a man, because as I see it, it's simply a sort of stopping up a big hole with small bits of cement, or (if you like!) not very effectively stopping up the cracks in a broken heart. His feeling for that girl will always be first, and whatever he feels for me would come way after. That's not for me, I assure you. I'd rather go without. I'd rather go a long way away and forget him altogether."

To prevent her aunt from pursuing the matter, Charlotte used her remaining strength to persuade Aunt Elizabeth to recognize Derek's marriage to Patsy Wakeman. "She'll be good for him—she's honestly devoted to him, I think, and he adores her," Charlotte pleaded.

Aunt Elizabeth was unconvinced and didn't commit herself. She said she would see Derek. "Are you sure you won't unbend and tell me what all this trouble is about, Charlotte?" she pressed.

"Ask Derek," Charlotte said, feeling suddenly too weary.

"Dr. Berrington *is* in love with you," Aunt Elizabeth insisted, as a last shot, at the door. "You should have seen that man's stricken face when he saw my chauffeur carrying you back to my car. All I can say is, it's a good thing I was caught in a traffic jam and happened to see you at that moment!"

Charlotte didn't argue. She just wanted to sleep now. She slept a good deal during the next day or two, but she was young and healthy and resilient, and the blow on her head had been a glancing one. She was very glad to be back on the wards and active again, and out of the immediate orbit of the RMO.

There was a great deal of teasing among the men when she first appeared on the ward. "Low company you keep, love!" they chipped. But she was quick to notice that it was in a subdued tone and she soon knew why: Granfer Trippick had taken a turn for the worse, and was in a very low condition.

Somehow he heard that she was back again and feverishly asked to see her. "It's my Jill," he moaned.

"Mr. Trippick, I did speak to her," Charlotte told him earnestly, holding tightly to his free hand. "I urged her to stop seeing Mears, and I think she will. Don't worry!"

He rolled his head listlessly from side to side, and didn't say any more, but to Charlotte's surprise Jill herself asked to see her when she next came to the hospital.

She looked terribly distressed. Charlotte took her into one of the waiting rooms and made her sit down. "Would you like a cup of tea?"

Jill shook her head, "No, you don't understand. He thinks I'm in trouble—well, I mean, the sort of trouble—well, he thinks Mears is married but he's got it all wrong and I can't tell him what I'm worried about! Well, I don't want to worry him—see? What I wondered was, would you tell him it's all right?"

"But how *can* I, if it isn't? Suppose you are in real trouble later on, Jill, and he gets to hear of it? He'll never trust me again!" Charlotte said earnestly. "Tell me all about it."

But Jill wouldn't go so far as that. She was shivering and suddenly she said, "Maybe I will have that cup of tea!" so Charlotte left her and went to the kitchen. But it was just an excuse, for when Charlotte went back with a good hot cup of tea for her, Jill had gone.

Charlotte did her best with the old man and managed to convince him that Mears wasn't a married man, but all the time she kept remembering the Cubs and their maps, and the marking on one which showed a blonde girl, so frightened, in the woods. It seemed to her now that it might well have been Jill Trippick, waiting to meet Mears. Why hadn't she thought of it before? Perhaps Jill had seen who had shot Derek! That would have scared her, surely?

The realization of this made her so restive, she could hardly concentrate on her work. She decided to speak to Derek when she went in with his tea.

Since she herself had been off sick, there had been a marked change in him. Patsy Wakeman was allowed to visit him whenever she could get time off, and he seemed a different person now that his love affair was straightened out.

Nonetheless, he appeared rather wary when he saw Charlotte's serious expression that afternoon. "I say, what happened to you?" he began. "They're saying you were knocked out, but that's all a lot of hoo-ha, isn't it?"

"No, my lad, it isn't. It's all to do with this business, I'm sure, and if you don't want me to be knocked out again, you had better tell me a few things!" she said firmly.

"Oh, help, I thought it'd come to this," he grumbled. "All right, I suppose you want to know why I didn't catch on about that name—Fay Iverbury? Well, I was feeling pretty rotten at the time, and I frankly didn't recognize Patsy in those awful clothes and those glasses. She wears a pretty snappy dress when she's working, or going out in the evening, and those glasses do make her look different, you must admit!"

"Yes, I know all about that, Derek, but it doesn't explain how it was you couldn't remember that Patsy's boss was this Fay Iverbury!"

"Well, I couldn't," he said bluntly. "It's her private name and the only place I've seen it is above the door where it says 'Licensed to sell beer and spirits etc.' A chap doesn't think of that when he's feeling as rotten as I was! They call her Betsy for some reason, at the King's Head."

"All right, Betsy or Fay Iverbury, it's all one to me—what I want to know is, who said you must see her?"

"Oh, some chaps—on the race-course," he said carelessly.

"Is that why Uncle George looked so sick when I mentioned her name?" Charlotte said wrathfully. "Is that all this highly blown-up business is—a matter of racing debts, trouble on the race-course? And you're involved too?"

"Stow it, Charlotte, just because a chap's getting better!" he begged. "I don't know that that *is* it. That's what I want to find out. I only know what I told you I heard Uncle George say on the telephone. It's clear to me he's being blackmailed and you know what Aunt Elizabeth would have to say to that if she found out. She does go on and on and on!"

"Well, speaking of Aunt Elizabeth, did she come and see you when I was off sick?" Charlotte demanded.

"Yes, she did," Derek said ruefully.

"That's how I found out you'd been knocked out. No one else would tell me! I say, the old girl does get up on her high horse, doesn't she? She really was rotten about Patsy. But there, it doesn't matter to me. I'm going to marry Patsy and I don't care about Aunt Elizabeth—all I care about is that Isabel won't hurt Patsy. You know how spiteful she can be, in that well-bred way of hers. Patsy doesn't understand that sort of thing. She really is a nice girl, Patsy," he urged.

Charlotte made an impatient gesture. "Derek, if that's how you want it, it's up to you, but it isn't an end of everything. Who shot you?"

"I say, you *are* in a tizz today! What's wrong? It won't help anyone to know that now—it's all over! even the police have washed their hands of it—"

"Never!"

"Well, they have, seeing as I told 'em it was an accident, a chap cleaning his gun while he was talking to me—"

"Was that true? Cleaning his gun in the woods?" Charlotte was scandalized.

"Derek, who are you protecting?"

He looked embarrassed but was determined not to speak. Charlotte made a decision. She left his room and asked permission to go back and talk to him and she took the maps.

"Oh, lor," Derek moaned when she appeared the second time. "You're on the war-path, Lotta!"

"Yes, I am. I've been gentle with you in the past, my lad, because they warned me you weren't very well. But since I've been off sick, you have taken such a turn for the better that we don't have to be so gentle with you. Now, I've got something to show you!" and she spread the maps out in front of him.

"Good grief, where did these come from?" he said weakly.

"You wanted to meet me in the woods, to tell me something so urgent that you got shot during the course of your waiting for me. Right, that's good enough for me! I said I'd sort it out for you and this is what I've done so far. The Cubs were all over the woods that day. They're learning to make maps and map-read so it was all part of the exercise, and just look what they saw—people and places and the times marked."

Derek studied them and went ashy pale. Charlotte pounced on him. "Now, Derek, you're a lot better and things won't improve outside unless you are honest and come clean! Tell me what you know, old chap, and let's get it cleared up before Aunt Elizabeth finds out!" Charlotte pleaded.

He shook his head. "This is mostly news to me," he said faintly. He stabbed at Brenda Newey's name. "What was *she* doing here, for heaven's sake? And you just can't mean that anyone saw old Endon out of the house—in the woods. No!"

"I believe the Cubs, Derek. If you say you don't know what those people were doing there, I shall have to believe you. But you must tell me who shot you!"

Derek lay back and grinned helplessly. "Okay. That's me there, yes? Well, it was them," and he pointed to the place where one of the Cubs had marked in the two scared boys. The running boys that the

RMO felt were being chased by a gamekeeper.

"Them?" Charlotte echoed blankly. "But why, why?"

"Well, there you are!" Derek said. "No reason, no reason at all. Just an accident. Like I said. I'd been talking to them earlier, poor little brutes. They were strangers. Asked me a few directions. Pretty scared when I gently pointed out it was a private property. They'd lived in a manufacturing town all their lives and thought they'd like to come south. Hitched a lift and all that. I suggested where they might get work and I showed them how to look for traps—didn't want 'em to run into trouble before they got to our boundaries."

"But why did they shoot you?"

"Well, it seems that in looking on the ground for traps as they went, they found an old army pistol. When I showed up again they were struggling for possession of it. It went off and I was the unlucky target."

"You might have been killed!" she said in horror.

"That's what they thought. I couldn't

persuade 'em to run for it at first, but in the end they went. I thought I'd be all right, seeing as you'd be along pretty soon. I must have passed out, and of course, you might have passed me a dozen times and just not seen me, lying there in the bushes."

"Oh, Derek! Why couldn't you have said all this before?"

"I don't know! Fellow feeling, I suppose. They'd have been picked up and shoved in an approved school or something. Couldn't do it, Lotta. They were orphans, like me. Never had a father or a decent chap to talk to one. Well, you can't say Uncle George was ever much comfort to a lad, can you? I had a vague hope that people would forget about my gunshot wound."

"Well, they haven't, but I'm glad it's cleared up. But where do we go from here? We still don't know the answers to all the other questions, do we?"

"No, but that's what I've been waiting patiently to ask you about. I think old Endon knows. Go and see her, will you?"

Charlotte stiffened. "Go to Ferndale House—me? I will not! And you ought to know better than to ask me, Derek! I've tried once, to see Uncle George, and where did it get me?"

"Go round by the kitchen quarters," he persuaded. "See old Endon privately. Our housekeeper's always liked you. I think she's just waiting for the chance to tell you all the things she wouldn't dream of telling the police. The things she knows that took her out there, on the day in question," he finished ruefully.

It wasn't any use trying to refuse Derek when he was in a wheedling mood. When Charlotte left him it was in a rather depressed mood, having promised Derek she would do as he wanted. She did hesitate before leaving, feeling she ought to tell Keith Berrington, since he had expressed the hope that she wouldn't go in those woods again. But she couldn't find him.

It was all very well for Great-Aunt Elizabeth to say roundly that the RMO was in love with Charlotte. Charlotte thought she herself was in a position to know better about that; it was Charlotte who had seen his cold looks in her direction since she had been knocked out in the alley—quite clearly the RMO hadn't relished chasing all over the place trying to find her when he hadn't found her waiting at his table in the teashop. It didn't take much to annoy him and he probably felt she was engaged in something she was keeping from him, to get involved in such an incident.

So Charlotte shrugged and made her own way to Ferndale House, by means of the car of one of the local farmers, which she had happened to see in the High Street. The lad knew her well enough and Charlotte was glad of the lift.

The visit was doomed from the start, however. The kitchen quarters were empty. Charlotte, going slowly through the house, was puzzled to find no evidence of anyone. It was still, uncannily still, until she followed a queer clicking sound to the Green Saloon and finally realized that they were all in their watching a ciné film of the latest horse trials. Miriam would be showing it.

Charlotte almost laughed aloud in her

relief. At any other time it wouldn't have seemed odd to find the house empty, but now—with so much that was queer going on—such a thing automatically seemed sinister.

Charlotte went back the way she had come, intending to wait in the kitchen for the housekeeper, when she heard voices in the library. One was Isabel's. Low, muted, as if she were standing far across the room, by the fireplace. The other, thick masculine, one that Charlotte couldn't place—not Uncle George.

Charlotte stood still, rooted to the spot in surprise, when she realized Isabel was talking about her.

"You'd think now she's a nurse in the hospital we'd be shot of her, but no! That Derek has kept in touch. Anyone else would just listen, and do nothing, but no, that Charlotte has to get busy and energetic, *doing* something about things."

The man't voice rumbled.

Isabel, answering, said, "What *can't* she do! She's going around with Rosemary's left off beau—the RMO. Another one keen on interfering! I tell you, it would have all been all right, if that stupid Derek hadn't got shot and taken into her hospital. Now I shan't sleep another wink!"

Again the man's voice rumbled, and Isabel in answer said, "Rory Utting was quite satisfied with the heirloom—oh, I don't know what it's worth. We call it the heirloom rather cynically—it's just a Georgian snuff-box. Its worth is what you can get out of some unsuspecting buyer with more money than sense. He could have discharged most of his debts in time, only now—"

But at that point the door of the Green Saloon clicked open and the people in there were coming out. Charlotte had to run for it, which was a pity. She was no eavesdropper, but time was at a premium and she was desperate enough to do anything to find out what was going on at home. Now she wouldn't know for ages, perhaps never.

She waited for the housekeeper as long as she dared, but then she heard Isabel come towards the kitchens, remarking that she had to make tea when the housekeeper was off duty, Charlotte had only one course left open to her: she made a quick exit by way of the woods.

The most familiar short cut she knew was the one where she had run out to the RMO's car that night. She took it unthinkingly, turning over the things she had found out this afternoon, and she was surprised to find him there, sitting in his car.

"Now don't tell me you were waiting for me on the off-chance of finding me here!" she said, scandalized.

He was so very angry. "No, I was told by your cousin Derek where you'd gone. It seemed likely you'd come out this way. Can't you keep a promise? Are you like everyone else?"

"I couldn't do much else about it today," she frowned, wondering why he did get so very cross with her for the least thing, "I'll tell you, if you like," and when he didn't answer, she did tell him, because she wanted his opinion.

It was galling to find he merely intended to drive her back to the hospital in grim silence. "Well?" she exploded. "I would like an opinion on all that!"

"Your good aunt practically commissioned me to keep an eye on you—how on earth can I, when you won't even honour a bargain to tell me when you intend to go near these woods so that I can arrange to be with you?"

"I think," Charlotte said, fighting her own anger, "that it might be as well if you forgot about any obligation (real or fancied) to look after me. You don't have to feel responsible on my behalf. I'm a big girl now. I can look after myself!"

"Can you!" Keith Berrington snorted. "I doubt that very much, after the sight of you in that alley some days ago! If you think I care for the sight of you in that condition you are very much mistaken."

"It was just a glancing blow. I'm tough," she said, with a confidence she didn't really feel.

"It isn't that entirely! I want to know why someone should feel he had to attack you in such a way!"

He made it sound as if she kept bad company. She was so angry, so hurt that

Keith Berrington of all people, should talk to her like this, that she was stung to retort: "Has it occurred to you that someone might have intended that blow for the person who *was* to have met you, so urgently, and who didn't come?"

That was, of course, a mistake, and she could have bitten her tongue out the moment she said it. A childish retort, springing from her anger, but it drew from Keith the cold comment, "Whatever else Rosemary Deane may have done to displease me, she never did rash or ill-mannered things. I could rely on her for that!" and it drove a further wedge between them.

And later that ill-starred day, after Charlotte had been back in the hospital only half an hour, she heard of a further incident in the woods, which would gratify Keith further, she had no doubt, in showing how right his anger had been. Another accident in the woods—a man knocked out with a blow that might or might not have been from a fallen elm branch: Warren Jeakings!

10

LENNY QUEXFORD wasn't so well. Keith Berrington came to see him, the surgeons were all round his bed but he was too weak to stand another operation, and that uneasy flutter went round the ward when an old patient who has been there longer than any of the others, shows signs of failing. Charlotte couldn't remember when the men had been so quiet, not even when Granfer Trippick had had his last bad turn. Granfer Trippick had a trick of recovering again which was rather remarkable, but Lenny hadn't the stamina.

Sylvia said, "I wonder if they'll let him have visitors today?" and Linda said, "He hasn't got anyone, only that miserable little clerk person that Charlotte seems to dislike so much!" and she looked at Charlotte as she said it.

Charlotte's lunch had never seemed so

unattractive a meal that day. Keith Berrington didn't appear to notice her and she hadn't heard a word from Aunt Elizabeth since she had made that lightning visit to the sick bay when Charlotte had been knocked out in the alley. Warren Jeakings lay in a coma and no one came to visit him, not even Miriam, and it was all very wretched. She was almost moved to ask to see him herself.

"Oh, don't go soppy over everyone who gets hurt in your family's woods," Linda begged bluntly. "Everyone will come rushing to see him soon, and then you'll wish you hadn't."

"Besides, his accident wasn't sinister, was it?" Sylvia reasoned. "Everyone seems satisfied that that elm branch fell on him and that could happen to anyone."

"Except that you told me that they had had a quarrel, he and Miriam," Charlotte pointed out worriedly to Sylvia.

"Well, you don't think his lady love could have wopped him one on the head, do you, and left him for dead in the woods? Is your Miriam that sort of person?"

"Don't joke, Sylvia. I don't know what I think. It just isn't the same since the day Derek got shot, and I'm sure I don't know why, now that he's explained that it was just an accident and could have had no bearing on anything else at all!"

They would have forgotten about it, in the pressure of a big intake that afternoon, if Lenny Quexford hadn't been allowed his one visitor—Harris, who worked in the solicitor's office. Lenny, looking very ill indeed, lay silently, listening to Harris, who didn't appear to realize how ill Lenny was. Harris had troubles of his own. Yates, plucking anxiously at Charlotte's sleeve, said hoarsely, "Miss, that poor bloke shouldn't be worried like that, should he?"

Charlotte frowned. "I'll see," she promised. "Isn't your boy here today, Mr. Yates?"

"No, he couldn't get here, nurse, but I'll be all right. I can study my racing form. Don't often get a bit of peace for it."

Charlotte nodded, and went over to Lenny Quexford's bed, but at that moment Harris got up and said he would have to go and that he was sorry he couldn't stay longer.

Lenny looked rather bothered. Charlotte went over to him and put a hand on his forehead. "Take it easy," she begged him. "I'll call Sister. I didn't think your visitor would—"

"Nurse, don't go," Lenny gasped. "Want to tell you! You know he's in your solicitor's place, don't you?"

"Yes, I know," she soothed. "It's all right, really it is. You just lie still while I go and fetch Sister."

"No, it's not all right! You must listen, Nurse! He was fed-up because he's got sacked, for letting out secrets—about your family!"

Beads of perspiration stood out on Lenny's forehead and his skin was the curious colour of old parchment. "It's all right, really it is," Charlotte insisted, and left him, although she would have given the world to know what Harris had betrayed about her family. Oh, well, time enough for that later, she thought, as she found Sister and hastily explained what had happened.

The curtains were pulled round Lenny, and the RMO called, and when the visitors' hour was over, the curtains were still pulled round Lenny.

"What's up?" Sylvia whispered, as they passed while giving out the patients' teas.

"Lenny upset by his visitor," Charlotte said briefly.

"Yates is upset by his visitor, too," Sylvia retorted. "Seen who it is?"

Charlotte hadn't, and got a shock when she was told by Sylvia, the next time they passed. "It was that man who sat by No. 3, when he was asleep that day!"

Yates was on Charlotte's side of the ward and he did look unhappy, she thought, when she gave him his tea.

"What's the matter, Mr. Yates?" she asked him, as she pumped up his pillows and pulled up his bed table. "Did your visitor upset you, too?"

He looked sharply at her. "See him, did you, Nurse?"

"I was told he was the same man who sat by No. 3, that day," she said evenly. "It seems you knew him all the time!"

"No! No, straight I didn't, nurse! Nor I don't know him now! But he knows me and he knows my boy! And I wish him to Jericho, I don't mind telling you!"

"Mr. Yates, is Tom in trouble?" Charlotte asked sternly.

"No, Nurse, not really! The trouble is, he's smart—a bit too smart. I'm always telling him. I didn't like his snooping with field glasses on the big house and I told him so. But there—the young folk don't take any notice of the old ones!"

Charlotte, remembering the way Tom's father had done his share of gossiping about the Ferndales not so long ago, said nothing to that. Yates looked quickly at her, seeming to read her thoughts. "Well, I'll admit I've been as inquisitive as my boy in the past. The Ferndales have only got themselves to blame for doing the things as gets 'em talked about. But I do draw the line at taking money for information received, which is what that chap wanted me to do!"

"Who was he?" Charlotte asked.

"One of your Uncle's creditors," Yates

said unhappily. "They're going to have your uncle, you know, Nurse! Better tell him! And it's none of my doing. And you can't lay the blame on my boy, neither—it's my word against yours."

"Don't be silly, Mr. Yates," Charlotte said, feeling distinct relief. "If that's all he is, it really doesn't matter all that much. He only has to present his bills to the solicitors and they get paid, in time, so don't you worry. It isn't your affair, after all."

"Well, it is, then, seeing as my boy has been opening his big mouth too much, and seeing as you don't seem to have the latest news about that rich aunt of yours, Nurse," he snapped. "No, it's no use asking me. I've said enough. Best ask *him*, and he nodded towards the closed curtains of Lenny's bed. "It's him as has all the latest from the solicitors, and from what I've seen of that chap and the way he spills everything that's supposed to be private in his boss's office, I'm glad I don't have to take any business of mine to any solicitor."

"They're not gossips usually," Charlotte said sharply. "And if you know anything, you owe it to me to tell me!"

But Yates would say no more just then, so she left him. But later when she came to take his tea-things away, he seemed to have thought better of it.

"Nurse, there's just one thing—my boy overheard a quarrel between your uncle's step-sister, Miriam, don't they call her?"

"Well?" Charlotte said coldly.

"Well, if your folks will shout at the tops of their voices, they must expect people to hear, and my boy heard. I don't know who else he's told, but he heard an earful that day, which I doubt if you know about!"

Charlotte coloured with shame that her family should put themselves into such a position. "I've no doubt I do know, but what is more to the point, who else has Tom told about it, and how much did you tell that man today?"

"It's no good going for me, Nurse," Yates said anxiously. "I'm only doing my best to make things right, if I can. I didn't tell that chap much, if you must know, because I didn't like his manner. But I don't suppose it mattered much. He told me fair and square that he came here in the first place to try and get a word with the nurse who was George Ferndale's niece, and after he got here, he found he could pick up so much gossip about the family by just sitting, that he found a patient with no visitor and just let the rest of us do what he wanted."

"Oh, really, Mr. Yates, I don't think anyone could have known much that would interest a creditor of my uncle's."

He eyed her, with a gleam that made her rather uneasy. "Not (for instance) the information that Miss Deane, who was engaged once to the RMO, is in possession of fake hunting prints for which she was dunned the price of the originals?"

That really shook her. She couldn't believe it. He pressed his advantage by remarking, "The Deanes were friends of your uncle's step-sister, so it's not likely that the fakes got there on purpose. In fact, I've heard tell that that row in the barn was really about that."

"Yes, well, really, Mr. Yates I hardly

think—" Charlotte began, but he hardly seemed to hear her.

"Your uncle really is in a spot, you know. I don't think you do know. He needs so much cash he give Rory Utting one of the family's heirlooms to shut him up, but that's only one thing—he's still after raking in big money, real big money, and he can't seem to satisfy himself. Folks are asking what he wants so much for."

"But it's no one else's business!" Charlotte whispered.

"Perhaps you're right, Nurse, but it seemed to me you ought to be told what's going on. Don't seem right that outsiders know and you don't. You see, that row they had—the one in the barn which my lad heard most of—that was over a brooch. Seems your Uncle George had been pestering his step-sister for money to help him and that brought to light the business of the fakes being sold to the Deanes. Seems she had to pawn the originals to tide her over, and someone unknowingly sold the copies as originals. Not a nice thing to happen to a lady."

"Mr. Yates, I beg of you, forget you heard all this!" Charlotte said distractedly. "It isn't your business! It isn't anyone else's. I don't even know if it's true! I've only got your word for it!"

He leaned over the side of his bed. "Ask your cousin Derek—that's what I'd do, Nurse! He knows more than he'll say! I daresay he'll know about that Miriam promising your uncle that brooch of hers, just to tide him over. Ask him about that!"

She was shaking when she left him. She felt horrified, undressed, as if all the eyes in the ward were on her. How could Uncle George have allowed things to get like this, so that outsiders knew all about him?

It seemed logical to speak to Derek. There was no one else she could talk to. No one at Ferndale House that she could privately discuss this thing with, and certainly it wouldn't do to try to speak to Great-Aunt Elizabeth, or in fact the solicitors—if that man Harris were around. His perfidy alone made her feel sick. She couldn't think what he had been telling people. And even if he had already left them, who was to say how loyal or otherwise the rest of the staff were?

She felt curiously alone and vulnerable, and it was this feeling at last that drove her to Derek's bedside.

He wasn't alone. The adoring Patsy was with him. They had the silly-happy look of declared lovers in their eyes, in their faces. Charlotte hardly had the heart to ask him if she could speak to him alone.

"Oh, I say, Lotta, can't it wait? Patsy hasn't got long. Talk to me when she's gone, if you must. Well, what's wrong with talking while she's here? That's an idea! Well, she's going to be in the family soon, aren't you, love?"

"But she isn't in the family yet, Derek, and I don't suppose she will want to hear what I have to say to you. It's about what you were wanting to tell me, the day you got shot."

He slowly took his arm from round Patsy's shoulders, and although Patsy looked adoringly hopeful at him, he seemed to have forgotten her presence. He stared at his cousin with no great liking, and at last he said, "For heaven's sake, can't that business be allowed to die a natural death now?"

"No, it can not!" Charlotte said vigorously. "It was important to you then and after what I've heard today it must be doubly important to you now! I go off duty soon, so please, Patsy, be a dear and go out. I only want five minutes with him!"

Patsy hesitated, started to rise, then sat down again. "Tell her, Derek," she said softly.

"Tell me what?" Charlotte asked, shrinking. Surely Patsy Wakeman didn't know all the family's shabby little secrets too?

It seemed that she didn't. She was concerned with something quite different. Derek, flushing a little, said, with that sullen air he had always had when caught out in not being entirely honest or admirable, "Well, the fact is, it was only important to me because of the possibility of inheriting the old girl's money—this thing I wanted to tell you about that day in the woods," he added hurriedly.

Patsy put in softly, "It's all right, Charlotte—I don't know what the secret is. I wouldn't want to. I only want Derek and our life together."

Derek made an impatient movement. "The fact is, I can't see a hope in the world of getting Aunt Elizabeth's cash—anyway, it's like Patsy says. She doesn't want to be rich. She doesn't want to have anything to do with Ferndales. She just wants to marry me, and for us to go off and spend our lives together."

"But you haven't got an income, Derek, or a career!" Charlotte said blankly. "What do you propose to live on?"

Patsy stood up and faced Charlotte. In her soft, myopic way, she was really very pretty without those glasses. "You don't understand, Charlotte," she said. "He's going to have a job. We're both going to work when we're married."

"A job?" Charlotte said blankly. Derek? Derek, who had been destined for the law, after his term at college, if he didn't do too badly. Derek, who was to have had a brilliant future like his dead father. "What sort of job?" she asked awfully.

Patsy looked a little ashamed, but said firmly enough, with a glance at the adoring Derek, "He's going to work at the King's Head, with me—for Fay Iverbury."

11

"CHARLOTTE!" The RMO's voice bit quietly into her thoughts as she went out of the gate. "Wait for me. I've been looking for you."

He caught her up and took her arm. She met his eyes with difficulty. "I thought you were cross with me, avoiding me," she said. "I was going to slip out somewhere and try to think."

"And I was going to let you go—after what your Great-Aunt said to me when she came to the hospital and saw you in Sick Bay—but I couldn't. Promise or no promise, I couldn't leave you to get out alone, not after that affair in the alley. There's a limit to what I can take."

She missed the intense note in his voice and thought only of the improbable idea of Aunt Elizabeth talking to him and extracting a promise from him. "I thought you said she wanted you to keep an eye on me?

What did she make you promise?"

He hesitated. "It's irrelevant at this stage. Tell me instead where you intended to go."

"Oh, I don't know. Somewhere—anywhere, where I could be quiet and think. There doesn't seem to be any peace any more in the hospital. Everyone gossiping about me. People staring, and I can see from their eyes that they're speculating on what they've heard about me, about our family." She glanced at him. "I expect you've heard about my cousin Derek and what he intends to do?"

He hadn't, and as they walked, she told him about Derek's new manner, his being so wrapped up in Patsy Wakeman, his intention of throwing up his studies to marry that girl and work for Fay Iverbury in the King's Head.

He hadn't heard that, but he didn't appear to be surprised or unduly concerned. He said, "I'd like to drive you in my car to the King's Head—we've said all along that we ought to see this Fay Iverbury—but I'm not sure that I should.

Your great-aunt doesn't want us to—er—be alone together, is how she delicately put it."

He looked keenly at Charlotte, who reddened furiously. "You can't mean that! But that's an awful thing to say! Besides how can you keep an eye on me if you're not with me?"

"You don't know why she said that?"

"No! Do you? You don't seem much put out about it, KB!"

"Did you refer to me in that way when you spoke to her?" he wanted to know.

"I don't think so. It's personal and private, isn't it? I think I avoided mentioning you, so far as I could."

"Ah, well, that may have had the same effect," he said obscurely. "Personally I always go by the things people leave unsaid, rather than the things they carefully allow themselves to say."

"Now you're being all uppish and adult," she said crossly. "Anyway, surely Aunt Elizabeth wouldn't want me to catch my death of cold? Well, look at the sky! It's going to rain buckets any minute now!"

"That settles it. It's emergency," he grinned. "Come on, I left my car in the garage just ahead. We'll collect it."

In a way that little conversation served to break the ice that had recently formed between them, and when he had collected his car, Charlotte settled in beside him to tell him, while he was driving towards the King's Head, all the things that had happened to her since she had gone back on the wards.

Lenny Quexford's visitor intrigued him, but he was as angry as Charlotte had been, over the disclosures made by Tom Yates' father, mainly she surmised, because Yates had embarrassed her by telling her on the ward. "He never lowers his voice."

"As for Derek, he so shocked me, what he intended to do, that I forgot all about asking him if it was true about Miriam and the brooch and the fake hunting prints."

"As to that," Keith said, rather grimly, "I know that to be true. Rosemary wanted to speak to me about it that day she didn't come to the Copper Kettle. She's told me since."

"Oh." Charlotte felt dashed. So he *was* still seeing Rosemary! Well, it did rather confirm all she had felt about him, and why Aunt Elizabeth should have to worry about him, Charlotte couldn't think. "So," she said with spirit, "my ill-timed remark about me getting the wallop on the head that had been intended for Staff Nurse Deane, might well have been correct, don't you think?"

He didn't care for that. "Why should anyone want to hit Rosemary on the head?"

"Well, come to that, why should they want to hit me? What have *I* done? I tell you what I haven't done—I haven't been silly enough to pay a high price for hunting prints that weren't the originals, and if I had, I should have taken it on the chin, not made a fuss about it, as I've no doubt she is! Perhaps someone thought a dot on the head might warn her to shut up!"

Now she *had* done it. She was half glad, half ashamed for what now seemed a rather childish outburst. But it did seem unfair to her that Rosemary, who had jilted the RMO and gone off with what struck her as the better bargain, should be able to claim his attention and his allegiance just when she felt like it. But Keith didn't seem to be furious.

"Don't be catty, Charlotte," he said mildly. "It doesn't suit you. Besides, do you really see your relative, this Miriam, lurking in an alley to hit Rosemary with something?"

"Now you're laughing at me! Of course I don't. And in point of fact, I really can't see Miriam going to any pawnshop with possessions of hers, to raise money. Much more likely the originals were stolen and replaced by copies that Miriam, in a hurry, didn't detect. Well, she wouldn't expect to find copies in her precious frames, would she?"

"It is so easy to find such good copies?" he asked.

"I don't know! I expect so! They say that for every original there's a copy, made to be sold as such to people who can't afford the real thing. Though why anyone should want hunting prints I can't think—I loathe the dreary things personally."

"Me, too," he said unexpectedly, and she caught the tail end of a smile lurking round his mouth as she glanced at him. "However, it seems to me that we can't do a thing about that until this Miriam visits Warren Jeakings—as no doubt she will. You might like to speak to her then, Charlotte. She ought to be told about her business being talked about on the wards, of course."

"What I want to know about," Charlotte said vehemently, "is this clerk Harris. Lenny did try to tell me but he collapsed. Poor man, he was so upset. I'm sure Harris has been most dreadfully indiscreet, to get sacked for it, but what could he have *said*?"

"Well, you won't hear it from Lenny, Charlotte," Keith said quietly. "He might last the night out, but he won't talk any more, I'm afraid."

And yet they did hear about Harris the clerk, that day, and in such an odd way. Charlotte, dashed about Lenny as most of the nurses on that ward were, didn't really care if they got to the King's Head or not, but it turned out to be a very large and prosperous pub, in rather nice country surroundings, with several bedrooms, a good restaurant and a gloss about it that spoke of good steady trade and room for improvement. Charlotte was surprised, and thought again of Derek. After all, he was young, good-looking, energetic. He and this unknown Fay Iverbury might suit each other well, as employer and employee.

And when she met Fay Iverbury, she wondered what on earth she had expected, and why she hadn't thought of such a thing. Pieces of the puzzle began to slip into place, for she had once caught a glimpse of this woman in her Uncle George's car. From then on, everything seemed a lot easier to understand.

Fay was a big handsome redhead, a shrewd business woman with a great deal of charm and generosity in her make-up.

"That's a Ferndale face if ever I saw one," she remarked with some amusement, when she had personally supervised their meal in the empty parlour just off the private bar. They were too late for a meal in the restaurant but she promised to rustle them up something.

"I'm Charlotte Arrowsmith," Charlotte said. "To be honest, I've only just heard that my cousin Derek Ferndale is to work here when he's fit, and—"

"So you came to look the place over," Fay said with a smile. "What I'm wondering is what his Uncle George will say when he hears about it. Still, the lad's of age, so why should anyone get excited?"

"Because he was studying for a career and since he met Patsy, he's thrown all that overboard," Charlotte said, not without heat.

Fay smiled at Keith Berrington. "You're pretty quiet. Aren't you in on the family fight yet?" and she looked from one to the other of them as if she quite expected to find them looking guiltily showing signs of a romance or a pending engagement. Charlotte said shortly, "This is Dr. Keith Berrington, the RMO at the hospital. He just drove me in here today. Derek's his patient."

"I see," Fay said, with the sort of smile

that suggests she had already made up her own mind about their relationship.

Charlotte waited, but Keith didn't add anything to that, but merely watched Fay guardedly, so she said defiantly, "And my Great-Aunt Elizabeth has asked him to keep an eye on me."

She wished she hadn't said that, because Fay looked most interested, and said, "She did, did she!" Charlotte was beginning to dislike that knowing look of Fay Iverbury's.

"But only, I assure you," Dr. Berrington broke in smoothly, "because Charlotte has had one or two—er—unlucky accidents. She was hit on the head in an alley, fortunately sustaining only a minor injury, but she also had the frightening experience of being chased in the Ferndale Woods."

"My, you live dangerously!" Fay commented. "You didn't tell the police about this? When was it, by the way?"

Charlotte said shortly, "The day Derek was shot!" She was beginning to dislike Fay Iverbury very much.

Fay the shrewd, noticed this. She knit

her brows. She had a lot to lose by antagonising one of the Ferndales, so she said, "Don't take on, honey—I was merely getting it in focus. As it happens, you wouldn't have come to any harm. That was your old Uncle George chasing you. He told me about it. He was pretty wild because you wouldn't stop. He wanted you."

"Uncle George!" Charlotte ejaculated. "Why would he want to do that? He had only to call me, in civilized fashion!"

"Civilized? Honey, no one was feeling civilized in the woods that day, nor that night, either! I know. I was there, too," she admitted ruefully. "Well, you won't want me staying here talking to you. Eat your food and I'll see you later!"

Charlotte thought that meant she had said too much, and that Fay wouldn't come back. She said as much to Keith.

"I think she'll come back, if I leave you," Keith said shrewdly. "She isn't the type to want an audience. Don't show your dislike to her so much, my dear. We need her, or rather, we need to know what she knows, and it seems to me that she knows an uncomfortable amount."

"I hate her! I don't believe she knows my uncle so well," she said fiercely, but catching the RMO's quizzical eye, she had to smile at herself. It was more than likely that Uncle George had a woman friend. He was a lusty, hard-drinking, hard-riding man who, in spite of his seniority of Isabel, would hardly be likely to be satisfied with that frigid person. Isabel, Charlotte had often felt, asked for all she got.

Keith Berrington proved to be right later, when Fay drifted back. "Hello, where's your doctor pal?" she asked, and grinned.

"I sometimes think he likes his car more than me," Charlotte said coolly. "He's out there with her now, head under the bonnet!"

"That's as maybe," Fay said dryly. "Still, I wanted to talk to you on your own. You won't want everyone to know about your family, I'm sure! The fact is, I wanted to warn you. Those solicitors of your old aunt's, they've got a clerk there who can't keep his mouth shut."

Harris! Charlotte forced herself to say nothing and wait. Fay said, "I was there one day (and in case you wonder what on earth I was doing in a solicitor's office, I was trying to buy some land to enlarge my little show here) and I heard someone talking over the telephone in one of the empty rooms. Mighty furtive, he sounded. He'd got the door locked—I went and softly tried it—so I had to content myself with listening ear to the wall, and I nearly got caught. Still, as he was talking to my friend, George Ferndale, I thought it interested me too."

She twinkled at Charlotte, daring her to be indignant or disgusted. Charlotte stared stonily at her and waited.

"You didn't know I was your Uncle George's friend, did you? Did you know he was to be sole heir to your rich old auntie?" Charlotte did, but she didn't feel inclined to admit it. Fay continued, "In the old days Auntie didn't mind debts so long as there was no scandal, so my friendship with Georgie was kept Very Secret. Nowadays, it seems, the old girl is hot on debts as well, so there's a mad scramble going on for

Georgie to pay up his debts, warned by his dear friend Harris."

"So that's what he was doing," Charlotte murmured.

"Yes. He reminded George of how much he owed. I gather George was scandalized at the thought of paying up all at once." She glanced quickly at Charlotte. "What's the matter?"

"Nothing, nothing. I just thought of something, that's all," Charlotte choked, but she had remembered what Derek had heard his uncle saying to someone on the telephone. Derek must have been listening at one end, Fay at the other. Derek had said his uncle had ejaculated that the person at the other end must be mad if he thought that all that much could be paid up at once. Poor Derek had thought it was a blackmailer, when it had merely been Harris, issuing a friendly warning. Or was it so friendly? "I'm just wondering what this devoted legal clerk expected to get out of my uncle for the warning," she said.

Fay nodded, approvingly. "I see you're not so innocent as you look, my girl. Anyway, the whole point is, George is in the past tense. We are not friends any more, which is what I'm coming to. You needn't be scared about what he was doing in the woods that night, in case you've heard about the threatening letters."

"Threatening letters?" Charlotte whispered. Did Derek know about those, for heaven's sake?

"That's right," Fay said, amusement crinkling her face. "George didn't play fair with me. So I thought I'd give him a scare so I sent one or two anonymous letters to him, threatening to tell his dear wife about us. I knew he'd be in a terrible state, because if Isabel went to the old girl and told her, then George would get nothing. Of course, I was cutting off my nose to spite my face, in a way, because I'd always been more keen on your uncle than anyone else, and if he'd come into the money, he would have shared with me. Generous, he always was, to his friends."

Lady friends, Charlotte thought, angrily, but said nothing.

Fay went on, "I had a stroke of luck. It

seems someone else got hold of them, all except one, and that was the mildest of the lot, but it stipulated that George was to wait in the woods for someone. Well, that someone didn't turn up—I meant to give him a run for his money. But I think he guessed it was me, or some woman, or else why did he chase you?"

"Why are you telling me all this?" Charlotte said.

Fay shrugged. "I want something of you, of course! I wouldn't tell you for fun, would I? See, the thing is, I do impulsive things then I'm sorry. I can't think who got hold of those letters (unless it was Isabel, which I doubt!) but the thing is, I got an attack of conscience and when your Uncle George came to me and begged me to help him find some cash to pay up his debts, so he would be solvent when your old aunt died and her Will was proved, although I hadn't got the ready cash just then (on account of me buying that land I told you about) I did have one very good piece of jewellery. A brooch given me by, well, another friend. I let George have it, to sell, or raise money on. I was sorry after, because my other friend wanted to know where it was."

Charlotte waited, and as Fay looked expectantly at her, she burst out, "Don't tell me you want me to try and get the brooch back! Well, do you suppose my Uncle George would have kept it all this time? When did you let him have it?"

"I want you to find out if he's parted with it or merely given it as security. You never know, with George. If it's still in his possession, I want it back, to wear at a dinner. If I can just have it to wear, so my friend can see me with it, then I'll send it back to George. Don't look so staggered, duckie! These things happen! People like us *live*, they don't just vegetate in a hospital, taking folks' temperature and such!"

"Money," Charlotte said wrathfully, getting up. "All this scramble for poor old Aunt Elizabeth's wealth! I hope she leaves it to an animals' Home."

"Don't say that, dear! Money's all right if you know how to handle it. A bad master but a good slave. That's why I want to keep in with your Uncle George, in case he gets it. That, and me always having had a soft spot for him. Besides, I might want to go back to him. Don't look so shocked, love! I'll tell you another old saying—never burn your bridges. I never do. Don't listen to people who say it's never wise to go back—that's silly. I've got no false pride. If my new friend doesn't turn out all right, I'd go back to old George, like a shot. So do your best, dear, and get me that brooch."

Charlotte struggled briefly with herself. She was sick and ashamed of her family; desperately afraid to hear the Ferndale Woods mentioned, in case she heard of something else that had been going on in them, but at the same time, if she could prevent an open scandal by getting the brooch back, she would.

Fay watched the play of emotions in Charlotte's smooth young face with interest. "That's right love, I knew you'd come round to my way of thinking," she said, as Charlotte began to say she would. "You're a nice kid. The best Ferndale of the lot, I'd say. And if you ever want any help yourself, don't hesitate to come to me. And I mean that! Well, you never know what help you might want! No one knows."

Charlotte went out into the sunlight. Keith was just strolling towards her. "Oh, there you are. Got all you came for?"

"I'm not sure," Charlotte said. "There is something else I want to do—at least, that I think I ought to do—before I go back to the hospital."

"Come and tell me all about it. It might just be that I could do it for you. You look a bit strained."

She smiled, briefly. "I don't think you'd want to do this thing, KB I'm quite sure I don't *want* to do it."

He drove her out of the yard of the King's Head and down the long lane to the common. Here there was the calm, soothing vista of open land, gorse bushes, the little church and scattering of red roofs belonging to the nearest village; peace, no sound of the nearest main road. Charlotte eased out, collected her thoughts, and told him in a rush what Fay had said to her.

He was indignant. "But you're not

going to get that brooch back? You surely won't have anything to do with such a business?"

Charlotte shifted restlessly. "To avoid a scandal? Oh, I don't want any help from someone like Fay Iverbury, ever, in spite of what she says, but there is my cousin Derek. She's to be his employer, his wife's employer—oh, yes, he'll marry Patsy Wakeman, no matter what my old aunt says. And I think that with someone like Derek, if he wants to marry someone, he should be allowed to. He'll be happy and settled if he gets the wife he wants; if he doesn't, he'll probably drift around and become like my Uncle George. I couldn't bear that. And if he likes Fay, she'll probably mother him; well, be a good friend to him, and to Patsy. Well, I can try to find out what's happened to the brooch, can't I? It's the least I can do."

"I wish you wouldn't," he said earnestly.

Charlotte leaned back and looked at him, steadily, trying to assess what he felt about her. If Great-Aunt Elizabeth was right, and he did love Charlotte, then why didn't he say so? If he had said then, "Charlotte, I love you and I don't want you to have anything to do with this business", she would have done as he asked, and been glad to. But he didn't. He looked away from that steady regard of hers, and murmured that he hadn't any right to ask her but he wished she wouldn't.

No, Charlotte thought, Aunt Elizabeth's wrong. He does still care for Rosemary, though there's nothing in it for him. Well, that doesn't give him any right to interfere with anything I may feel I have to do.

"I'm sorry, KB," she said, "but I feel I must do this, and it doesn't really concern you, does it?"

He looked as if he had taken a blow between the eyes. He recovered a moment later, and said cheerfully, "Very well, if you think you know what you're doing, I'll drive you there. Do you want me to wait for you?"

She would have loved to say no, but she was still afraid of the woods. She suddenly remembered that the woods had been filled with Cubs, and not one of them had recorded having seen Uncle George there that day.

12

ISABEL had to go out sometimes, if only to get her hair done, and by the greatest good luck she happened to be out when Keith Berrington drove Charlotte right up the drive to the front of the house. Charlotte had forgotten to warn him that she never went in that way, but it wouldn't have made any difference. He didn't care for hole-and-corner methods, such as slipping through the woods to the back door and creeping through the kitchen regions.

There was no one in but Mrs. Endon, but the housekeeper was frankly pleased to see Charlotte. "Come into my sitting-room, Miss Charlotte, and have a nice cup of tea. You were the last person I expected to see today!"

She was a nice woman, who had been with the Ferndales most of her life. She looked worried when Charlotte said what she had come for, to talk about what was going on in the house.

Mrs. Endon looked past her to the drive, now empty since Keith Berrington had succumbed to Charlotte's pleading and driven back to the hospital, to pick her up later. "I had hoped it would all die down," the housekeeper said. "I had hoped you wouldn't know anything about it. I had hoped . . ." Her eyes were misty. "Miss Charlotte, I don't know how much you know about it, but I sometimes feel this family is breaking up. It doesn't seem right for everyone to be hanging on to the span of life of one person, waiting to scrabble for her things when she goes. It's not decent."

"No, but it isn't unknown. It must be happening in a lot of places all the time."

"You sound like the rest of the Ferndales," the housekeeper said reproachfully. "I had thought you were different. I had thought that you and Master Derek were the two best of the whole lot and that you'd both make a match of it, and it'd all be good and wholesome again, and I'd have served you both."

"You're being sentimental, Endy," Charlotte smiled. "You know we wouldn't be here if we had made a match of it. This is Uncle George's house, and I expect it will go to Isabel if anything happens to him, and you work here. You always have done. Besides, Derek's in love with someone else, and so am I. Not, mark you, that my affair will come to anything."

"Not Dr. Berrington? I saw him drive you up to the door," Mrs. Endon said, in concern.

"It's all right, Endy, I know he's still silly over Rosemary Deane. Be a dear and don't let it get to her ears."

"She knows," Mrs. Endon said flatly. "I didn't believe it when I heard her telling the mistress the other day. But if you say so, then it must be so."

"What did she tell Isabel about it?" Charlotte asked, white to the lips.

Mrs. Endon hesitated. She had heard Rosemary say in that soft little voice of hers, but with drips of ice in it, "I hate that girl, that Charlotte. She doesn't bother to make anything of herself and all the boys go for her, including *him* and I'd love to make him go off her, I really would."

Isabel had said, "Why, darling? You've got the better bargain of the two. Your consultant has prospects and money."

"You don't understand at all, Isabel," Rosemary had said softly. "When Keith was with me, he looked like a silly dog frantic for a bone it could never reach, but when he's with her he looks like a victorious dog that's reached its bone and is being gloriously protective over it, not letting any other dog come near. I don't like him to be like that over her! He never was with me."

"Perhaps you never let him," Isabel had said in amusement.

"I can't see *her* letting him, either," Rosemary had said. "She just makes him feel she has. I loathe her!"

Thinking over all that, Mrs. Endon decided to be diplomatic, so she said, "She was very bitter, dear, because it is obvious that Dr. Berrington is very taken with you, and you don't dress up or do anything to attract the gentleman."

"Oh, is that all?" But it satisfied Charlotte, who could now turn her mind to other things. "Endy, Derek asked me to meet him in the woods, the night he was shot, because he was worried about what was going on at home. I was sick with anxiety because no one seemed able to find out what was going on, and in the end I asked the Cubs to help me. Don't look alarmed—they were learning to make maps and show where they were at different times, so I turned the exercise to good use and asked them to make maps of their movements that day, and who they saw in the woods. Now what's the matter, Endy? I know you were there! It's all right!"

Mrs. Endon had started up out of her chair and then sat down again, looking rather ill. "Please, Endy," Charlotte begged, "it's perfectly all right. Just tell me what you were doing, so I can write you off, and then I can turn my attention to the others who weren't really supposed to be there."

Mrs. Endon said, rather breathlessly, "Well, my dear, if I'm to tell you why I was there, I suppose I might as well tell you the rest. Dear, oh, lor, if the Cubs know about it, then it's true—the whole of Ewbrook St. Peter must know!"

"Everyone seems to know, except me," Charlotte said.

"Well, of course, it all started with your dear Aunt, Miss Elizabeth, having a few quiet words with me, the last time she came here. Caught us all on the hop, she did, by not announcing her arrival, and everything at sixes and sevens, and what she didn't see that day, I'm sure I don't know. And she told me she'd altered her mind again. Not a penny would she pay out for this graceless family any more, she said, and what was more, she was going to alter her Will. Debts, she said, she would not have."

"But Endy, why were you in the woods?" Charlotte pressed.

"Well, I was so worried. You see, your aunt caught me—the only one in the house. After she'd gone, I went to find Brenda Newey, and she was in the woods with a man. A very nasty type called Rory Utting. I knew him because of seeing him in the library with your Uncle George one day. A bookmaker, he was said to be, but I don't know—not the sort for that girl's mother to learn she'd been meeting in the woods, even in these days, and I was responsible for her while she was with us."

"Wait a minute, Endy—do you mean to say that Aunt Elizabeth visited this house the day all that happened in the woods?"

"Yes, more's the pity. Any other day would have been bad enough, but that day! Oh, she didn't stay long. You know what those lightning visits of hers are like! But it's been on my conscience because I've never told your uncle that she came. He was so upset about your cousin Derek being shot like that."

"And to think it was just an accident! Those two boys struggling for the gun they found," Charlotte fretted.

Mrs. Endon didn't seem to notice. She said, half to herself, "It isn't possible for me not to notice what's going on in this house. I do try not to appear to be prying, but when you've been in a place so long—well, when I see them doing foolish things I want to advise them, try and make them see where they're going wrong. Your Uncle George's wife, so silly being friends with that man—"

"Which man, Endy?"

"I don't know his name. I only know there *is* a man and she's restless and bored, and so suspicious about what everyone else is doing. If your Uncle George finds out—but there, I don't suppose he'd say much, in case she found out about *his* friend. I suppose you've guessed, from what you said—"

"That Fay Iverbury," Charlotte said wrathfully.

"Yes, and it doesn't begin and end there. Seeing as I know so much about it, I feel I ought to do something, but I'm sure I don't know what. Your Uncle George isn't easy. You see, Miriam, now—she's another difficult one. Horses, that's all she lives for, and I must say I was happy when she began to be friends with that Mr. Jeakings. Well, someone of her very own. But she's not easy, either. And when your uncle begins to go mad to get his debts paid up, well, he just hadn't got the cash and he asked her to let him have some. Well, how can I *not* hear what's going on—this family do raise their voices so!"

"I know, Endy, I know! Go on!"

"Well, this particular day I took in his tray of tea-things, I'd been out in the garden cutting some parsley for the fish casserole for that evening and I didn't hear Miriam come in and they must have been quiet, looking at something, so in I sailed with his tray, and then it was too late to draw back."

"Did they see you?" Charlotte asked, puzzled.

"No, they had the old screen back over the door. I almost knocked it over. You know, the one with the cutout pattern in the wood at the top. I could see them through it but they didn't notice me. Your uncle had been showing her this brooch—oh, it was a fine-looking thing, even at that distance. I distinctly heard him say he'd been given it by a friend of his to raise some cash on, and Miriam looked daggers at him."

"Why? Wouldn't she let him have any money?" Charlotte began, and then realized why Miriam couldn't—she was so hard up that she had had to let her original prints go.

"No! It wasn't that. It was because the brooch belonged to her! I'd heard her ringing up her Mr. Jeakings asking him to get it for her—he'd taken it to be repaired. In a fine way she was, because apparently he hadn't got it back. Of course, she didn't tell him she wanted to let her step-brother have it or why, because there's no love lost between those two. Well, so now you can see, can't you, from what you've said, Miss Charlotte! Your Uncle had got it from that Fay Iverbury, and how had *she* come by it, if not from that Mr. Jeakings? And Miss Miriam knew it, and there was a fine old hammer-and-tongs row about it between her and Warren Jeakings next time he came, only they had to go and have it outside, for all the world to hear! Really, this family!"

"In the barn, or the stable, I'm not sure which," Charlotte murmured. And as the housekeeper looked at her with raised eyebrows, Charlotte said, "You're filling in a lot of vital bits for me, but you won't like to know how I got my information. But I'll tell you, so you'll know why I'm so miserable and ashamed. Endy, I heard about that row from a man in my ward—his boy is our Tom Yates, and he heard the row!"

Mrs. Endon was shocked and wrathful.

"And," Charlotte continued, "another man on my ward, who is dying, was allowed a visitor, who is Harris, in our solicitor's office and he told him all about letting Uncle George know about getting his debts paid off—he knew that Aunt Elizabeth had changed her mind."

"Oh, Miss Charlotte!"

"And there's another old man who's got a granddaughter who is flighty and she's going around with Mears. The poor old man is so worried, he asked me to speak to her about it, but it did no good. She was rather rude to me, and she certainly didn't give Mears up."

"She should have. He's a married man," Mrs. Endon said wrathfully. "Is she a fair girl? That would be the one I saw that day. I did try to reach her, because she looked so scared, and I knew about Mears, but she went behind some bushes and I lost sight of her."

"Oh, Endy, everyone's talking about us and it's all so sordid and horrible. It was bad enough when one of my friends told me all the nurses knew about Uncle George's drinking habits, but now—well, I don't think I want to stay on at the hospital any more."

"But you liked it so much," Mrs Endon said thoughtfully, "and that nice Dr. Berrington is there, and he'll help you. Besides," she said, brightening, "it's the least of your worries—your patients will go, and the new lot won't know about all this, but here the situation will stay the same, only you won't have to worry about it. You'll be married and happy and—"

"No, Endy, you don't understand. It isn't finished yet. That Warren Jeakings got himself in the way of an elm branch—"

"Yes, funny thing that, wasn't it?" Mrs. Endon mused. "I never did understand that. It didn't *sound* right."

"And Miriam isn't visiting him—"

"Well, it's all over, dear."

"Yes, but Endy, that wretched Fay Iverbury asked me to get the brooch back for her, just for one night. Oh, that's odd! If *he*'s her new friend, she won't want it for his benefit because he's still in our hospital."

"Your uncle's sold it," Mrs. Endon said flatly. "So that takes care of that worry for you."

Charlotte felt a wave of relief go over her. She hadn't like that at all. "I'm so deeply in it, though, what with Derek and the business of Miriam's hunting prints. That Rosemary Deane won't let it go, you know. She thinks Miriam is dishonest."

"Well, she isn't," the housekeeper said with a smile. "She is anything but that. I can tell you she's selling everything she's got, to get them back for Miss Deane, to put that right! You know Miss Miriam's temper; she isn't going to have *that* girl saying she was dunned by her!"

"I hope she manages to tidy it up," Charlotte said. "I don't think I'd care for dear Nurse Deane to be carrying tales around about me, in that soft little voice of hers. Oh, Endy, it's been so nice talking to you. It's cleared up so many things. But I must go now, or Isabel will be back. What's the time? Oh, almost time for the RMO to pick me up. I mustn't keep him waiting!"

The housekeeper hid a smile. That gentleman was starting in the way he meant to go on, she thought, even if Charlotte wouldn't allow that he was in love with her.

Keith Berrington arrived on the minute he had said he would be there, and he let Charlotte talk, until she had told him everything, and then he said quietly, "Well, now that's off your back, and now I have to tell you something you won't like. Lenny died while we were out, Charlotte."

"Oh, no!" Charlotte cried.

"Well, we expected it. And old man Trippick collapsed. Will you go and see him? He asked for you. His granddaughter is with him. She's gone to pieces. Her type always do. It isn't helping him, poor old man."

"Oh, KB, I know Sister Tut said we weren't to get involved with the patients, and I haven't minded too much about others, but those two—they've been with us so long."

"I know, my dear—I feel like it, myself. Especially about Trippick. Never mind, do what you can for him."

The old man was lying very still, looking rather dignified and remote and free from pain. He opened his eyes a little and looked at Charlotte as she took his hand, but that was all.

Presently the RMO touched her arm, to get up and come away, and somehow she didn't feel so bad about it then. But Jill was another thing she had to deal with, and Sister took her into her office to talk to the girl.

Cups of hot sweet tea did little to revive her. Jill was hideously conscience stricken, filled with a guilt that Charlotte thought nothing would shift. "I should have told him," she sobbed, "but I couldn't bring myself to! I couldn't!"

"Told him what, Jill?" Charlotte asked patiently.

"It was that Mears—Granfer was so upset about him and I—I don't want him any more. I hate him!"

"Who do you hate? Albert Mears? But I thought—"

Jill shook her head and sobbed harder than ever, but when she was able to speak clearly, she explained with an impatience that took Charlotte's breath away and made her feel very helpless, because for all her painstaking questioning, and baffled reasoning, and piecing facts together, she had missed so much in her family's tangle that should have been obvious, and which she herself should have seen.

"It was since the day that Mr. Jeakings was fetched in here from the woods!" Jill said savagely.

"That you hated Mears?" Charlotte asked in bewilderment.

Jill nodded vigorously. "I would have *told* Granfer right away but he did go on and on and I was scared Sister would have blamed me for upsetting him."

"Told him what, Jill?" Charlotte persevered.

"That I'd done with Mears! I couldn't go on with a chap like him! He scared me!

After what he'd done! And I saw him do it! But then, me not telling Granfer then, I couldn't tell him afterwards, because he would have been wilder. You know what Granfer's like. And now I can't tell him ever!"

"Tell him what? What had Mears done?" Charlotte asked blankly.

Jill looked scornfully at her. "Don't you know anything? It's all this money—everyone's grabbing after it. Mears had a row with that Mr. Jeakings, didn't he? Well, it got worse, and then Mears hit him on the head with that elm branch. And I saw him do it!"

13

AS if it were not enough to see the empty beds of Granfer Trippick and Lenny Quexford, there was a three-star disaster that evening in the town, and the ward had to take in a lot of really sick people. As always in such a circumstance, those who were gently recovering, found they were given the chance to go home sooner to make room for the serious cases. Tom Yates' father was among these.

"I've only just started going out to the bathroom, and here they are, throwing me out!" he complained to Charlotte.

"You'll be coming to Out Patients for quite some time yet," she said by way of consolation, but that wasn't what he meant.

No. 3, was put in one of the cots down the centre of the ward; he would be sent home in two days. So many others were in either of these two categories that the ward became filled with strangers. Even Brenda

Newey's brother-in-law was to go—to a rehabilitation centre outside Ogmarsh. And with the new face of the ward, a lot of Charlotte's tension went.

Derek was getting up and about now, too. As soon as she had the chance, Charlotte tackled him about the threatening letters, but as with Charlotte, Derek, too, felt that the thing was easing out, blowing over. "Yes, that's right, I did find one," he admitted. "In fact, that was really what I wanted to tell you about, that night in the woods. You can see I couldn't have hoped to telephone you about it. The local switchboard is no more private than our telephone at home. But then it suddenly didn't seem to matter."

"Not matter!" Charlotte, busy cleaning the bath out, a job the juniors should have done, paused to ease her back and flare at him. He was a stranger. She had thought when he had been lying so pale and ill, that all she lived for was to see him on his feet again, vigorous, laughing, his old self. Well, here he was on his feet again, with some colour back in his cheeks, leaning against the bathroom door lazily watching her, but he wasn't the same person. He didn't even talk like the same person. "I've been worrying sick about it!" she told him.

"I'm sorry, Lotta," he said, with real regret, "but the fact is, when Patsy told me that it was only Fay Iverbury writing them, to settle an old score with Uncle George, it didn't matter so much. It wasn't as if it were some sinister crook waiting to do the old boy in, if you see what I mean!"

"You're not the same any more," Charlotte complained.

"No, I'm not," Derek agreed. "How could I be, love? I've grown up since I've been in here. I can't afford to racket around any longer. I'm going to be married. I've got to look after Patsy. Well, Fay Iverbury's going to be my boss, so it isn't in my interest to make a fuss about the things she does."

Charlotte accepted it. And during the next few days Derek was discharged from the hospital and a very sick elderly man came in his place and lay white and ill staring up at his wife and saying nothing. No one at all knew the secrets that had been flung around. Even Mr. Overton had been sent to the hospital's convalescent home, and if Mrs. Overton still gossiped about the family, at least it was a good way from the hospital.

Because of the accident, the RMO worked overtime, but at the end of the week he told Charlotte he had some time off due to him, and he felt they should celebrate.

"Celebrate what, KB?" she asked blankly. For her, the trouble was still in the background. Money was still very short and who knew to what subterfuges her uncle was descending to get more? What had happened to Miriam's brooch? Charlotte didn't even know if Miriam had managed to put the affair of the hunting prints right. And Derek had slipped quietly away and married his Patsy at a registry office, with only Fay Iverbury and the man from the local garage as witnesses. He had telephoned Charlotte afterwards to tell her about it, and he had flatly refused to contact Aunt Elizabeth and tell her.

Keith Berrington looked quizzically at her. "Celebrate a cessation of our anxieties until you fall into more trouble!" And on a different note, he pleaded, "Say you will! Let's go mad and slip down to the coast for the day. No? Well, somewhere miles away from anyone. Do you like exploring old churches? I do!" So to please him she had agreed. But she felt there would be no pleasure in going out with a man who kept on the strict friendship line, reserving his heart to grieve over the loss of someone else, while Charlotte herself had to exercise grave care so that he shouldn't see how she felt about him.

But it was a nice day, as it happened. The weather was warm and sunny, and the RMO was in holiday mood; a rare thing. After they had had lunch at one of those places off the beaten track which he had a genius for finding, they walked over a track of common land between gorse bushes, following a "ride" that led them into woodland that had an air of innocence that the Ferndale Woods would never have. There was a stream that was just a stream, not a miniature waterfall as at home. The little bridge over it was just a plank, not an elaborate stone bridge as the one built by some other Ferndale long since dead and gone, who had more money than sense. Charlotte said contentedly, "I'm liking this."

"Are you really," the RMO said softly. "And what is it you are liking exactly? The weather, the holiday, the escape from hospital and reality, or the neat tidying up of the secrets that have plunged our existence recently? Or could it be that you like being out with old KB?"

She chuckled at that, but she flushed a little and turned her head away.

He stopped and pulled her round to face him. "Charlotte, look at me, my dear," he said, taking her chin in his hand and upturning it. "Do you like me or loathe me?"

"Don't be silly, KB. Why this inquisition?"

"Because it's suddenly important that I know," he told her. "Up till now, we've been having fun, sorting out your problems."

"I expect I shall get into hot water again soon, or have an outstanding problem that you want to solve," she said chokily, and felt for the first time in her life, rather out of her depth. If he didn't like her specially, why was he acting like this? And if he did like her as much as Aunt Elizabeth and Mrs. Endon seemed to think, why didn't he say so?

"Is that what I'm relegated to, the OC for getting Charlotte Ferndale out of trouble?" he asked softly.

"I don't know, KB. What do you want to be?" she asked rashly. "KB, don't look like that! I had a right to say that, because I fancy that every time we get close to each other in friendship, the face of Rosemary Deane looks over your shoulder. It's no good getting all nettled with me for mentioning her. I believe you still care for her and you don't even know it."

"I did ask you a question—what you wanted, Charlotte!" he reminded her.

She thought in bewilderment, what does

he want me to say? That I'm crazy about him?

She shrugged a little. "I don't know what answer you want to that. Perhaps we'd better just walk on, and enjoy the day. We may not get another like this."

But of course, the best had gone out of the day. It wasn't the same after that. It couldn't be, because she was all shaken and could still feel the touch of his fingers on her chin, upturning her face for what could surely have only been a kiss. What had happened to that kiss? And why did she have to go to pieces at the thought of his kissing her? Other men had kissed her, without the sky falling in!

The day deteriorated weatherwise, soon after that, and they had to run for the shelter of the car and they went back early, and when they got back, there was unwelcome news for Charlotte. News that took all the sunshine away. Aunt Elizabeth had died.

Charlotte just stood there, looking stupidly at Home Sister, who told her the news. Charlotte felt helpless. She could still hear the hum of the RMO's car as he was manoeuvring it into the Residents' Car Park at the back of the Nurses' Home, but he had never felt further away than he did now, and she wanted him so much. Wanted his support. There had been too many people she knew, leaving her lately, and now Aunt Elizabeth who had looked nowhere near her age, and had vigorously got about in her car, bullying her chauffeur, bullying her relatives and making certain lives very uncomfortable indeed because of their expectations in all that wealth of hers. And she had died in her sleep, helplessly, with no one within call. Not like Granfer Trippick, in a ward full of people, with everyone grieving at his passing. Not like Lenny Quexford even, who had no one belonging to him but many friends. Alone, Aunt Elizabeth had died, with nothing but her money to comfort her.

Charlotte staggered to her room, but her friends were out. The girl next door volunteered the information that both Sylvia and Linda were going steady and didn't Charlotte know? She looked curiously at

Charlotte, so Charlotte thanked her and pushed her out, and cried into her pillow until she was exhausted, because she knew the kind of loneliness Aunt Elizabeth had suffered. It was Charlotte's now.

The whole of that evening she resisted the temptation to call the RMO on the telephone. Ferndale House, too. She had expected someone there to telephone her, but they didn't, and they must have been informed, for Derek telephoned her. The solicitors had found his new telephone number somehow and told him of his aunt's death.

Derek said, "Charlotte! Fancy the old girl going off quickly like that! I would never have believed it!" He had no grief, only a lively interest in who would get Aunt Elizabeth's money.

Charlotte ought to have known that everyone would be wanting to know that—waiting; creditors and family alike. She supposed drearily that Uncle George would inherit, because it was most reasonable that he should. She wished she didn't have to go to the funeral—that she could slip over to the graveside and quietly pay her last respects to Aunt Elizabeth without having to see any of the rest of the family.

But that wasn't likely, and she knew it. In deep mourning hastily procured (because Aunt Elizabeth for all her modern exterior believed in such things) Charlotte went over to the great ugly house hemmed in by evergreens, backed by tall gloomy cypresses, where Aunt Elizabeth had lived. Charlotte had forgotten how ugly it was inside as well as out, and how many servants there still were, and how many relatives, distant as well as close, would be invited there. It was a chilling afternoon. The RMO had been on call, so Charlotte hadn't even said goodbye to him. She had caught a taxi and boarded a train. And here, in the purple and olive green drawing-room, with the curtains drawn against the offending sunlight, Charlotte was stunned to hear that she herself had inherited everything. Everything. There were a few modest bequests to the staff, but it seemed as if Aunt Elizabeth in that last Will of hers had fallen over backwards to leave as much as possible to Charlotte. Not, she noticed, in stupefaction, Charlotte mentioned by name but "to the one among all my relatives who has not been in debt once during the past year", and so far as that went, Aunt Elizabeth might just as well have mentioned Charlotte. There were the farms which Aunt Elizabeth owned, and the two streets of mean houses in Rolborough; the big town house and the ugly one in the country. There were the collections of silver and china which (Charlotte heard from her staggered and displeased relatives) would set dealers by the ears, and what was she going to do with them? There was the period furniture which Aunt Elizabeth had collected in her youth and the pictures of the French period Aunt Elizabeth had so much admired and collected in her middle years. And there was a very great deal of money.

Charlotte was so staggered she couldn't think. Staggered and not at all happy. She was featured in the press because to be young and pretty and suddenly inheriting such a fortune was news. She was featured on the television for the same reason, and she didn't like having to tell strangers how she felt about it. Home Sister was frigid, but Matron really charming. The RMO kept out of sight altogether. And her relatives discovered that they had always liked Charlotte very much but had somehow managed to give her the wrong impression.

Matron suggested that Charlotte should take her leave to help the solicitors clear up everything. Matron seemed to be quite sure that Charlotte wouldn't want to stay on as a nurse, and rather put out when Charlotte said that she did.

"Well, think it over, my dear," Matron said.

Sylvia and Linda were a little odd in their manner when she went to say goodbye, and when she went to find Keith Berrington, he wasn't alone; Rosemary was with him.

Rosemary! Was she tired of Oscar Verrall already, Charlotte asked herself furiously. She explained that she was going on leave and had merely come to say goodbye, so he said goodbye, without making an opportunity of seeing Charlotte alone. True,

Rosemary hung on to his arm and did a lot of the talking for him, and said it was so nice for Charlotte to have come into money, adding, "But of course, personally, I would rather not be so rich, because I would never know if anyone, but *anyone*, wanted me for myself or my money!" and she smiled up at Keith as if he too, were in complete agreement with that sentiment.

Aunt Elizabeth's chauffeur was there to drive Charlotte away. The solicitors, with one very old clerk who would never in a hundred years have debased himself to betray a client's secrets as Harris had done, were very much at Charlotte's service. Everyone was eager to help her and smooth her path, but, she told herself ruefully no one wanted to love her. She had stepped into Aunt Elizabeth's shoes and inherited, with all the rest, Aunt Elizabeth's isolation, her loneliness.

The house grew more and more oppressive, so when she had done all the duty things she felt she ought to, and the solicitors had been instructed about what to sell and what to keep, she felt she was free to please herself so she went to a small hotel she had once stayed at on the coast.

It ought to have been quiet and pleasant. She went by train and taxi, much to the indignation of her chauffeur, and took only a suitcase, but on the day of arrival she saw her picture on the front of a newspaper in connection with a sale of pictures, and word got around who she was, so there was no more peace. In desperation she decided to go back to the hospital. But first she telephoned Keith Berrington.

His voice made her pulse leap. Now he was on the line she didn't know what to say to him. She wanted to say, "KB, I'm so lonely. Come and cheer me up!" but after two weeks of giving orders to people and receiving respect from them, she had lost the art of saying baldly what she meant. She couldn't say that any more, so she managed: "How are you?" and he said, in an equally stilted tone, "Very well. And you?" which wasn't how they had been at all.

Even the familiar "KB" stuck in her throat, so she said with a little rush, "Do you think you could spare me a little time? There's something I would like to discuss with you."

He sounded guarded, and said at last, "I really do think that the sort of help you need now would come better from your solicitors, don't you?"

"It isn't that," she choked. "It's . . . well, I want to come back and finish my training, but it struck me that Matron didn't seem too keen on the idea. What do *you* think?"

He said, "I don't think I can add anything to that. After all, what Matron says and does is the important thing."

Frustrated, she quietly put down the receiver, telling herself she was all sorts of a fool. He had probably got Rosemary beside him, listening to all that was being said on the telephone.

From out of her loneliness, Charlotte went home to Ferndale House. This time she went in her car, driven by her aunt's man, but the sight of him, behind the wheel of that car, gave the worst impression possible. They didn't see it that Charlotte couldn't drive, and wouldn't have attempted to drive that great ungainly vehicle if she could. They didn't see, either, that she was tired and dispirited. She had worked hard on doing the duty things that Aunt Elizabeth had done. Charlotte had soon learned that her great-aunt had spoken no less than the truth when she had once said that owning a fortune was hard work. George and the rest of the family only saw money as a means of getting rid of creditors, or a means of gambling with no anxieties, a means of acquiring horses and dogs, all the things they wanted. The would have been shocked to think hard work was required of them in connection with it.

The atmosphere was frosty from the start, and even when Charlotte in desperation, offered to put Ferndale House and the stables in order for her uncle, that did no good.

"I don't want you to do things for me, my girl," he said. "I wanted her money and I had a right to it, but as I haven't got it, then there's an end of it."

"But it's in the family, isn't it?"

Charlotte said blankly.

"No. It's yours, and what you do with it is your business, do you understand? Ferndale House, on the other hand, is mine, and if I want it to fall down about my ears for want of repair, that also is my business."

"But you always said if only you had the money to repair it—" Charlotte began, but he cut in coldly.

"You never began to understand, did you? I didn't want Aunt Elizabeth dispensing largesse to me. None of us did. What we wanted was her money, in toto, by inheritance, which was what we had always been led to believe. Well, we haven't got it. So there is an end of it."

Isabel went further and suggested that Charlotte must have "got round" the old lady, for this thing to happen.

"Are you saying that you want nothing from me, too, Isabel?" Charlotte asked quietly.

"None of us do. Don't worry, George won't let the house fall to pieces. He'll get it put in order, if only by selling those nasty woods for development. I'm sure we'll all be very glad to see that happen. And then we can sell the house, too, and go abroad under our own steam. We don't want you for anything."

Even Derek echoed that. "I'm happy now, Charlotte. Patsy and I have got everything we want."

Charlotte ran into Jill Trippick in Ogmarsh High Street on the way from seeing Derek. She tapped at the window and invited Jill into the car to talk to her, but Jill refused. But the memory of the old man and his anxiety over his granddaughter was so strong that Charlotte was moved to ask the girl if she could help her.

"Why would you want to do that, miss?" Jill asked bluntly.

"Because when I was a nurse on your grandfather's ward he used to talk to me about you and I know he would have been a lot easier in mind if he could have been sure someone would be there for you to turn to for financial help if you needed it. I couldn't have helped you then—I was so hard-up. But I'm not now—"

"It makes no difference," Jill broke in. "I wouldn't take help if I needed it, but it so happens I don't. My boss is ever so kind to me, since my grandfather died, and—well, to tell you the truth, he's offered to marry me, and I've said yes, so you don't need to worry. I'm all right."

Even Jill Trippick, Charlotte thought, as she signalled the worried chauffeur to move the precious car out of all that unseemly traffic. Did Aunt Elizabeth feel that people didn't want her help? Was that why she hadn't been happy?

Never in her life had Charlotte felt so wretched, and like a homing pigeon, she left the car in Rolborough's car park, to wait for her, and walked the last two streets to the hospital. Only the sight of Keith Berrington marching across the grass, his coat tails flying, made any sense to her, and she hurried towards him.

"I'm so glad to see you," she said sincerely. "I've had such a nasty day. Could we have a meal together when you come off duty, or are you busy?"

She didn't understand the way he looked

at her. "Why has it been nasty, Charlotte?" he asked her.

She told him. "No one, not even Jill Trippick, wants anything to do with me! I wonder if Aunt Elizabeth felt like this?"

"Yes, she did. She told me so. We had a long talk that day when you were in the sick bay. I told you."

"Oh, yes, when she made you promise something. What was it? You do owe it to me, don't you, to tell me now?"

He hesitated. "She told me she was making you her heiress, and she didn't want me hanging around you to spoil your chances. I see what she means."

"Well, you did keep your promise, didn't you?" Charlotte said, with a gasp. "Even when you took me out that day, there was a nice barrier between us!"

"And there's going to be," he nodded. "No one, no one at all, is going to label me a fortune-hunter." And his anger communicated itself to her, like a living thing, leaving her cold and shivering and a little afraid. It wasn't Great-Aunt Elizabeth who had produced this; it was Rosemary, Charlotte told herself. Rosemary had got at him.

And this seemed to be confirmed later, after visiting her one-time friends in the Nurses Home, when she saw Keith Berrington walking Rosemary to the Car Park, his hand tucked under her arm, and later Keith driving Rosemary out of the hospital gates. Why couldn't he say he'd gone back to Rosemary again, for heaven sake? Why couldn't he be honest?

Sylvia and Linda were full of their marriages. They were giving up nursing just as soon as they decently could. They both sedulously avoided mentioning Charlotte's inheritance, and tried not very successfully, to pretend that everything was still as it had once been.

"Remember the gossip on the ward," Linda said in her old tactless way, and Sylvia kicked her, as a reminder, just the way she had always done. And yet it wasn't quite the same. The difference was that Charlotte didn't belong any longer.

She accepted the invitations to their weddings, knowing very well that she wouldn't go and that they didn't really expect her to.

She went round to see all her old friends, but they were busy, and she hadn't much heart, so at last she went to see Matron and arranged to leave right away. Matron was obviously relieved.

"Well, nurse, I'm glad, because the gossip on your ward must have made you very uncomfortable, and who knows when the grapevine may well flare out again? No, I believe your decision is the right one. Perhaps at some other hospital, a larger one perhaps—in London, where everything is impersonal."

Impersonal, yes, where no one knows each other, and couldn't care less. Such a bleak prospect chilled Charlotte even more than the thought of going back to Great-Aunt Elizabeth's house and starting to entertain the people who would be willing to know her; the ones Great-Aunt Elizabeth had said you couldn't be sure of—did they want you for yourself or your money?

Rolborough at this time of the day was pepping itself up for the nightly exodus from work. The traffic rumbled by and it was practically impossible to cross any road. She couldn't see a way to reach the car park and the car, so she just walked on until she came to the bridge over the network of railway lines. As she walked, she asked herself where the days had gone when it had been fun to be a nurse? When she had slipped in and out of trouble, and where in the background a craggy face had watched her although she hadn't been too much aware of it at the time, a face which had slipped into laughter wrinkles when she came out of trouble unscathed, and which had slipped into a frown of anxiety when it looked as if she wouldn't be so lucky.

Where had they gone, those days filled with interest, in patients who didn't gossip, but who were nice to know? In the days before Derek had sent that message to her to meet him in the woods? Only the taint of scandal, the sticky touch of intrigue and underhanded dealings, had made life impossible for her, and she had only been trying to help Derek, who had been like a brother to her. And overnight, he had slipped away, to range himself beside Patsy—so she need not have been drawn into the thing at all, Charlotte told herself in dismay.

And now it was all too late, because Great-Aunt Elizabeth had done the final tarnishing act by leaving her burden of wealth to Charlotte. Was it possible, she asked herself, to give it all away? And to whom? The family would hate her even more if she split it up among them, because they hated her for having been chosen to inherit it in the first place.

She stood staring at a poster, not seeing it at first but seeing instead Keith Berrington walking beside an elated Rosemary, towards the Residents' Car Park.

Had he gone back to Rosemary? She couldn't see the poster, clearly. And then her vision cleared and she looked at it and read that the world was pitted with pockets of distress and malnutrition. Photographs of starving children and sick adults in a dozen different parts of the globe, stared down at her and she was riveted to the spot. People might not want Charlotte Ferndale here in Rolborough, but there were multitudes who might—those people who had the disease which had always interested her.

China, Africa, the Americas—where should she choose to go, she asked herself? At once, because it didn't matter now. Time was on her side. She had it in abundance because Rolborough had rejected her.

She was so lost in her own reflections about the poster that she had no thought of the traffic behind her. Later she learned that a wheel had come off a lorry, causing it to skid straight at her. At the time she was just confusedly aware of a multitude of raucous sounds behind her, a rush of wind, and of a blow in the back that shattered pain all over her and swept her off her feet. And the wall, with its poster, which had interested her so much, crumbled and vanished with a splintering, crunching sound, and she could see the railway lines, only they were where the sky ought to be.

During her time in Casualty, Charlotte had seen the receiving end of many street accidents, but never had she seen the start of one. She lay, pinned by her leg, poised perilously over the edge where the wall had been, afraid to move, terrified at the thought of not being able to get away. High above her, like a crumpled tattered mountain, the lorry was poised at a drunken angle. From the cab, the driver's arm hung, swinging a little, as if he were unconscious. Slumped over the driving wheel. Objects that filled the lorry were steadily falling out, now a few, now a lot, in little rushes. A sea of faces were beyond, and all the traffic stopped on the bridge, the only sound being voices, conflicting voices, all with different ideas of what to do, and no one willing to put a single one of those ideas into practice, for fear the lorry moved, with Charlotte underneath it.

Someone pushed through the crowd, inches taller than the other people. In wonderment Charlotte recognised the RMO—alone, agonised when he recognized who it was under the lorry. She saw his face, his mouth ludicrously frame her name, and then another rush of the objects from the lorry came past her head, and she felt a stinging blow on the temple and darkness closed over her.

It only seemed a minute or two before she opened her eyes again, but now it was quiet, and nothing reared itself above her. The lorry had gone, and in its place a bowl light hung, and it wasn't turned on. The only light came from the glass partition to the corridor and that was dim. Someone sat beside her, and a nurse moved about the room. Charlotte croaked, in an effort to speak, and the nurse said she'd call Sister and went out. Charlotte turned to the person beside her, thinking it was Derek, or perhaps Uncle George, but it was Keith Berrington.

He said, in a husky voice so unlike his own that she couldn't believe at first that it was him, "You're all right! Just your leg caught it. Now take it easy!" and then, before she could ask any of the things she wanted to ask, he burst out, "Charlotte, for heaven's sake, how did you get *into* that mess? Can't I let you out of my sight for five minutes?"

"How unjust," she heard herself say.

"You didn't want me—you went off with Rosemary Deane. I saw you."

"Good grief, yes, to give her a lift to the station. She *asked* me—just when I was making up my mind to forget that promise to your aunt, and to find you and tell you I didn't care what people said. If you could just have some idea of how I *felt* when I saw you under that lorry—"

He broke off, on a queer note. Sister was coming back with the nurse, but Charlotte had the feeling that even if they hadn't been interrupted, he wouldn't have been able to continue, he was so upset.

It was a pity, because he went out without a backward glance, and Sister took over.

"Well, Nurse Arrowsmith, things do seem to happen to you, don't they?" she said cheerfully. "Everyone is talking about you! No one has seen such an escape! To think you could have such a thing happen to you, and to get away with only your leg broken!"

Charlotte said, "They won't take it off?"

"Bless you, no! Why should they? A

couple of breaks, but you're a strong and healthy young woman, if a foolish one. Now, just keep still while I—"

Jabs. Everything truly did happen to her, Charlotte thought drearily, as the darkness closed over her again.

Inactivity in a place where she had once been so active, became the worst of Charlotte's troubles, but it had its compensation, for whenever he had a minute and was near, Keith Berrington dropped in for a chat. One day he said, "I imagine you can talk about the accident now, Charlotte? What were you *doing* on that bridge, of all places?"

She told him, baldly, with pain in her eyes and voice. "I still mean to continue what I was planning when that lorry hit me," she said. "I don't want the money. I never did. But now I've found people who do."

"You mean you'll go out to those places?" he asked her.

She nodded. "I'd like to. Because I want to see for myself just what they need and when. I'd rather do it that way than just hand over the money for other people to dispense. Aunt Elizabeth always used to say, money is a duty to be handled by the owner. I think she'd like me to do that."

He nodded, but the thing she wanted to hear, just didn't come. Desperate, she said, "KB, don't you want to tell me something?"

He smiled ruefully. "I am not in love with Rosemary."

"I didn't mean that, but it helps. Don't you want to tell me I need advice and assistance from someone who knows more about the subject than me—you, for instance?"

He looked surprised, and then he laughed. "Why, you little wretch—yes, as it happens, that's just what I do want to say!"

"I accept your help," she told him. "And I expect you want to say that Rolborough won't be nearly as interesting as one of those countries I was looking at on the poster, now there's plenty of money free to do some really good work?"

"Yes, I do—"

"And that you're ready and willing to pack up and come with me, as soon as my wretched leg's fit to make the journey?"

"Yes, Charlotte, I do indeed—"

"And that you're a plain-speaking man and there won't be any pretty speeches whatever—"

"Charlotte! Really!" he exploded, then he took her hand in his and turned it over, and put his lips to it. "But I would like to propose to you myself, if I might be allowed to say a few words."

"Yes, please," she said happily, wriggling down in the bed. "Go on, KB!"

"Will you marry me, Charlotte, even though everyone will brand me as a fortune-hunter?"

"Yes, I will," she said, with something of her old vigour, "and if I hear them say it, I shall have a thing or two to say to them!"

He started to say something, then altered his mind and gathered her into his arms. His face buried in her dark hair, he said, in a choked voice, "Charlotte, I don't think I could bear to let you out of my sight again, for fear of wondering what was happening to you."

"Oh, is that all I am—a responsibility?" she retorted.

He was silent for a while, then he said, a hint of amusement back in his voice, "What else do you want to be?"

"Do I have to say it?" she said, a hint of tears in her voice.

"But you must know that I love you, Charlotte," he said, still keeping his face hidden. "I have been ashamed at times of the way I trailed around after you, unable to let you out of my sight, and unhappily conscious of everyone else seeing what was so obvious. You must know that you come first, even though I might sit all night holding some frightened injured young woman's hand—you must know the RMO doesn't usually make it his life's work to keep one especial nurse out of possible danger and let the others do as they like?"

"KB, you've made a speech," she whispered, delighted.

"The sort you wanted to hear?"

"Yes, oh, yes, and it was so original, too.

KB, I'm going to be like every other engaged girl, you know—jealous and catty and possessive and all those things—"

"You don't happen to love me, I suppose?" he murmured.

"Now isn't that what I'm telling you, darling?"

The nurse bringing Charlotte's water jug backed out hurriedly, scarlet to the ears. She had heard all that. Sister said, "Is Nurse Arrowsmith alone?" and opened the door, but averted her eyes. The RMO was kissing Charlotte as if nothing else in the world mattered. "Well, never mind, nurse, take that jug in later," Sister said.

THE END

Other titles in the Linford Series:

HEAVEN IS HIGH
by Anne Hampson

The new heir to the Manor of Marbeck had been found—an American from the Rocky Mountains! But it was rather unfortunate that when he arrived unexpectedly he found an uninvited guest, complete with Stetson and high boots, singing "I'm an old cowhand . . . Here I am, straight from those jolly ole Rockies . . ."

LOVE WILL COME
by Sarah Devon

June Baker's boss was not really her idea of her ideal man, but when she went from third typist to boss's secretary overnight she began to change her mind.

ESCAPE TO ROMANCE
by Kay Winchester

Oliver and Jean first met on Swale Island. They were both trying to begin their lives afresh, but neither had bargained for complications from the past.

ISLAND FIESTA

by Jane Corrie

Corinne found herself trapped into marrying Juan Martel. He expected her to behave as a docile Spanish wife, and turn a blind eye to his affairs. How on earth could Corinne cope with this mess?

THE CORNISH HEARTH

by Isobel Chace

Anna was not pleased when she ran into Piran Trethowyn again. She had no desire to further her acquaintance with such an insulting and overbearing character.

NOW WITH HIS LOVE

by Hilda Nickson

Juliet hoped that Switzerland would help her to get over her broken engagement, but all that happened was that she fell in love with Richard Thornton, who was not interested in her.

SHADOW DANCE
by Margaret Way

When Carl Danning sent her to interview the elusive Richard Kauffman, Alix was far from pleased—but the assignment led her to help Richard repair the situation between him and his ex-wife. If only she could sort out the situation between herself and Carl!

WHITE HIBISCUS
by Rosemary Pollock

"A boring English model with dubious morals," was how Count Paul Santana Demajo described Emma. But what about the Count's morals, and who is Marianne?

STARS THROUGH THE MIST
by Betty Neels

Secretly in love with Gerard van Doorninck, Deborah should have been thrilled when he asked her to marry him. However, he had made it clear that he wanted a wife for practical not romantic reasons.

TIME FOR LOVING
by Kathleen Treves

When two young men are saved from their capsized boat and brought to Honeybank Farm House to recover, their arrival causes upheaval in the family, and Deborah has to cope with many problems until she finds time for loving!

THE SPOTTED PLUME
by Yvonne Whittal

"I can only stand females in small doses," the arrogant Hunter Maynard told Jennifer. That was alright by Jennifer, her career as a nurse would come first in her life. Or would it?

SURGEON'S SECOND WIFE
by Kay Winchester

At thirty-eight, Senior Surgeon Nicholas Kent, feels himself to be the odd man out at St. Hyria's Hospital. A widower for some years, his life changes when he literally bumps into Venny who is only eighteen years old.

ventolin

LAND OF TOMORROW
by Mons Daveson

Nicola was going back to the little house on the coast near Brisbane. Would her future also contain Drew Huntley? He was certainly part of her present, whether she wanted him to be or not.

THE MAN AT KAMBALA
by Kay Thorpe

Sara lived with her father at Kambala in Kenya and was accustomed to do as she pleased. She certainly didn't think much of Steve York who came to take charge in her father's absence.

ALLURE OF LOVE
by Honor Vincent

Nerida Bayne took a winter sports holiday in Norway. After a case of mistaken identity, entanglements and heartache followed, but at last Nerida finds happiness.

Olympic Dreams

A Journey to Gold. Part-1

ELIO E

ElioEndless

ELIO ENDLESS PUBLISHERS

For more information or to book an event, please contact: elioendleeshouse@gmail.com

Book design by Kai

Cover design by Tyson

Paperback ISBN:

ebook ISBN:

To Dad, Mom, and my supportive colleagues,Your love, guidance, and unwavering support have been the driving force behind my journey as a writer. Thank you for believing in me and encouraging me to pursue my dreams. Your presence in my life has made all the difference.

With heartfelt gratitude,

ELIO.E

Preface

Hey there, "wave"! How's it going? I'm your friendly neighborhood book editor, here to tell you about this amazing book that just landed on our shelves. It's a gem that our awesome publishing company has brought to life. Now, as part of my job, I get to dive into countless books, and I must say, this one is an absolute delight. No need for any unnecessary delay, let me give you a sneak peek into what makes it so worthwhile. Are you ready? Let's jump right in with the introduction.The Olympic Games, which are sometimes referred to as simply The Olympics, are the most prestigious international multi-sport athletic tournament that takes place on a worldwide scale. This spectacular competition, which takes place once every four years, is designed to highlight the abilities of athletes from all around the world. What was once an age-old custom has evolved into a modern festival that honors the achievements of humankind. This festival is split into two parts: the summer games and the winter games, which take place every two years apart. This schedule is a departure from the previous tradition, which, prior to 1992, consisted of holding both the summer and winter games in the same calendar year.The origins of the Olympic Games may be traced back to Olympia, Greece, around the year 776 B.C.E., where they stood as a stunning exhibition of sports skill for almost a millennium until its demise in 393 C.E. The appeal of the ancient Greek games was so strong that even warring groups would temporarily put their differences aside to enable their athletes to partake in the games. The development of the Roman Empire, on the other hand, brought forth a more vicious and exciting kind of gladiatorial fighting, which caught the attention of the people and ultimately overshadowed the more subdued attraction of the Greek games. The later Christianization of the Roman Empire led to a perception of the Olympic Games as being similar to pagan festivities. This contributed further to the Olympic Games' diminishing popularity.Greek benefactor Evangelos Zappas, who funded the first modern international Olympic Games in 1859, was the driving force behind the revitalization of the Olympic heritage in the 19th century. Zappas's charitable activities allowed him to realize his aim of reviving the Olympic legacy. The beginning of a new era in Olympic history was marked by the formation of the International Olympic Committee (IOC) in 1894, which paved the way for the first modern Olympic Games to be held in 1896 in Athens. Athletes from virtually every region of the world are now eligible to compete in the Olympic Games thanks to the expansion of the event throughout time. The emergence of cutting-edge communication technology, such as satellite transmission and global telecasts, elevated the Olympic Games to the status of a colossal media event, which in turn inspired towns all over the globe to compete with one another for the prestigious opportunity to host the games.When the modern Olympic Games were revived in 1896, there was a fervent wish that the massive athletic competition that they represented may one day act as a unifying force for the world. People all over the world, from distant villages to booming metropolis, saw competitive sports as a platform through which to exhibit human brilliance, self-mastery, and collaborative effort. This fostered links between people living in different parts of the world. These athletic competitions served as a uniting influence since they cut over religious, socioeconomic, and ethnic lines. The tumult of two world wars in the twentieth century and the split caused by the Cold War put the Olympic dream's high ideals to the test. Despite this, the Olympic hope persisted for a period of time. Throughout its history, the Olympic Games have been plagued by controversies including cheating, nationalistic triumphalism, and rampant commercialism. However, the Olympic Games continue to instill pride in human accomplishments and encourage mutual respect among political opponents. This is true despite the fact that the Olympics have yet to fulfill its ultimate goal to transcend political boundaries and symbolize human aspirations.

Acknowledgements

I would like to take this opportunity to extend my heartfelt thanks to all the individuals who have played a significant role in the creation of this non-fiction book. Your unwavering support, valuable advice, and constant encouragement have been invaluable throughout this journey. I am deeply grateful to those who have provided me with aspirational direction, constructive criticism, and kind advice. Your feedback has been instrumental in shaping the content and direction of this book. I genuinely appreciate your candid insights into my project.I am particularly grateful for the exceptional assistance of Mr. Jaffer and Mrs. Sameena at Endless Publishers. Their continuous support, dedication, and guidance have been instrumental in helping me overcome obstacles and improve the quality of my work. I am sincerely appreciative of their tremendous efforts and unwavering belief in this project.I would also like to express my heartfelt appreciation to Mr. Ahmed, my project's external advisor from Ahmed Corporation. His invaluable advice, insightful critique, and vast wisdom have played a pivotal role in refining my thoughts and enhancing the overall quality of this book. I am truly grateful for his guidance and expertise.Furthermore, I would like to acknowledge Ms. Sultana and every individual who has contributed to obtaining the necessary resources and making this initiative possible. Your assistance, whether it was in sourcing information, conducting research, or providing logistical support, is deeply appreciated. This book would not have come to fruition without your invaluable contributions.I cannot overlook the individual who initially sparked the flame of inspiration within me to embark on this book-writing endeavor. Your unwavering belief in my abilities, continuous motivation, and unending support throughout this artistic process have been instrumental in my journey. I am forever indebted to you for being my constant source of inspiration.I want to express my deepest gratitude to every person who has contributed to this project, no matter how small their role may have been. Each and every one of you has played a part in making this book possible, and your contributions have not gone unnoticed. Your support, encouragement, and assistance have been instrumental in bringing this book to fruition.Finally, I would like to give special credit to Kai, B.EE, and Tyson, the pen names that have accompanied me on this writing adventure. Your creativity, distinct perspectives, and unique insights have added depth and character to this book. I am honored to have had the opportunity to collaborate with you.To all of you who have been a part of this remarkable journey, I extend my deepest gratitude. Your unwavering support, guidance, and friendship have been invaluable. Thank you for believing in me and for contributing to the realization of this non-fiction book.With

sincere appreciation,

Elio Endless

EDITOR NOTE

1. Publisher Notes: This edition is a product of inspiration from other works, with a portion of its content derived from public domain sources. Elioendless, the creator, editor, and publisher of the ebook edition, utilized manuscripts, select texts, and illustrative images from public domain archives. Members can acquire this ebook from our website for personal use. However, please note that any form of commercial storage, transmission, or reverse engineering of this file is strictly prohibited.

Contents

Chapter One
Introduction

Brief overview of the Olympic Games and their significance

The Olympic Games, which are sometimes referred to as simply The Olympics, are the most prestigious international multi-sport athletic tournament that takes place on a worldwide scale. This spectacular competition, which takes place once every four years, is designed to highlight the abilities of athletes from all around the world. What was once an age-old custom has evolved into a modern festival that honors the achievements of humankind. This festival is split into two parts: the summer games and the winter games, which take place every two years apart. This schedule is a departure from the previous tradition, which, prior to 1992, consisted of holding both the summer and winter games in the same calendar year.

The origins of the Olympic Games may be traced back to Olympia, Greece, around the year 776 B.C.E., where they stood as a stunning exhibition of sports skill for almost a millennium until its demise in 393 C.E. The appeal of the ancient Greek games was so strong that even warring groups would temporarily put their differences aside to enable their athletes to partake in the games. The development of the Roman Empire, on the other hand, brought forth a more vicious and exciting kind of gladiatorial fighting, which caught the attention of the people and ultimately overshadowed the more subdued attraction of the Greek games. The later Christianization of the Roman Empire led to a perception of the Olympic Games as being similar to pagan festivities. This contributed further to the Olympic Games' diminishing popularity.Greek benefactor Evangelos Zappas, who funded the first modern international Olympic Games in 1859, was the driving force behind the revitalization of the

Olympic heritage in the 19th century. Zappas's charitable activities allowed him to realize his aim of reviving the Olympic legacy. The beginning of a new era in Olympic history was marked by the formation of the International Olympic Committee (IOC) in 1894, which paved the way for the first modern Olympic Games to be held in 1896 in Athens. Athletes from virtually every region of the world are now eligible to compete in the Olympic Games thanks to the expansion of the event throughout time. The emergence of cutting-edge communication technology, such as satellite transmission and global telecasts, elevated the Olympic Games to the status of a colossal media event, which in turn inspired towns all over the globe to compete with one another for the prestigious opportunity to host the games.When the modern Olympic Games were revived in 1896, there was a fervent wish that the massive athletic competition that they represented may one day act as a unifying force for the world. People all over the world, from distant villages to booming metropolis, saw competitive sports as a platform through which to exhibit human brilliance, self-mastery, and collaborative effort. This fostered links between people living in different parts of the world. These athletic competitions served as a uniting influence since they cut over religious, socioeconomic, and ethnic lines. The tumult of two world wars in the twentieth century and the split caused by the Cold War put the Olympic dream's high ideals to the test. Despite this, the Olympic hope persisted for a period of time. Throughout its history, the Olympic Games have been plagued by controversies including cheating, nationalistic triumphalism, and rampant commercialism. However, the Olympic Games continue to instill pride in human accomplishments and encourage mutual respect among political opponents. This is true despite the fact that the Olympics have yet to fulfill its ultimate goal to transcend political boundaries and symbolize human aspirations.

Ancient Olympics

It is said that the legendary Heracles, who was worshiped as a heavenly hero, was the one who came up with the idea for the famous Olympic Games. This assertion may be found in the domain of legend and lore. Heracles attempted a task of enormous proportions after successfully completing the arduous Twelve Labors because he had an intense need to show his adored father Zeus his gratitude. As a way to show his respect for the all-powerful god Zeus, he painstakingly constructed the magnificent Olympic stadium as well as the buildings that surround it.As the mythical story progresses, Heracles is shown to have set out on an important voyage, during which he walked deliberately in a line for a total of four hundred paces. In the ancient Greek language, this particular measured distance was given the name "stadion," and it later developed into a standard unit of measurement. This particular measurement has been used to meticulously determine the circumferential length of modern stadiums, and this standard has been carefully maintained over the ages.Beliefs that were prevalent in ancient Greece are intertwined with the origin of the Olympic Games, including the holy notion of, also known as Olympic Truce. Warring city-states momentarily put down their arms in a gesture of tremendous importance, creating a climate in which athletes might congregate and take part in the splendor of the Games. This allowed athletes from all over the world to compete.

Although scholarly discourse gives a range of estimations running from 884 B.C.E. to 704 B.C.E., historical agreement often places the first Olympic Games in the year 776 B.C.E., which was a sacred year in Greek history. Regardless of the specific dates, it is certain that the Olympic Games rapidly expanded into an important institution over the entirety of ancient Greece, reaching their pinnacle during the sixth and fifth centuries before the common era (B.C.E.). The festivities had significant theological connotations, with heated competitions interspersed with holy ceremonies and tributes paid to both the enormous god Zeus, whose statue loomed magnificently at Olympia, and Pelops, the divine hero and mythical monarch of Olympia. The rites and tributes were dedicated to both of these figures.This momentous occasion began with a straightforward footrace, then grew to incorporate wrestling and the pentathlon, and finally reached its zenith with a grand total of twenty distinct competitions. As the size and significance of the celebrations increased, they were extended over a period of many days and became decorated with the glory of athletes who had won, who were glorified via poems and statues. These competitions took place once every four years, and the interval between them was known as a "Olympiad," which was a span of time that marked the progression of history and was carefully documented in the annals of Greek culture.Young males, their bodies exposed in reverence to the honoring of human physical accomplishment, stood as the torchbearers of athletic power within this ancient tapestry. To emerge triumphant from the Games was to advance to the highest possible level of status, to be awarded not only with olive leaves but also with accolades that will last forever. A solitary character arose as an icon in the sixth century B.C.E. among the pantheon of famed athletes. This figure was Milo of Croton, the venerable wrestler, who etched his name in the annals of history as the only athlete to win in six consecutive Olympics. Milo of Croton was the lone athlete to win in six consecutive Olympics.Despite this, the ancient world was being swept by a wave of change at the same time as the Games were captivating the hearts of many. The rise of Rome coincided with the beginning of the Games' decline as a major cultural event. The transition of the Roman Empire to Christianity as its official religion resulted in a widening gap between the ancient pagan celebrations and the ethos of the new faith. In the year 393 C.E., Emperor Theodosius I put an end to the tradition that had been going on for a millennium, so relegating the Games to the depths of history's forgotten past.We bear witness to a testament to human accomplishment, an intermingling of myth and reality, and a legacy that continues in the annals of history, continually leaving an indelible stamp onto the fabric of human existence as we contemplate the exquisite tapestry of the ancient Olympic Games.

Revival

A significant athletic competition that came to be known as the "Olympic Games" was first held in the early seventeenth century in the charming town of Chipping Campden, which is located in the beautiful English Cotswolds. This event took place in this town. This event captivated the imagination of the locals and continued on for a number of years, so establishing the groundwork for the modern Cotswold Games, which are now profoundly ingrained in the cultural fabric of the region.

Moving forward in time to the year 1850, in the picturesque community of Much Wenlock, which was at the time located in the county of Shropshire in England, an ambitious endeavor was launched. An "Olympian Class" was established, which is considered to be the progenitor of what would later become the prestigious "Wenlock Olympian Games" in the year 1859. Remarkably, these games are still held yearly as a celebration of sports skill and community spirit under the auspices of the Wenlock Olympian Society. This is a monument to the games' ability to continue to grace the current calendar.

At the same time, on the other side of the world in London, the tireless Dr. William Penny Brookes, the brains behind the Much Wenlock project, was putting the finishing touches on a national Olympic competition. This remarkable event, which marked a crucial milestone in the history of athletics and leisure pursuits, took place in the ancient Crystal Palace in the year 1866.In the meanwhile, a rich Greek philanthropist by the name of Evangelos Zappas arose as a beacon of support for the rekindling of the first contemporary international Olympic Games. Evangelos Zappas was located in a distant place that resounded with the memory of the ancient Olympics. In 1859, the first edition was published, and it was supported monetarily by Zappas. The publication was unveiled in the center of a city plaza in Athens. Notably, the old Panathenian stadium, which Zappas' support helped to magnificently rebuild, served as the venue for the Olympic Games in 1870 and 1875. These games brought together athletes from a variety of cultures and backgrounds, including Greece and the Ottoman Empire.In the middle of the nineteenth century, industrious German archaeologists uncovered the legendary remains of ancient Olympia, which provided a significant push for the rekindling of interest in reestablishing the Olympics on a worldwide scale. Baron Pierre de Coubertin, in light of this historical discovery, undertook the colossal job of founding the International Olympic Committee (IOC). The tragic Congress that took place at the Sorbonne University in Paris from June 16 to June 23, 1894 resulted in a critical decision: the first Olympic Games hosted by the International Olympic Committee would be held in Athens, the city that gave birth to this illustrious sports history, in the year 1896.In order to ensure the success of this momentous occasion, Demetrius Vikelas was selected to serve as the first President of the International Olympic Committee. In this capacity, he was tasked with carrying out Pierre de Coubertin's original goal. After undergoing painstaking restorations, the legendary Panathenian stadium, which had previously served as a witness to Olympic grandeur in the years 1870 and 1875, stood once more as a tribute to the eternal heritage of the Olympic Games during the spectacular spectacle that took place in Athens in 1896.Even though there were fewer than 250 athletes competing at the first IOC Olympic Games, which is a very low number when compared to modern standards, these games were the most prestigious international athletic event that had ever been held at the time. The zeal and excitement that was shown by Greek politicians and the general people was obvious, which ignited a desire to have a monopoly on the privilege of hosting future Olympic competitions. However, the International Olympic Committee had other ideas, and the following Olympic Games were held in Paris. This was the first time that women were given the chance to compete, ushering in a new era of inclusiveness and sports achievement.

Modern Olympics

In the years that followed the Olympic Games' first successful launch, organizers confronted a number of difficult obstacles. The successive editions of the Olympics were able to partially overshadow the original success of the modern Olympics. The splendor of the World's Fair displays, which included the Olympic Games, partly eclipsed the celebrations that took place in Paris (1900) and St. Louis (1904). Both of these cities hosted the Olympic Games. A further attempt to revitalize the Olympic spirit took place in 1906 with the Intercalated Games, which were held in Athens during an off-year from the normal Olympic cycle. This endeavor took place in the midst of an off-year from the usual Olympic cycle. The International

Olympic Committee (IOC) initially recognized and supported the Games of 1906; but, at the present time, the IOC does not formally consider the Games of 1906 as being part of the Olympic canon.

However, the 1906 Games were successful in attracting athletes from a variety of countries all over the world, mirroring the achievements of the 1896 Games. This represented a significant turning point, and it signaled the beginning of a continuous growth in both the popularity of the Games and the magnitude of the event, despite the absence of formal recognition from the IOC. Over 11,000 athletes from 202 countries competed in the 2004 Summer Olympics, which were held in Athens for the second time. The Olympics began with a very modest participation of 241 athletes representing 14 nations in the year 1896. Since then, the competition has grown dramatically. In contrast, the Winter Olympics, although being a notable sports event, attracted a lesser contingent of competitors, with 2,633 athletes from 80 nations competing in 84 events during the Winter Olympics held in Turin, Italy, in 2006.Notably, the Olympics have evolved into one of the most widely covered events in the history of media anywhere. Over 16,000 journalists and broadcasters were present in Sydney for the Olympic Games in 2000, setting a new record for such a gathering. The number of people that watched the games on television was nothing short of amazing, with an estimated 3.8 billion individuals turning in to witness the action. The Olympic Games are facing an increasing number of obstacles as a result of its rapid expansion in magnitude and worldwide reach. Despite the fact that permitting professional athletes and gaining sponsorships from big multinational organizations helped reduce financial burden in the 1980s, the growing number of athletes, media employees, and spectators has made hosting the Olympics a difficult and expensive endeavor for host cities.The current number of countries that take part in the Olympic Games is 203, which is much more than the 193 states that are officially recognized by the United states. This difference is a result of the International Olympic Committee's (IOC's) policy of allowing colonies and dependents to field their own Olympic teams and athletes, even though these competitors hold the same citizenship as another member nation. Specifically, this regulation allows for the United States to compete in the Olympics with its own athletes. This further exemplifies the international and welcoming character of the Olympic movement, which welcomes participants from a wide variety of countries and territories in the spirit of cooperation and sportsmanship.

Amateurism and professionalism

The ancient Greeks and Romans held the view that participation in athletics was an essential part of a well-rounded education. During the later half of the nineteenth century, public schools in England emerged as key influencers in the world of sports. This attitude was in line with the ancient

Greek and Roman philosophy. The concept that physical activity not only fostered physical strength but also nourished character and discipline is firmly entrenched in classical ideas, and these institutions championed the idea that physical activity did all of these things.

The Olympic Games served as a focal point for athletic competition and were seen as the pinnacle of the spirit of amateurism during this time period. At the beginning of its history, the Games strictly enforced a ban on the participation of professional athletes in order to preserve the purity of amateur competition. Nevertheless, for a limited time, there was a loophole for fencing coaches and teachers. The Olympic Games have never been open to professional athletes, which has given rise to a number of contentious debates throughout the years. Jim Thorpe, the outstanding winner of the pentathlon and decathlon at the 1912 Olympic Games, faced the possibility of disqualification after it was discovered that he had previously participated in semi-professional baseball. This was a famous instance. It wasn't until 1983 that the International Olympic Committee, after taking into account humane reasons and recognising the extraordinary accomplishments that Thorpe had already accomplished, reinstated his position as a champion.In the annals of Olympic history, events such as the boycott of the 1936 Winter Olympics by Swiss and Austrian skiers shed light on the strict adherence to the amateurism regulations that were in place at the time. These skiers organized a protest against what they saw as an unjust treatment of their skiing teachers, who were not allowed to compete because of the financial benefits they derived from the sport and were therefore considered to be professionals.As more time passed, the amateurism regulations gradually became less stringent and more flexible. This was largely owing to the awareness that these regulations had grown out of date, especially with the appearance of "full-time amateurs" from Eastern-bloc nations who were funded by their individual states. This was the primary reason for this change. The inequality and ineffectiveness of the amateurism ideals were brought to light by the comparison between these athletes who were supported by their respective states and the self-financed amateurs from Western nations. In addition, this gap was responsible for the drop in popularity of various Olympic competitions, since the lack of elite athletes caused audience interest to decrease.The Olympic Charter went through a period of major change in the 1970s, during which the restrictions that athletes compete in Olympic events as amateurs were removed. The responsibility of overseeing the professional involvement of athletes has been given to the international federations that are specific to each sport. Boxing remained the only sport to not adopt the professional model by the year 2004, when practically all other sports had done so. Even in men's football (soccer), where limitations were put on the number of players above the age of 23, a recognition was given to the changing terrain of sports and the developing status of athletes. This move eventually transformed the dynamics of Olympic competition, aligning it with the growing views towards athleticism and embracing the diversity and experience that professionals brought to the global sports arena. This transition occurred in the 1960s and was largely responsible for the rebirth of the modern Olympic Games.

Olympic sports

At the moment, the Olympic program is comprised of a wide variety of athletic competitions. It now includes a grand total of 35 different sports, 53 different competitions, and an incredible number of over 400 individual events. This extensive display of athletic prowess is broken down into two primary categories: the Summer Olympics, which include 28 different sports and a total of 38 different disciplines; and the Winter Olympics, which include seven different sports and a total of 15 different specializations.

This tremendous athletic gathering can be traced all the way back to the first modern Olympic Games, which were staged in 1896 in Athens, Greece. Nine different sports were featured on the Olympic program when it was first established. These disciplines were athletics, cycling, fencing, gymnastics, weightlifting, shooting, swimming, and wrestling. In addition, there were competitions in rowing scheduled to take place, but they were forced to be postponed due to the unfavorable weather conditio ns.Throughout the course of the development of the Winter Olympics, there have been a few sports that have remained a mainstay, serving as the foundation of the many frigid disciplines. Since the very beginning of the Winter Olympics, the following events have always been mainstays: cross-country skiing, figure skating, ice hockey, Nordic combined, ski jumping, and speed skating. Surprisingly, figure skating and ice hockey were originally part of the Summer Games until the Winter Olympics were eventually established as their own event.

The International Olympic Committee (IOC) has, in recent years, made a concerted effort to strategically expand the Olympic program by including current sports that are popular among younger audiences. Snowboarding and beach volleyball are two notable sports that have been included with the intention of piqueing the attention of a more diverse group of people. However, due to the expansion of the Olympic repertoire, careful curating has become necessary. As a result, certain sports that are less popular or more financially demanding, such as white water canoeing and the modern pentathlon, may lose their status in the Olympic program. The International Olympic Committee (IOC) made the decision to adapt and advance the sporting showcase by removing baseball and softball from the Olympic program beginning in 2012. This move is notable because it reflects the IOC's commitment to adapt and advance the sporting showcase.The Olympic Charter, especially Rule 48.1, requires that there be a minimum of 15 Olympic sports competed in at each and every Summer Games. This is done to preserve a sense of equilibrium and to guarantee an all-encompassing sporting event. However, each sport may have a wide variety of competitions, including weight divisions, styles, and events that are open only to participants of a certain gender. After the Games in 2002, the International Olympic Committee (IOC) set a limit of 28 sports, 301 events, and a maximum of 10,500 competitors for the Summer Games. These limitations allow for more efficient operation of this massive athletic event.Rule 46 of the Olympic Charter lays forth the requirements for a sport to be considered for participation in the Olympic Games. This rule defines Olympic sports as those that are controlled by international federations. Rule 47 places an emphasis on the exclusive inclusion of Olympic sports within the program. This helps to reinforce the IOC's determination to protecting the Olympic brand and advancing recognized federations to Olympic status through the use of a two-thirds majority vote.After each Olympiad, the Olympic program is subjected to in-depth analysis and consideration for prospective changes, which helps to ensure that it is both adaptable and current. Through this procedure, a simple majority is all that is required to include a new Olympic sport or to reintroduce an Olympic sport that was not chosen for a given Games. This enables the Olympic showcase to be periodically updated and to continue to develop. This dedication to vitality is highlighted by the forward-looking strategy taken by the International Olympic Committee (IOC), which will see 26 other sports added to the schedule for the Olympic Games in London in 2012.It is essential to keep in mind that the Olympics featured demonstration sports up until the year 1992. These were competitions that attempted to extend the attractiveness of the games and attract a larger audience. Despite the fact that the winners of these competitions did not earn the right to be called Olympic champions, this exhibition served as a platform for sports that are well known on a local as well as a global scale to increase their profile and explore the possibility of becoming full-fledged medal events in the future.

Olympic champions and medalists

In the domain of athletic competition held during the Olympic Games, the ceremonial bestowal of medals is the embodiment of the heroism and honor granted to the top competitors in their respective events. The remarkable athletes and teams who demonstrate exceptional proficiency in their particular competitions are honored and celebrated by the international community by virtue of the awarding of medals. This act of symbolic significance represents their victorious successes and ensures that their outstanding performance will live on in the annals of Olympic history.

The athletes were presented with medals as a concrete representation of their victory, which would forever immortalize both their names and their accomplishments. Gold, silver, and bronze medals are highly sought after emblems of achievement, and they are awarded to the top three finishers in each competition. Those who triumph and reach the peak of achievement are awarded the prestigious "gold medals." The move from being produced from pure gold up to the year 1912 to being crafted from silver that has been gilded is an interesting and noteworthy aspect of the history of these medals. This process continues to this day.

The competitors' remarkable effort was recognized with the awarding of the silver medal, which places them in the runner-up position. Athletes that finished in third place and demonstrated great perseverance and talent are awarded the bronze medal. However, in competitions organized as single-elimination tournaments, such as boxing, it may be difficult to identify a winner who deserves clear third place. When this occurs, both of the competitors who did not advance to the final round are awarded bronze medals as a token of appreciation for their heroic efforts and persistence on the Olympic stage.The practice of presenting medals to the top three finishers in a competition was first begun in 1904, and since then, it has been an integral part of the celebration and acknowledgement of extraordinary athletics. In contrast, the first Olympic competition was held in 1896, when only the first two competitors in each event were awarded medals (silver and bronze, respectively). The succeeding Games in 1900 saw the introduction of a variety of awards, which contributed to the further evolution of the system of acknowledgment for extraordinary accomplishments.Beginning with the Olympics in 1948 and continuing ahead, incremental steps were taken in order to broaden the scope of recognition. Awarded to the athletes who placed fourth, fifth, and sixth were awards that were suitably dubbed "victory diplomas." This action not only broadened the scope of those deserving athletes who were recognized, but it also highlighted the athletes' unwavering commitment to the profession in which they compete. Since the Olympics in 1976, this accolade has been granted to the individuals who ultimately won a medal. In the Olympics held in 1984, the honor was further expanded such that it included seventh- and eighth-place finishers as well, so encompassing a broader percentage of the community of Olympic athletes.An extra component of recognition was implemented in time for the Summer Olympics that were staged in Athens in 2004. Not only were the top three finishers awarded medals, but they were also honored with wreaths, which are a sign of triumph and glory. As a result of this enhancement to the ceremonial acknowledgement, the honor of being an Olympic medalist has been elevated to a higher level, which further emphasizes the significance of the accomplishment.The significance and worth that sportsmen and people all around the world ascribe to Olympic medals are unmatched. Athletes will tell you that winning an Olympic medal is more meaningful to them than winning a world championship or a medal from any of the other international competitions they've competed in. Achieving the title of Olympic champion has elevated a great number of athletes to the prestigious position of national heroes, earning them tremendous affection and adoration within their own nations.On a more global scale, the International Olympic Committee (IOC) uses a medal tally table that has been painstakingly created to rank countries based on their performance at the Olympics. The amount of gold medals that a nation has won is the major consideration in this ranking method. In situations when states have an identical number of gold medals, the count of silver medals and then bronze medals is used to determine the order in which the states are ranked. This approach enhances the competitive spirit among nations, which helps to cultivate healthy rivalries and spurs athletes to push the boundaries of their skills all in the sake of achieving Olympic glory.

Olympic Movement

The coordination of the Olympic Games requires the participation of a large number of organizations that come together to form what is collectively referred to as the Olympic Movement. This complicated network functions in accordance with the regulations and procedures that are outlined in the comprehensive Olympic Charter, which outlines the limitations within which they are allowed to operate.

The acclaimed International Olympic Committee (IOC), which is frequently regarded as the governing body of the Olympics, is at the forefront of this international movement. The International Olympic Committee (IOC) is entrusted with the task of managing day-to-day operations and possesses the ability to make important decisions, such as choosing the city that will serve as the host for the Olympic Games and compiling the schedule of Olympic competitions.

Taking a deeper dive into a more specific field, there are three major types of organizations that make substantial contributions:To begin, the worldwide Federations (IFs) act as the governing body for a variety of sports. This function is shown by organizations such as FIFA, which is the IF that presides over football (also known as soccer), and the FIVB, which is the worldwide governing institution for volleyball. Both of these organizations are examples of IFs.Second, the National Olympic Committees (NOCs), which are responsible for overseeing the Olympic Movement inside the borders of their individual nations, play a significant part in this regulatory process. The significance of the United States Olympic Committee (USOC), the nation's national Olympic committee, in this broad movement is exemplified by the fact that it is one of the organizations listed above.Last but not least, the job of painstakingly arranging and directing a specific celebration of the Olympics falls on the arranging Committees for the Olympic Games (OCOGs). These committees must ensure that all components are integrated in a way that is seamless in order to maintain the event's grandiosity.There are now 202 National Olympic Committees (NOCs) and 35 International Federations (IFs) affiliated with the Olympic Movement, demonstrating the movement's extensive worldwide reach and impact. The Olympic Movement also boasts an amazing roster. Notably, once the Olympic Games have come to an end, the OCOGs gracefully wrap up their obligations and bring their activities to a close after ensuring that all necessary paperwork and post-celebration chores have been finished.The phrase "Olympic Movement" refers to a more inclusive group that includes a wide variety of stakeholders. This broadens the scope of what is being discussed. This includes regulatory bodies of national sports, athletes, members of the media, and the crucial sponsors who contribute to the splendor of the Olympic Games, which bring the globe together through the spirit of sportsmanship and competitiveness on a worldwide platform.

Olympic symbols

The Olympic movement, which is an expression of the visionary ideas of Pierre de Coubertin, comprises a wide variety of symbols, each of which is loaded with significant significance. The most recognizable of these emblems is the set of five interlocking rings known as the Olympic Rings. These rings represent the cohesion of the five inhabited continents that make up our planet. It is interesting to note that despite the fact that North America and South America are two separate continents, they have been combined into a single entity for the sake of this symbolic portrayal. over the Olympic Flag, a visually attractive insignia is formed by these five rings, which are embellished in vivid colours of red, blue, green, and yellow, as well as black, and which entwine over a background of pure white.

There was a lot of thought that went into selecting the colors for the Olympic rings. This was done to make sure that every nation that took part in the Olympic Games would have at least one of these colors represented in their national flag. When the Olympic Flag was originally publicly accepted in 1914, this symbolic inclusion and unity was formally created for the first time. However, it made its first appearance at the Antwerp Games in 1920, where it bravely flapped in the wind and embodied the Olympic spirit. Since then, it has been used at consecutive celebrations of the G ames.In addition to the rings that have come to symbolize the Olympic movement, the official motto of the Olympic movement is "Citius, Altius, Fortius," which is a Latin phrase that poetically translates to "Swifter, Higher, Stronger." This motto is another way that the Olympic movement mimics the thought of Pierre de Coubertin. This statement captures the core values that are at the center of the Olympic movement, which are the goal for continual progress and the pursuit of perfection.In addition, Coubertin's values are eloquently expressed in the Olympic Creed, which is a tribute to the concept that success does not lay in winning but rather in participation and effort that is given with one's full heart. It upholds the spirit of the conflict by highlighting how important it is to fight to one's full potential despite the uncertainty of the outcome.The presence of the Olympic Flame, which was lit in the ancient Greek city of Olympia, lends an air of mystique to the rites and rituals that take place during the Olympic Games. The significance of this flame, which was brought to the host city by a relay of runners carrying the torch, will become clear at the opening ceremonies of the competition. The custom of lighting a torch on fire dates all the way back to 1928, but it didn't become well known until 1936, when the relay was first introduced.The Olympic mascot is a relatively recent addition to the Olympic tradition. It was first used in 1968 and consists of either a person or animal figure representing the rich cultural legacy of the country that is playing host to the games. Since its incorporation into the Games in 1980, the Olympic mascot has played an essential part in developing a sense of cultural pride and contributing to the overall atmosphere of celebration. This has been the case ever since the mascot was first introduced.In conclusion, the Olympic movement celebrates linguistic variety by designating French and English as its official languages. This practice echoes the global spirit of inclusion that serves as the foundation for the Olympic Games. This language contradiction highlights the desire for worldwide peace and unification, which is reflective of the main goals of the Olympic movement.

Olympic ceremonies

Opening

In addition to the usual elements that are essential to the beginning of the Olympic Games, the nation that will be hosting the event will customarily be responsible for putting on a magnificent artistic performance that will include both theater and dance and will serve as a representation of the nation's cultural identity and legacy. The opening ceremonies of the Olympic Games are steeped in history. They begin with the solemn hoisting of the flag of the host country and the performance of that country's national hymn, which evokes a sense of national pride and solidarity among its citizens.

Athletes, representing their different countries, march joyfully into the stadium during the traditional portion of the opening ceremony, which is known as the "parade of nations." Each athlete is followed by a notable athlete who has been chosen to wear their nation's flag. This segment of the event is one of the most anticipated parts of the opening ceremony. This symbolic procession's purpose is to bring together all of the many nations participating in a show of good sportsmanship and unity.

Greece, which is traditionally recognized as the birthplace of the Olympic Games, has the privilege of leading the march as an homage to its pivotal role in the origins of the Games. This honor was bestowed to Greece because of its historical significance. On the other hand, the nation that is hosting the parade is given the place of honor and anticipation that comes after the final one in the procession. The parade continues with the other participating nations going in alphabetical order, which is decided by the language that is most commonly spoken in the host country; alternatively, if the host country's language does not adhere to a particular alphabetical order, the parade will go in either English or French alphabetical order.When all of the countries have completed their spectacular entrances, the president of the Olympic Organizing Committee for the country that is hosting the games will take the stage and give an important speech. After that, the President of the International Olympic Committee

(IOC) will take the stage. Towards the end of their address, they will present the acclaimed person who will be in charge of formally starting the Games. This distinction is often given upon the Head of State of the country that is hosting the Games since they are best able to symbolize the spirit of the Games via their ceremonial role.After then, the internationally recognized Olympic flag is displayed in a horizontal orientation, a custom that has been followed ever since the Summer Olympics in 1960. The notes of the Olympic Anthem resonate throughout the stadium as the audience is entranced by the sight; this serves to emphasize the significance of this historically significant event. The flag bearers from each country gather around a central platform, where an athlete and a judge take the Olympic Oath in a serious manner to renew their dedication to competing and adjudicating in line with the rules and ideals that have been created.The arrival of the Olympic Torch, a representation of the unending flame that has come to represent the Games, is the highlight of the opening ceremony. The Olympic Torch is a symbol of the eternal flame that has come to represent the Games. After being ceremonially passed from one athlete to another, the Torch eventually reaches its ultimate bearer, who is typically a notable athlete from the nation that is hosting the games. This person is responsible for lighting the fire in the cauldron that is located within the stadium. This hypnotizing performance ushers in the formal beginning of the Games and serves as a tribute to the legacy of the Olympics. This custom dates all the way back to the Summer Olympics in 1928.The lighting of the Olympic Flame has been accompanied by a variety of different rituals over the course of its history. One of these ceremonies, which was performed for a substantial amount of time after World War I and continued all the way up until 1988, was the symbolic releasing of doves, which represented a wish for worldwide peace. As a result of the regrettable injury that was inflicted upon the doves at the opening ceremony of the 1988 Summer Olympics, this practice was eventually abandoned. This marked a shift in tradition while yet keeping the everlasting spirit of the Olympic Games.

Closing ceremonies

During the magnificent closing ceremonies of the Olympic Games, which serve as a climax that takes place once all of the competitive events have achieved their exhilarating finishes, a number of time-honored rituals and practices are brought to completion for the first time in modern times. This amazing event, which is steeped in history and adored by millions of people all around the world, has an aura that bears a quality that eloquently captures the spirit of togetherness and sportsmanship.

As the last act of this global extravaganza draws to a close, a parade of flag bearers from the many countries that are taking part in it begins. These envoys, marching in a single line, create the way for a deep demonstration of solidarity as the athletes follow without any distinction of nationality, reinforcing the notion of a unified human race. As the athletes follow, the envoys walk in a single file. This treasured custom was initially dreamt of at the 1956 Summer Olympics in Melbourne, Australia, and was introduced by John Ian Wing, a perceptive youngster. His goal was to cultivate a feeling of oneness among the athletes that would transcend political and geographical divides.In the midst of the awe-inspiring environment, three national flags are raised with elegance atop flagpoles while their respective national anthems play in the background. On the pole on the right, the Greek flag is displayed as a tribute to the country that gave birth to the

Olympic Games, while the flag of the country that is hosting the event proudly adorns the pole in the center. It is important to note that the flag of the nation that will soon be hosting either the Summer or Winter Olympic Games is placed on the left-hand pole. This symbolizes the continuity and longevity of this significant event. One notable exception to this rule was made during the Olympic Games that were held in Athens in 2004, when a single Greek flag was flown in recognition of the historical significance of the city that was hosting the event.

The historically significant "Antwerp Ceremony," which can be traced back to the Summer Olympics held in Antwerp in 1920, lends an air of distinction to the proceedings. At this point in the proceedings, a key person, the mayor of the host city, hands a unique Olympic Flag over to the president of the International Olympic Committee (IOC). After then, the mantle of duty is passed on to the mayor of the next city that will serve as host. The mayor of that city will then wave the flag eight times to represent continuity and the passing of this prestigious honor. The Antwerp flag, the Oslo flag, and the Seoul flag are examples of these one-of-a-kind flags. Each of these banners has a significant historical background and contributes to the complex web of Olympic custom by including a fringe made up of six different colors and being affixed to a flagpole with six different ribbons of the same hue.An artistic display that was first used during the 1976 Games, the unveiling of the future host nation is now intricately woven into the fabric of the ceremony. The globe gets a sneak peek at the wonderful tapestry that will be waiting for them in the next Olympic adventure through enthralling performances of dance and theater that are indicative of the culture and tradition of the forthcoming host nation.As the event continues, the president of the Olympic Organizing Committee of the nation that is playing host to the games walks up to the microphone and addresses the audience, offering heartfelt thanks and expressing enthusiasm for the trip that lies ahead. After this, the president of the International Olympic Committee will take the stage and bring the event to a close by making an official declaration of closure. While doing so, he will invoke the spirit of tradition and encourage the youth of the world to unite once more in a few short years for the subsequent beautiful gathering of athleticism and goodwill.In the midst of the resonating echoes of the Olympic Anthem, the softly flickering Olympic Flame is extinguished, and the Olympic Flag, a symbol of togetherness and hope, is lowered from its towering flagpole. Both of these events take place in the Olympic Stadium. It is a sad moment, representing the conclusion of a magnificent chapter in the history of mankind, while promising the beginning of another unprecedented epic in the search of excellence and unity. Although it marks the end of one chapter, it also promises the beginning of a new chapter in the history of humanity.

CHAPTER TWO

The Path to Qualification

How athletes qualify for the Olympics

A seat on an Olympic squad is a coveted goal for many athletes, but even reaching the qualifying requirements does not necessarily guarantee a berth on the team. This is an important point to keep in mind since it underscores the magnitude of the accomplishment. The path to possibly competing in the Olympics is a difficult one, and for the 11 Brigham Young University (BYU) affiliates who have completed these qualifications, this is only the beginning of their drive to achieve their goals.

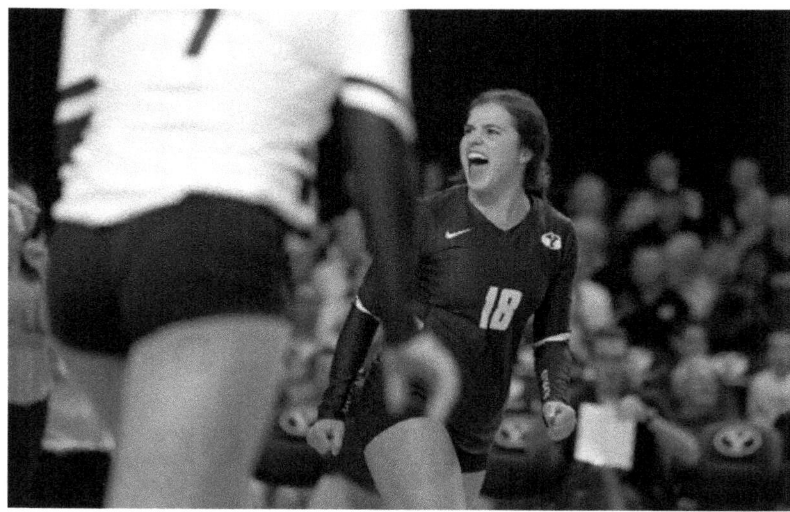

Mary Lake, one of 11 Olympic qualifiers affiliated with BYU, is currently playing in her last collegiate season before possibly going pro. (Hannah Miner)

The illustrious city of Tokyo in Japan is going to play home to the Olympic Games for the very first time since it played host to those historic games in 1964. This international athletic spectacular, which is slated to take place between the 24th of July and the 9th of August in 2020, has been widely anticipated. In spite of this, the definitive answer to the question of who will be included on the official squad roster will not be known until around two weeks before the opening ceremony of the Olympics.

It is one of the most fascinating features of this procedure that the participating countries are not required to name their official teams until the beginning of July, with the precise dates differing depending on the sport in question. The number of sports that will be competed in at the Olympic Games has increased from 32 to 33 as a consequence of the addition of five new events for the Olympic Games in 2020. As a result of this exciting growth, the Olympic competition now includes the sports of baseball and softball, karate, skateboarding, sport climbing, and surfing.A constraint has been placed on the amount of athletes that each nation may bring for each event. This restriction is intricately woven into the sophisticated method that is being used. Each sport that is part of the Olympic Games is governed by an international committee, which is charged with determining the criteria that must be met in order to compete on a global level. This criterion takes on a greater level of significance for larger countries like the United States, since the number of athletes that qualify for Olympic teams frequently exceeds the number of slots that are actually available on such teams. As a consequence of this, a stringent selection procedure is put into place in order to narrow down the pool of possible applicants until the necessary number has been reached.The United States of America, which is consistently a strong competitor on the Olympic stage, conducts its own Olympic trials throughout the month of June in order to locate and choose its best possible candidates. This tough testing phase is of the utmost importance in identifying which athletes are most qualified to represent their country on the international stage. On the other hand, in nations with a smaller population, the majority of athletes who meet the requirements to qualify for the Olympics are awarded the prestigious chance to participate in the Olympic competition.Track and field, swimming, and volleyball are three sports in which BYU-affiliated athletes have a good chance of competing at the 2020 Olympics in Tokyo. There is a lot of promise for these athletes in these three sports. However, the route to gaining a spot on the Olympic roster for each of these sports varies in terms of the expectations and conditions that must be met. Because of this, the trip is one that is unique and difficult for every athlete who hopes to compete in the Olympics. The eagerness and resolve of these competitors is still obvious as they prepare to embark on this life-altering Olympic journey. They are sincerely wanting to make a name for themselves on the most prestigious sports platform in the world.

Track and field

The qualifying procedure for track and field has undergone a substantial transition, adopting a more complex two-tiered approach to select which athletes gain a berth. Previously, competitors had to meet a single set of requirements to be eligible for competition. Athletes must first satisfy a set time criteria in order to qualify for this new method. Thereafter, the remaining spaces are assigned depending on the athlete's position in the global rankings.

When calculating an athlete's world ranking, it is important to take into account not only the quality of their timed performance but also the prestige or reputation of the competition in which they competed. The length of the competitions in which athletes specialize has a direct bearing on the complexities of the ranking system used for those athletes.

Men	Event	Women
10.05	100m	11.15
20.24	200m	22.80
44.90	400m	51.35
1:45.20	800m	1:59.50
3:35.00	1500m	4:04.20
13:13.50	5000m	15:10.00
27:28.00	10,000m	31:25.00
13.32	110m Hurdles / 100m Hurdles	12.84
48.90	400m Hurdles	55.40
8:22.00	3000m Steeplechase	9:30.00
2.33	High Jump	1.96
5.80	Pole Vault	4.70
8.22	Long Jump	6.82
17.14	Triple Jump	14.32
21.10	Shot Put	18.50
66.00	Discus Throw	63.50
77.50	Hammer Throw	72.50
85.00	Javelin Throw	64.00
8350	Decathlon / Heptathlon	6420
1:21:00	20km Race Walk	1:31:00
3:50:00	50km Race Walk	
2:11:30	Marathon	2:29:30

International track and field qualifying times for the 2020 Tokyo Summer Olympics. (IAAF.org)

The standings of the athletes in the 10,000-meter race are determined by taking their two best performances, which places a premium on maintaining excellent performance across a greater distance. In contrast, the ranks of participants in the 5,000-meter race only take into consideration their best three scores. This highlights the need of maintaining a high level of performance over the course of the race, which is considered a middle distance event.In competitions lasting up to 1,500 meters, participants are judged based on the five best times they've posted in the previous year's worth of competitions. This criteria highlights how important it is to maintain a high level of performance in the events that are shorter and more intensive.The evaluation procedure takes on a unique character when applied to marathon runners. Due to the arduous nature of the marathon and the amount of time necessary to effectively train for and compete at the top level, marathon runners are given a longer evaluation period of 18 months within which their performances are evaluated. This is in recognition of the fact that marathons are run at the highest level. Their rankings are determined by combining the points they earned for their two finest performances throughout the course of this lengthy time. In addition, athletes who run marathons also have the opportunity to qualify through an alternate route, which requires them to place in the top ten of a World Marathon Major competition, such as the prestigious Boston Marathon.The addition of additional time requirements is another modification that has been made to the process of qualifying for the position. The new criteria are designed to be more stringent in order to set a higher standard for athletes and guarantee that only the very best will be allowed to compete in the Olympic trials. As a consequence of this, the quota for each race is now lower than it was in previous years, making the battle even more intense and highlighting the importance of extraordinary performance in order to win a slot.Jared Ward, an adjunct statistics professor at Brigham Young University (BYU), shows the effort and aptitude necessary to obtain a coveted slot in the track and field qualifying process in its current iteration, which has undergone significant changes. His entry into the U.S. Olympic trials will take place on February 29, 2020, and he qualified by achieving a fantastic eighth-place finish in the prestigious Boston Marathon. This type of outstanding performance is what enables an athlete to get entry into the U.S. Olympic trials. The laborious road that athletes must travel in the quest of Olympic glory is now characterized by a precise and competitive two-tiered qualification system. Jared Ward's journey stands as a testament to the difficult path that athletes must walk in order to achieve Olympic success.

Swimming

The Fédération Internationale de Natation (FINA), which is the global regulatory organization for aquatic sports, has very specific requirements that swimmers need to fulfill in order to be eligible to compete in the renowned Olympic Games. Competitors are required to attain particular timing standards during officially sanctioned swimming meets, such as the prestigious Winter Nationals, in order to fulfill these conditions and qualify for the competition. This pursuit of qualification is open until the closure date of June 29, 2020 for solo athletes, however the cutoff for relay athletes is May 22, 2020, which is a little bit sooner than the individual athletes' deadline.

Following the qualification standards to the letter is necessary if one want to participate in the Olympic trials that will be held in the United States. Athletes have the ability to qualify in a number of different competitions; however, they are only allowed to participate in the trials for those competitions in which they have achieved the qualifying times. This guarantees that athletes have the appropriate level of ability and performance to successfully compete in the difficult Olympic trials. At least once over the course of the trials, every contestant will be given the opportunity to demonstrate their abilities in the water.

Men's		Event	Women's	
Olympic Qualifying Time (OQT / "A" Time) – 2 Entries	Olympic Selection Time (OST / "B" Time) – 1 Entry		Olympic Qualifying Time (OQT / "A" Time) – 2 Entries	Olympic Selection Time (OST / "B" Time) – 1 Entry
22.01	22.67	50m Freestyle	24.77	25.51
48.57	50.03	100m Freestyle	54.38	56.01
1:47.02	1:50.23	200m Freestyle	1:57.28	2:00.80
3:46.78	3:53.58	400m Freestyle	4:07.90	4:15.34
7:54.31	8:08.54	800m Freestyle	8:33.36	8:48.76
15:00.99	15:28.02	1500m Freestyle	16:32.04	17:01.80
53.85	55.47	100m Backstroke	1:00.25	1:02.06
1:57.50	2:01.03	200m Backstroke	2:10.39	2:14.30
59.93	1:01.73	100m Breaststroke	1:07.07	1:09.08
2:10.35	2:14.26	200m Breaststroke	2:25.52	2:29.89
51.96	53.52	100m Butterfly	57.92	59.66
1:56.48	1:59.97	200m Butterfly	2:08.43	2:12.28
1:59.67	2:03.26	200m Individual Medley	2:12.56	2:16.54
4:15.84	4:21.46	400m Individual Medley	4:38.53	4:46.89

International swimming qualifying times for the 2020 Tokyo Summer Olympics. (FINA.org)

Only the most talented individuals are able to advance to further phases of the competition in this extremely cutthroat environment. After the preliminary rounds of each competition, the top 16 swimmers in each event move on to compete in the semi-finals, where they attempt to earn one of the coveted spots in the finals. The top eight participants in terms of their speed will move on to the next round, which will set the scenario for a heated battle in the championship round. The most exciting part of the competition is when the top two swimmers in each event compete against one another to see who will earn a spot on the United States Olympic squad.The sport of swimming is one of the events that takes place in the world's most prestigious athletic competition, the Olympics. Each nation is given the opportunity to send a team consisting of 26 men and 26 women to compete in this event. This distribution helps to develop a sense of global inclusion by ensuring that each participating nation will have a fair representation in the event. These rules apply to everyone, including the mighty United States Swimming Team, which is a dominant force in the sport of swimming. The level of competition is quite high since there are a large number of skilled swimmers who are fighting for a spot on the coveted Olympic squad.As the trip continues, a considerable number of talented swimmers have successfully reached the strict qualifying requirements, pushing them into contention for a berth on Team USA's acclaimed swimming team. As the journey unfolds, a substantial number of talented swimmers have successfully met the stringent qualifying standards. It is remarkable that six of these talented athletes attended Brigham Young University (BYU), which is a testimonial to the extraordinary talent that is rising from the academic sphere.The culmination of a historic process that will choose the final members of the United States Olympic swimming squad is scheduled to take place on July 6, 2020. The lucky few who will be able to represent their nation on the greatest athletic platform and carve their names into the annals of swimming history will see their ambitions come true on this momentous event, which will be a turning point in the sport's history.

Volleyball

In the world of athletics, each sport has its own different methods of selection and qualifying, which are based on the particular aspects of the game that make it stand out from the others. Volleyball, in contrast to sports such as swimming and track and field, has a qualification process that is significantly different from the others. This is due to the absence of strict time and measurable results in volleyball.

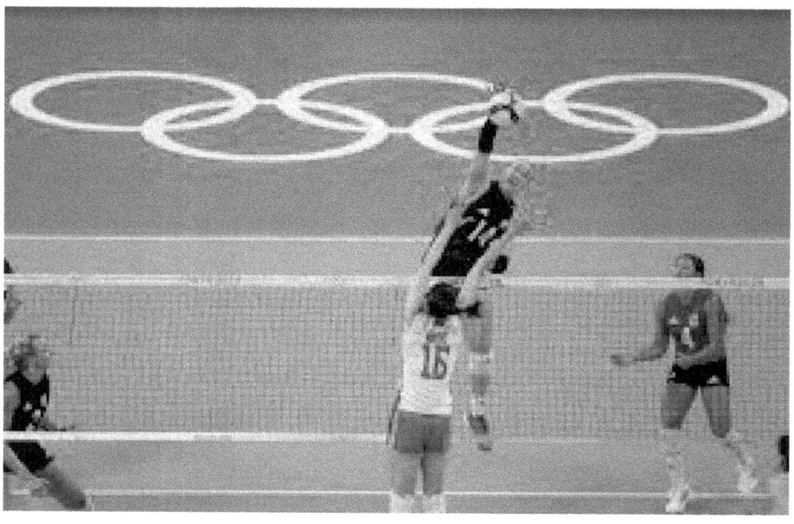

Volleyball, in contrast to timed sports in which exact measurements and records play a vital part in deciding qualifications, is determined by means of a painstaking selection procedure. Establishing a talent pool is the first step in this procedure. From this pool, the head coaches will carefully choose individuals to nominate for the official squad as well as prospective substitutes.

Athletes that have a varied and extensive amount of experience playing for their country's national team will be given priority during this procedure. Not only does such previous experience indicate the players' competence, but it also gives useful insight into their capacity to succeed in high-stakes competitive contexts.In addition, the appraisal of volleyball players takes into account more than just their athletic capability alone. It includes a thorough evaluation of how effective they are in attacking, blocking, digging, setting, serving, and passing across all six of the most important facets of the game. The complex approach that is utilized in team construction is highlighted by the fact that the priority that is placed on each domain differs depending on the position that a player is given within the team.This evaluation takes into account a wide variety of elements, many of which inquire into the athletes' fundamental characteristics and behavior. Elements such as teamwork, attitude, adaptability, maturity, and receptivity to coaching instruction are essential components of this complex evaluation. An evaluation of this comprehensive nature seeks to assure not only the brilliance of each individual member of the team but also the cohesion and harmony of their dynamic.Mary Lake and Taylor Sander are both well-known athletes who have earned their place in this pool of potential because to the illustrious contributions they have made to Team USA. Their previous participation on a national platform is a tribute to their expertise as well as their potential, which positions them advantageously within the selection process.Volleyball fans who are interested in Team USA are anxiously awaiting the forthcoming announcement despite the growing amount of anticipation. At some point on or before July 2, 2020, the drapes will be pulled back, revealing both the squad that was nominated and the replacements who were selected. This will mark the beginning of an exciting new era of volleyball competition and national representation.

Main character's early athletic career and dedication to their sport

To instill in a person the motivation and aptitude to carry out particular activities or provoke particular feelings is what we mean when we talk about inspiring them. This act of inspiration bears tremendous relevance in the sphere of human accomplishment and athletics, where the narratives of athletes have repeatedly worked as catalysts for acting as a source of motivation for others.

The annals of sports history are filled with examples of outstanding sportsmen who have achieved greatness not just through their physical prowess, but also by becoming beacons of inspiration for the general populace. One way in which these athletes have reached greatness is by being role models for the general populace. Their incredible travels and victories have frequently extended beyond the boundaries of their particular sports, leaving an everlasting impression on society and inspiring the emotions of countless individuals in the process.Magic Johnson, a legendary character in the sport of basketball, serves as a model of tenacity and a living illustration of the victory of the human spirit. As a result of overcoming obstacles and doing very well in spite of difficulties, Johnson became a symbol of inspiration for a large number of young athletes with aspirations of making it big in their sport. He exemplified the transformational power of commitment and determination.

In the world of baseball, Lou Gehrig is and will continue to be revered as an enduring emblem of grit and bravery. Gehrig's unflinching determination and indomitable will continue to inspire others, highlighting the strength of character and the capacity to survive even in the most trying of situations. Despite suffering from a crippling disease, Gehrig's unyielding tenacity and indomitable will continue to inspire individuals.The incomparable talent and dogged perseverance that Tiger Woods possesses have cemented his place in the annals of sports history. Woods is a legend in the sport of golf. His spectacular ascension to the peak of golfing excellence, along with his persistence and fortitude during difficult times, has served as an inspiration to a vast number of aspiring golfers and people from other fields as well.As we explore further into the huge tapestry that is the world of sports, we come across a wide variety of motivational individuals. These sportsmen have become icons of endurance, fortitude, and the persistent pursuit of perfection. Their accomplishments range from the historic exploits that Jesse Owens accomplished in track and field to the flamboyant defiance that Muhammad Ali displayed in boxing. Their stories strike a chord with the human psyche, igniting dreams and inspiring folks to work toward accomplishing great things for themselves.In light of these incredible tales, we have compiled a detailed list of the 25 sportsmen who have been the most inspiring figures in the annals of sports history. Every name on this list not only exemplifies extraordinary physical capability but also a profound capacity to kindle the fire of determination and resiliency that lies dormant within each and every one of us. These people have made an unmistakable mark on the world of sports, and the stories they have to tell serve as lighthouses that guide us toward our own objectives and goals. They also illustrate the potential for remarkable achievements that lies inside each and every one of us.

Kurt Warner

Kurt Warner, a former quarterback in the National Football League (NFL), has cemented his place in the annals of American sports history as the protagonist of one of the most incredible comeback stories that has ever been played out on the gridiron. Warner's narrative. His rise from the lowly aisles of a grocery store, where he painstakingly stacked shelves and bagged groceries, to the highest level of professional football ended in his achieving the coveted title of Super Bowl-winning quarterback. His journey began in the aisles of a grocery store.

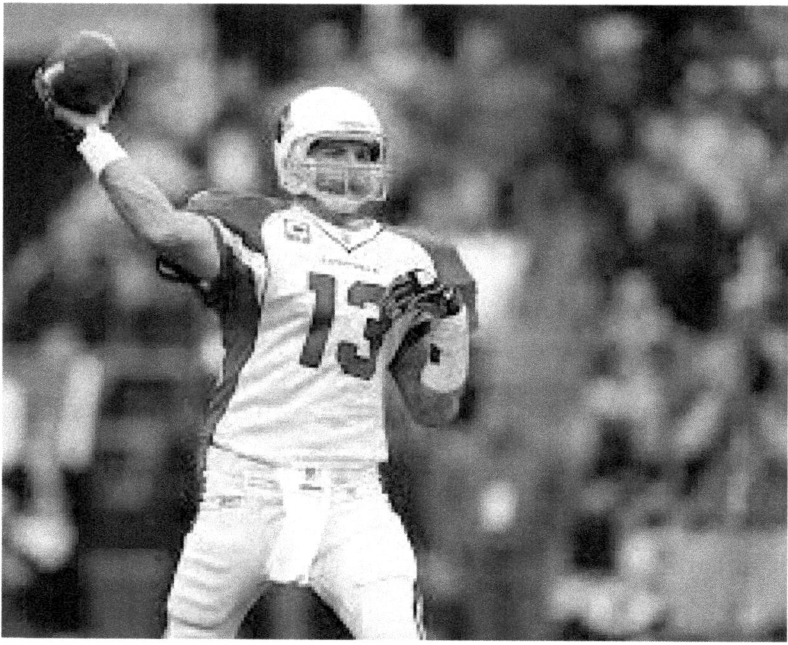

In the earlier parts of his life, Warner's goals were not centered on the high-pressure environment of the football world, but rather on the values of hard work and endurance. The echoes of his drive reverberated through the daily routine of a grocery shop, where he handled clients with diligence and merchandise with immaculate organization. It was in the middle of these unremarkable circumstances that the germination of a gigantic ability lay dormant, waiting for its chance to blossom into its full potential.

Warner felt an irresistible pull toward the world of football and its opportunities. He responded to the invitation, impelled by an unyielding yearning to achieve success in the world of professional athletics and rise above the limitations that were imposed on him by his surroundings. He was unfazed by the difficulties that were still in front of him, so he committed himself to perfecting his talents, practicing over and over again, and cultivating the untapped potential that would one day be displayed on the main stage.As luck would have it, Warner's journey brought him to the highly competitive environment of the National Football League (NFL), where his skills and resilience were put to the very best test possible. Despite the severe challenges that preceded his trip, he was able to emerge victorious and triumphant, standing tall amidst the cheering audience as a Super Bowl champion. This win was not merely the climax of ability; rather, it was a monument to the resiliency of the human spirit and the triumph of the underdog despite all odds being stacked against them.The motivational journey that Warner has been on has reverberated among aspiring quarterbacks all around the world, well beyond the confines of the football field. His life acts as an inspiration and a living proof that if one is willing to devote themselves fully, is relentless in their resolve, and maintains a strong work ethic, it is possible to make one's aspirations come true. In the same breath, his story discovers kindred spirits in the likes of Tom Brady, another prominent figure whose path shares the colors of tenacity and triumph against hardship.To repeat Warner's story is to take part in a tale that retains its fascination no matter how many times it's told. The stories of this unassuming guy who rose to become a football legend are an evergreen source of encouragement. They serve as a constant reminder that the human spirit, when equipped with desire and tenacity, is capable of conquering the highest peaks and leaving its mark in the annals of history.

Pat Tillman

Pat Tillman rose to prominence as a model of patriotism within the sphere of athletic skill, standing as the perfect personification of unflinching commitment to the United States. Tillman was killed in action while serving in the United States Army. This outstanding demonstration of patriotism became a reality when, in the year 2002, he took the courageous decision to enroll in the Army of the United States of America. After a very productive fourth season with the Arizona Cardinals, which is a franchise in the National Football League, this important choice came after the season.

When Pat Tillman put on the uniform and committed himself to a life of service, the intricate fabric of his dedication to his country began to weave itself into the tapestry of history. This began to happen as soon as he put on the uniform. The fundamental change in his purpose that occurred as a result of his shift from a recognized football player to a soldier was symbolized by his devotion to a cause that was greater than himself. However, this voyage was cut short in the year 2004, about two years after he enlisted in the service, when he was serving in Afghanistan. This tragic and unfortunate event occurred during his deployment in Afghanistan.The tragic series of events that transpired, which ultimately resulted in Tillman's untimely death, was a gut-wrenching consequence of friendly fire that occurred among the merciless battlefield environment. The passing of this exceptional person was lamented to a great extent, and it has left an indelible impact on the hearts and minds of those who held dear the ideals that he advocated for and the efforts that he put forth.The significance of Pat Tillman's legacy extends far beyond the realms of his sports accomplishments and his time spent in the military. His story has echoed through the annals of history, motivating generations of people with the tale of the ultimate sacrifice he made in the sake of the country that he cherished so much. Tillman's incredible commitment and steadfast dedication continue to resound, motivating many others to ponder on the genuine nature of patriotism and the sacrifices that it may entail.

Reggie White

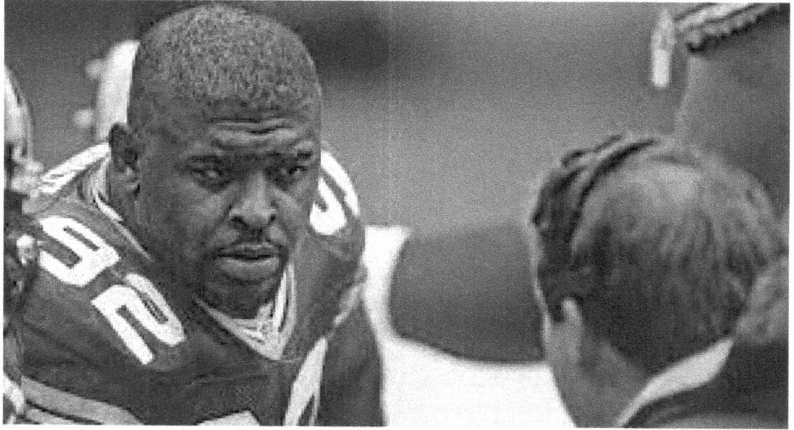

When Reggie White used to play football in the National Football League (NFL), he was a defensive juggernaut for the Green Bay Packers and the Carolina Panthers. He was able to fascinate audiences wherever he went. This extraordinary athlete, who was born and raised in Chattanooga, Tennessee, established himself as an almost unbeatable force on the defensive line throughout the course of his storied 15-year professional career. During that time, he racked up an amazing total of over 200 s acks.Affectionately known as "The Minister of Defense," White got this title not just for his impenetrable presence on the gridiron but also for his off-field image as an ordained minister. Together, these two aspects contributed to White's reputation as "The Minister of Defense." In the course of his life, he led a great number of people to a relationship with Jesus Christ by means of this spiritual calling, leaving an indelible impression on the world outside the sphere of football.Michael Irvin, a player who is now enshrined in the NFL Hall of Fame, said something that wonderfully captured the spirit of Reggie White when he said, "He was a gift from God, and that's all you need to know about Reggie White." Indeed, White's skill on the field was similar to a gift from the gods; he left an enduring legacy that reached well beyond the domain of athletics, one that continues to reverberate in the hearts and minds of people he inspired both on and off the game. This legacy can be traced back to individuals he motivated both on and off the field.

Roberto Clemente

During his time spent sporting the legendary Pittsburgh Pirates uniform, Roberto Clemente cemented his legacy as an unrivaled athlete and became an unforgettable source of motivation for generations to come. Throughout his successful career in the major leagues, he displayed a singular and awe-inspiring mastery both in the outfield and at the plate, demonstrating that his prowess and skill went well beyond the realm of simple talent.

Clemente was a strong force in the world of baseball, and he displayed a virtuosity that frequently left fans and his fellow sportsmen in awe of his abilities. He was able to navigate the outfield with pinpoint accuracy and quickly cover territory in order to make catches that appeared to be impossible, which increased his position as an elite player in the game. At the same time, his talent at the plate was nothing short of spectacular, as he routinely delivered tremendous hits and showed an unprecedented level of elegance in the way he approached the game.But beyond his accomplishments in the world of sports, Roberto Clemente was a model of what it means to be a remarkable individual away from the constraints of the baseball pitch. His personality shone as a dazzling monument to the intrinsic nobility and generosity that he had, serving as a light of hope and compassion that shone across his neighborhood and beyond. An enduring legacy that transcends the confines of athletics has been left by Roberto Clemente as a result of his philanthropic and generous deeds as well as his unyielding commitment to the advancement of humanitarian causes.Late in 1972, a gloomy occurrence resulted in the untimely passing of this shining example of mankind. Tragically, he was snatched from this world. The plane that was transporting Clemente and relief materials for earthquake victims in Nicaragua met a tragic end when it crashed, and he was one of the people who lost their lives in the incident. The death was strongly felt not just inside the sporting arena but also around the globe, leaving behind an everlasting emptiness and a painful reminder of the precarious nature of life. In spite of the tragedy, Clemente's legacy endures, and he continues to be an unending source of motivation for young athletes and others who want to have a meaningful effect on the world.

Josh Hamilton

Outfielder Josh Hamilton, who plays for the Texas Rangers, has experienced a trip that can only be characterized as a relentless odyssey from the depths of despair and the victorious ascension towards redemption throughout the course of his thirty-year lifetime. This adventure is intricately woven into the complex tapestry that is Hamilton's life.

Hamilton, who was once a hopeful draft selection for the Tampa Bay Rays, found himself trapped in the clutches of drug addiction in the early chapters of his life. Hamilton was formerly a member of the Rays. The conflict with this tremendous opponent lasted for years, casting a persistent shadow over all of his hopes and desires.

On the other hand, buried deep inside his spirit was a glimmer of optimism that called out for a metamorphosis and a fresh start. In the face of the crushing weight of his addictions, Hamilton set out on a journey of introspection and a search for liberation from the grasp of his demons. In his pursuit of atonement, he looked for comfort and direction from a higher power, and he turned to God as a source of inspiration and fortitude to guide him on the road to recovery.Hamilton was able to escape from the gloom that had formerly enveloped his life as a result of his unrelenting commitment to his religion and his relentless desire to break free from the constraints that held him. The reminders of his previous hardships helped only to strengthen the resiliency that was already present in him, which in turn propelled him to accomplish great things on the baseball pitch.In the midst of those difficult days, the tale of Hamilton took a turn that was both inspirational and motivating. His unwavering dedication to sobriety and personal development drove him to the zenith of his career, which finally resulted in the coveted achievement of an American League Most Valuable Player (AL MVP) title. His dedication to sobriety and personal development catapulted him to the pinnacle of his career. This honor served as a symbol not only of his brilliance on the field, but also of his successful conquest over the significant obstacles that had previously threatened to derail his destiny.Through the passing of the years, Hamilton remained a ray of light for an incalculable number of people who were going through struggles that were comparable to their own. His life serves as a powerful illustration of the transformational potential of faith, resiliency, and the unconquerable spirit of the human race. Not only did Josh Hamilton emerge from the labyrinthine turns of fate and the furnace of his own personal troubles as a baseball icon, but he also emerged as a living witness to the capacity for atonement that lives within each and every one of us.

Ted Williams

Ted Williams was an extraordinary example of the unusual combination of intrinsic brilliance and great proficiency across a wide variety of fields. Because of the breadth and depth of his talents, he was recognized as a genuine polymath not just in the field of baseball but also in the wider world of sports.

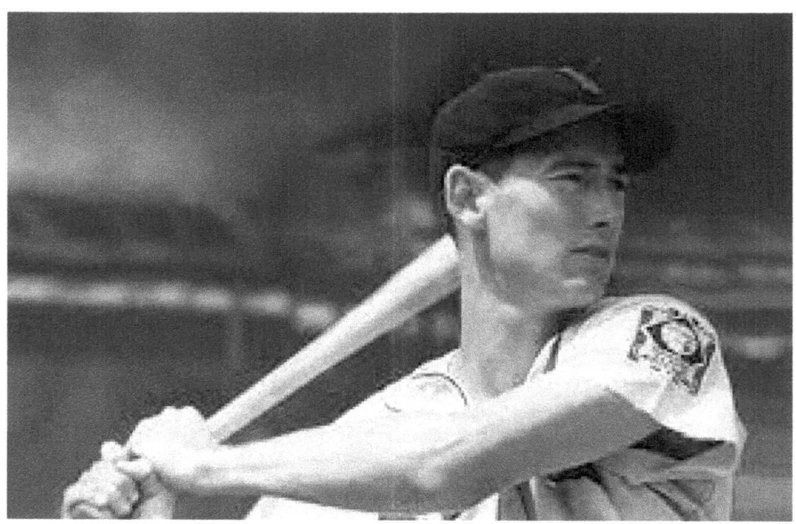

Williams, popularly known as "Teddy Ballgame," emerged as a star in the history of Major League Baseball. He accomplished the amazing distinction of being selected an All-Star an astounding 19 times. However, his influence was not restricted to the revered baseball grounds; rather, he served as an example of unflinching devotion to his country via courageous military duty.The life narrative of Williams is filled with acts of bravery and selflessness, as evidenced by the fact that he participated in no fewer than 39 combat missions throughout the turbulent years of World War II and the Korean War. He was a talented pilot, and he flew to the air without any trepidation, facing the dangers of battle with an unbreakable will.When one considers the grand tapestry of history, it becomes increasingly unlikely that we will ever be witnesses to the emergence of another individual who possesses the unique blend of talent, dedication, and valor that defined Ted Williams' remarkable tenure in Major League Baseball and his courageous service in the military. This is especially true when one considers how unlikely it is that we will ever see another individual possess the unique blend of talent, dedication, and valor. His accomplishments will forever leave an indelible mark on the annals of athletics and bravery, serving as an example for future generations.

Lyman Bostock

In spite of Lyman Bostock's relative obscurity in the annals of sports history, his story is one that is not only intriguing but also relevant, and it is reminiscent of the extraordinary experiences of well-known sportsmen.

In the rich fabric of baseball legend, the year 1978 was a watershed year because it was the year when Bostock, who was a shining star for the Minnesota Twins during his prime, made headlines. It was during this season when an incredible act of bravery emanating from his character surfaced, one that echoed the honor of a genuine sportsman. In the midst of a battle with his performance, during which he was batting an exceptionally low.150, he made a move that stunned the whole sports community. The extraordinary sense of accountability and sportsmanship that Bostock displayed was on full show when he offered to give up his whole paycheck for the month of April. He had a genuine passion to both his profession and his team, and he wanted to show that dedication by making apologies for his subpar performance.Gene Autry, the respected owner of the California Angels at the time, was the intended recipient of this astonishing offer. Due to the fact that Bostock was aware of his poor performance, he made an effort to ease the financial strain that was being placed on the company. This exemplifies Bostock's unmatched sense of honesty and accountability. Autry turned down the offer, despite the fact that the person behind it had good intentions and wanted to help others. As a result, Bostock was able to put the money toward philanthropic causes. This selfless deed further highlighted Bostock's dedication to making a good effect in the world outside of the domain of baseball.Bostock's life was cut tragically short later on in that awful year, and his passing came far too soon. In spite of this tragic conclusion, the legacy of his magnificent act of generosity lives on and will be permanently carved into the collective consciousness of everyone who witnessed it. This unselfish act by Bostock transcends the sport and serves as an example of the power of empathy and compassion when confronted with hardship. It is a reminder to all of us of the importance of these qualities. His life offers as a powerful illustration of the qualities that catapult sportsmen to the level of genuine heroes, affecting the lives of a great number of people and leaving an unforgettable impression on the whole globe.

Magic Johnson

The year 1991 was a pivotal juncture in both the life and professional trajectory of the former point guard for the Los Angeles Lakers, who is widely regarded as one of the most influential players in the annals of the history of his position. It was in that year that he was given a diagnosis that would change the course of his life forever. He tested positive for the Human Immunodeficiency Virus (HIV), a discovery that forced him to put a protracted halt in his burgeoning basketball career and drove him to reevaluate the way his life was going to progress.

Following the shocking revelation, he was forced to take a lengthy break from playing basketball. During this time, he had to redirect his attention away from the court and onto the fight for his health and wellbeing. Fans and admirers were left in a state of bewilderment after the abrupt and unanticipated end to his career. At the same time, the globe struggled to come to terms with the news that this legendary athlete was facing a significant health crisis. In spite of this, he produced a spectacular comeback to the Lakers' lineup during the finishing portion of the 1995-1996 NBA season, signifying an incredible rebirth in the face of adversity. He did this by exhibiting tenacity and drive.After he had finished his career in the world of active athletics, he devoted his time, energy, and influence to becoming a steadfast champion for increasing awareness of AIDS. This change exemplified his unyielding dedication to bringing attention to this life-threatening condition, which continues to have a negative impact on a great number of people all over the world. His efforts to educate and enlighten the general public about the complexities of HIV and AIDS have not only been powerful, but they have also motivated and educated others, which has fostered a better awareness of the disease as well as the significance of early identification, treatment, and community support. The fact that he was able to go from reaching the pinnacle of athletic achievement to becoming a powerful spokesperson for AIDS awareness has, without a doubt, left an indelible mark on both the world of sports and the realm of public health advocacy. This goes to show that adversity can in fact serve as a catalyst for remarkable transformation and an impact that will last for a long time.

Michael Jordan

In the history of professional basketball, Michael Jordan is remembered as a seminal figure because he is so frequently regarded as the embodiment of all that is great about the game of basketball. His unrivaled talents and accomplishments firmly establish him as possibly the greatest professional basketball player of all time, leaving an indelible impact on the history of the sport and an everlasting legacy that continues to inspire generations. His legacy is one that will continue to inspire generations to come.Jordan won a remarkable total of six NBA championships throughout the course of his storied career, an accomplishment that puts him in a class all by himself and puts him in a league of his own. His path to reaching this exalted rank was characterized by unyielding tenacity, unyielding resiliency, and an unyielding enthusiasm for the game. Jordan displayed an unshakable will that spurred him to enhance his talents and finally conquer the summit of the sport, despite the fact that he experienced setbacks early in his life, the most notable of which was getting cut from the basketball team he played for in high school.The sheer drive that Michael Jordan showed in the face of adversity is maybe one of the most intriguing elements of his story. In spite of the deep loss of his father and the struggle to come to terms with the unmet desire of playing professional baseball, he was able to convert these problems into inspiration for succeeding in the sport that he loved the most, which was basketball. Not only did his amazing ability to turn obstacles into stepping stones demonstrate his physical talent, but it also demonstrated the strength of his character and his capacity to bounce back from adversity.Failure and setbacks are not obstacles but rather stepping stones on the way to achievement. Jordan's rise to prominence serves as a beacon of light for aspiring sportsmen, emphasizing that failure is not a roadblock but rather a stepping stone. His biography exemplifies the significance of unyielding devotion, unrelenting hard work, and an unshakable belief in oneself. As a result, he has left an indelible impact on the history of athletics and has motivated other people to pursue their aspirations with zeal and conviction.

Mia Hamm

It is undeniable that Mia Hamm has a preeminent position in the domain of women's soccer, and she has left an indelible stamp on the history of soccer in the United States. It is a testimonial to her outstanding skill and proficiency on the field that she has engraved her name at the top of the U.S. soccer record books with a stunning total of 158 goals scored for the United States in international competition.

In addition to the incredible things that she has accomplished, Mia Hamm continues to exert a profound effect even in the present day, when she serves as a genuine soccer ambassador. Because of her position, she is able to pass on the excitement and allure of the sport to future generations, which will ensure the activity's continuous development and success. Her path has become a guiding light for young female soccer players all throughout the country, igniting a fire within them to pursue their ambitions with perseverance and unshakable determination. Her story has become a beacon of inspiration. She continues to enhance the prestige of women's soccer by her accomplishments and her passion to the sport, so opening opportunities for numerous others and busting preconceptions along the way.

Marathoners challenging USATF over Olympic trials' noon start

A meeting with Max Siegel, the Chief Executive Officer of USA Track and Field, has been set for this coming Thursday, and many of the most accomplished marathon runners in the United States have gotten together to prepare for the meeting. The U.S. Olympic trials for 2024 are scheduled to take place in Orlando, Florida, and the goal of this conference is to address a germane concern over the start time of noon that has been assigned for those trials. The runners voice their concerns about the possibility for the heat that is prominent throughout the middle of the day to have a negative impact on their athletic performance as well as their general wellbeing.

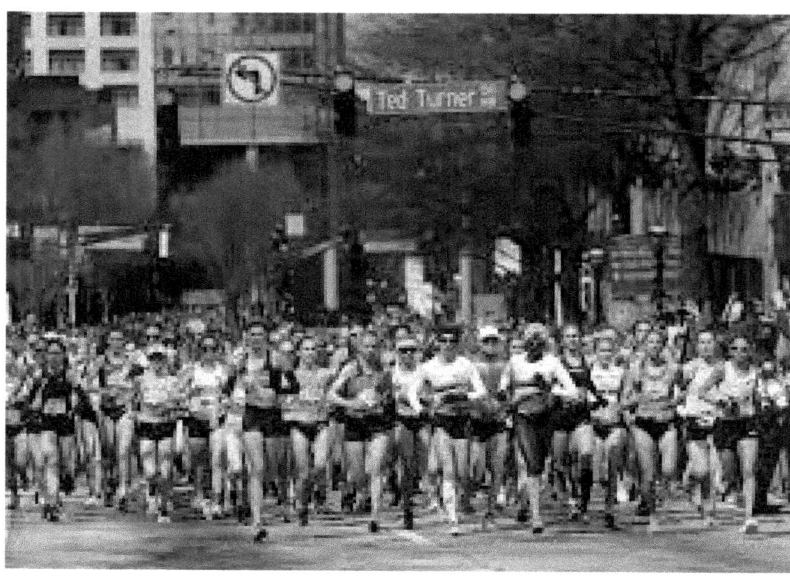

According to Citius Mag, on September 15 around one hundred runners collaborated to write a letter to USATF highlighting the increased dangers to the competitors' health caused by beginning the race at noon on February 3. The letter was sent to the organization in an effort to bring attention to the issue. Their principal argument is on the want for more favorable weather conditions, which they believe will make it easier for athletes to obtain qualifying times for the Olympics that are far quicker. The runners referred to the weather data from February of the year before, stating that there was not a single day in February that had a recorded high temperature that was lower than 70 degrees Fahrenheit, and that this was accompanied by continuously high levels of humidity. In addition, they called attention to the weather patterns that occurred in the year 2023, when the average daily high temperature was 78 degrees Fahrenheit, and it regularly exceeded the threshold of 80 degrees. The prospective location of the race, in conjunction with the planned start time of noon, seems to guarantee that participants will be subjected to weather that is extremely hot and humid, and will be exposed to the sun for an extended period of time. These are conditions that are vastly different from the typical surroundings in which elite marathoning races are typically competed.At this time, the start of the men's race is scheduled to take place at 12:10 pm, while the start of the women's race is scheduled to occur at 12:20 pm. Jared Ward, a member of the USATF Athletes Advisory Committee, responded to the concerns expressed by the athletes by communicating that Max Siegel, the CEO of USATF, has demonstrated a willingness to participate in meaningful discussions with athletes. He stressed the necessity for Siegel's intervention to bring about a good adjustment in the start time, recognizing the essential relevance of this change in protecting the athletes' well-being and optimizing their performance. He underlined the need for Siegel's involvement to bring about a favorable adjustment in the start time.

Olympian Mary Lou Retton has pneumonia, fighting for her life

Mary Lou Retton, the famous gymnast who won the gold medal in the women's all-around event at the 1984 Summer Olympics in Los Angeles and became a common name across America, is really sick right now. Her daughter, McKenna Kelley, wrote a touching post on social media about how her bravely facing a serious and rare form of pneumonia in intensive care at a Texas hospital.

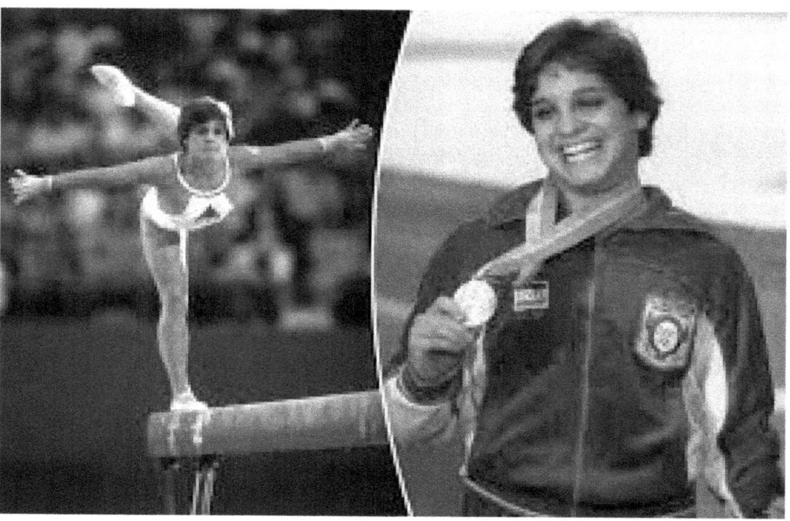

In an emotional Instagram post, Kelley told the sad news that Retton is having a hard time breathing on her own because of how sick she is. The family is still holding on to hope, and they said that Retton is getting great medical care as she fights to get better. The fact that the famous athlete has been in intensive care for more than a week shows how serious the situation is.

During this tough time, Kelley has started a fundraising campaign to help pay for her mother's medical bills. She stresses that Retton does not have health insurance at the moment, which makes the campaign even more urgent and necessary.When we think about Retton's amazing gymnastics career, it's important to remember how important her accomplishments were in the history of the sport. She wowed the world of gymnastics when she was only 16 years old, making history as the first American, male or female, to win an Olympic medal in gymnastics. The gymnast from Fairmont, West Virginia, was the best of the best. She got two perfect 10s in the all-around competition and won the gold medal. She also won two silver and two bronze medals in the Los Angeles Olympics.Remembering her success at the 1984 Olympics, Retton and Ecaterina Szabo of Romania were in a very close race for first place in the all-around. While meeting difficulties, Retton showed unwavering drive, making up lost time and eventually being on the verge of winning a gold medal. During the vault rotation, when everything had to be just right, the important moment came. Retton did an amazing feat of skill and bravery when she did a perfect full-twisting layout Tsukahara. She got a perfect 10.0 and won the gold, making her name famous in the history of gymnastics.Former teacher Bela Karolyi summed up the effect of Retton's performance by saying that she changed the idea of what a gymnast should be like by showing strength, energy, and unmatched physicality in her routines. After her win, she was named The Associated Press amateur athlete of the year in 1984. This award shows how much she has contributed to the world of sports. After that, she got the respect she earned when she was inducted into the International Gymnastics Hall of Fame in 1997 and the USOC Olympic Hall of Fame in 1985. She also made history as the first woman to appear on the famous Wheaties box, solidifying her status as an American sports star.

Sapporo abandons 2030 bid, to consider hosting future Olympics

Sapporo, a city located in northern Japan, has made the decision to pull out of the competition to host the Winter Olympics in 2030. This is a huge development. During a press conference that took place in Tokyo, the Mayor of Sapporo, Katsuhiro Akimoto, and the President of the Japanese Olympic Committee, Yasuhiro Yamashita, announced this decision together. The rampant corruption and bid-rigging linked with the Tokyo Olympics had a negative influence, which is the fundamental reason behind this withdrawal. As a result, the faith and support of the population was diminished as a result of these actions.

It was stressed by Mayor Akimoto that the lack of support and comprehension on the part of the residents was a significant factor in this withdrawal. The populace, who were still dealing with the consequences of the corruption investigations tied to the 2020 Tokyo Games, possessed feelings of disquiet and worry over the possible financial difficulties involved with hosting the Winter Olympics. The already soiled reputation of the Olympics in Japan was further damaged by the incident, which resulted in Sapporo's chances of hosting the renowned event decreasing even more.

A former executive from the powerful advertising business Dentsu who joined the Tokyo Olympic organizing committee in 2014 is at the center of the controversy that is at the heart of this issue. Haruyuki Takahashi has maintained his innocence, despite the fact that his trial has not yet begun. Takahashi had a large amount of influence in the process of coordinating sponsorships for the Games. In relation to the bribery case, a total of fifteen persons hailing from five different firms are now being tried. Companies such as Aoki Holdings, which was in charge of providing the uniforms for Japan's Olympic squad, Sun Arrow, which was responsible for creating the mascots for the Olympics, and Kadokawa, which is a Japanese publishing firm and whose boss was recently found guilty of bribing Takahashi, are just some of the notable companies that are engaged.The financial aspect of this choice also has some weight, as seen by the fact that Japan officially spent around $13 billion on hosting the Tokyo Olympics, while a government audit revealed that the true cost may be twice as much as that amount. As a direct result of this, the magnitude of this financial commitment along with the implications of the corruption scandal have strongly impacted the decision to withdraw Sapporo's application for the

Winter Olympics in 2030.In looking to the future, despite the fact that there is an intention to investigate the viability of Sapporo's candidacy for future Olympic editions, notably the Winter Olympics in 2034, the chances appear to be poor. In light of the recent developments, the possibility of hosting the 2034 Olympics might be interpreted as an effort to save the city's image despite the current state of affairs. The International Olympic Committee is expected to choose Stockholm as the host city for the Winter Olympics in 2030 and Salt Lake City as the host city for the Winter Olympics in 2034. In the meanwhile, Salt Lake City looks to be a near-shoot for the 2034 event.

IOC to vote on flag football for 2028 Los Angeles Olympics

On Monday, the National Football League (NFL) gained a huge boost in their ongoing efforts to capture international notice when it was announced that the organizers of the 2028 Los Angeles Olympics made a proposal to include flag football in the tournament. This move comes at the same time when the Summer Games are being held in the United States once again after a break of 32 years, further underscoring the NFL's goal to appeal to an international audience.

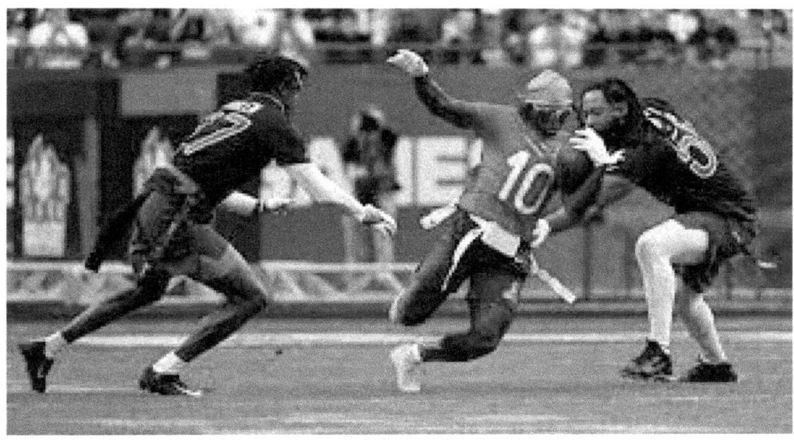

Baseball and softball were both included in the plan, which will be considered by the International Olympic Committee (IOC) during their sessions in Mumbai, India, which will begin later this week. Votes will also be taken on the idea. Over the course of Olympic history, these competitions have been on the schedule less frequently than other sports. In addition, the games of lacrosse, squash, and cricket were shown, demonstrating the wide variety of sports that are played across the world, each of which has its own level of popularity.

Casey Wasserman, the chairman of the organizing committee for the Los Angeles Olympics, emphasized that these new sports have a great deal of relevance, are innovative, and are deeply ingrained within communities. These new sports are played in a variety of settings such as backyards, schoolyards, community centers, stadiums, and parks not only in the United States but also all over the world.The National Football League (NFL) has been actively promoting flag football, a tamer version of the well-loved sport that is played in the United States, in Europe, Mexico, and Japan for many years. This season, the National Football League (NFL) planned to play a number of games in London and Germany to increase exposure for the sport. In flag football, players make tackles by removing a flag from a belt that is worn around their waist. Flag football is normally played on a field that is 50 yards long and has a 5-on-5 matchup with no offensive or defensive lines. The United States of America men's team won the World Games and took home the gold medal, but the United States of America women's team was beaten by Mexico in the championship game.The presence of cricket offers a striking contrast to the more well-known sport of flag football, which would likely be more familiar to the local audience. Cricket is a sport that is extremely well-liked in certain nations, such as India, Australia, and Britain, but it is still a sport that is not very well-known in the United States. Twenty20 cricket is a suggested addition to the program for the Olympic Games in Los Angeles since it is a condensed version of the original game. Only once, all the way back in Paris in the year 1900, did the sport ever compete in the Olympic Games.It is important to note that breakdancing, which will make its debut at the Olympic Games in Paris in the year after next, was not selected for the program in Los Angeles. In a similar vein, the proposed program did not include any events involving racing, kickboxing, or karate.Given the addition of five team sports, which would naturally lead to an increase in the total number of participants, the question of whether or not other sports will need to reduce the number of disciplines in order to comply with the limit of 10,500 athletes at a Summer Olympics that has been set by the International Olympic Committee remains unanswered.

CHAPTER THREE

Training and Preparation

Olympic Day home workout

Olympic stars like Rommel Pacheco, PV Sindhu and Martin Fourcade united to sweat and celebrate with a special workout on Olympic Channel.

On June 23rd, athletes originating from all different parts of the world joined together in a coordinated effort to compete in a strenuous 24-hour training session. This event took place in a communal effort. This event served as a moving monument to the day when the International Olympic Committee was established in 1894. It was a symbolic confluence of devotion and togetherness in the world of sport, and this event paid homage to that day.

As a way to commemorate this event, the Olympic Channel has compiled a special home exercise video that has been specifically designed to correspond with the significance of the day. Fans were invited to participate in this fitness endeavor and worked out alongside Olympic greats such as the accomplished gymnast from the United States of America, Laurie Hernandez, the remarkable biathlete Martin Fourcade, the taekwondo maestro Lutalo Muhammad, the formidable wrestler Vinesh Phogat, and the athlete from Tonga who is universally adored, Pita Taufatofua, amongst many other illustrious names.Even though Olympic Day has come and gone, the spirited motivation behind these energizing activities should not be allowed to die out. Individuals are welcome to explore the original exercise session that has been given below, or they may choose their favorite Olympian-led sessions from the playlists. This is done in recognition of the idea that maintaining one's fitness level should be an ongoing commitment. The rallying cry continues to be #StayHealthy, #StayStrong, and #StayActive, reiterating the evergreen spirit of Olympic Day and the tenacity required to maintain a healthy lifestyle.As a throwback to Olympic

Day 2020, individuals all over the world were issued an open invitation to #StayActive by participating in dynamic live workouts that were presented by elite athletes located in different parts of the world. This was done in the spirit of Olympic Day 2020. This event was a celebration of human resiliency, a symphony of drive, and a presentation of the steadfast dedication of players who are acknowledged as some of the most influential personalities in the world of sports. It was an exciting day packed with exhilarating appearances that provided viewers with a window into the world of sports as seen through the eyes of some of the most prominent figures in the athletic world.

Improve mental health

The regular performance of vigorous physical activity, in particular exercise, possesses a significant potential for the development of better mental well-being and the promotion of a pleasant mood. In periods marked by uncertainty and a persistent negative environment, indulging in physical activities, particularly inside the confines of one's house, might prove to be crucial in assisting in the cleansing of one's mind of thoughts that are damaging.

Exertion of the muscles causes the body to produce a number of important chemicals, which together form a chain reaction known as a neurochemical cascade. These substances include serotonin, norepinephrine, endorphins, and dopamine. These bioactive compounds play a crucial part in elevating mood and generating a state of relaxation, which eventually contributes to the reduction of stress and a decreased propensity to become depressed.The National Health Service in the United Kingdom highlights the significance of this connection by highlighting the fact that individuals who participate in a consistent regimen of physical activity exhibit a remarkable reduction in depression risk, with estimates suggesting a substantial 30 percent decrease in the likelihood of experiencing depressive episodes. This connection highlights the significance of the significance of this connection.In addition, the beneficial effects of exercise include reducing the severity of symptoms linked with anxiety disorders and making them more manageable. Individuals have the ability to actively control and reduce the impact that anxiety symptoms have on their lives by incorporating regular exercise into their lifestyles, which in turn strengthens their general mental resilience and well-being. This combined benefit, which targets both anxiety and sadness, highlights the overall advantages of adopting a more active lifestyle.

Improves thinking skills

Participating in an exercise routine on a consistent basis is the answer for everyone who wants to keep their cognitive function at its peak, strengthen their ability to remember information, and improve their thinking abilities in general. The physiological reaction that is induced by exercise, which involves the release of numerous chemicals inside the body, has a significant effect on the health of the brain by strengthening the fundamental structure of this crucial organ.

The United Kingdom's National Health Service (NHS), which is recognized as a reliable source of medical information, highlights the enormous advantages of engaging in physical exercise on a consistent basis. People who make regular exercise a part of their lifestyle have shown to have a significant decrease of up to 30 percent in the chance of acquiring dementia, which is a concerning ailment that has a negative impact on a person's cognitive abilities and memory. The findings of their study and the insights of their experts support this assertion.In summary, the numerous benefits that come from exercising go well beyond simply improving one's physical health. The act of partaking in regular exercise not only adds to a strong body, but it also functions as a shield for mental clarity and cognitive performance. This is because exercise releases endorphins, which are feel-good chemicals in the brain. The complex interaction of physiological processes that is induced by exercise manifests as a robust defensive system. This defense mechanism protects the delicate nuances of the brain and preserves its optimal function throughout time. Therefore, adopting exercise as a component of a holistic health practice is an investment in one's mental as well as their physical well-being.

Helps with sleep

The respected National Library of Medicine in the United States of America highlights the substantial significance that physical activity has in the domain of sleep. It sheds light on the fact that indulging in physical exercise may hasten the beginning of sleep, as well as prolong its restorative hold, so improving the overall quality of your nocturnal repose by increasing the amount of time you spend sleeping. Endorphins are natural sedatives that are released into the body as a response to physical effort during exercise. Endorphins help to relax both the mind and the body in preparation for a more peaceful transition into sleep.

In addition, physical activity possesses the extraordinary ability to not only hasten the process of falling asleep but also to increase the depth to which one sleeps. By engaging in consistent physical activity, you may pave the way for a more restorative night's sleep. This allows you to go into the deeper stages of the sleep cycle, which is when the body carries out the necessary repairs and rejuvenation processes.

However, time is everything, so be judicious. The esteemed Mayo Clinic warns against indulging in strenuous physical activity too close to bedtime, stating that this might lead to sleep problems. Although it is unquestionably healthy to exercise, participating in strenuous physical activity in the later hours of the day might unwittingly inject a burst of energy into the system, making it more difficult to fall asleep. This is especially true for people who exercise in the evening. It may be difficult for the body, which is now pumped up from the exertions, to make a smooth transition into a condition of calm slumber in a timely manner.To summarize, physical activity is a powerful ally in the pursuit of undisturbed sleep; nevertheless, the timing of these physical pursuits as well as the intensity of these activities require careful attention. Your search for refreshing sleep will be successful if you strike a balance between the advantages of exercise and the prudent timing of your activities. This will usher in a night of restorative slumber and guarantee that you rise feeling rejuvenated to embrace the new day.

QUALITIES OF A GREAT SPORTS COACH

The process of coaching an athlete is not reducible to a single, universally applicable strategy due to its complexity and intricacy. Each coach has their own individual teaching style, which is a conglomeration of their own personal experiences, ideas, and body of knowledge, making it completely one-of-a-kind and impossible to replicate. The history of a coach, the ideas they have, and their level of comprehension of the sport they are instructing all contribute to the formation of their unique style.

The world of coaching is one in which a variety of coaching approaches is not only tolerated but actively promoted. It highlights the uniqueness of the person and the creative potential that is inherent in the human experience. It is the flexibility of a coach to a variety of circumstances as well as their capacity for innovation in response to the ever-changing dynamics of the athletic domain that contribute to the particular coaching style of that coach.

In spite of the many different ways that coaching may be done, there are a few essential qualities that distinguish great coaches from good ones. These characteristics serve as the foundation for any successful coaching approach, regardless of the specifics that make it stand out from the others. Great coaches are defined by their unyielding dedication, boundless enthusiasm, and deeply ingrained love for the athletes they mentor in addition to the sport itself. They have an insatiable appetite for learning and are always looking for new ways to better their coaching techniques, demonstrating that they have an expansive grasp of the sport overall.I n addition, successful coaches have exceptional communication abilities, which allow them to effectively express their thoughts and directions to the players under their tutelage. They cultivate a climate of mutual respect, understanding, and trust among the athletes, creating a setting in which players feel encouraged and driven to perform to the best of their abilities. These coaches are also excellent observers who are able to critically analyze performances and discover areas for growth. As a result, they are able to personalize their instruction to fulfill particular requirem ents.The characteristic of a great coach is an amalgamation of devotion, flexibility, enthusiasm, effective communication, and acute observation. While coaching approaches can vary considerably, the hallmark of a great coach stays consistent: an amalgamation of these qualities. These common characteristics serve as a bridge across the various coaching environments and constitute the foundation upon which the athlete-coach relationship thrives and develops.

UNDERSTANDING THE SPORT

It is very necessary to have a thorough and all-encompassing understanding of the sport in order to perform admirably in the function of a competent instructor. This entails having a comprehensive understanding of the fundamental abilities, an in-depth knowledge of advanced tactics and strategies, and a keen awareness of the delicate interplay between the sport's many different aspects. The potential to successfully express one's knowledge and skills is further enhanced by the acquisition of experiential insights gained from a noteworthy career spent actively participating in the sport.

The painstaking planning and preparation that coaches put in during the whole of the athletic season is of equal importance. This necessitates a strategy with several facets, one that takes into account the gradual nature of training adaptation, and one that combines this knowledge. A coach is responsible for adjusting training regimens in accordance with the progression and development of athletes. This ensures a steady but significant improvement in an athlete's skills and capacities. Knowledge of the sport's rules and regulations is essential since it enables coaches to direct athletes in conformity with the established parameters, therefore encouraging fair play and good sportsmanship.In addition, developing and sustaining an atmosphere that is conducive to the academic growth of athletes is an art form in and of itself. It is the responsibility of the coaches to create an environment that is uncomplicated yet well-structured in order to promote success. Optimising several aspects, such as the organization of training sessions, the dissemination of pertinent ideas, and the provision of constructive criticism, is required. The best coaches create an atmosphere in which their athletes may flourish, hone their skills, and realize their full potential by employing strategies that are well-organized and have a specific goal in mind.

EAGERNESS TO LEARN

A competent coach has a wide-ranging knowledge of the sport they are coaching; yet, the route to success requires a continuous commitment to gaining new information and perfecting creative training approaches. As part of this commitment, it is necessary to be current on the most recent research, trends, and advances that can improve the coaching process. This pro-active attitude is one of the hallmarks of a genuinely excellent coach, who is always looking for new ways to deepen their study of the subject matter and improve their skill in it.

An exceptional coach is one who exemplifies this devotion by actively engaging with a variety of topics that are important to the field of sports coaching, so strengthening their ability to instruct. Beyond the constraints of the game itself, diving into interdisciplinary subjects such as sport psychology gives essential insights into the mental fortitude and psychology of players. When a coach has a solid grasp of the subtleties of exercise and nutrition physiology, they have the ability to help their players achieve their full potential in terms of both performance and health. A coach can improve their capacity to design comprehensive and efficient training regimens by expanding their knowledge of a wide variety of disciplines. Attending specialist classes appears to be a wise technique in order to aid this continual learning process and make it more manageable. These seminars provide an organized and expert-guided approach, so guaranteeing that coaches are armed with the most modern information and practices. Because of the vast amounts of material that can be accessed through various educational channels, coaches have a variety of opportunities to develop and improve their coaching methods.A fantastic coach is one who understands that the path to mastery is essentially an endless search for new information and ways to develop oneself. Not only does it need having a solid foundation in the sport's fundamentals, but it also necessitates adopting lifelong education and making an active effort to include a wide range of specialized knowledge. This never-ending path will, in the end, result in the improvement of coaching skills and the realization of the full potential of the athletes who are coached by those skills.

SHARING KNOWLEDGE

Acquiring new information is an essential step in the progression of any athlete's career, but it is just as important for them to be able to articulate their thoughts clearly and seek out a variety of viewpoints, particularly those that go outside the constraints of their specific sport. This characteristic is a priceless asset, and it is one of the characteristics that separate excellent coaches apart from the rest of the competition. These coaches exemplify a great understanding of their position, as they are well aware that the core of their responsibility entails the transmission of information and education to the athletes under their tutelage.

In the world of competitive sports, players frequently find themselves involved in solo practice sessions, during which they devote a sizeable amount of their time to honing their abilities and perfecting their methods. Within the context of this individualized goal, having a comprehensive awareness of the complexities of their training routine is of the utmost importance. The fact that they are aware of what they are doing and, more importantly, why they are doing it, contributes to the improved quality of the training and practice sessions that they participate in. Athletes may discover a plethora of information that guides their approach to training by delving deeper into the reasoning behind each exercise, the mechanics of their motions, and the scientific underpinnings of their training routines.

Athletes have the ability to make educated decisions regarding their training when they have a thorough understanding of the physiological and biomechanical components of their sport, which allows them to perform at their peak level of efficiency and effectiveness. In addition, having a thorough understanding of the 'why' behind their activities cultivates a greater feeling of drive and devotion on their part. Athletes who are equipped with this information have a greater chance of maintaining their unwavering dedication to their trade. This is because they are strengthened by an intellectual comprehension of the goal behind each tough exercise and each methodical practice session.This comprehensive awareness goes well beyond the confines of simple technique and reaches into the realms of strategy, sports psychology, and even nutrition. Athletes who study deeply into the complexities of their sport are better suited to participate in meaningful conversations and seek insights from a wide variety of sources that extend beyond the traditional realm of their sport. They further expand their own approach to their athletic activities by adopting a mindset that is open to a diverse range of viewpoints since this allows them to get access to novel ideas and creative techniques.Athletes are propelled closer and closer to the peak of their potential by virtue of the symbiotic link that exists between the acquisition of information and the confidence to investigate, discuss, and incorporate a variety of points of view. Because of this complex interplay, training may be transformed into an intellectual and physical adventure, which lays the groundwork for not only competency but mastery in the field of sports.

MOTIVATIONAL SKILLS

A competent coach is one who possesses the special capacity to motivate and animate their team by maintaining a positive attitude and an enduring love for the sport and the athletes that participate in it. The ability of a coach to instill in his or her charges a burning desire to perform at the highest possible level is the fundamental component of motivation in coaching. By skillfully fanning this flame, a coach inspires the individuals under their tutelage to strive for their own best, concentrating on accomplishing set performance milestones rather than becoming fixated on the final outcomes. This strategy assures that a player will concentrate on the process at hand, allowing them to hone their abilities and improve their technique, which will ultimately result in improved overall performance.

A skillful coach will always put more of an emphasis on the achievement of performance goals as opposed to outcome goals. A growth mentality is developed in the athletes as a result of this deliberate emphasis on quantifiable successes rather than end results, which instills resilience and fosters a continuing drive for development. In this context, the coach assumes the role of a guide as well as an educator, assisting the athlete in charting a course that will lead to unending improvement and accomplishment.In addition, one of the most important aspects of being a great coach is to cultivate an atmosphere in which happiness and amusement are the fundamental building blocks. A more fulfilling and memorable experience is provided to an athlete by their coach when the latter combines training with aspects of fun and excitement. This not only results in an increased sense of involvement, but it also helps to cultivate a real passion for the activity, which in turn helps to enhance long-term commitment and devotion.The core of the art of coaching goes beyond only having competence in certain tactics. It incorporates the capacity to create drive, nurture growth, and inject delight, all of which combine into a journey that is transforming for the coach as well as the athlete. By using such an all-encompassing approach, a coach may morph into a guiding light, pointing athletes in the direction of their full potential while also ensuring that the sport continues to be a source of joy and success for them.

KNOWING THE ATHLETE

Achieving success in coaching requires first and foremost an in-depth comprehension of, as well as a recognition of, the broad spectrum of individual variations that exist among players. It is essential to have a fundamental understanding of the many different emotional landscapes that athletes go through. Athletes are susceptible to a wide range of effects due to the powerful role that their emotions play in their performance in competition. What motivates and encourages one athlete may have the opposite effect on another, leading them to feel disheartened and lose their drive. Recognizing these uniquely personal emotional responses is therefore absolutely necessary.

When it comes to coaching, a cookie-cutter method of communication and motivation will never be able to satisfy the complex requirements of the athletes you work with. The most important thing is to customize each athlete's communication and motivating techniques so that they take into account their individual traits and sensitivity levels. This individualized approach not only improves performance, but it also reduces the likelihood of accidentally undermining an athlete's sense of self-worth and motivation.A skilled coach pays careful attention to the emotional spectrum, as well as the capabilities and limitations, of each and every athlete who is under their supervision. This attentiveness goes beyond the physical prowess and skill set, and instead delves into the psychological and emotional components of the situation. When a coach does this, they not only create an environment that is supportive and favorable to growth, but they also maximize the athlete's potential for both growth and success. It is the responsibility that comes with being a competent coach to recognize and accommodate the unique qualities of each player that sets them apart from other coaches and drives them to achieve the highest levels of coaching success.

COMMUNICATION

An successful communicator exudes an air of legitimacy, competence, respect, and authority; this is one of the defining characteristics of a skilled coach. One of the most important aspects of this talent is the skill of expressing one's thoughts in a way that is understandable to others. This clarity depends on a few different pillars, including the ability to create well-defined goals, offer feedback that is both straightforward and constructive, and continuously reaffirm essential ideas. In addition, a knowledgeable coach is aware of the significance of acknowledging and praising accomplishments as an essential component of efficient communication within the context of the coaching dynamic. Language, a fundamental component of coaching, plays an essential part by highlighting the need to keep things simple and ensuring that all communication is kept in a format that is simple to take in and comprehend. This helps to ensure that coaching is as successful as possible.

LISTENING SKILLS

The ability to pay close attention to what is being said is one of the most important skills that a coach may possess in order to facilitate good communication. To fully flourish in this position, one has to establish a true sense of compassion and openness towards an athlete's remarks, questions, and suggestions. Only then can one hope to realize their full potential. A skilled coach not only takes into account the unique viewpoints and knowledge that athletes have to offer, but also actively seeks out this information from the athletes in their charge. A sense of inclusiveness and cooperation within the coaching dynamic may be cultivated by cultivating an environment that is welcoming and open. Athletes are not merely accommodated, but they are really encouraged to voice their views and opinions when such an environment is fostered. This symbiotic relationship between the coach and the athlete is supported by a shared knowledge of the value of active involvement and polite discourse, which results in an experience that is both more rewarding and more productive for the coaching.

DISCIPLINE

Athletes take part in a world that is organized by a core set of rules, which govern their behavior both in the heat of competition and for the entirety of their life. In the interest of achieving the highest possible level of performance in a sports event, these laws provide a behavioral playbook that acts as a set of guiding principles. The observance of these norms is not just an expectation but also a legally obligatory obligation, highlighting the importance of taking a thoughtful approach to disciplinary measures. Trust emerges as the keystone in this complicated tapestry of athlete-coach connections, an intangible essence that is essential for establishing a flourishing coaching partnership. This trust, which is both fragile and strong, serves as the foundation around which successful coaching is constructed. It is the very definition of dependability and faith, a firm conviction that the coach would act in the athlete's best interest both on and off the playing field.

The effectiveness of coaching is dependent not just on words but also on actions; a good coach is one who expresses their expectations in a way that is easy to understand and who establishes a clear set of guidelines for behavior from the very beginning. This code functions as a moral compass, directing athletes through the maze of decisions they face along their path as competitors in their respective sports. It acts as a standard against which their actions are evaluated, a compass pointing in the direction of the moral high ground.Nevertheless, establishing regulations is simply the first step; the subsequent implementation of those norms is of as or even greater significance. Discipline is not a one-time occurrence but rather a regular and continuing process that ensures obedience to these principles. Discipline is the method by which adherence to these norms is achieved. The annals of behavioral psychology provide evidence that corroborates the requirement of a certain strategy to the implementation of discipline. In order for discipline to be really transformational, it must possess these three important characteristics: gentleness, promptness, and consistency.

Mildness suggests a prudent and controlled approach, avoiding too severe language while yet communicating the seriousness of the situation. Mildness is the opposite of harshness. It seeks to rectify conduct without excessively reprimanding the individual, so increasing comprehension and progress. On the other hand, promptness emphasizes the significance of the necessity of quick intervention. Delays in resolving transgressions can dilute the impact and efficacy of discipline, perhaps allowing unfavorable habits to become entrenched in a person's behavior.The importance of maintaining uniformity in the application of discipline is emphasized by consistency, which is possibly the most important factor in effecting change in behavior. It guarantees that the repercussions for comparable violations stay consistent, providing a climate that is predictable and allowing athletes to realize the direct relationship between the acts they do and the results that they receive. This, in turn, fosters a feeling of accountability and cultivates a culture of responsibility, which lays the groundwork for long-term changes in behavior and creates the framework for long-term behavioral change.In the arena of athletics, the subtle interplay of rules, trust, and discipline leads to a connection that is both nurturing and productive between the coach and the athlete. The balance that is reached by conscientiously adhering to a clearly defined code of conduct and the wise use of discipline leads to the achievement of this equilibrium. In the world of sports, the road to long-term success and continued expansion is paved with a relationship that is founded on trust, that is led by norms that are unchanging, and that is reinforced via discipline that is constant and fair.

LEADING BY EXAMPLE

When it comes to coaching, a successful mentor is someone who not only shares their expertise and knowledge with their athletes, but also embodies the values and standards that they want their players to keep. It is a vital belief that a coach should follow the same standards that they set for their athletes. This is because when a coach does this, they develop a culture of honesty and mutual respect among their players.

A coach who wants to win the respect of their team must, first and foremost, demonstrate what it means to behave in a respectful manner. This entails exhibiting polite demeanor, carefully listening to the problems and suggestions of their athletes, and recognizing the viewpoints of their athletes. Because of this, a coach who treats his or her players with respect will increase the likelihood that they will treat the coach with respect in return, which will contribute to the development of a good and cohesive team dynamic.Additionally, one of the most important aspects of coaching is having good communication skills. A coach who wants to teach discipline and attentiveness in their players can model such traits themselves by paying close attention to what their athletes have to say. To listen attentively means to give sincere consideration to the ideas and viewpoints expressed by the athletes, to acknowledge their strengths, to address their concerns, and to incorporate their input into the training schedule. When a coach engages in active listening, they display empathy and understanding, which helps to cultivate an environment within the team that is conducive to trust and collaboration.A coach, in essence, serves as a role model for the athletes they work with by influencing the athletes' conduct and the values they hold via the coach's own actions and attitudes. To be a good coach, one must maintain the same high standards of behavior and conduct as are expected of those who are working under one's tutelage. A coach sets the scene for a team that not only performs in their specific sport but also grows as individuals, bringing these principles beyond the playing field and into their life beyond. These attributes include respect, active listening, and fair treatment. A coach embodies these qualities by actively listening to his or her players.

COMMITMENT AND PASSION

The most successful coaches in the industry of sports coaching are those who have worked their way to the top thanks to a profound passion for the field in which they work. Their commitment extends much beyond a simple choice of profession; rather, it is a genuine passion that directs each and every one of their actions. These remarkable coaches not only have a strong dedication to the sport and the pursuit of success, but they also represent an unrelenting commitment to the health and development of individual athletes. This is a commitment that they have shown throughout their careers. Their job as coaches does not need them to adhere to a rigid timetable; rather, it is an undertaking that demands their undivided attention 24 hours a day, seven days a week. They have coaching ingrained in their very beings, and the art of coaching permeates every element of their life. They are distinguished by their unwavering commitment as well as their passion for coaching, which enables them to achieve success and motivate others outside the realm of sports.

PSYCHOLOGICAL PREPARATION IS KEY TO OLYMPIC PERFORMANCE

Being at the Olympics is like being a child in a candy store. You must figure out how to enjoy yourself and taste the candy, but not eat so much candy that you get sick.

An important turning point that occurred in May 2012 in the bucolic environment of Chagrin Falls, Ohio, put light on the myriad of obstacles that are encountered by Olympic coaches. The underlying complexities of this high-stakes profession were highlighted by a well-known Olympic athlete from the United States who had an outstanding track record of competing in several Olympic Games and winning a variety of medals, the most of which were gold. Their astute observation acts as a guidepost for comprehending the challenging nature of the work that these coaches are responsible for.

"This quote," stated the illustrious Olympic athlete, "resonates deeply within the realm of Olympic coaching. " The fundamental heart of this endeavor is in striking a balance between the requirement of obtaining peak physical, technical, and emotional proficiency in athletes and safeguarding against the hazards of overtraining in order to avoid overtraining. It is a delicate dance that takes place in the middle of a complicated tapestry of diversions and demands.Daniel Gould, Ph.D., CC-AASP, a renowned figure in the field of kinesiology who is linked with Michigan State University, is the one who expressed these thoughts. Dr. Gould, who is a Fellow of the highly regarded Association for Applied Sport Psychology (AASP) and a former President of the organization, was the driving force behind a number of extensive research projects. These in-depth examinations, which were commissioned by the United States Olympic Commission (USOC) and lasted the course of three Olympiads, served as a foundational component in developing a knowledge of the complex dynamics that are present during Olympic coaching.A variety of new ideas arose as a result of conducting individual interviews, discussions in focus groups, and in-depth surveys with athletes and coaches. Dr. Gould's study investigated a wide range of characteristics that are intertwined with performance. Specifically, he examined the physical, psychological, and environmental aspects that are responsible for success on the great Olympic stage. The insights, which were both deep and illuminating, are now being distributed throughout the United States in the form of clinics and courses on the training of psychological abilities. Athletes and coaches all around the world stand to benefit from the sharing of this information, which has the potential to improve both their performance and their health. International organizations also stand to gain from the dissemination of this information.

Research provides valuable knowledge, strategies for preparing to perform well at the Olympics

The general audience is enthralled by the visible performance elements that undoubtedly affect an athlete's fate on the world stage when they tune in to see the magnificent spectacle that is the Olympic Games. When they do so, they are fascinated by these characteristics. However, despite all of the attention and glory that an athlete receives, their performance is significantly impacted by a variety of factors that are less well recognized and are kept hidden behind the scenes.

Extensive study has helped shed light on these behind-the-scenes influencers, which are generally disregarded. A snoring roommate, attendance at the famous Opening Ceremonies, unanticipated transportation delays, and personal familial issues have been identified as possible game-changers, capable of changing the direction of an athlete's ultimate outcome in the Games. These are just some of the seemingly insignificant factors that have been shown to be potential game-changers.The result of this study has led to some insightful findings and inventive solutions, which have imparted a useful lesson that transcends beyond the arena of Olympic competition. The significance of these discoveries is immense; they provide a compass that can be used to navigate not only the path of highly accomplished athletes but also that of people from all walks of life. Dr. Gould, a notable researcher in this field, graciously offered important lessons drawn from this long study, highlighting their relevance and possible applicability in the day-to-day lives of both athletes and non-athletes alike. This study was conducted by Dr. Gould and colleagues.

Dealing with distractions

It is one of the most major obstacles to reaching optimum performance in the lead-up to and during the Games to properly manage a variety of distractions, and this is one of the most significant obstructions. These diversions include a broad range, including contacts between athletes from less prominent sporting disciplines and some of the world's most famous sports people within the crowded confines of the community dining hall in the Olympic village. In addition, these distractions include encounters between athletes from less prominent sporting disciplines and athletes from less prominent sporting disciplines. In addition, complications caused by traffic disturbances, which can have a significant negative effect on the normal training routine of an athlete, further exacerbate the problem.

Athletes have to struggle with a variety of situations that have the ability to disrupt their attention and preparation when they are competing in this environment of distractions. For instance, living in close quarters with roommates who snore might make it difficult to get adequate rest and interfere with the healing process. Athletes may also discover that they are scheduled to participate toward the end of the Games while living in a village where the majority of their fellow competitors have already finished their competitions and are enjoying post-competition celebrations. This scenario presents a number of challenges for the athletes involved.Extens ive study has shed light on the proactive techniques that elite athletes and teams adopt in order to efficiently handle these distractions. In spite of their natural optimism, these athletes recognize the inevitability of distractions and have made a firm commitment to ensuring that such distractions do not interfere with their best possible preparation for peak performance. Despite their innate optimism, these athletes accept the inevitability of distractions. This devotion extends to their capacity to handle the organizational complexities of the event as well as the ubiquitous media attention that accompanies the Olympic Games, all while keeping steadfast concentration on the ultimate athletic goals they have set for themselves. A combination of having a strategic attitude and planning everything out in minute detail allows these athletes to try to improve their performance despite the tornado of distractions that surrounds them, with the ultimate goal of excelling on the enormous platform that is the Olympic Games.

Expect the unexpected

At the Olympic Games, the difference between successful athletes and their less successful peers was not only apparent in their physical capability but also in how they mentally approached the obstacles that lay in wait for them. The victorious athletes approached the massive stadium with a positive view and a well-framed mindset. They were aware that throughout the tough trip, they would encounter unanticipated events. They were successful in large part due to the mental readiness they possessed.

In addition to having a constructive frame of mind, effective athletes were experts in both preparing for and reacting to unforeseen circumstances. They were able to respond in an effective manner when confronted with unanticipated obstacles because they had perfected their coping techniques via past experiences and training. For example, if a wrestler found himself outside the specified boundaries of the mat, he would take a minute to collect his thoughts and breathe deeply in order to concentrate his concentration on the essential steps to carry out a certain maneuver.

Before reentering the middle of the mat to restart the bout, he can discreetly repeat a selected term such as "penetrate," enabling it to underline his devotion and plan. Because of the unpredictability of the high-stakes competition, these coping methods were essential skills for the athletes to use in order to keep their performance focus.On the other hand, competitors who were less successful tended to come into the Games with exaggerated expectations of immaculate performance. They failed to account for the likelihood of hitting obstructions since they anticipated a path free of problems. As a consequence of this, when unanticipated problems presented themselves, individuals were taken aback and their concentration wandered, which resulted in a decrease in their performance. They were unable to maintain their competitive edge because they were unable to quickly adjust and refocus when faced with such challenges. This exemplifies the critical role that mental toughness and flexibility play in the arena of athletic accomplishment.

Develop and stick to your routine

When it comes to improving athletic performance, there is a resounding consensus across athletes and coaches about the value of developing preperformance physical and mental preparation routines. This consensus reflects the importance of building routines. Those who achieve greater levels of success are more likely to stress the need of sticking to a regimented daily schedule. It is interesting to note that this urge does not change, regardless of the quality of the opponent, whether it in the preliminary rounds against opponents who are less fearsome or in the decisive finals against an opponent who has been around for a long time.

An experienced athlete offered a significant explanation of this philosophy when they emphasized the fundamental significance of maintaining a consistent routine, despite of the dynamic shifts that are characteristic of the Olympic Games. This provided a profound insight into this philosophy. Athletes, in their own words, require a well-established routine, a trustworthy refuge to which they can withdraw among the maelstrom of changes that characterize the atmosphere of the Games. The Olympics, being an event that is distinguished by extraordinary dynamism, provide a unique difficulty in maintaining consistency. This is especially the case owing to the numerous departures from the usual and typical competitive atmosphere that occur throughout the Olympics.This viewpoint sheds light on the athlete's persistent commitment to maintaining a consistent routine, which serves as a pillar of stability among the whirlwind of unknowns that are presented during the Games. Recognizing the difficulties of this duty inside the Olympic arena, where a spectrum of changes often deviate substantially from an athlete's usual competing settings, the focus that is placed on avoiding eleventh-hour adjustments is vital. This is because the difficulty of this task is acknowledged. Dr. Gould, who is shining light on this topic, gives essential insights into the delicate fabric of athletes' preparations and advocates for the consistent adherence to established routines in order to maximize performance on the great stage that is the Olympic Games.

Opening Ceremonies – energizing or energy zapping?

Participating athletes, particularly those who are scheduled to participate in the next 24 to 48 hours, are required to give significant thought to the possibility that they may be there for the Opening Ceremonies of the Olympics. After doing considerable study, we have come to the conclusion that the outcome of this choice is dependent on the intricate interaction of a number of elements, which elicits a variety of responses from athletes.

Some athletes find that participating in the Opening Ceremonies gives them the opportunity to have a remarkable and exhilarating experience, which in turn inspires them and fills them with wonder. They might be propelled toward peak performance on the main stage by the increased excitement as well as the motivation it provides.

On the other hand, there is a contingent of athletes who are concerned about the possible downsides that come along with taking part in the Opening Ceremonies. They may have a major drain on their energy as a consequence of the lengthy periods of standing and waiting that take place throughout the ceremony. As a result, their future performance may suffer, and the outcomes may be less than stellar. The delicate harmony that must be maintained between the attraction of the ceremony and the requirement to save energy in order to provide one's best performance calls for considerable thinking and specific attention on the part of each participant.In light of these findings, Dr. Gould stresses how important it is to have athletes participate in an in-depth conversation regarding the benefits and drawbacks of attending the Opening Ceremonies. This conversation need to be carried out with the utmost care and attention, with a careful balancing being done between the potential beneficial effects and the potential negative impacts on their athletic aspirations. Having such a conversation helps to empower athletes to make an informed decision that is in line with their performance goals and ensures that they are at their peak level of well-being throughout this key time period leading up to the Olympics.

The influence of family and friends

Our investigation led us to discover an unanticipated component that shed light on the considerable influence that family and friends may have on the success of athletes and teams. In response to this unexpected finding, the researcher who was in charge of the project, Dr. Gould, made the following observation: "The effect of family and friends on athlete and team performance is a facet we had not previously considered. It is of critical importance to the overall dynamics of the athletes' experiences.

The participation of an athlete's family and friends in an athletic event, such as the Olympics, may become a significant source of delight as well as an essential kind of social support for the athlete. They are able to play to the best of their abilities on the main stage thanks in large part to the support structure that they have in place. According to Dr. Gould, "The emotional encouragement and backing from loved ones can be a powerful motivator, instilling a sense of confidence and determination."On the other hand, it became out that the extent to which an impact can differ from athlete to athlete became clear. Some people feel that the engagement of their parents and friends accidentally distracts them from the game. Their well-intentioned enquiries regarding the results of performances, forthcoming opponents, or the ramifications of victories and defeats draw their attention away from the game.

In light of this discovery, a preventative solution was developed, which consisted of an educational strategy targeted at informing athletes' family and friends about the responsibilities they play in assisting them in achieving their best performance at the Games. According to Dr. Gould, "We recognized the need to provide education and guidance to families and friends, helping them comprehend how they can best support their athlete's performance."Establishing a disciplined mechanism for the distribution of tickets to family and friends was one option that was offered. This would ensure that the presence of the athlete's loved ones would be orderly and favorable to the athlete's ability to concentrate and perform. In addition, standards were established for the management of contact between athletes and their family and friends throughout the Games. These guidelines were intended to ensure a degree of engagement that was balanced and did not intrude on the players' privacy.In addition, it was essential to make sure that the athletes' parents were aware that, while there would be times throughout the Games when it would be appropriate for their children to connect with them, there would also be times when it would be important to limit contact with them in order to improve performance. This delicate balance was intended to maximize the athletes' performance by matching the demand for attention and concentration during key sports undertakings with the support that the players receive from their families.To summarize, the unexpected discovery that family and friends have a significant impact on the performance of athletes and teams led to the creation of individualized educational strategies to strengthen these vital support networks. These strategies ultimately contribute to an athlete's optimal performance and overall well-being during major sporting events like the Games.

Summary

The origins of the Olympic Games, a momentous occasion with deep roots in history and culture, can be traced back to ancient Greece, the site of the first recorded games, which took place in 776 BC in Olympia and were dedicated to the Greek deity Zeus. These ancient competitions, known as the Olympic Games, played a vital role in the development of Greek civilization by bringing together athletes from a variety of Greek city-states and cultivating a sense of national pride. However, throughout the course of time, the ritual fell into disuse until its renaissance in the current period. The ancient Olympic Games were revived on a global scale in 1896 with the opening ceremonies taking place in Athens, Greece. This brought the spirit of the original games back to the modern world. Pierre de Coubertin, a forward-thinking French educator and sports fan, was the driving force behind this rekindling. He believed in the potential of athletics to bring people together and promote harmony and understanding across the world.The process to qualification for the contemporary Olympic Games is an extremely difficult and cutthroat competition that is unique to each event. Athletes put in a lot of work in the gym and compete in a variety of events, both locally and nationally and internationally, that are specific to their sport. Performance and conformity to predetermined criteria are required in order to be qualified. Famous athletes who have left enduring legacies include Kurt Warner, Pat Tillman, Reggie White, Roberto Clemente, Josh Hamilton, Ted Williams, Lyman Bostock, Magic Johnson, Michael Jordan, and Mia Hamm. These athletes are examples of athletes who are dedicated and passionate about their sports, and they serve as role models for other athletes who aspire to be successful in their chosen fields.The most recent Olympic news provides light on critical talks that have been going on. Concerns raised by marathoners about the start time of the Olympic trials being at noon bring attention to the ongoing conversation around the best possible circumstances for athletes. The fight against pneumonia that Olympic athlete Mary Lou Retton had to put up with sheds light on the resiliency that is necessary to be a part of the Olympic group. In addition, recent events, such as Sapporo withdrawing its candidacy for the 2030 Olympics and the possibility of flag football being included in the 2028 Olympic Games in Los Angeles, highlight the ever-changing landscape of Olympic bids and the range of sports that are on offer at the Olympics.Athletes who aspire to compete at the Olympic level participate in extensive training that covers not only their bodies but also their minds and their mental and emotional states. Workouts designed specifically for Olympic Day are performed at home as part of their specialized routines. In addition, the important role that a good sports coach plays is underlined, with a particular emphasis on the importance of attributes like as devotion, enthusiasm, and psychological preparation as fundamental components for reaching one's full potential in Olympic competition. When it comes to Olympic preparation and performance, one of the most important aspects is undoubtedly the level of devotion that is displayed by both athletes and coaches.Olympic Sports and Events

The Olympic Games feature a diverse range of sports and events that captivate audiences worldwide. From track and field to swimming, gymnastics, soccer, basketball, and more, these sports showcase the pinnacle of athletic achievement. Athletes undergo extensive training specific to their disciplines, fine-tuning their skills and strategies to compete at the highest level. The Olympic events are a testament to human determination, skill, and sportsmanship, uniting athletes from different cultures and backgrounds on a common platform.

Olympic Champions and Medalists:

Over the years, the Olympics have seen numerous champions and medalists who have etched their names in sporting history. These individuals have displayed extraordinary talent and dedication, earning gold, silver, and bronze medals and leaving a lasting legacy in the annals of Olympic achievement. Their stories of triumph and perseverance continue to inspire generations, embodying the Olympic spirit of striving for excellence.

Olympic Movement and Symbols:

The Olympic Movement, guided by the International Olympic Committee (IOC), aims to promote Olympic values such as friendship, respect, and excellence. The five interlocking rings, representing the continents of the world, symbolize unity and solidarity among nations. The Olympic flame, lit during the opening ceremony and extinguished during the closing ceremony, represents the enduring spirit of the games and the pursuit of peace and understanding through athletic competition.

Olympic Ceremonies:

Olympic ceremonies are grand and elaborate spectacles that mark the beginning and end of the games. The opening ceremony is a celebration of culture, history, and athletic achievement, featuring performances, parades of athletes, and the lighting of the Olympic cauldron. The closing ceremony is a reflection on the successes of the games and a passing of the torch to the next host city, symbolizing the continuity of the Olympic tradition.

Conclusion

The Olympic Games, which are a tradition that has been going on for centuries but is still growing, perfectly capture the everlasting spirit of human accomplishment and solidarity. The ancient Olympics were a celebration of human achievement in the realms of athleticism, cultural harmony, and devout service to the gods. They were held in Olympia, a city in ancient Greece. The modern Olympics were resurrected in 1896, and since then, they have evolved into a worldwide spectacle that celebrates athletic prowess, international friendship, and cultural variety.Athletes originally competed for honor and the love of the game, but now they often also compete for financial incentives and celebrity. This contrast between amateurism and professionalism has transformed the character of Olympic sports. Nevertheless, the quest for success and the exhibition of remarkable abilities continue to be the driving forces behind the Olympic Games, regardless of the age.The Olympic Movement is a shining example of good sportsmanship and worldwide collaboration because of the principles it upholds, which include friendship, respect, and excellence in athletic performance. The Olympic rings and torch are symbolic representations of the globe coming together in peace through the common bond of athletic competition. The opening and closing ceremonies of each Olympic Games are huge spectacles that combine innovation and tradition. These events bring the entire globe together in a spirit of joy.Athletes put a lot of time and effort into pursuing their goals of Olympic success, and that is clear when one examines the process by which they might qualify for the Olympics in their respective sports. Athletes demonstrate devotion, enthusiasm, and resiliency in their quest of Olympic qualifying, which can be seen in everything from the challenging trials in track and field to the fierce rivalry in swimming and volleyball.When we consider the beginnings of the sports careers of famous people like Mia Hamm, Pat Tillman, and Kurt Warner, we are reminded of the great efforts and devotion that are necessary to attain the highest levels of athletic performance. The characteristics of endurance, sacrifice, and commitment are what set Olympic competitors apart from the rest of the world. These stories serve as a monument to those characteristics.In conclusion, it is impossible to place enough emphasis on the significance of training and preparation for an athlete's trip to the Olympics. Workouts performed at home on Olympic Day, the presence of a competent sports coach, and mental conditioning are all important factors that contribute to the final result of an athlete's performance on the Olympic stage. Athletes' ability to perform well at the most difficult levels of competition is directly correlated to the degree of dedication, passion, and mental toughness they demonstrate during their preparation.In its most basic form, the Olympic Games continue to serve as a symbol of human potential and worldwide solidarity. They are able to transcend both time and culture in order to encourage future generations to achieve greatness, accept difference, and work toward achieving global harmony through the celebration of sport.

The Olympic Games serve as a living monument to both the adaptation and development of human civilization, since they continue to develop over time. The Olympic Games are continually updated to reflect the changing times by adding new competitions and making other organizational improvements. The dynamic nature of the Olympic Movement, which is continually looking ahead and evaluating new options, is exemplified by the recent consideration of flag football for the 2028 Olympics in Los Angeles and the abandoning of Sapporo's candidacy for the 2030 games. Both of these developments occurred quite recently.E ven the strongest and most determined athletes are not immune to life's hardships; the struggles and tribulations endured by Olympians, such as Mary Lou Retton's battle with pneumonia, serve as a reminder of this fact. However, by highlighting the remarkable power of the human spirit to persevere in the face of hardship, these tales of overcoming adversity give readers reason to hope.In conclusion, the Olympic Games continue to serve as a tremendous platform that bridges the gap between different nations, cultures, and different types of people. Athletes from many walks of life come together to compete in the Games; what brings them together is a passion for athletics and the drive to be the best they can be. Friendship, respect, and excellence are three core values that are championed by the Olympic Movement. These values may serve as guiding principles for a world that is consistently working toward greater harmony and compreh ension.The Olympic Games will definitely continue to develop in the years to come, rising to meet new challenges and seizing new opportunities, but never straying from its fundamental goals of advancing world peace, fostering inclusiveness, and showcasing the power of sport to bring people together. via the unifying power of sport, the Olympic Games will leave a lasting legacy that will encourage future generations to pursue their goals, overcome obstacles, and create a better world via the universal language of sport.

Milton Keynes UK
Ingram Content Group UK Ltd.
UKHW020905201123
432908UK00020B/3116

THE BOURNONVILLE SCHOOL

THE BOURNONVILLE SCHOOL

THE DAILY CLASSES

THE DAILY CLASSES

Technique, Exercises, Combinations

Text by Kirsten Ralov
Foreword by Walter Terry

Edited by Sandra Caverly

NOVERRE PRESS

First published in 1979 by Dance Books Ltd

This facsimile reprint published in 2012 by
The Noverre Press
Southwold House
Isington Road
Binsted
Hampshire
GU34 4PH

ISBN 978-1-906830-53-3

**To the memory of Valborg Borchsenius and Karl Merrild
in gratitude for what they taught me
about Bournonville choreography**

Acknowledgments

This work was made possible by generous grants from:

Her Majesty Queen Margrethe and Prins Henrik's foundation
The Danish Ministry of Culture
Consul Georg Jork's foundation
The Carlsberg Foundation
The Danish National Bank Foundation
The Doll Foundation
S. A. Eibeschütz Foundation
Herman Isacs III
The Pittsburgh Ballet Theatre
The Association of American Dance Companies

Foreword

Kirsten Ralov, together with her husband and frequent partner, Fredbjørn Bjørnsson, soared toward the audience with open arms in that exuberant Danish leap which I always think of as an *embrace-in-air*. The site was the very old (1766) Court Theater in Christiansborg Castle in Copenhagen, the dance was the Pas de Deux from August Bournonville's *Flower Festival in Genzano* (the most frequently performed Danish duet in the entire world), and the occasion was the farewell performance by Kirsten Ralov who, at forty, had danced with the Royal Danish Ballet for thirty-three years!

During those years, Kirsten, trained in the Bournonville school, became one of the foremost Bournonville-style dancers of her era. She entered the Ballet School of the Royal Theater the last year that musical accompaniments were provided by violin instead of piano and the lilt and legato of a stringed, rather than a percussive, musical instrument remained with her throughout her career. Her favorite teacher, Valborg Borchsenius, became the pupil and subsequent partner of Hans Beck, who had been an ardent student of the master choreographer himself. Beck was present when Kirsten graduated from the Royal School into the Royal Ballet and, having seen her dance a Bournonville piece for her graduating exercise, predicted a great future for her as an exponent of Bournonville. She has made his prediction come true.

As Beck himself sought to preserve the legacy of Bournonville's ballet masterpieces—of Bournonville's output of close to 150 ballets, he succeeded in passing 15 of them on to a later generation—and of the Bournonville technique, style, and movement qualities through training methods in the classroom, so Kirsten Ralov today has dedicated her career to a spirited but almost scientific preservation and exposition of the unique art of August Bournonville. Somewhere in her text she will define in her own words that exuberant leap which she mastered at the Royal School when she was a child and which marked her farewell at the Royal Court Theater, transformed from a theater museum back to a performing stage in her honor for her farewell. She will describe the leap in technical terms: grand jeté en attitude (with arms à la seconde). But most of us realize that it is truly a Danish dance embrace for all the dancers in the world. This is Kirsten Ralov's salute to her great Bournonville ballet heritage; her ballet gift to us.

Walter Terry

Introduction

The idea of publishing a book telling about August Bournonville and his technique is not new. Actually we already have just such a book in published form, the book by Lillian Moore and Erik Bruhn: *Bournonville and Ballet Technique*. This is a book which gives a very good introduction to Bournonville, his technique and style. But my idea is to go further. My experience teaching Bournonville for the last fifteen years and dancing many of his ballets during my extensive career as a dancer has convinced me that Bournonville's technique and choreography are indeed unique, but that an in-depth exposition of how to "teach" Bournonville has been missing. This book endeavors to provide that necessary service.

Since the Royal Danish Ballet started to tour, and foreign reporters visited Copenhagen, there has been a great interest in Bournonville's repertory of great ballets. During the last twenty years Bournonville ballets and divertissements have been staged in most parts of the world. In order to become familiar with his choreography it is essential to take lessons in his special style, and for that reason teachers who really know Bournonville's technique have been in great demand by many companies and schools.

With reference to his technique and style, I feel that there has been a lack of understanding, especially of his style. I have seen productions and classes being taught and danced with mannerisms, because the teacher or the dancer had the feeling that they should try to make it look "authentic—old-fashioned." That is a great, *fundamental mistake*. Bournonville writes in his book that he does not accept affectations and mannerisms and he will not permit steps to be danced for special "circus-effect." We have seen old paintings of ballerinas depicting very bent arms; we forget they were painted by artists who wanted the ballerinas to look feminine, charming, and picturesque. Bournonville stands for natural movements. He wants male dancers to look like males and the females to look feminine. You do not look feminine just because you are dancing with spread fingers and bent elbows.

Bournonville is not different because of any kind of old-fashioned or "stylish" look, but because his steps are choreographed in a different way. He knew what was necessary to build the technique and physique, so he choreographed long enchaînements with musical phrasing which allowed the steps to be more interesting. He never composed a variation in class or on stage where the dancer would merely walk or run from one corner to another (in order to prepare the next phrase). He made the dancer dance at all times, even with the back to the audience. All Bournonville's variations are built on classical steps: changement, assemblé, jeté, etc. He did have favorite steps which are not so common elsewhere, but you will find them in Cecchetti or the French or Russian schools.

The Bournonville school, as it exists today, is a collection of steps Bournonville taught when he was Maître de Ballet. His successors realized how important these enchaînements were and selected some of the steps, arranged music to fit, and made a class-program for each weekday built in the same way as Bournonville had himself done: adagio, tendu, pirouettes, allegro, jumps, etc. The collection we have today has been taught from one generation to the next, and I was lucky enough to be taught by a former ballerina† who was actually a pupil of a pupil of Bournonville himself. Many of my colleagues as well as I have mastered all these variations; thus it gives me the urgent desire to make sure that the authentic classes are preserved for the future, as indeed this is a school of great importance to the world. We must agree that the Royal Danish Ballet itself over the last twenty years has been influenced by other teachers and choreographers, which is, of course, necessary to keep ballet alive and in strong competition with other companies. As countries, cities, and habits all over the world are getting more alike, so it happens in the arts. The Danes want to deal with modern, Russian, Spanish, and other styles, and other countries in turn like to share in our tradition.

The Bournonville program is difficult and it is essential to master the phrasing in order to do it well. That is yet another reason for working out a system enabling the dancer to learn it. So far no teacher of Bournonville has done just that. In Denmark we have an international ballet-seminar where teachers (I have been teaching there for many years, too) give classes for three weeks in some of the classwork from the repertory that we use in the Royal Danish Ballet. The dancers and teachers who have participated are very interested in absorbing as many enchaînements as possible, and the more experienced dancers are actually able to dance the variations. But the teachers who want to notate the variations in order to teach them later on in the United States or elsewhere might get into difficulties with their students. You must build up to the variations through a system leading from basic Bournonville into the more complicated enchaînements. For that purpose I have recommended a number of enchaînements as preparatory exercises (see page 9).

My advice to teachers and dancers who want to deal with Bournonville is that they start with basic steps for beginners, as one does in Cecchetti, Vaganova, or other systems (or a mixture of several). It is essential that all classical foundation in ballet be alike, i. e., the positions, the placement, etc. I am not dealing further with this matter, as it is well known fundamentally to be the most important. When the student knows the placement and moves with ease, the teacher might begin with the short enchaînements I have selected out of the Bournonville classes. When the student is familiar with the phrasing and the variations, that are so specially Bournonville, the instructor might begin to teach the Bournonville classes. I recommend that Monday's Class, being the least complicated, be the logical starting point.

Kirsten Ralov

†Valborg Borchsenius, 1872-1949.

Contents

CONTENTS

CONTENTS

Friday's Class

Saturday's Class

Illustrations

THE BOURNONVILLE SCHOOL

INTRODUCTORY MATERIAL

Ballet Terminology

While traveling around the world it becomes evident that teachers in different companies and schools use a variety of ballet terms to express the same movement. This poses no problem as long as the teacher is present and can explain what he means. However, faced with the task of writing the step, it is important that the terminology chosen can be easily, accurately, and widely understood. Fortunately, this dilemma does not occur in Parts 3 and 4 (Benesh Notation and Labanotation, respectively), where the movement will be perfectly clear.

To ensure that the terms will be understood, I shall offer explanations of certain movements and positions. Simple terms such as assemblé, jeté, changement, rond de jambe, etc. are universally recognized. However, the term *changement battu* is used here instead of *entrechat royale*, and *assemblé battu* instead of *brisé fermé*. When teaching inexperienced students, one can substitute simple changements and assemblés, adding the beat as they become more advanced. The combination will remain the same.

The term *coupé* is distinguished from *posé* in the following way: Coupé refers to the change of weight, under or over sur place, whereas posé means stepping outwards in a specified direction.

e.g., standing on the right with left attitude derrière, then *the left steps under* will read "left coupé dessous."

e.g., standing in 5th with right devant, then *the right steps forward* will read "right posé en avant."

Chassé should be executed as a step followed by a closing, e.g., step right, close left.

The following are further descriptions of frequently executed Bournonville steps, written in the text in simplified form:

Chassé Contretemps

The Bournonville contretemps has a unique quality and is executed differently from the contretemps we use in other styles and methods.

Stand on the right with left tendu derrière, left coupé dessous, right posé en avant, and jump while simultaneously beating the left in 5th behind and then immediately passing left forward into croisé devant, transferring weight onto the left.

The entire "look" of the step must be light—not high, but travelling and finishing in 4th croisé devant on a demi-plié. After the beat in the air, it must not have the rebounding quality of a cabriole. This step is usually a preparation for glissade grand jeté or for another contretemps.

BALLET TERMINOLOGY

Coupé

Dessus (step over) transferring the weight by "cutting" the working foot in front.
Dessous (step under) transferring the weight by "cutting" the working foot behind.

Glissade Through 4th

This is a common movement often leading into jeté en attitude. It has the quality of a running step.
e.g., starting with weight on left, right derrière
and right posé en avant
one left passes through to 4th position devant
and right brushes forward
two land from grand jeté en avant with left in attitude derrière.

Grand Port de Bras as preparation for pirouette en dedans

4th position croisé on the right with slightly bent knee, left derrière with heel lowered, left arm in 4th en haut. Arms pass through 5th en avant, left opens to 2nd while right rises to a slightly curved position in front of the face, head looking over shoulder on right side of right arm. The right arm then lowers to the rounded position in front of the chest, i.e., 4th en avant, in preparation for pirouette.

Jeté

When this term is used by itself, it implies jeté with a brush.

Petit Jeté

A small jeté without a brush.

Jeté en Tournant generally named *Saut de Basque*

e.g., right posé de côté and while making a half-turn right, brush left à la seconde; jump and land on left with right retiré devant while completing another half-turn en l'air to the right.

Pas de Bourrée Couru

A running step in 1st position when travelling forward or backward, in 5th position when travelling sideways.

Pas de Valse

This consists of three movements in the count of 1 "one-and-two," e.g., after landing from jeté dessus on the left, coupé dessous onto right extending left devant, slightly step onto left keeping it extended—weight remaining on right, step again onto right.

Piqué

Used as a term to mean stepping onto demi-pointe or pointe into a position, e.g., attitude.

BALLET TERMINOLOGY

Porté (carried)

Refers to an allegro movement which travels, e.g., assemblé porté. Another term with the same meaning is *élancé*.

Posé

A step in any direction.

Posé Chassé

Used when the posé should have a quality of sliding the working foot before transferring the weight.

Renversé

Used in this text to mean a pirouette en dedans with the preparation of the working leg being a movement outwards before coming in to the knee. (N.B. When the text states "pirouette en dedans," the working foot moves directly to retiré.)

Retiré

Generally at knee level, otherwise indicated, e.g., petit retiré.

Sissonne Simple

Also known as sissonne retombée

Sur le Cou-de-Pied

This position occurs continuously in the Bournonville enchaînements. The working foot touches the supporting leg below the calf with the heel at the side and the toe behind. It is not a "wrapped foot" as the arch is fully stretched and the heel is at the side instead of the front.

Author's Notes

When I was a child studying in the Bournonville classes, we were taught to place the working foot sur le cou-de-pied in all pirouettes except renversé, which was at knee level in front. The arms were always placed in 1st during the turn. In the text, for easy reading I have omitted instructions of how to place the foot and arms. However, to remain aware of the original Bournonville training, it is very important for one to remember this placement of the limbs.

For pirouettes I have not analyzed the arm movement. Bournonville does require a very special style. The preparation is from 4th en avant, and the arms are placed in low 5th or 1st while turning.

In the Bournonville style, when arms open from 5th en haut through 2nd to bras bas, the palms do not turn to face down before reaching 2nd position. The turning of the hand is very smooth and does not disturb the flow of movement.

Fixed Points of the Classroom or Stage

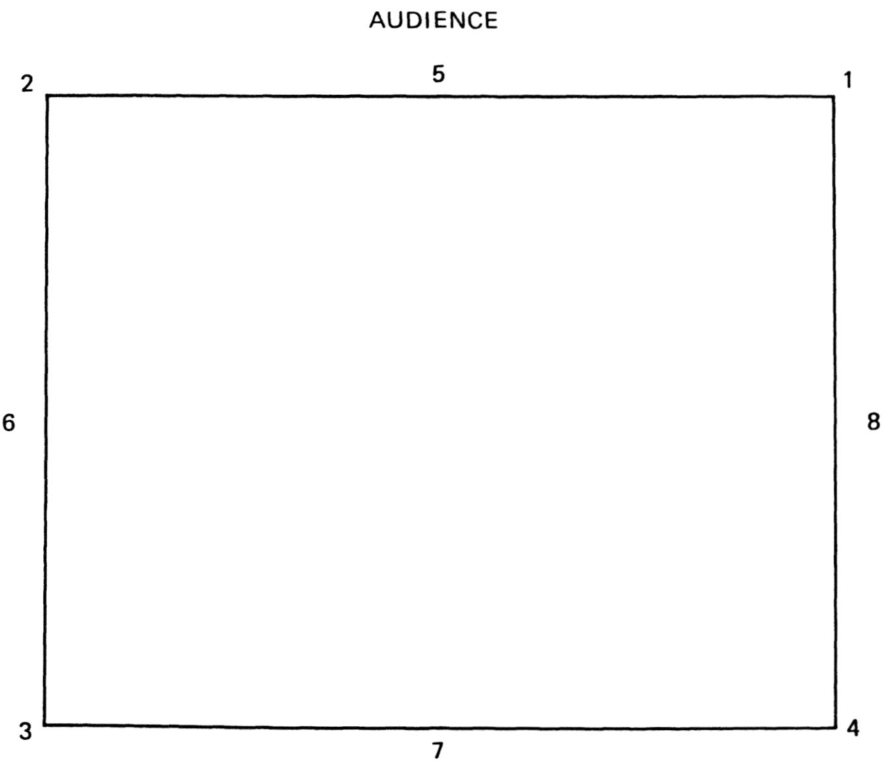

Arm Positions

drawings by Henrik Bloch

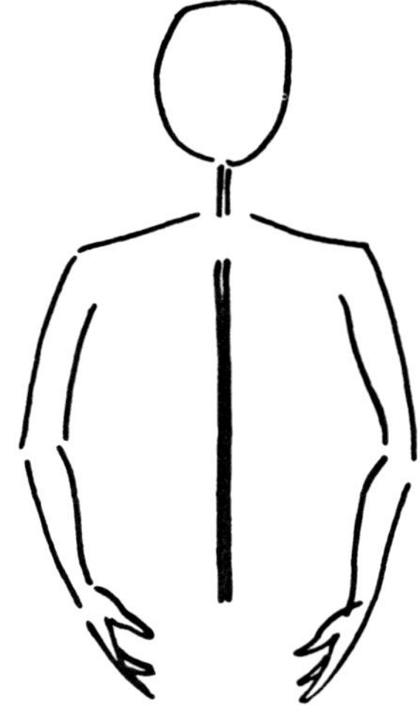

Bras bas

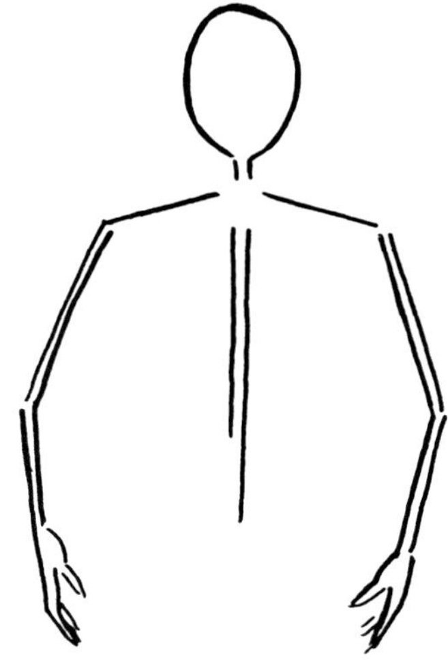

First position

Demi-seconde

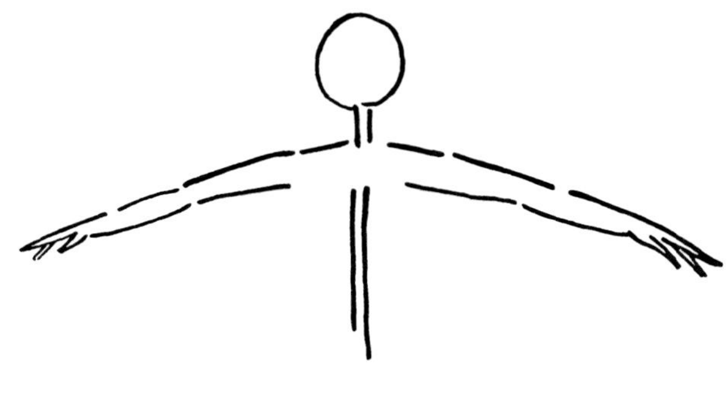

Second position

Fifth position en avant

Fifth position en haut

Fourth position en avant
(third position is like fourth position lowered)

Fourth position en haut

Fourth position crossed
(à la lyre)

First arabesque

Third arabesque

Adorés

Enchaînements Recommended as Preparatory Exercises

The following is a list of enchaînements or parts of enchaînements which are recommended as preparatory steps leading eventually to more difficult and complicated variations.

		Bars
Adagio	Monday No. 1	1-24
	Saturday No. 3	1-32
Port de Bras	Monday No. 2	1-32
	Wednesday No. 2	1-32
Grand Port de Bras (with Pirouette)	Friday No. 3	1-16
Tendu	Monday No. 4	1-16
	Thursday No. 5	1-32
	Friday No. 9	1-16
	Saturday No. 4	1-16
Relevé with Tendu	Tuesday No. 4	1-16
Petits Sauts and Allegro		
Échappé Sauté with Pirouette	Monday No. 5	1-8
Ballonné	Monday No. 7	1-8
Glissades	Monday No. 7	9-16
Travelling Jeté with Hold	Monday No. 9	1-32
Brisé Volé	Monday No. 17	1-16
Changement Enchaînement	Monday No. 18	9-16
Petits Sauts	Monday No. 18	1-8
Changement	Tuesday No. 8	1-16
Tendu with Pirouette	Tuesday No. 9	1-16
Jeté Enchaînement	Tuesday No. 16	1-16
Batterie	Wednesday No. 11	1-16
Grand Pirouette	Wednesday No. 10	1-16
Petits Sauts	Friday No. 11	1-16
Pirouette Enchaînement	Saturday No. 5	1-16

RECOMMENDED ENCHAÎNEMENTS

		Bars
Echappé Sauté with Pirouette	Saturday No. 6	1-32
Ballonné	Saturday No. 9	1-32
Pointe Enchaînement	Wednesday No. 15	1-24
	Saturday No. 12	1-32
Grand Allegro		
Chassé Grand Jeté en Tournant	Monday No. 15	1-16
Sissonne Fermée	Monday No. 15	17-24
Grand Changement	Tuesday No. 6	1-8
Grand Plié with Changement	Tuesday No. 7	1-16
Sauté en Attitude	Wednesday No. 13	1-16
Heavy Échappé	Saturday No. 7	1-16

Classification of the Enchaînements and Variations

Adagio	Monday Nos. 1 and 3 Tuesday Nos. 1 and 3 Wednesday Nos. 1 and 4 Thursday Nos. 1 and 3 Friday Nos. 1, 3, and 4 Saturday Nos. 1 and 3
Port de Bras	Monday No. 2 Tuesday No. 2 Wednesday No. 2
Pirouette	Monday Nos. 5 and 13 Tuesday Nos. 9 and 13 Wednesday Nos. 3 and 10 Thursday Nos. 6 and 7 Friday Nos. 5, 10, and 13 Saturday Nos. 5 and 6
Tendu	Monday No. 4 Tuesday No. 4 Wednesday No. 5 Thursday No. 5 Friday No. 9 Saturday No. 4
Posé Chassé, etc.	Tuesday Nos. 5 and 18 Wednesday Nos. 7 and 7a Thursday No. 4 Friday No. 8
Petit Sauts, Batterie, Brisé Volé, etc.	Monday Nos. 17 and 18 Tuesday Nos. 8, 11, 15, and 16 Wednesday Nos. 8 and 11 Friday Nos. 6 and 11 Friday No. 19a

CLASSIFICATION OF ENCHAÎNEMENTS AND VARIATIONS

Rond de Jambe Sauté	Monday Nos. 6 and 14 Wednesday No. 6 Thursday Nos. 8 and 9 Friday No. 18
Jeté Échappé, etc.	Monday No. 9 Tuesday Nos. 10 and 12 Thursday No. 10 Saturday Nos. 6 and 7
Ballonné, Ballotté, Temps de Flèche, Pas de Basque, etc.	Monday Nos. 7 and 11 Monday Nos. 20 and 21 Tuesday Nos. 6 and 7 Thursday Nos. 11 and 16 Friday No. 12 Saturday No. 9
Allegro Enchaînements	Tuesday No. 21 Wednesday No. 14 Saturday Nos. 8 and 10
Glissade and Chassé Grand Jeté, Chassé Contretemps, etc.	Monday Nos. 15 and 19 Monday Nos. 22 and 23 Tuesday Nos. 14, 17, 19, and 22 Wednesday Nos. 13 and 16 Thursday No. 21 Friday No. 16 Saturday Nos. 11 and 13 Saturday No. 14 and 23
Girls' Enchaînements	Monday Nos. 12 and 16 Wednesday Nos. 12, 17, 19, 20, and 22 Thursday Nos. 13, 15, 17, 18, and 20 Saturday Nos. 15, 18, 21, and 22
Boys' Enchaînements	Tuesday No. 24 Thursday Nos. 12, 14, and 22
Female Variations	Monday No. 25 Tuesday No. 23 Friday Nos. 7 and 12a Friday Nos. 15 and 17 Saturday Nos. 16 and 20

CLASSIFICATION OF ENCHAÎNEMENTS AND VARIATIONS

Male Variations	Monday No. 24 (*La Ventana*) Tuesday No. 21 (*La Sylphide*) Wednesday Nos. 18 and 21 Friday No. 14 (*Konservatoriet*) Saturday Nos. 17 and 19 (*Flower Festival in Genzano*)
Pointe	Monday No. 10 Wednesday No. 15 Saturday No. 12

"Enchaînements" are distinguished from "variations" as the first constitutes exercises for the classroom and the second, choreography suitable for the stage.

Only a few complete enchaînements are designated as "pointe work"; however, a bourée, piqué, or relevé found within the context of other sequences should be executed on pointe.

In Bournonville's choreography, pointe work was not the focus of attention; rather, movements on pointe were blended into variations to contribute to the overall quality.

Nicknames for the Enchaînements

The nicknames for the enchaînements appeared little by little in the classes: a dancer loved (or hated) a particular step, or a rhythm inspired a name. Saturday's last exercise was nicknamed "The Door Step" since you could step out of the classroom after dancing the variation!

Monday

No. 8	Aplomb	
No. 9	Hel Kineser	The Chinaman
No. 18	Syvtrin	Seven-Beat-Step
No. 19	Louise-Vals	(The name of the composition)
No. 22	Vinterstorm	The Winter Storm
No. 23	Det Tre-Delte	The Three-Part Step

Tuesday

No. 10	Pirouette i 3	Pirouette in 3 Beats
No. 11	Sjasketrin	The Scamped Step
No. 12	Rosamunde	Rosamunde
No. 16	Thychsen	(Named after a dancer)
No. 17	Det Spanske	The Spanish Step
No. 19	Korstrin	The Crossing Step

Wednesday

No. 11	Det Mørke	The Dark Step
No. 13	Den Store Vals	The Big Waltz
No. 17	Drejetrin	The Turning Step
No. 21	Il Bacio	Il Bacio (Italian for "The Kiss")
No. 22	Spøgetrin	The Joking Step

NICKNAMES FOR THE ENCHAÎNEMENTS

Thursday

No. 10	Halv Kineser	Half Chinaman
No. 16	1ste Ballontrin	1st Elevation Step
No. 16a	2det Ballontrin	2nd Elevation Step
No. 19	Charlotte Skovsgaard	(Name of a dancer)
No. 21	Det Store Bagvendte	The Big Wrong-Way Step

Friday

No. 5	Ved Vintertid	Wintertime

Saturday

No. 8	Sommertrin	Summer Step
No. 13	March-Solo	March-Solo
No. 14	2det Sommertrin	2nd Summer Step
No. 16	Japaneren	The Japanese Step
No. 17	Spansk Vals	The Spanish Waltz
No. 22	Det Store Spøgetrin	The Big Joking Step
No. 23	Dørtrinnet	The Door Step

MONDAY'S CLASS

Court Theater Museum, Copenhagen

No. 1 Adagio 4/4

Bar	Beat	Feet and Direction	Arms
Starting Position		5th right devant facing 2	bras bas
	4	left fondu with right tendu croisé devant	right 3rd
1	1-2-3	rond de jambe à terre en dehors with right into 4th position devant–demi-plié facing 1, left tendu effacé derrière looking towards 2	change directly across to left 3rd
	4	left through 1st and 5th derrière into	
2	1-2-3	4th position croisé derrière–demi-plié facing 2, right tendu croisé devant	change directly across to right 3rd
	4	right fermé 5th devant	
3	1-2	right rond de jambe à terre en dehors while turning towards 1	through 2nd to bras bas
	3-4	right fermé 5th derrière–demi-pointe changing into 5th devant when lowering heels	
4	1-2	left développé into attitude effacé derrière, looking to left	through 5th en avant to left 4th en haut
	3-4	extend en arrière and left fermé 5th devant	through 2nd to bras bas
	and	right fondu with left tendu croisé devant	left 3rd
5-7		repeat bars 1-3 to other side	
8	1-2	repeat bar 4, beats 1-2 to other side	
	3-4	right passé retiré and posé into 4th croisé devant with left tendu croisé derrière	through 2nd, bras bas and 5th en avant to left 4th en haut
	and	left fermé 5th derrière–demi-plié facing 5	left through 2nd
9	1-2	left posé chassé en arrière to 4th with right tendu devant	
	3-4	right fermé 5th devant	bras bas
10	1-2	right petit retiré devant on left relevé	
	3-4	lower left heel	
11		right développé devant and grand rond de jambe to 2nd	through 5th en avant to 2nd
12	1-2	turn left to face 6 in 1st arabesque	left 1st arabesque
	3-4		change through 5th en avant to 2nd arabesque
13-14		right to attitude derrière and promenade en dehors ending to face 1 (1-1/4 turns)	right directly to 4th en haut

No. 1 (continued)

Bar	Beat	Feet and Direction	Arms
15	1-2-3	right tombé croisé en arrière into 4th–demi-plié, left tendu devant bending backwards looking to 2	change through 5th en avant to left 4th en haut
	4	left fermé 5th devant–demi-plié	bras bas
16		left posé chassé en avant into 4th with right tendu croisé derrière	through 5th en avant to right 4th en haut
	and	right fermé 5th derrière–demi-plié facing 5	
17-24		repeat bars 9-16 to the other side, remaining facing 2 at the end of bar 24	
25	1-2-3	left posé de côté with right tendu à la seconde facing 2, incline body left and look down to left	through 2nd to right 4th en haut with left 4th en avant
	4	right fermé 5th devant–demi-plié	right through 5th en avant to bras bas
26	1-2	right rond de jambe à terre en dehors into 5th derrière–demi-pointe while turning to face 1	
	3-4	change to 5th right devant when lowering heels	
27	1-2-3	left développé into attitude derrière effacé	through 5th en avant to left 4th en haut
	4	right fondu with left sur le cou-de-pied	through 2nd to bras bas
28	1	right relevé with left développé croisé devant	through 5th to right 4th en haut
	2	right fondu with left sur le cou-de-pied	
	3-4	left posé croisé en avant into 4th with right tendu croisé derrière	
29-32		repeat bars 25-28 to other side	
33		left tendu croisé derrière bending body to the right,	left lowers directly to 4th en avant,
34	1-2-3	turn to the left so the left becomes tendu croisé devant	through en avant to right 4th en haut
	4	left fermé 5th devant	
35	1-2	left rond de jambe à terre en dehors into 5th derrière–demi-pointe facing 2	through 2nd to bras bas
	3-4	change to left 5th devant when lowering heels	

(continued)

No. 1 (continued)

Bar	Beat	Feet and Direction	Arms
36		right développé to attitude effacé derrière	through 5th en avant to 5th en haut
37		promenade en dedans	
38		finishing to face 5	
39		extend right en arrière, grand rond de jambe en dedans to croisé devant on left demi-plié, facing 2	through 5th en avant to 2nd 5th en avant
40	1-2	hold	
	3-4	right fermé 5th devant, left dégagé into attitude derrière	bras bas through 5th to left 4th en haut
41		left passé retiré into développé attitude effacé devant	change through 2nd to right 4th en haut
42		left rond de jambe en l'air en dehors through 2nd and retiré ending effacé devant	
43		promenade 1/4 to the right to face 1	
44	1-2-3	left passé retiré into attitude derrière	through 2nd–1st–5th to left 4th en haut
	4	left fermé 5th derrière	through 2nd to bras bas
	and	right failli into	1st
45		left piqué croisé en avant with right petits battements sur le cou-de-pied	
	3-4	right dégagé effacé devant into tendu and fermé 5th devant facing 2	bras bas
46		right développé to 2nd	through 5th to right 4th en haut
47	1-2	right rond de jambe en l'air en dehors	
	3-4	repeat beats 1-2	
48	1-2-3	right grand rond de jambe en dedans while turning towards 6 and développé through to 3rd arabesque	through 5th en avant to left 3rd arabesque
	4	right fermé 5th derrière facing 5	lower to bras bas
Coda			
49		left développé à la seconde	through 5th en avant to 2nd
50	1-2	right demi-plié	
	3-4	left fermé 5th derrière	bras bas
51		pas de bourrée couru sur les pointes in a semi-circle to the right	through 5th en avant to right 4th en haut

No. 1 (continued)

Bar	Beat	Feet and Direction	Arms
52	1-2	when facing 2, right posé croisé en avant into 4th with left tendu derrière	through 2nd, bras bas and 5th en avant to left 4th en haut
	3-4	left fermé 5th derrière	through 2nd to bras bas
Note Bar 51		boys walk in the semi-circle	right 4th en avant

No. 2 Port de Bras 3/4

	Feet and Direction	Arms
Starting Position	5th right devant facing 2	bras bas
Intro		
1	relevé	
2	demi-plié	
3	right posé croisé en avant into 4th with left tendu derrière	through 5th en avant to left 4th en haut
1-2	lower left heel and demi-plié on right circular port de bras—the body bends forward as left arm moves through 4th en avant, sideways to left and backwards as right arm moves to 4th en haut, sideways to right and straighten as left arm changes to 4th en haut	
3-4	repeat bars 1-2	
5-6	change right arm to 4th en haut and repeat rotation of the upper body to the other side	
7-8	repeat bars 5-6	
9-10	bring arms to 2nd and bend forward bringing arms to 5th en avant, straighten through the upright position and bend backwards with arms 5th en haut, straighten and open arms to 2nd	
11-12	repeat bars 9-10	
13-14-15	left dégagé to attitude croisé derrière, grand rond de jambe en dedans while turning to right to face 1, left leg extended devant	through 5th en avant to 2nd 5th en avant

(continued)

No. 2 (continued)

Bar	Beat	Feet and Direction	Arms
15	3	demi-plié on right with left sur le cou-de-pied	bras bas through 5th en avant
16		posé croisé en avant with right tendu derrière	to right 4th en haut
17-32		repeat bars 1-16 to other side	

No. 3 Adagio Andante 4/4

Starting Position		5th right devant facing 5	bras bas
1		grand plié	
2	1-2-3	pirouette en dehors, starting from full plié, finishing	
	4	right développé effacé devant–demi-hauteur facing 1	through 5th en avant to left 4th en haut
3	1-2	left fondu with right sur le cou-de-pied	through 2nd to bras bas
	3	right posé effacé en avant	through 5th en avant
	and	left fermé 5th derrière	
	4	right posé de côté	to
4		left posé through 5th devant into 4th croisé with right tendu derrière	right 4th en haut
5	1-2	left relevé with right attitude derrière	
	3-4	left fondu placing right 4th croisé derrière heels lowered, begin	
6		grand port de bras into:	
7		pirouette en attitude on left ending facing 5	5th en avant
8		extend right derrière grand rond de jambe en dedans into 2nd and fermé 5th derrière,	through 2nd to bras bas
9-16		repeat 1-8 to other side	
17		grand plié	
18	1-2	pirouette en dedans, starting from full plié, finishing with	
	3-4	left attitude effacé derrière facing 1	through 5th en avant to left 4th en haut
19	1-2	right fondu with left sur le cou-de-pied	through 2nd to bras bas

No. 3 (continued)

Bar	Beat	Feet and Direction	Arms
	3	left posé effacé en arrière	
	4	right fermé 5th devant	
	and	left posé de côté	
20		right through 1st into 4th croisé derrière	through 5th en avant to 4th right en haut
21	1-2	left relevé with right attitude derrière	
	3-4	left fondu placing right 4th croisé derrière, begin	
22		grand port de bras into:	
23		pirouette en attitude en dedans on left	5th en avant
24	1-2	lower heel in attitude derrière facing 2	right 4th en haut
	3	extend right	through 2nd to
	4	right fermé 5th derrière facing 5	bras bas
25-32		repeat 17-24 to other side	
33		grand plié	
34	1-2	pirouette en dehors, starting from full plié ending	
	3-4	right développé à la seconde (90°)	through 5th en avant to 5th en haut
35		promenade to the left with right retiré passé to effacé devant, facing 3 looking over the right shoulder	through 2nd bras bas and en avant to left 4th en haut
36		left relevé and turn 1/2 to the left so the right becomes attitude croisé derrière facing 1, looking to 2	change to right 4th en haut
37	1-2	left relevé in attitude	
	3-4	left fondu placing right 4th croisé derrière, begin	
38		grand port de bras into:	
39		pirouette en attitude en dedans on left ending:	5th en avant
40	1-2	1st arabesque facing 6	left 1st arabesque
	3-4	right fermé 5th derrière facing 5	bras bas
41-48		repeat 33-40 to other side	

(continued)

No. 3 (continued)

Bar	Beat	Feet and Direction	Arms
49		grand plié	
50	1-2	pirouette en dedans, starting from full plié, ending left	through 5th en avant
	3-4	développé à la seconde (90°)	to 5th en haut
51		promenade to the right with left retiré passé to développé devant facing 8	through 2nd and bras bas to 5th en avant
52		right relevé and turn to the right so the left becomes arabesque, facing 6	to right forward in 1st arabesque
53		left coupé dessous with right retiré, lower the left heel and place right 4th croisé derrière, begin	right 4th en haut
54		grand port de bras into:	
55	1-2-3	pirouette renversé en dedans on left	
	4	left fondu facing 5	
56	1-2	left relevé with right développé à la seconde	5th en haut through 2nd to
	3-4	right fermé 5th derrière	bras bas
57-64		repeat 49-56 to other side	

No. 4 Tendu Allegretto 2/4

Bar	Beat	Feet and Direction	Arms
Starting Position		5th right devant facing 5	bras bas
1	1	right tendu devant	
	and	left fondu with right sur le cou-de-pied	
	2	right tendu de côté	
2	1	right fermé 5th derrière	
	2	left jeté dessous	
3	1	right posé de côté	through 5th
	and	left fermé 5th derrière	en avant to
	2	right posé de côté	2nd
4	1	left coupé dessous	
	2	right assemblé dessous	bras bas
5-8		repeat 1-4 to other side	
9-16		reverse bars 1-8	

No. 4 (continued)

Bar	Beat	Feet and Direction	Arms
17	1	right posé de côté	
	2	left fermé 5th derrière–demi-plié	
18	1	left posé de côté	
	2	right fermé 5th devant–demi-plié	
19	1	right tendu devant	
	2	right jeté dessus	
20	and-1	left glissade en arrière	
	2	left assemblé dessus	
21-24		repeat bars 17-20 to other side	
25-32		reverse bars 17-24	

No. 5 Pirouette 2/4

Starting Position		5th right devant facing 5	bras bas
1	and-1	échappé sauté into 2nd	
	2	sauté fermé 5th right derrière	
	and	changement	
2		grand plié	
3		pirouette en dehors, start from plié	
4		right fermé 5th derrière	
5-8		repeat 1-4 to other side	
9	and-1	assemblé porté dessous–effacé en avant	
	2-and	2 changements	
10	1	temps levé onto right with left derrière	left 3rd
	2	extend left facing 1	
11		left piqué effacé en arrière into pirouette en dedans	5th en avant
12		right fermé 5th derrière facing 5	bras bas
13-16		repeat 9-12 to other side	
17	1	right posé chassé de côté	through 5th
	2	left fermé 5th derrière	en avant to
	and	right posé de côté	2nd

(continued)

No. 5 (continued)

Bar	Beat	Feet and Direction	Arms
18	1	place left in 4th devant	right 4th en avant
	2	demi-plié	
19		pirouette en dehors on left	
20		right fermé 5th derrière	bras bas
21-24		repeat 17-20 to other side	

No. 6 Rond de Jambe Sauté 6/8 (count 2)

Starting Position		5th right devant facing 5	bras bas
1	1-2	left fondu with right petit retiré devant	
2	and-1	rond de jambe sauté en l'air en dehors with	
	2	right assemblé dessous	
3	1	left développé à la seconde	through 5th en avant to 2nd
	2	left fermé 5th derrière	
	and	sissonne de côté onto right	
4	1	left coupé dessus	1st
	2	right jeté dessous	left 4th en avant
	and	extend left effacé facing 2	
5		into tombé and pirouette en dedans	
6	1	right fermé 5th derrière	bras bas
	2	échappé sauté into 2nd	left 4th en avant
7		pirouette en dehors on right	
8	1	left coupé dessous	
	2	right assemblé dessous	bras bas
9-16		repeat 1-8 to other side	

No. 7 Ballonné 6/8 (count 2)

Starting Position		5th right devant facing 5	bras bas
1	and-1	right ballonné dessous	
	2	hold	

No. 7 (continued)

Bar	**Beat**	**Feet and Direction**	**Arms**
2	and-1	right ballonné dessus	
	2	hold	
3	1	right posé en avant	through 5th en avant
	2	left fermé 5th derrière	to 5th en haut
4	1	assemblé right dessous	through 2nd to bras bas
	2	hold	
5-8		repeat 1-4 to other side	
9	and-1	right glissade de côté left fermé devant	left 3rd
	2	hold	
10	and-1	right glissade de côté left fermé derrière	right 3rd
	2	hold	
11	and-1	right glissade de côté left fermé devant	1st
	2	right jeté dessus	
12	1	left assemblé dessus	bras bas
	2	hold	
13-16		repeat 9-12 to other side	
17-24		reverse bars 1-8	

No. 8 Grand Rond de Jambe 4/4 March

Starting Position		5th right devant facing 5	bras bas
1	1	left fondu with right tendu devant	through 5th to 2nd
	2-3-4	hold	
2	1	right dégagé devant, demi-hauteur	left to 4th en haut
	2-3-4	hold	
3	1	right to 2nd	2nd
	2-3-4	hold	
4	1	right extends derrière	right 4th en haut
	2-3-4	hold	
5	1	right to 2nd	2nd
	2-3-4	hold	

(continued)

No. 8 (continued)

Bar	Beat	Feet and Direction	Arms
6	1-2	right extends devant	left 4th en haut
	3-4	right fermé 5th devant	through 2nd
7	1-2	relevé	to 1st
	3-4	demi-plié	
8	1-2	changement	
	3-4	hold	
9-16		repeat to other side	
17-32		reverse	

No. 9 Travelling Jeté with Hold 6/8 (count 2)

The following step has been called "The Chinese Step" because we were taught to have pointed fingers in front of shoulders with bent elbows. This was good for practice, but the arms can move in the manner indicated here.

Starting Position		5th right devant facing 1	bras bas
1	and-1	right jeté en avant landing in demi-plié with left sur le cou-de-pied	left 3rd
	2	hold	
2		hold	
3		hold	
4		hold	
5	and-1	left jeté en arrière landing in demi-plié with right sur le cou-de-pied, facing 2	right 3rd
	2	hold	
6		hold	
7		hold	
8		hold	
9	and-1	right jeté en avant landing demi-plié with left sur le cou-de-pied, facing 1	left 3rd
	2	hold	
10		hold	
11		as bar 5	
12		hold	
13		as bar 1	
14		as bar 5	

No. 9 (continued)

Bar	Beat	Feet and Direction	Arms
15	and-1	right jeté en avant	1st
	and-2	left jeté en arrière	
16	and-1	right jeté en avant	
	and-2	left ballonné dessus turning 1/4 left to face 2	demi-2nd bras bas
17-32		repeat 1-16 to other side	

No. 10 Girls' Pointe Enchaînement Allegretto 2/4

Bar	Beat	Feet and Direction	Arms
Starting Position		5th right devant facing 2	bras bas
Intro	1	relevé	
	2	demi-plié	
	1	right posé croisé en avant into 4th with left tendu derrière looking to the right	through 5th en avant to left 4th en haut
	2-and	left chassé de côté	2nd
1	1	left piqué de côté with right dégagé à la seconde	
	2	right posé de côté	1st
2	1	left piqué croisé en avant into attitude facing 1	through 5th to right 4th en haut
	2-and	right chassé de côté	2nd
3		repeat 1 to other side	
4	1	right piqué croisé en avant into attitude	through 5th to left 4th en haut
	2-and	left pas de bourrée to:	left through
5		4th position, demi-plié facing 3	2nd to right 4th en avant
6	1	relevé turning to right to 4th right devant facing 1	left 4th en avant
	2	turn left to 4th left devant, demi-plié facing 3	right 4th en avant
7	1	left relevé with right développé devant facing 1	through 5th to left 4th en haut
	2	right coupé dessus	

(continued)

No. 10 (continued)

Bar	Beat	Feet and Direction	Arms
8	1	left assemblé battu dessus	bras bas
	2-and	right chassé de côté	2nd
9-16		repeat 1-8 to other side, but hold beat 2 of bar 8 and remain facing 5	
17	1	entrechat quatre	
	2	left piqué effacé en arrière with right petits battements sur le cou-de-pied ending	right 3rd
18	1	dégagé effacé devant	through 2nd
	2	right fermé 5th derrière in demi-plié	to bras bas
19		repeat bar 18 to other side	
20	1	left dégagé effacé devant	left 3rd
	2	right fondu with left retiré derrière	bras bas
21	1	left coupé dessous	right 3rd
	2	temps levé on left with right petits battements sur le cou-de-pied (dessous-dessus) travelling effacé en arrière	
22	1	repeat bar 21 beat 2	
	2	repeat once more	
23	1	left relevé with right développé à la seconde facing 2	through 5th to right 4th en haut
	2	right coupé dessous, left posé de côté (pas de bourrée)	2nd
24	1	right posé into 4th devant, left tendu derrière facing 2	right 4th en avant
	2	right fondu with left petit retiré derrière	
25	1	left coupé dessous	
	2	right glissade en avant facing 1	5th en avant
26	1	right piqué en attitude, left derrière	left 4th en haut
	2	right fondu	2nd
27		repeat bar 25	
28	1	right piqué into 1st arabesque	1st arabesque
	2	right fondu	
29	1	left coupé dessous with right petit développé effacé devant	left 3rd
	2	right jeté dessus	
30	1-2	left tombé effacé en arrière into pirouette en dedans	
	and	left fondu facing 5	bras bas

No. 10 (continued)

Bar	Beat	Feet and Direction	Arms
31		left relevé with right développé à la seconde	through 5th to 5th en haut
32		right fermé 5th derrière	bras bas

No. 11 Ballotté 6/8

Starting Position		5th right devant facing 1	bras bas
	5-6	left fondu with right développé devant	through 5th to 2nd
1	1-2-3	right jeté dessus with left développé derrière (ballotté)	
	4-5-6	right temps levé with left développé croisé devant	
2	1-2-3	right temps levé with left développé effacé derrière	low 5th en avant
	4-5-6	temps de flèche landing left with right attitude derrière	through 2nd to right 4th en haut
3	1-2-3	right ballonné dessus landing facing 3	1st
	4-5-6	right ballonné dessous landing facing 1	
4	1-2-3	right glissade en arrière facing 5	
	4	right jeté dessous facing 2	bras bas
5-16		repeat on alternating sides	

No. 12 Girls' Enchaînement 2/4

Starting Position		on the left with right tendu derrière facing 1	bras bas
	and	pas couru en avant	
1	1	right dégagé devant à terre on left demi-plié	through 5th to left 4th en haut
	2	left temps levé with right petit retiré derrière	1st
	and	pas couru en avant	

(continued)

No. 12 (continued)

Bar	**Beat**	**Feet and Direction**	**Arms**
2	1	right dégagé devant à terre on left demi-plié	through 5th to left 4th en haut
	2	right jeté dessus	1st
3	1	left coupé dessous facing 5	
	2	right pas de basque ending left 5th devant	
4	1	entrechat quatre	bras bas
	2	entrechat trois onto right, left derrière	
	and	pas couru en avant facing 2	
5-8		repeat 1-4 to other side	
	and	pas de bourrée couru en	
9	1	arrière into 4th position right derrière, demi-plié facing 5	
	2	entrechat trois onto left with right derrière	
	and	pas de bourrée couru en arrière into	
10	1	4th position right derrière	
	2	entrechat trois onto right with left derrière	
11	1-2	repeat bar 3	
12	1-2	repeat bar 4	
13-16		repeat 9-12 to other side	

No. 13 Pirouette 3/4

Starting Position		5th right devant facing 5 standing close to corner 1	left 4th en avant
1		pirouette en dehors on right (towards front foot)	
2	1-2	end pirouette demi-pointe with left développé à la seconde	through 5th en avant to 2nd
	3	right fondu with left petit retiré derrière facing 1	left 3rd
3		left piqué effacé en arrière into pirouette en dedans ending:	5th en avant
4	1-2	left demi-pointe with right développé 2nd	5th en haut
	3	right coupé dessous	
5		left chassé contretemps facing 2	through 2nd

No. 13 (continued)

Bar	**Beat**	**Feet and Direction**	**Arms**
6	1-2	ending right 4th devant	to right 4th en avant
	3	left glissade éffacé	5th en avant
7		en arrière facing 1	
8		left assemblé battu dessus facing 5	bras bas
9-32		repeat on alternating sides	

No. 14 Rond de Jambe Sauté 3/4

Starting Position		5th right devant facing 1	bras bas
	2-3	rond de jambe sauté en dehors with right	
1		landing left with right extended devant	
2		right jeté dessus	5th en avant
	3	begin	
3		left glissade en arrière, cabriole into	
4	1-2	1st arabesque on right	right 1st arabesque
	3	left coupé dessous	
5		right chassé contretemps landing	left through bras bas to
6	1-2	left 4th devant	4th en avant
	3	begin	
7		right glissade de côté with left dessous facing 5	2nd
8	1	right jeté dessous facing 2	bras bas
9-31		repeat 1-7 on alternating sides	
32		left assemblé dessous facing 5	bras bas
Polonaise			
1	1	entrechat cinq onto right with left petit retiré derrière	
	2	left glissade en arrière	
	3	left jeté dessous	right 4th en avant
2	1	right posé de côté	2nd
	2	left jeté en tournant dessous	right 3rd
	3	right assemblé dessous	bras bas

(continued)

No. 14 (continued)

Bar	Beat	Feet and Direction	Arms
3-8		repeat alternating sides	

No. 15 Grand Jeté en Tournant 3/4

Bar	Beat	Feet and Direction	Arms
Starting Position		on right with left tendu derrière, facing 1	left 4th en avant
1			
2	2-3	left chassé en arrière	2nd
1		left posé en arrière	bras bas
2	1	grand jeté en tournant en attitude landing on right	through 5th en avant to 5th en haut
	2-3	pas couru into	2nd
3		4th left derrière,	
4		from 4th entrechat trois onto left with right derrière, facing 2	right 4th en avant
	2-3	left chassé en arrière	
5-15		repeat alternating sides	
16		from 4th changement battu ending right 5th devant	bras bas
change to 6/8			
17	1-2-3	right sissonne fermée en avant en attitude with left derrière	through 5th en avant to left 4th en haut
	4-5-6	changement battu to face 5	through 2nd to 1st
18-20		repeat alternating sides	
21	1-2-3	left sissonne fermée croisée en avant en attitude with right derrière facing 1	through 5th en avant to 5th en haut
	4-5-6	entrechat quatre facing 5	through 2nd to bras bas
22-24		repeat alternating sides	

No. 16 Girls' Enchaînement 3/4

Bar	Beat	Feet and Direction	Arms
Starting Position		on left with right tendu croisé derrière facing 1	1st
	2-3	right glissade en avant (posé right-left)	
1		right piqué effacé en avant with left extended derrière (demi-hauteur)	through 5th to 2nd
2		left into 4th position devant in demi-plié	right 4th en avant
3-4		slow pirouette en dehors on left	right 4th en haut
5		right glissade de côté with left fermé 5th devant	2nd
6		right glissade effacé en arrière into left 4th position derrière facing 2	bras bas
7		left relevé bringing right through 1st to 1st arabesque	through 5th en avant to 1st arabesque
8	1	right fermé 5th derrière, demi-plié	1st
	2-3	sissonne onto left with right effacé derrière	
9	1	right posé croisé en avant into 4th	through 5th en avant to right
	2-3	cabriole landing right in 2nd arabesque	2nd arabesque
10		pas de bourrée en avant (posé left-right)	1st
11		left dégagé à terre effacé devant	through 5th to right 4th en haut
12	1	left coupé dessus	through 2nd
	2-3	pas couru en arrière (right-left) to:	
13		4th position right derrière–demi-plié	1st
14	1	entrechat cinq onto left with right derrière	
	2-3	pas couru en arrière (right-left) to:	
15		4th position right derrière–demi-plié	
16	1	entrechat trois onto right with left derrière	
	2-3	left glissade en avant (posé left-right) facing 2	
17-32		repeat to other side	

No. 17 Brisé Volé 6/8

Bar	Beat	Feet and Direction	Arms
Starting Position		on right with left tendu devant, facing 1	1st
	and	posé left en avant	
1	1	brisé volé en avant landing right with left devant	
	2	hold	
2		hold	
3	1	brisé volé en arrière landing left with right derrière	
	2	hold	
4		hold	
5	1-2	as bar 1	
6	1-2	as bar 3	
7	1	as bar 1 (beat 1)	
	2	as bar 3 (beat 1)	
8	1	right glissade en arrière facing 5	
	2	jeté battu en arrière landing right with left derrière, facing 2	
9-16		repeat 1-8 to other side	

No. 18 Petits Sauts 2/4

Bar	Beat	Feet and Direction	Arms
Starting Position		5th right devant facing 1	bras bas
1	1	right posé en avant	through 5th
	2	left fermé 5th derrière	en avant
	and	temps levé on left with right devant	slowly to right 4th
2		repeat bar 1	en haut
3	1	right posé en avant	slowly
	and	left coupé dessous	through 2nd
	2	right ballonné dessous	
	and	right ballonné dessus	
4	1	right petit jeté dessous facing 5	demi-2nd
	and	left petit jeté dessous	
	2	right assemblé dessous facing 2	bras bas
5-8		repeat to other side, finish facing 5	

No. 18 (continued)

Bar	Beat	Feet and Direction	Arms
9	1-and-2	3 changements turning 1/2 to the right to face 7	slowly to 5th en haut
10	1-and-2	3 changements turning 1/2 to the right to face 5	slowly to 2nd
11	1	temps levé on left with right derrière	1st
	and	right coupé dessous with left dégagé à la seconde	
	2	left coupé dessous	
	and	right assemblé dessous (porté de côté)	bras bas
12	1	sissonne de côté onto right with left à la seconde, demi-hauteur	1st
	and	left coupé dessous	
	2	right assemblé dessous	bras bas
13-16		repeat 9-12 to other side	
17-24		reverse 1-8, but with the same arm movements	

No. 19 Grand Allegro 3/4

Starting Position		5th right devant facing 5	bras bas
Intro: 4 bars			
1	1	sissonne ouverte en attitude onto right with left derrière facing 1	left through 5th to 4th en haut
	2-3	left pas de bourrée couru in 5th derrière facing 5	2nd
2	1	left coupé dessous with right dégagé à la seconde	right 4th en avant
	2-3	right chassé de côté	
3		right posé de côté	2nd
4		left jeté en tournant dessous, facing 5	
5	1-2	right ballonné dessous facing 2	1st
	3		
6		right glissade en arrière	5th en avant
7		cabriole onto left in 1st arabesque	left 1st arabesque
8		right assemblé dessous	bras bas

(continued)

No. 19 (continued)

Bar	Beat	Feet and Direction	Arms
9-15		repeat 1-7 to other side	
16	1-2	left glissade en arrière	1st
	3	temps levé on right bringing left rond de jambe en dedans, demi-hauteur into:	demi-2nd
17	1	posé into 4th croisé devant	right 4th
	2-3	left temps levé with right rond de jambe en dedans to:	en avant
18	1	4th devant	left 4th en avant
	2-3	left pas de bourrée couru in 5th derrière	
19		left coupé dessous facing 5	1st
20		right ballonné battu finishing derrière facing 1	right 4th en avant
21		right glissade en arrière	5th en avant
22		grand jeté en attitude turning to right to face 2	5th en haut
23		left glissade croisé en arrière	through 2nd to
24		left jeté dessus	1st
25-30		repeat 17-22 to other side	
31		right glissade en avant facing 1	through 2nd, 1st, 5th to
32	1	right grand jeté en avant landing on right	left 2nd arabesque
	2-3	left chassé en arrière	through 5th en avant
33		left posé en arrière	
34	1-2	grand jeté en tournant landing right facing 1	5th en haut
	3	left coupé dessous	through 2nd, bras bas and 5th
35	1	right piqué effacé in 1st arabesque	to 1st arabesque
	2-3	hold	
36	1	hold	
	2-3	left chassé en arrière	5th en avant
37-39		repeat 33-35	
40	1	right fondu with left retiré derrière facing 5	lower slowly
	2-3	left pas de bourrée with left 5th derrière	to
41		left coupé dessous	
42		right ballonné dessous	
43		right assemblé dessous	bras bas

No. 19 (continued)

Bar	Beat	Feet and Direction	Arms
44	1-2	sissonne ouverte en attitude onto left facing 2	through 5th to right 4th en haut
	3	right coupé dessous	right through 2nd to 4th en avant
45		left chassé contretemps	
46	1-2	right into 4th devant	
	3	begin	
47		glissade en avant (left-right)	
48		grand jeté en avant landing arabesque on left	right 2nd arabesque
49-62		repeat 33-46 to other side	
63	1-2	glissade en avant (right-left)	
	3	right jeté en avant	bras bas
64	1	right relevé in attitude with left derrière	through 5th en avant to left 4th en haut
	2-3	hold	

No. 20 Allegro Enchaînement Allegretto 6/8 (count 2)

Girls' Version

Bar	Beat	Feet and Direction	Arms
Starting Position		5th right devant facing 5	bras bas
1	1	échappé sauté to 2nd	right 4th en avant
	and	left temps levé with right retiré devant turning right to face 7	5th en avant
	2	right coupé dessus	
2	1	temps de flèche (grand jeté en tournant) landing on left with right attitude derrière turning right to face 5	through 2nd to right 4th en haut
	and-2	right pas de bourrée dessous-dessus en tournant to face 1	through 5th en avant to bras bas
3	1	left glissade en arrière	5th en avant
	2	cabriole landing on right in 1st arabesque	right 1st arabesque
4	1	left glissade effacé en arrière	
	2	left jeté battu dessus to face 5	bras bas
5-16		repeat 1-4 alternating sides	

(continued)

No. 20 (continued)

Bar	Beat	Feet and Direction	Arms
Boys' Version			
Starting Position		5th right devant facing 5	bras bas
1		as for Girls	
2	1	temps de flèche (grand jeté en tournant) landing on left with right attitude derrière turning right to face 1	through 2nd to right 4th en haut
	and-2	glissade en avant (right-left)	through 5th en avant to
3	1	right grand jeté en avant en attitude with left derrière turning right to face 2	left 4th en haut
	2	left assemblé dessous facing 5	bras bas
4	1	right rond de jambe sauté en l'air en dehors	through 5th en avant to 2nd
	2	right ballonné dessous	bras bas
5-16		repeat alternating sides	

No. 21 Rond de Jambe Sauté and Pas de Basque 3/4

Bar	Beat	Feet and Direction	Arms
Starting Position		on left with right tendu devant facing 2	bras bas
1		right rond de jambe sauté en l'air en dehors	demi-2nd
2		right jeté dessus	right 4th en avant
3	1	left coupé dessous	
	2-3	right pas de basque finishing	
4		left 5th devant facing 5	bras bas
5		right temps levé with left derrière facing 1	
6		left glissade en arrière	5th en avant
7		temps de flèche landing left with right attitude derrière	right through 2nd to 4th en haut
8	1	right coupé dessous	
	2-3	left pas de basque to	1st
9		right 5th devant facing 5	
10		left temps levé with right derrière	
11		right coupé dessous with left développé à la seconde	through 5th en avant to 2nd
12		left into 2nd position demi-plié	left 4th en avant

No. 21 (continued)

Bar	Beat	Feet and Direction	Arms
13		pirouette en dehors on right ending:	
14		fondu with left dégagé croisé devant facing 1	right 4th en avant
15		left posé croisé en avant	
16		brisé onto right with left devant, demi-hauteur	bras bas
17-32		repeat 1-16 to other side	

No. 22 Grande Cabriole Fouettée Sautée 3/4

Bar	Beat	Feet and Direction	Arms
Starting Position		on right with left tendu devant facing 1	bras bas
1	1	left posé en avant	5th en avant
	2-3	right dégagé en avant into cabriole devant turning in the air (fouetté) to land:	
2	1-2	left in 1st arabesque facing 6	left 1st arabesque
	3	left temps levé	
3-4		repeat 1-2 to other side	
		repeat ad lib (temps levé on the 3rd beat can be omitted)	

No. 23 Jeté Enchaînement 3/4

Bar	Beat	Feet and Direction	Arms
Starting Position		5th right devant facing 1	bras bas
	2-3	left fondu with right développé devant	
1		right jeté en avant	5th en avant
2		right temps levé with left petit développé croisé devant	slowly to
3		left jeté croisé en avant	2nd
4		left temps levé with right petit développé effacé devant	
5	1-2	right jeté dessus	lower slowly to
	3	begin	

(continued)

No. 23 (continued)

Bar	Beat	Feet and Direction	Arms
6		left glissade en arrière	
7		left jeté dessus	bras bas
8		right petit jeté dessous facing 2	
9-16		repeat 1-8 to other side	
17		right posé de côté	demi-2nd
18	1-2	left jeté en tournant dessous to face 5	right 4th en avant
	3	begin	
19		right glissade en avant through 4th facing 1	5th en avant
20	1-2	right grand jeté en attitude facing 1	left 4th en haut
	3	begin	
21		left glissade en arrière	
22	1-2	left jeté dessus	bras bas
	3	begin	
23		right glissade en arrière facing 2	
24		right jeté dessous	
25-32		repeat 17-24 to other side	
33		right jeté en avant, fermé 5th left derrière facing 1	1st
34		left temps levé with right devant	
35		right jeté en avant, fermé 5th left derrière	
36		right temps levé with left derrière	
37	1	left coupé dessous	
	2-3	right pas de basque finishing	
38		left 5th devant	
39		entrechat cinq onto left with right derrière	
40		right petit jeté dessous to face 2	
41-48		repeat 33-40 to other side	

No. 24 Male Variation from *La Ventana* 6/8 (count 2)

Bar	Beat	Feet and Direction	Arms
Starting Position		on left with right tendu croisé derrière facing 1	bras bas
1	1	right jeté en attitude en avant	
	2	left jeté en attitude en avant	
2	1	right glissade en avant	through 5th
	2	right grand jeté en attitude en avant	en avant to left 4th en haut
3-8		repeat with alternating legs making a circle: 1st part towards 8, 2nd towards 2, 3rd towards 7 and last ending facing 5	2nd
9	1	right coupé dessous	
	2	left jeté dessus	bras bas
10	1	right assemblé battu dessus	
	2	hold	
11	1	right assemblé devant	
	2	entrechat six	
	and	temps levé onto right with left derrière facing 2	
12	1	left piqué croisé en arrière with right développé devant	through 5th en avant to right 4th en haut
	2	right tombé en avant	
13	1	left coupé dessous	2nd
	2	right ballonné dessous	demi-2nd
14	1	right petit jeté dessus	1st
	2	left assemblé dessous	
15	1	sissonne onto left with right beating behind landing with right attitude derrière facing 2	through 5th to right 4th en haut
	2	right assemblé battu dessus	bras bas
16	1	repeat bar 15, 1st beat	
	2	right jeté dessous with left petit développé effacé devant,	right 4th en avant
	and	left jeté dessus	
17	1	right chassé en arrière	1st
	2	right posé en avant facing 4	2nd
18	1	left jeté en tournant landing with right dégagé devant facing 2	left 4th en avant
	2	right assemblé dessus	bras bas

(continued)

No. 24 (continued)

Bar	Beat	Feet and Direction	Arms
19-22		repeat 15-18	
23	1	tour en l'air landing 5th left devant	
	2	temps levé onto left with right derrière	left 3rd
	and	pas de bourrée with 5th right derrière (right-left-right)	demi-2nd
24	1	left posé en avant facing 2 with right dégagé devant	left 4th en avant
	2	right ballonné dessous	1st
25	1	right petit jeté dessus facing 5	
	2	left petit jeté dessus	
	and	pas de bourrée to the left with right 5th derrière (right-left-right)	
26	1	repeat bar 24, 1st beat	
	2	left temps levé with right retiré passé into effacé derrière	change to right 2nd arabesque
	and	right chassé en arrière	2nd
27	1	right posé effacé en arrière	
	2	grand jeté en attitude en tournant landing on left facing 2	through 1st, 5th en avant to 5th en haut
	and	right chassé en arrière	2nd
28	1	right posé en arrière	through 5th
	2	grand jeté en tournant en attitude landing on left facing 2	en avant to 5th en haut
	and	right chassé en arrière	2nd
29	1-2	repeat bar 28 but land facing 5	
	and	right chassé en avant	
30	1	right posé en avant	demi-2nd
	2	temps levé on right with left attitude derrière	
31	1	left jeté dessus with right attitude derrière	1st
	2	right jeté dessus with left attitude derrière	
	and	pas de bourrée to right with left 5th derrière (left-right-left)	
32	1	right posé effacé en avant with left dégagé croisé devant facing 1	right 4th en avant
	2	left ballonné dessous	1st
33	1	left jeté dessus facing 5	
	2	right jeté dessus	
	and	left coupé dessous	2nd

No. 24 (continued)

Bar	Beat	Feet and Direction	Arms
34	1	right posé effacé en avant onto demi-plié with left dégagé croisé devant	right 4th en avant
	2	right relevé with left retiré passé into effacé derrière	left to 2nd arabesque
	and	left chassé en arrière	2nd
35	1	left posé en arrière	
	2	grand jeté en tournant en attitude landing right with left derrière facing 1	through 5th en avant to 5th en haut
36	1	left glissade en arrière	2nd
	2	left jeté dessous	bras bas
37		right tombé effacé en avant into pirouette renversé to face 5	
38		left fermé 5th devant	1st

No. 25 Female Variation–Mazurka 3/4

Starting Position			
Intro			
1-2		run forward	
3		right assemblé devant	demi-2nd
4	1-2	relevé 5th right devant	
	3	demi-plié	bras bas
1	1	right relevé élancé in 1st arabesque facing 1	right 1st arabesque
	2	hold	
	3	left fermé 5th derrière in demi-plié	bras bas
2	1	right relevé with left petit retiré derrière	left 4th en avant
	2	hold	
	3	left fermé 5th derrière in demi-plié	bras bas
3	1	right relevé with left retiré derrière	through 5th en avant to
	2-3	hold	5th en haut
4	1	left coupé dessous facing 5	2nd
	2	right assemblé dessous	bras bas
	3	temps levé onto right with left derrière facing 1	left 4th en avant

(continued)

No. 25 (continued)

Bar	Beat	Feet and Direction	Arms
5	1-2	left posé effacé en arrière with right tendu devant	5th en avant
	3	right coupé dessus	
6	1-2	left posé effacé en arrière with right tendu devant	left 4th en haut
	3	right fermé 5th devant	bras bas
7	1	left temps levé with right derrière facing 2	
	2	right posé en arrière with left tendu devant	5th en avant
	3	left coupé dessus	
8	1-2	right posé effacé en arrière with left tendu devant	right 4th en haut
	3	left fermé 5th devant	through 2nd to 1st
9-13		repeat 1-5 to other side	
14	1-2	right posé effacé en arrière with left tendu devant	right 4th en haut
	3	left tombé effacé en avant	2nd
15		right soutenu en dedans	
		ending 5th left devant	bras bas
16	1	changement	
	2	hold	
	3	left petit retiré derrière facing 2	
17	1	left coupé dessous	through 5th en avant
	2-3	2 petits sauts on left with right rond de jambe en dehors to 2nd–demi-hauteur	and 2nd
18		right piqué with left retiré devant facing 1	bras adorés
19	1	left tombé de côté	through 5th
	2-3	2 petits sauts on left with right rond de jambe en dedans	2nd to
20		right piqué croisé en avant facing 2	5th en haut
21	1-2	left coupé dessous	
	3	right assemblé dessus	2nd
22	1-2	relevé 5th facing 5	bras bas
	3	demi-plié	
23	1-2	échappé to 2nd sur les pointes	1st
	3	right fermé 5th devant	demi-2nd
24	1	changement	bras bas
	2	hold	
	3	right retiré derrière	

No. 25 (continued)

Bar	Beat	Feet and Direction	Arms
25-31		repeat 17-23 to other side	
32	1	changement	
	2-3	hold	
33	1	right dégagé à terre devant facing 1	right 4th en avant
	2	hold	
	3	petits battements sur le cou-de-pied with right	
34	1	right dégagé à terre devant bending slightly forward	
	2	hold	
	3	right coupé dessus with left dégagé effacé en arrière demi-hauteur, looking over left shoulder	change to left 4th en avant
35	1	left fermé 5th derrière	
	2	right glissade effacé en avant	1st
	3	right assemblé porté en avant facing 1	5th en avant
36	1	right relevé élancé in 1st arabesque	1st arabesque
	2	hold	
	3	left coupé dessous	bras bas
37	1	right posé en avant making 1/4 turn right to face 4	left 4th en avant
	2	left dégagé devant, demi-hauteur	right 4th en avant
	3	right fondu with left petit retiré derrière making 1/2 turn right to face 5	
38	1	left coupé dessous with right tendu devant	2nd
	2	hold	
	3	right fermé 5th devant—demi-plié	right 4th en avant
39		pirouette en dehors on left	
40		right fermé 5th derrière	bras bas
41-46		repeat 33-38 to other side	
47	1-2	pirouette en dehors on right	
	3	left fermé 5th derrière	bras bas
48		left tendu croisé derrière	demi-2nd

TUESDAY'S CLASS

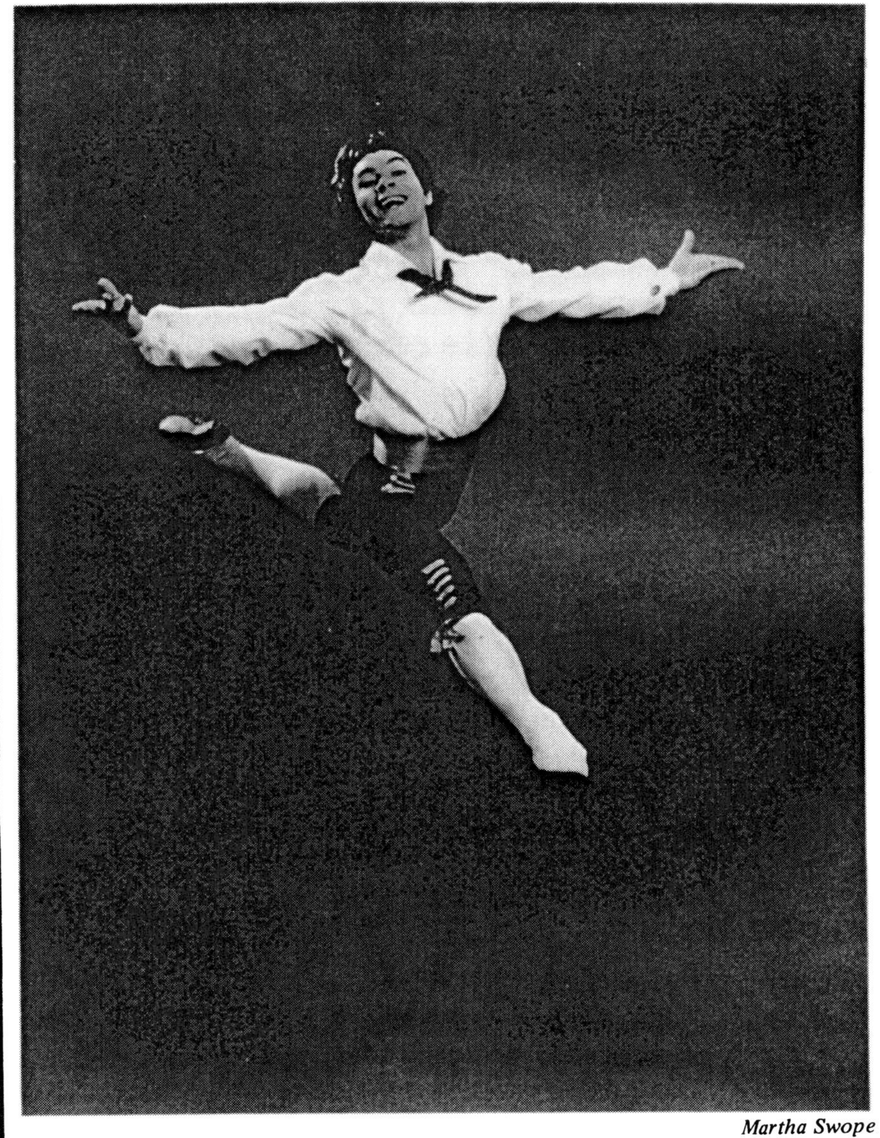

Martha Swope

TUESDAY'S CLASS

No. 1 Adagio 4/4

Bar	**Beat**	**Feet and Direction**	**Arms**
Starting Position		5th right devant facing 5	bras bas
1-2		grand plié and straighten	demi-2nd, bras bas
3-4		repeat	
5-6		right développé devant	5th en avant
7		right grand rond de jambe into 2nd	2nd
8		right fermé 5th derrière	bras bas
9-16		repeat 1-8 to other side	
17-32		reverse 1-16	
33		grand plié and straighten	
34		left développé into attitude derrière facing 1	through 5th to left 4th en haut
35	1-2-3	promenade en dedans	
	4	extend left derrière facing 5	5th en avant
36	1-2-3	left grand rond de jambe en dedans into 2nd	2nd
	4	left fermé 5th devant	bras bas
37-40		repeat 33-36 to other side	
41		grand plié and straighten	
42		left développé into attitude derrière facing 2	through 5th to left 4th en haut
43		promenade en dehors and when facing 8 leave the leg towards 6 but continue the	through 5th to
44	1-2-3	promenade to face 5 so the left becomes 2nd	2nd
	4	left fermé 5th devant	bras bas
45-48		repeat 41-44 to other side	
49		grand plié and straighten	
50		right développé devant facing 1	through 5th to left 4th en haut
51		promenade en dehors	
52	1-2-3	right opens to 2nd facing 5	slowly to 2nd
	4	right fermé 5th derrière	bras bas
53-56		repeat 49-52 to other side	

No. 1 (continued)

Bar	Beat	Feet and Direction	Arms
57		grand plié and straighten	
58		right développé croisé devant facing 2	through 5th to left 4th en haut
59		promenade 1/4 to the left to face 3, looking over right shoulder towards 2	
60	1-2	turn 1/2 to the left to face 1 so the right leg becomes attitude derrière	through 5th en avant to 5th en haut
	3	extend right derrière	through 2nd to
	4	right fermé 5th derrière	bras bas
61-64		repeat 57-60 to other side	

No. 2 Port de Bras

Starting Position	5th right devant facing 2	bras bas
Intro 1	relevé	
2	demi-plié	
3	right posé croisé en avant into 4th with left tendu derrière	through 5th en avant to left 4th en haut
1-2	lower the left heel and demi-plié right, circular port de bras—the body bends forward as left arm moves through 4th en avant, sideways to left and backwards as right arm moves to 4th en haut, sideways to right and straighten as left changes to 4th en haut	
3-8	repeat 1-2	
9-10	bring right arm to 4th en haut and make the rotation of the upper body to the other side	

(continued)

No. 2 (continued)

Bar	Beat	Feet and Direction	Arms
11-16 Extra 2 beats into:		repeat 9-10	
17-18		bring arms to 2nd and bend forward bringing arms to 5th en avant. Straighten through upright position and bend backwards with arms 5th en haut, straighten while opening arms to 2nd	
19-20		repeat 17-18	
21-22		left dégagé attitude croisé derrière and grand rond de jambe en dedans in 1/2 turn to the right, facing 1, left extended devant on right demi-plié	through 5th en avant to 2nd 5th en avant
23-24		left to sur le cou-de-pied and posé croisé en avant with right tendu derrière	right 4th en haut
25-48		repeat 1-24 to other side.	

No. 3 Adagio with Pirouette 4/4

Starting Position		5th right devant facing 5	bras bas
1		grand plié finishing down	left opens slightly
2	1-2-3	pirouette en dehors (start turn from plié) ending	throught 5th to
	4	right tendu effacé devant	left 4th en haut
3	1-2-3	right rond de jambe à terre into soutenu en dehors, face 5	through 2nd
	4	remain demi-pointe, 5th right devant	to bras bas
4	1-2-3	left dégagé derrière and rond de jambe en dedans–demi-hauteur into croisé devant	
	4	lower the right heel and place left tendu croisé devant facing 1	through demi-2nd to right 4th en haut
5	1-2	left fermé 5th devant, demi-pointe	
	3-4	right into 4th croisé derrière, heels lowered	
6		grand port de bras into:	

No. 3 (continued)

Bar	Beat	Feet and Direction	Arms
7		pirouette en attitude en dedans ending facing 2	5th en avant to right 4th en haut
8	1-2	lower left heel	
	3	extend right derrière	2nd
	4	right fermé 5th derrière facing 5	bras bas
9-16		repeat 1-8 to other side	
17		grand plié finishing down	left opens slightly
18	1-2-3	pirouette en dedans (from plié) ending	
	4	left tendu effacé derrière facing 1	through 5th to left 4th en haut
19	1-2-3	left rond de jambe à terre into soutenu en dedans facing 5	through 2nd to bras bas
	4	remain demi-pointe 5th right devant	
20	1-2-3	right dégagé devant and rond de jambe en dehors demi-hauteur into croisé derrière facing 1	through 5th to right 4th en haut
	4	lower left heel and place right tendu croisé derrière	
21-22		grand port de bras into:	
23		pirouette en attitude en dedans ending facing 2	5th en avant
24	1-2	lower left heel	5th en haut
	3	extend right derrière	through 2nd to
	4	right fermé 5th derrière facing 5	bras bas
25-32		repeat 17-24 to other side	
33		grand plié finishing down	left opens slightly
34	1-2-3	pirouette en dehors from	
	4	plié ending attitude croisé derrière facing 1	through 5th to right 4th en haut
35	1-2	right posé de côté with left through cou-de-pied to	
	3-4	tendu effacé devant on right fondu, facing 2	through 2nd to right 3rd
36		on demi-pointe turn into 2nd arabesque facing 8	through en avant to left 2nd arabesque

(continued)

No. 3 (continued)

Bar	Beat	Feet and Direction	Arms
37	1-2	right relevé with left attitude derrière facing 2	left 4th en haut
	3-4	place left 4th croisé derrière when lowering right heel	
38		grand port de bras into:	
39	1-2	pirouette renversé	
	3	right fondu with left retiré facing 5	5th en avant
	4	right relevé with left développé à la seconde	5th en haut
40		left fermé 5th devant	bras bas
41-48		repeat 33-40 to other side	

No. 4 Relevé with Tendu 2/4

Starting Position		5th right devant facing 5	bras bas
1	1	left relevé with right développé à la seconde	through 5th to 2nd
	2	hold	
2	1	left fondu with right sur le cou-de-pied	bras bas
	2	hold	
3	1	right tendu à la seconde	
	2	right fermé 5th devant	
4	1	left assemblé dessus	
	2	hold	
5-8		repeat 1-4 to other side	
9	1	left relevé with right développé attitude effacé derrière facing 2	through 5th to right 4th en haut
	2	hold	
10	1	left fondu with right sur le cou-de-pied	bras bas
	2	hold	
11	1	right tendu croisé devant	through 5th left 4th en haut
	2	right fermé 5th devant	bras bas
12	1	left assemblé dessus facing 5	
13-16		repeat 9-12 to other side	

No. 5 Posé Chassé, Assemblé 4/4

Bar	Beat	Feet and Direction	Arms
Starting Position		5th right devant facing 5	bras bas
1	1-2	right posé-chassé en avant	5th en avant
	3-4	left fermé 5th derrière	2nd
2	1-2	right assemblé dessous	bras bas
	3-4	hold	
3-4		repeat 1-2 to other side	
5-8		reverse 1-4 (arm movements the same)	
9	1-2	right posé chassé de côté	5th en avant
	3-4	left fermé 5th derrière	2nd
10	1-2	right assemblé dessous	bras bas
	3-4	hold	
11-12		repeat 9-10 to other side	
13-16		reverse 9-12 (arm movements the same)	
17	1-2	right posé chassé en avant facing 1	5th en avant
	3-4	left fermé 5th derrière	left 4th en haut
18	1-2	right assemblé dessous facing 5	bras bas
	3-4	hold	
19-20		repeat 17-18 to other side	
21-24		reverse 17-20 (arm movements the same)	
25	1-2	right posé chassé croisé en avant facing 2	5th en avant
	3-4	left fermé 5th derrière	5th en haut
26	1-2	right assemblé dessous facing 5	bras bas
	3-4	hold	
27-28		repeat 25-26 to other side	
29-32		reverse 25-28 (arm movements the same)	

Repeat in all directions as follows:

Bar	Beat	Feet and Direction	Arms
33	1-2	right posé chassé en avant	slowly through
	3-4	left fermé 5th derrière	5th en avant
34		repeat bar 33	to 2nd

(continued)

No. 5 (continued)

Bar	Beat	Feet and Direction	Arms
35	1-2	right tendu devant	
	3-4	right fermé 5th devant	
36		left assemblé dessus	bras bas
37-96		continue in pattern described above	

No. 6 Grand Changement 4/4

Starting Position		5th right devant facing 5	bras bas
1	and-1	grand changement landing in grand plié	
	2-3-4	gradually rise to	
2	1-2	right relevé with left sur le cou-de-pied	
	3-4	left fermé 5th devant	
3-8		repeat alternating legs	

No. 7 Grand Plié with Changement 2/4

Starting Position		5th right devant facing 5	bras bas
1-2-3		grand plié and push off for	
4	1	grand changement	
	2	hold	
5-16		repeat alternating legs	

No. 8 Changement 2/4

Starting Position		5th right devant facing 5	bras bas
1	1-and	2 changements	
	2	temps levé landing on left with right petit retiré derrière	right 3rd

No. 8 (continued)

Bar	Beat	Feet and Direction	Arms
2	1	right coupé dessous	
	and	left assemblé dessous	
	2	changement	bras bas
3-16		repeat alternating legs	

No. 9 Tendu, Pirouette 2/4

Starting Position		5th right devant facing 5	bras bas
1	1	right tendu à la seconde	through 5th to 2nd
	and	right fermé 5th devant	
	2	left posé into 2nd, demi-plié	right 4th en avant
2	1	pirouette en dehors on left	
	2	left fondu with right sur le cou-de-pied	bras bas
3	1	right piqué effacé en avant into attitude left derrière facing 1	through 5th to left 4th en
	2	left coupé dessous	haut
4	1	right assemblé dessous	through 2nd to bras bas
	and-2	2 changements	
5-8		repeat 1-4 to other side	
9	1	right tendu effacé devant facing 1	through 5th to left 4th en haut
	and	right fermé 5th devant	
	2	left posé into 4th position effacé derrière, demi-plié facing 1	left 4th en avant
10	1	pirouette en dedans on left	
	2	left fondu with right sur le cou-de-pied	bras bas
11	1	right piqué croisé en avant into attitude left derrière facing 2	through 5th to left 4th en haut
	2	left coupé dessous	
12	1	right assemblé dessous	through 2nd to bras bas
	and-2	2 changements facing 5	
13-16		repeat 9-12 to other side	

No. 10 Glissade, Échappé Sauté 3/4 Mazurka

Bar	Beat	Feet and Direction	Arms
Starting Position		5th right devant facing 5	bras bas
1	1	right glissade de côté, left fermé 5th derrière	through 5th
	2	échappé sauté into 2nd	2nd
	3	demi-plié in 2nd	right 4th en avant
2	1-2	pirouette en dehors on left	
	3	right fermé 5th derrière	bras bas
3-8		repeat alternating sides	
9	1	right glissade de côté, left fermé 5th derrière	through 5th en avant to 2nd
	2	right jeté with left dégagé croisé devant facing 1	left 4th en avant
	3	left tombé effacé en avant facing 2	
10	1-2	pirouette renversé on left closing right 5th devant	bras bas
	3	temps levé onto right with left retiré devant facing 5	
11-16		repeat alternating sides	

No. 11 Sissonne Fermée 6/8 (count 2)

Bar	Beat	Feet and Direction	Arms
Starting Position		5th right devant facing 5	bras bas
1	and-1	sissonne fermée to the left closing right 5th derrière	
	2	hold	
2	1-2	repeat bar 1 to other side	
3	and-1	sissonne fermée effacée en arrière closing right 5th devant facing 1	right 3rd
	and	sissonne ouverte en avant onto right	left 3rd
	2	left fermé 5th derrière	
4	1	right assemblé dessous facing 5	1st
	2	entrechat quatre	
5-8		repeat 1-4 to other side	
9-16		reverse 1-8	

No. 12 Jeté Enchaînement 4/8

Bar	Beat	Feet and Direction	Arms
Starting Position		on right with left tendu croisé devant facing 1	1st
Intro 3		left posé croisé en avant	
4		left petit temps levé with right ballonné dessus	
1	1	right jeté effacé en avant	left 4th en avant
	2	hold	
	3	left coupé dessous	
	4	right posé de côté	2nd
2	1	left jeté croisé en avant	right 4th en avant
	2	hold	
	3	right coupé dessous	
	4	left jeté battu dessus	demi-2nd
3	1	right jeté de côté with left devant facing 2	1st
	2	hold	
	3	left coupé dessus	
	4	right posé effacé en arrière	
4	1	left jeté croisé en arrière with right devant facing 2	
	2	hold	
	3	right posé croisé en avant	
	4	right petit temps levé with left ballonné dessus	
5-8		repeat 1-4 to other side	
9	1	right jeté effacé en avant, left fermé 5th derrière	left 4th en avant
	2	right petite sissonne ouverte en avant with left dégagé effacé derrière	
	3	left coupé dessous	
	4	right posé de côté	2nd
10	1	left jeté croisé en avant, right fermé 5th derrière	right 4th en avant
	2	left petite sissonne ouverte en avant with right dégagé croisé derrière	
	3	right coupé dessous	2nd
	4	left jeté battu dessus	

(continued)

No. 12 (continued)

Bar	Beat	Feet and Direction	Arms
11	1	échappé sauté into 2nd facing 8	left 4th en avant
	2	right temps levé with left retiré devant with 1/2 turn left to face 6	5th en avant
	3	left posé en avant facing 7	
	4	grand jeté en tournant en attitude onto right facing 5	through 2nd to left 4th en haut
12	1	échappé sauté into 2nd facing 6	right 4th en avant
	2	left temps levé with right retiré devant with 1/2 turn right to face 8	
	3	right posé en avant facing 7	
	4	left ballonné dessus to right to face 2	1st
13-16		repeat 9-12 to other side	

No. 13 Pirouette 2/4

Bar	Beat	Feet and Direction	Arms
Starting Position		5th right devant facing 5	bras bas
1	1	left relevé with right développé à la seconde	through 5th to 2nd
	2	place right in 2nd, demi-plié	right 4th en avant
2	1	pirouette en dehors on left	5th
	2	left fondu with right dégagé devant facing 2	right 4th en avant
3	1	right rond de jambe en dehors into attitude derrière continuing pirouette	right through 2nd to 4th en haut
	2	right coupé dessous	
	and	left posé de côté (beats 2-and-1—pas de bourrée en dehors en tournant)	through 5th en avant to
4	1	right coupé dessus	
	2	left assemblé dessus	bras bas
5-16		repeat alternating sides	

No. 14 Glissade, Jeté en Attitude 3/4 changing to 2/4

Bar	Beat	Feet and Direction	Arms
Starting Position		on left with right tendu croisé derrière facing 1	bras bas
1		glissade en avant through 4th	through 5th
2		right grand jeté en avant with left attitude derrière	to left 4th en haut
3		left assemblé dessous	through 2nd to bras bas
4		temps levé onto left with right derrière	right 4th en avant
5-8		repeat 1-4	
9		right glissade en arrière facing 5	1st
10		right jeté battu dessus	
11		left glissade en arrière	
12		left jeté battu dessus	
13		right tombé effacé en arrière into:	right 4th en avant
14		pirouette renversé on right	
15		left fermé 5th derrière facing 5	bras bas
16		place left croisé tendu derrière facing 2	
17-32		repeat 1-16 to other side	
Change to 2/4			
33	1	glissade en avant facing 1 (right-left)	
	2	right jeté en avant with left petit retiré derrière	left 4th en avant
34	1	left assemblé dessous	1st
	2	temps levé onto left with right derrière	right 4th en avant
35-36		repeat 33-34	
37	1	right glissade en arrière facing 5	
	2	right jeté battu dessus	bras bas
38	1	left coupé dessous	
	2	right jeté battu dessus	left 4th en avant
	and	left tombé effacé en arrière	2nd
39	1	pirouette en dedans on left	
	2	right fermé 5th devant	bras bas

(continued)

No. 14 (continued)

Bar	Beat	Feet and Direction	Arms
40	1	temps levé onto right with left derrière facing 2	
41-48		repeat 33-40 to other side	

No. 15 Brisé 2/4

Bar	Beat	Feet and Direction	Arms
Starting Position		5th right devant facing 1	bras bas
Intro		right petit retiré devant	
	1	place right 4th position croisé derrière demi-plié	
	2	left tendu croisé devant	
	and	left posé croisé en avant	
1	1	brisé onto right with left dégagé croisé devant	
	2	left posé croisé en avant	
2-3		repeat 1	
4	1	brisé onto right with left dégagé croisé devant	
	and	left coupé dessus, right fermé 5th derrière	
	2	left posé de côté, right coupé	
	and	dessus (pas de bourrée) facing 2	
5-16		repeat 1-4 alternating sides	
Boys only continue			
17		brisé volé landing right with left croisé devant facing 1	1st
18		brisé volé landing left with right croisé derrière	
19-22		repeat 17-18	
23		brisé volé landing right with left croisé devant	

No. 15 (continued)

Bar	Beat	Feet and Direction	Arms
24		left ballonné battu dessous facing 5	
25		left petit jeté battu dessus	
26-30		repeat bar 25 alternating legs and travelling backwards	
31		left assemblé dessous	
32		entrechat six	

No. 16 Petit Jeté and Changement 2/4 (Girls' Enchaînement)

Bar	Beat	Feet and Direction	Arms
Starting Position		on left with right tendu croisé derrière facing 1	1st
	and	right dégagé effacé en avant	
1	1	jeté en avant onto right with left dégagé croisé devant	
	and	jeté en avant onto left with right dégagé effacé devant	
	2	repeat beat 1	
	and	left assemblé en avant	
2	1-and-2	3 petits changements	
	and	temps levé onto left with right petit retiré derrière	right 3rd
3-4		repeat 1-2	
5	1-and	right coupé dessous, left posé de côté, right coupé dessous with left dégagé de côté (pas de bourrée) facing 5	left 4th en avant
	2-and	repeat 1-and to other side	
6		repeat bar 5 travelling backwards during bars 5 and 6	
7	1	right coupé dessous	bras bas
	and	left coupé dessous onto demi-pointe with right développé à la seconde	through 5th to 2nd
	2	place right in 2nd-demi-plié	right 4th en avant

(continued)

No. 16 (continued)

Bar	Beat	Feet and Direction	Arms
8	1	pirouette en dehors on left	
	2	right petit jeté dessus facing 2	bras bas
9-16		repeat 1-8 to other side	

No. 17 Mazurka 3/4

Starting Position		5th right devant facing 5	bras bas
Intro	3	right dégagé devant	
1	1	right assemblé en avant	
	2	entrechat six	
	3	temps levé onto left with right petit retiré devant	
2	1	right glissade de côté with left through 5th derrière	
	and	grand jeté de côté travelling to the right and landing on right with left 2nd demi-hauteur	through 5th to 2nd
	2	left through 1st and posé chassé into 4th position devant, right tendu derrière	through 1st to left 4th en haut
	3	right coupé dessous with left dégagé devant	through 2nd bras bas
3-6		repeat 1-2 alternating sides	
7	and	left coupé dessous in 1/4 turn right to face 4	left 4th en avant
	1	right posé en avant	
	2	right temps levé with left extended derrière	
	3	left glissade en avant through 4th	
8	1	left jeté dessus in 1/2 turn right to face 6	
	2	right jeté dessus facing 2	through 2nd
	3	left ballonné dessus facing 5	left 4th en avant
9	1	left chassé de côté with right fermé derrière	2nd
	2	left posé de côté	
	3	right jeté en tournant dessous	left 4th en avant
10	1	left tombé effacé en avant facing 2	2nd
	2	pirouette renversé on left	
	3	ending right attitude derrière facing 2	

No. 17 (continued)

Bar	Beat	Feet and Direction	Arms
11	1	right coupé dessous	bras bas
	2	left glissade effacé en avant, right fermé derrière	
	3	left posé en avant with right dégagé croisé devant facing 2	
12	1	right assemblé en avant	through 5th
	2	sissonne en attitude en avant with left derrière	5th en haut
	3	left assemblé dessous	through 2nd to right 4th en avant
13-16		repeat 9-12 to other side	

No. 18 Girls' Enchaînement 3/4 Mazurka

Bar	Beat	Feet and Direction	Arms
Starting Position		5th right devant facing 5	bras bas
1	1	right posé chassé de côté	through 5th
	2	left fermé 5th derrière	to 2nd
	3	right posé de côté	
2	1	left through 1st to 4th tendu croisé devant facing 1	right to 4th en haut
	2	left rond de jambe à terre into 4th effacé derrière	change to left 4th en haut
	3	left fermé 5th derrière, demi-plié facing 5	left 4th en avant
3	1	right posé de côté	2nd
	2	left fermé 5th derrière	
	3	right assemblé dessous	bras bas
4	1	sissonne en attitude onto right with left derrière facing 1	through 5th to left 4th en haut
	2	left coupé dessous	
	3	right assemblé dessous facing 5	through 2nd to bras bas
5-7		repeat bars 1-2-3 to other side	
8	1	sissonne en attitude onto left with right derrière facing 2	through 5th to right 4th en haut
	2	right coupé dessous	
	3	left ballonné dessous	through 2nd to bras bas

(continued)

No. 18 (continued)

Bar	Beat	Feet and Direction	Arms
9	1	left coupé dessous facing 1	through 5th en avant to right 4th en haut
	and-2	pas de valse on left derrière	
	3	right jeté battu dessus	right to 2nd, left to 4th en avant
10		repeat bar 9	
11	1	left coupé dessous	
	and-2	right glissade de côté—left fermé derrière	through 2nd
	3	right posé effacé en avant	1st, 5th to
12	1	left grand jeté en avant landing with right derrière	2nd
	2	right petit jeté dessus facing 5	
	3	left petit jeté dessus	bras bas
13-14		repeat 9-10 to other side	
15	1	right coupé dessous	
	2	left glissade de côté, right fermé devant facing 5	1st
	3	left glissade de côté, right fermé derrière	
	and	left développé à la seconde	through 5th en avant to 2nd
16	1	2nd position demi-plié	left 4th en avant
	2	pirouette en dehors on right	
	3	left fermé 5th derrière	bras bas

No. 19 Chassé Contretemps and Glissade Jeté 6/8 (count 2)

Bar	Beat	Feet and Direction	Arms
Starting Position		on right with left tendu derrière facing 1	bras bas
	and	left coupé dessous	
1		right chassé contretemps en avant to left 4th devant	left 3rd
2	1	right glissade en avant through 4th	through 5th to
	2	grand jeté effacé en avant landing on right with left en attitude derrière	left 4th en haut
	and	in the landing position bring left rond de jambe en dedans demi-hauteur into dégagé devant	open left to 2nd

No. 19 (continued)

Bar	Beat	Feet and Direction	Arms
3	1	facing 8: left coupé dessus	
	and-2	pas de bourrée couru in 5th left derrière	bras bas
4	1	right grand jeté en avant turning to the right landing with left derrière facing 3	through 5th en avant to 5th en haut
	2	left jeté dessus facing 2	through 2nd to 1st
5-8		repeat 1-4 to other side to be repeated ad lib	

No. 20 Girls' Enchaînement 3/4

Bar	Beat	Feet and Direction	Arms
Starting Position		on left with right tendu derrière facing 1	bras bas
1	1	right piqué effacé en avant with left petit retiré derrière	left 4th en avant
	2-3	hold	
2	1-2-3	3 petits jetés dessus (left-right-left)	bras bas
3-4		repeat 1-2	
5	1-2	right piqué de côté with left développé à la seconde facing 5	through 5th en avant to 2nd
	3	right fondu with left retiré derrière	left 4th en avant
6	1-2	left piqué pirouette en dedans en attitude	left 4th en haut
	3	left fondu facing 5	
7	1	right coupé dessous	
	2-3	left rond de jambe sauté en l'air en dehors into:	2nd
8	1	posé croisé en avant into 4th position right tendu derrière facing 1	through 1st to left 4th en avant
	3	right coupé dessous facing 5	bras bas
9-14		repeat 1-6 to other side	
15	1	left jeté dessous with right petit développé devant	2nd
	2	right petit jeté dessus	
	3	left glissade en arrière	
16	1	left assemblé en arrière	bras bas
	2	hold	
	3	temps levé onto left with right devant	right 4th en avant

(continued)

No. 20 (continued)

Bar	Beat	Feet and Direction	Arms
17	1-2	right posé de côté	2nd
	3	jeté en tournant landing left dessous	
18	1-2	right posé de côté	5th en avant
	3	left jeté en avant with right en attitude derrière facing 1	2nd
19	1	right coupé dessous	
	2-3	left ballonné en avant	bras bas
20	1	left piqué en avant into right attitude derrière	right 3rd arabesque
	2	hold	
	3	right petit jeté dessous facing 5	left 4th en avant
21-28		repeat 17-20 alternating sides	
29	1-2	left posé de côté	2nd
	3	jeté en tournant landing right dessous	left 4th en avant
30		repeat bar 29	
31	1	left posé de côté	2nd
	2-3	right ballonné en avant facing 5	bras bas
32	1	right piqué en avant with left en attitude derrière	2nd
	2	hold	
	3	left fermé 5th derrière	1st

No. 21 Male Variation from *La Sylphide* 2/4

Bar	Beat	Feet and Direction	Arms
Starting Position		on right with left tendu devant facing 1	right 4th en avant
1	1	left posé en avant	
	2	brisé landing right with left dégagé croisé devant	
	and	left posé en avant	1st
2	1	right assemblé dessus	
	2	left temps levé with right développé effacé devant	through 5th to right 4th en haut
	and	right coupé dessus	
3	1-2	left posé temps levé en avant, right extended derrière facing 3	through 2nd, 1st to right 4th en avant

No. 21 **(continued)**

Bar	Beat	Feet and Direction	Arms
4	and-1	right glissade en avant	
	2	right jeté in 1/2 turn left with left through retiré passé into croisé devant demi-hauteur facing 1	right 4th en avant
5-6		repeat 1-2	
	and	right coupé dessous to face 3	bras bas
7	1-2	left posé temps levé with right dégagé devant (turning to the left to face 5)	1st
8	and-1	right glissade en avant	
	2	right grand jeté en avant landing with left derrière	2nd
9	1	left coupé dessous	
	2	right jeté battu dessus	left 4th en avant
10	and-1	left glissade en arrière	bras bas
	2	left grand jeté en attitude turning left and landing facing 1 with right derrière	5th en avant to 5th en haut
	and	right coupé dessous	
11		left posé temps levé en avant facing 5	through 2nd and bras bas to
12	and-1	right glissade en avant	5th en avant
	2	right grand jeté en avant with left derrière	2nd
13-16		repeat 9-12	
17	1	left coupé dessous	1st
	2	right rond de jambe sauté en dehors	right 4th en avant
18	1	right coupé dessus	
	and-2	temps de flèche landing left with right attitude derrière	right through 2nd to 4th en haut
19	1	right coupé dessous	2nd
	2	left rond de jambe sauté en dehors landing with left extended devant	left 4th en avant
20	1	left jeté effacé en avant facing 2	open left forward
	2-and	right chassé effacé en arrière	through bras bas
21	1	right posé en arrière	and 5th to
	2	right fouetté sauté en tournant landing with left attitude derrière	left 4th en haut
22	and-1	left glissade croisé en arrière	through 2nd to 1st
	2	left jeté battu dessus	

(continued)

No. 21 (continued)

Bar	Beat	Feet and Direction	Arms
23	and-1-2	right coupé dessous, left chassé contretemps en avant	right 3rd
24	and-1	left glissade en avant	
	and	left jeté en avant landing right retiré derrière	5th en avant
	2	left relevé in attitude right derrière	right 4th en haut

No. 22 Demi-Contretemps, Assemblé Porté 3/4

Bar	Beat	Feet and Direction	Arms
Starting Position		on right with left tendu effacé derrière	bras bas
Intro		facing 1	
2	1-2	hold	
	3	right temps levé with left derrière	
1		left posé croisé en avant	1st
2	1-2	right assemblé dessus	through 5th
	3	right temps levé with left derrière	left 4th en haut
3		left posé croisé en avant	2nd
4	1-2	right assemblé porté effacé en avant with entrechat six landing right 5th devant	1st
	3	temps levé onto left with right derrière facing 5	
5	1-2	right chassé en arrière with left tendu devant facing 5	left 4th en avant
	3	left fermé 5th devant	
6		repeat 5	
7		right posé en arrière	
8	1	left assemblé dessus turning right to face 2	demi-2nd
	2	hold	
	3	left temps levé with right derrière	1st
9-15		repeat 1-7 to other side	
16	1	right assemblé dessus turning left to face 5	
	2-3	right chassé de côté	demi-2nd
17		right posé de côté	
18	1-2	left jeté en tournant landing dessous facing 5	5th en avant
	3	right posé en avant facing 1	

No. 22 (continued)

Bar	Beat	Feet and Direction	Arms
19		left posé croisé en avant	
20	1	right jeté en avant with left attitude derrière	left 4th en haut
	2-3	left coupé dessous–right posé en avant (pas de bourrée)	through 2nd
21	1	left coupé dessous with right dégagé devant	right 4th en avant
	2-3	right coupé dessus–left posé en arrière (pas de bourrée)	2nd
22	1	right coupé dessus with left dégagé derrière	left 4th en avant
23		left coupé dessous	
24	1	right jeté battu dessus facing 5	1st
	2-3	left chassé de côté	demi-2nd
25-31		repeat 17-23 to other side	
32	1	left jeté battu dessus	
	2-3	hold	

No. 23 Female Variation 3/4 Mazurka

Starting Position		5th right devant facing 5	bras bas
1	1	right assemblé porté dessous (to the right)	5th en avant
	2	right sissonne ouverte with left dégagé de côté (travelling to the left)	left 4th en avant
	3	left coupé dessous	2nd
2	1	right piqué de côté, right retiré devant	
	2	left fermé 5th devant sur les pointes	
	3	lower the heels	bras bas
3-4		repeat 1-2 to other side	
5	1	right tombé effacé en avant	demi-2nd
	and-2	pas de valse (left-right) to face 8	
	3	left piqué en dehors with right retiré devant to face 5	right 4th en avant
6		repeat 5	
7		pas de bourrée piqué sur les pointes–right dessus, left dessous, right posé de côté with left retiré devant	

(continued)

No. 23 (continued)

Bar	Beat	Feet and Direction	Arms
8	1	close left 5th devant sur les pointes	bras bas
	2	lower heels	
9-16		repeat 1-8 to other side	
17	1-2	right piqué tour en dedans	
	3	left coupé dessous, facing 1	
18	1-2	right posé effacé en avant with left tendu derrière facing 1	right 3rd arabesque
	3	bring left dégagé through 5th devant into:	left 4th en avant
19-20		repeat 17-18 to other side	1st
	3	right coupé dessus facing 5	
21	1	left coupé dessous	
	2	right glissade de côté, left fermé derrière	
	3	repeat beat 2	
22	1-2	right assemblé dessous	bras bas
	2	hold	
	3	temps levé on left with right derrière	left 3rd
23		repeat 21 to other side	
24	1	left assemblé dessous	bras bas
	2	hold	
	3	temps levé on right with left devant	left 4th en avant
25-32		repeat 17-24 to other side	

No. 24 Tours en l'Air 3/4

Starting Position	5th right devant facing 5	bras bas
1	relevé	
2	demi-plié	right 4th en avant
3	tour en l'air to the right landing 5th left devant	bras bas
4	hold	
5-16	repeat alternating sides	

A painting of August Bournonville by Carl Bloch belonging to the Royal Theater in Copenhagen. (*John R. Johnsen*)

Valborg Borchsenius in Bournonville's *Valdemar*. Borchsenius (1872-1949) was principal dancer with the Royal Danish Ballet. She was Hans Beck's partner for many years. After retirement she became a teacher (she was Kirsten Ralov's teacher from 1929). From 1940 to 1949 Borchsenius staged a number of Bournonville ballets together with Harald Lander (see text). (*Court Theater Museum, Copenhagen*)

Anna Thychsen (1853–1896) and Hans Beck (1861–1952) in *La Sylphide*. Beck was ballet master with the Royal Danish Ballet. Bournonville saw him dancing when he was 18. (*Court Theater Museum, Copenhagen*)

Fredbjørn Bjørnsson in *La Ventana*. (*Mydtskov*)

Anna Laerkesen and Jørn Madsen in *La Sylphide*. (*Mydtskov*)

Linda Hindberg, Vivi Flindt, Anne Sonnerup, and Mette Hønningen in *Napoli* in 1975. (*John R. Johnsen*)

Kirsten Ralov and Fredbjørn Bjørnsson in *Napoli* in 1960. (*Mogens von Haven*)

John R. Johnsen

WEDNESDAY'S CLASS

No. 1 Adagio 4/4

Bar	Beat	Feet and Direction	Arms
Starting Position		5th right devant facing 5	bras bas
Intro	3	relevé	
	and-4	lower left heel and petit retiré with right devant facing 1	
1		left fondu with right développé devant	5th en avant
2	1	right posé en avant into:	
	2	left attitude derrière	left 4th en haut
	3-4	hold	
3		promenade en dehors	left through en avant to
4	1-2	when facing 1 extend left derrière	2nd
	3-4	hold	
5		left retiré passé into:	1st and through
6	1-2	développé croisé devant on right demi-plié	5th en avant to right 4th en haut
7		left posé en avant into arabesque on demi-plié facing 5	through 2nd–1st to left 1st arabesque
8	1	left relevé in attitude with right derrière	left 4th en haut
	2	hold	
	and	right coupé dessous	
	3	left posé de côté	
	4	right fermé 5th devant facing 2	through 2nd to bras bas
9	1-2-3	right fondu with left développé croisé derrière	
	4	left fermé 5th derrière	
10		right développé croisé devant	through 5th to left 4th en haut
11		promenade 1/4 to the left and turn so the right leg becomes croisé derrière facing 1	gradually bring right to
12	1-2	bend right knee into attitude	5th en haut
	3-4	place right tendu croisé derrière	through 2nd to bras bas
13	1-2	turn to face 2 with right tendu à la seconde	1st
	3-4	right fermé 5th devant	through 5th
14		right développé à la seconde	to right 4th en haut
15		right into retiré passé and promenade en dehors	

No. 1 (continued)

Bar	Beat	Feet and Direction	Arms
16	1-2	when facing 6 extend to 2nd arabesque	right through en avant to 2nd arabesque
	3	left relevé in attitude with right derrière facing 5	right 4th en haut
	4	right fermé 5th derrière	through 2nd to bras bas
17		grand plié	
18	1-2-3	straighten	
	4	left petit retiré devant	
19	1-2-3	left développé à la seconde	through 5th to 2nd
	4	right fondu with left sur le cou-de-pied facing 2	bras bas
20	1-2	left into attitude croisé derrière	through 5th to left 4th en haut
	3-4	hold	
21-22		promenade en dedans	
23	1-2	when facing 5, extend left derrière	left 4th en avant to
	3-4	left into à la seconde	2nd
24	1	right fondu	through 1st
	2-3	left fermé 5th devant and soutenu en dedans to face 2	5th en avant 5th en haut
	4	lower heels in 5th right devant	through 2nd to bras bas
25	1-2-3	right développé croisé devant facing 2	5th en avant
	4	right fermé 5th devant	
26		left développé into attitude croisé derrière	left 4th en haut
27		promenade to the left leaving left leg so it becomes croisé devant facing 1	right slowly to 5th en haut
28	1-2	hold	
	3-4	left into tendu croisé devant	through 2nd to 1st
29	1-2	left dégagé croisé devant, demi-hauteur	5th en avant
	3-4	left retiré passé	
30		left développé derrière to 1st arabesque facing 8	right 1st arabesque
31		left retiré and promenade en dedans	5th en avant
32		when facing 5 left développé à la seconde	5th en haut
33		left through 5th derrière to développé effacé derrière on right fondu facing 1	through 2nd to bras bas

(continued)

No. 1 (continued)

Bar	Beat	Feet and Direction	Arms
34	1-2	left posé en arrière to	through 5th to
	3-4	right dégagé devant (90°)	left 4th en haut
35-36		promenade en dehors with right extended devant—finish facing 1	left opens slowly to 2nd
37		right retiré passé into	5th en avant
38	1-2-3	right attitude derrière facing 1	right 4th en haut
	4	left fondu	
39	1	left relevé	
	2	right coupé dessous facing 5	
	and	left posé de côté	2nd
	3	right tendu devant facing 2	left 4th en haut
	4	right fermé 5th devant	bras bas
40	1-2	right posé chassé en avant to 4th with left tendu derrière	5th en avant to left 4th en haut
	3	left fermé 5th derrière	through 2nd to bras bas
	4	hold	

No. 2 Port de Bras 3/4

Bar	Beat	Feet and Direction	Arms
Starting Position		5th right devant facing 1	bras bas
	3		demi-2nd
1		body bends forwards	bras bas
2		through upright position and bend backwards	through 5th en avant to 5th en haut and open in 2nd
3		repeat bar 1	
4	1-2	straighten and relevé in 5th	through 5th en haut
	3	change to 5th left devant when lowering heels, facing 2	2nd
5-8		repeat 1-4 to other side	
9-16		reverse, i.e., bend body backwards, upright, and forward, and straighten, ending facing 5	through 2nd to 5th en haut and 5th en avant to bras bas and return to 2nd

No. 2 (continued)

Bar	Beat	Feet and Direction	Arms
17		bend body right and straighten through upright position	through 5th en avant to left 4th en haut
18		look left	continue opening left to 2nd
19-20		repeat 17-18 to other side (without changing 5th)	
21-24		repeat 17-20	
25		bend body right	open through 2nd to right 4th en haut with
26		straighten, look left	left 4th en avant
27-30		repeat 25-26 alternating sides	
31	1-2	relevé in 5th	5th en avant
	3	demi-plié	
32	1-2	right posé chassé en avant facing 2 with left tendu derrière	left 4th en haut
	3	left fermé 5th derrière	bras bas

No. 3 Pirouette 2/4

Bar	Beat	Feet and Direction	Arms
Starting Position		5th right devant facing 5	bras bas
1	1	left fondu with right petit retiré devant	
	2	left relevé with right développé à la seconde	through 5th to 2nd
2		right into 2nd position demi-plié	right 4th en avant
3		pirouette en attitude on right	5th en avant
4		lowering heel in attitude effacé derrière facing 1	left 4th en haut
5	1	left fermé 5th derrière facing 5	2nd
	2	left relevé with right dégagé croisé devant demi-hauteur facing 2	left 4th en avant

(continued)

No. 3 (continued)

Bar	Beat	Feet and Direction	Arms
6	1	right posé croisé en avant	
	2	left dégagé into 2nd position demi-plié facing 5	change to right 4th en avant
7		pirouette en dehors on left	
8		right fermé 5th derrière	bras bas
9-16		repeat 1-8 to other side	
17	1	left fondu with right petit retiré devant	
	2	left relevé with right développé à la seconde	through 5th to 2nd
18		right into 2nd position demi-plié	right 4th en avant
19		pirouette renversé on right ending in	
20		1st arabesque facing 6	right 1st arabesque
21	1	left coupé dessous	1st
	and-2	right pas de basque ending left 5th devant facing 1	
22	1	temps levé on right with left devant facing 5	left 4th en avant
	2	left tombé effacé en avant to	2nd
23		pirouette en dedans	
24		right fermé 5th derrière	bras bas
25-32		repeat 17-24 to other side	
	and	left fondu with right petit retiré devant	
33		left relevé with right développé à la seconde	through 5th to 2nd
34		right into 2nd position demi-plié	right 4th en avant
35		left dégagé croisé derrière à terre into tendu 4th, bending to the right facing 2	change across to left 4th en avant
36		turn 1/2 to the left leaving left so it becomes croisé devant facing 1	through 5th to right 4th en haut
37	1	left fermé 5th devant	
	2	right jeté effacé en avant	left 4th en avant
38	1-2	left tombé effacé en arrière into pirouette renversé	
	and	left fondu with right retiré	through 2nd
39	1	left relevé with right développé à la seconde	5th en haut
	2	right fermé 5th devant	through 2nd
40	1	changement	to bras bas
	2	hold	
41-48		repeat 33-40 to other side	

No. 4 Adagio with Grand Jeté 4/8

Bar	Beat	Feet and Direction	Arms
Starting Position		right 5th devant facing 1	bras bas
Intro	1, 2	relevé, hold	
	3	left fondu with right petit retiré devant	
	and-4	right glissade en avant through 4th	through 5th to
1		grand jeté en avant landing on right with left attitude derrière	left 4th en haut
2	1-2-3	promenade en dedans bringing left through derrière to à la seconde	left through 4th en avant to 2nd
	4	right fondu	
3		pirouette en attitude en dehors	left to 4th en haut
4	1	lower right heel facing 2	
	2-3	hold	
	4	left coupé dessous	
5	1	right petit glissade de côté ending left 4th devant facing 1	bras bas
	2	right coupé dessous	
	and	left ballonné dessous	
	3	left piqué effacé en arrière with right retiré passé	5th en avant
	4	place right into 4th croisé derrière, heels lowered	right 4th en haut
6		grand port de bras into:	
7		pirouette en attitude en dedans	5th en avant
8	1	lower left heel facing 2	right 4th en haut
	2	hold	
	3	right fermé 5th derrière	bras bas
	and-4	left glissade en avant	
9-16		repeat 1-8 to other side	
17	1	right jeté en attitude with left derrière facing 1	through 5th to left 4th en haut
	2	right fondu with left extended effacé derrière	left 2nd arabesque
	3	left piqué effacé en arrière into pirouette en dedans	
	4	left fondu	bras bas
18	1-2	left relevé with right développé à la seconde facing 5	through 5th en avant to 5th en haut
	3	right jeté dessus	bras bas
	4	right fondu	

(continued)

No. 4 (continued)

Bar	Beat	Feet and Direction	Arms
19	1	left coupé dessous	
	2	right petit glissade de côté, left fermé 5th derrière	through 5th
	and	right petit développé à la seconde	2nd
	3-4	right into 2nd position demi-plié	right 4th en avant
20	1-2	pirouette en dehors on left	
	3	right fermé 5th derrière facing 2	bras bas
	and-4	left glissade en avant	
21-23		repeat 17-19 to other side	
24	1-2-3	repeat 20 to other side	
	4	hold	
25	1-2	changement into grand plié facing 5	
	3-4	from plié, pirouette en dehors on right ending:	through 5th
26	1-2-3	left développé à la seconde	5th en haut
	4	left coupé dessous	
27	1	right glissade de côté ending left 4th devant facing 1	2nd
	2	right coupé dessous	
	3	left glissade de côté ending right 4th devant facing 2	1st
	4	left coupé dessous	
28		left relevé with right grand rond de jambe en dehors into 4th croisé derrière facing 1	through 2nd to right 4th en haut
29		grand port de bras into	
30	1-2-3	pirouette en attitude on left	5th en avant
	4	lower heel facing 2	right 4th en haut
31	1-2	right soutenu en dedans ending left 5th devant demi-pointe facing 1	through 2nd to 5th en avant
	3	left tombé croisé en avant into right attitude derrière	5th en haut
	4	right coupé dessous	2nd
32	1	left assemblé dessous	
	2	changement facing 5	bras bas
	3-4	hold	
33-40		repeat 25-32 to other side	

No. 5 Tendu 2/4

Bar	Beat	Feet and Direction	Arms
Starting Position		5th right devant facing 5	bras bas
1	1	right tendu à la seconde	
	2	right fermé 5th devant	
	and	left relevé with right dégagé à la seconde, demi-hauteur	
2	1	right fermé 5th derrière	
	2	changement	
3	1	right posé en avant	
	2	left fermé 5th derrière	
4	1	right assemblé dessous	
	2	hold	
5-8		repeat 1-4 to other side	
9-16		reverse 1-8	
17	1	right tendu à la seconde	
	2	right fermé 5th derrière	
18		repeat bar 17 to other side	
19	1	right jeté effacé en avant landing demi-plié with left retiré derrière facing 1	left 4th en avant
	2	hold	
20	1	left coupé dessous	2nd
	2	right assemblé dessous facing 5	bras bas
21		grand plié	
22	1	changement	
	2	échappé sauté into 2nd demi-plié	right 4th en avant
23		pirouette en dehors on left	
24		right fermé 5th derrière	bras bas
25-32		repeat 17-24 to other side	
33	1	left tendu à la seconde	
	2	left fermé 5th devant	
34		repeat bar 33 to other side	
35	1	left jeté effacé en arrière landing demi-plié with right retiré devant facing 1	left 4th en avant
	2	hold	

(continued)

No. 5 (continued)

Bar	Beat	Feet and Direction	Arms
36	1	right coupé dessus	
	2	left assemblé dessus facing 5	bras bas
37		grand plié	
38	1	changement	
	2	échappé sauté into 4th right devant facing 1	left 4th en avant
39		pirouette en dedans on left	
40		right fermé 5th derrière facing 5	bras bas
41-48		repeat 33-40 to other side	
49	1	right posé de côté	
	2	left fermé 5th devant	
	and	right posé de côté	
50	1	left fermé 5th derrière	
	and	left relevé with right développé à la seconde	through 5th to 2nd
	2	right into 2nd position demi-plié	right 4th en avant
51		pirouette en dehors on left	
52		right fermé 5th derrière	bras bas
53-56		repeat 49-52 to other side	
57	1	left posé de côté	
	2	right fermé 5th derrière	
	and	left posé de côté	
58	1	right coupé dessus	
	2	left jeté en avant facing 2 landing right retiré derrière	right 4th en avant
59	1	right tombé effacé en arrière	2nd
	2	pirouette renversé on right	
60	1	left fermé 5th derrière facing 5	
	2	changement	bras bas
61-64		repeat 57-60 to other side	

No. 6 Rond de Jambe Sauté 2/4

Bar	Beat	Feet and Direction	Arms
Starting Position		5th right devant facing 5	bras bas
1	1	right rond de jambe sauté en dehors	
	2	right coupé dessous	
	and	left coupé dessous–right posé effacé en avant facing 1	
2	1	left posé croisé en avant	
	2	right jeté en avant landing with left retiré derrière	through 5th to left 4th en avant
	and	extend left derrière	
3	1	left tombé effacé en arrière	2nd
	2	pirouette renversé on left	
4	1	right fermé 5th derrière	bras bas
	2	hold facing 5	
5-8		repeat 1-4 to other side	
9	1	left rond de jambé sauté en dedans	
	2	left coupé dessus	
	and	right coupé dessus–left posé de côté	
10	1	right coupé dessous	
	and	left coupé demi-pointe dessous–right développé à la seconde	through 5th to 2nd
	2	right into 2nd position demi-plié	right 4th en avant
11		pirouette en dehors on left	
12	1	right fermé 5th derrière	bras bas
	2	hold	
13-16		repeat 9-12 to other side	
	and	left fondu with right retiré devant	
17	1	left relevé with right développé à la seconde	through 5th to 2nd
	2	right coupé dessus	
18	1	left assemblé battu dessus	bras bas
	and	échappé sauté into 2nd	left 4th en avant
	2	hold	
19	1	pirouette en dehors on right	
	2	right fondu	

(continued)

No. 6 (continued)

Bar	Beat	Feet and Direction	Arms
20	1	right relevé with left développé à la seconde	through 5th to 5th en haut
	and	left fermé 5th derrière–right posé de côté (pas de bourrée)	
	2	left fermé 5th devant	bras bas
21-24		repeat 17-20 to other side	
25	and	left fondu with right retiré devant	
	1	left relevé with right développé à la seconde	through 5th to 2nd
	2	right into 2nd position demi-plié	right 4th en avant
26	1	pirouette en dehors on left	
	2	left fondu	
27	1	left relevé with right développé à la seconde	through 5th to 5th en haut
	and	right fermé 5th derrière–left posé de côté (pas de bourrée)	
	2	right coupé dessus facing 2	right 4th en avant
28	1	left coupé dessous	2nd
	2	right assemblé battu dessous facing 5	bras bas
29-32		repeat 25-28 to other side	

No. 7 Posé Chassé 2/4

Starting Position		5th right devant	bras bas
1	1	right posé chassé de côté	
	2	left fermé 5th derrière	
	and	right assemblé dessous turning 1/2 to right to face 7	
2	1	left posé chassé de côté	
	2	right fermé 5th derrière	
	and	temps levé onto left turning 1/2 to right with right retiré devant to face 1	5th en avant
3	1	right posé effacé en avant	left 4th en haut
	2	left fermé 5th derrière	
4	1-and-2	3 changements facing 5	through 2nd to bras bas

No. 7 (continued)

Bar	Beat	Feet and Direction	Arms
5-8		repeat 1-4 to other side	
9	1	left posé chassé de côté	
	2	right fermé 5th devant	
	and	left assemblé dessus turning 1/2 to right to face 7	
10	1	right posé chassé de côté	
	2	left fermé 5th devant	
	and	temps levé onto right turning right with left retiré derrière to face 5	5th en avant
11	1	left posé effacé en arrière facing 1	left 4th en haut
	2	right fermé 5th devant	
12	1-and-2	3 changements facing 5	bras bas
13-16		repeat 9-12 to other side	
17	and		through 5th en avant to 5th en haut
	1	right posé chassé de côté	slowly to
	2	left fermé 5th derrière	2nd
	and	right assemblé dessous to face 1	bras bas
18	1	left posé chassé croisé en avant	through 5th to left 4th en haut
	2	right fermé 5th derrière	
	and	temps levé onto left with right retiré devant to face 3	through 2nd to right 4th en avant
19	1	right posé en avant	right 4th en haut
	2	left coupé dessous	
	and	right petit jeté with left extended devant facing 6	2nd
20	1	left posé de côté facing 5	5th en haut
	2	right fermé 5th derrière, demi-plié	
21-24		repeat 17-20 to other side	
25	1	left posé chassé de côté	2nd
	2	right fermé 5th devant	
	and	left assemblé dessus to face 1	bras bas

(continued)

No. 7 (continued)

Bar	Beat	Feet and Direction	Arms
26	1	right posé croisé en arrière	through 5th to right 4th en haut
	2	left fermé 5th devant	
	and	temps levé on right turning 1/2 to right with left retiré derrière to face 3	bras bas
27	1	left posé effacé en arrière	through 5th to left 4th en haut
	2	right coupé dessus	
	and	left jeté dessus turning 1/2 to right to face 5	right through
28	1	right posé chassé de côté	2nd to
	2	left fermé 5th devant	5th en haut
29-32		repeat 25-28 to other side	

No. 8 Sissonne Battue 2/4

Starting Position		5th right devant facing 5	bras bas
1	1	sissonne battue ouverte en avant onto left (beat right derrière) facing 2	right 4th en avant
	and	right coupé dessous	bras bas
	2	left assemblé dessous facing 5	
2	1	sissonne battue ouverte en avant onto right (beat left derrière) facing 1	left 4th en avant
	and	left coupé dessous	
	2	right assemblé dessous facing 5	bras bas
3	1	sissonne battue ouverte en arrière onto right (beat left devant) facing 2	left 3rd
	and	left coupé dessus	
	2	right assemblé dessous facing 5	bras bas
4	1	sissonne battue ouverte en arrière onto left (beat right devant) facing 1	through 5th to right 4th en avant
	and	right coupé dessus	
	2	left assemblé dessus facing 5	bras bas
5-8		repeat 1-4 to other side	

No. 9 Pas de Bourrée 2/4

Bar	Beat	Feet and Direction	Arms
Starting Position		5th right devant facing 5	bras bas
Intro	2-and	right dégagé de côté–and coupé dessous–left posé de côté	
1	1	right coupé dessous with left dégagé à la seconde	
	and	left coupé dessous–right posé de côté	
	2	left coupé dessous with right dégagé à la seconde	
	and	right coupé dessous–left posé en avant	
2	1	right coupé dessous with left dégagé effacé devant facing 2	
	and	left fermé devant–right posé en arrière	
	2	left coupé dessus with right dégagé effacé derrière	
	and	right coupé dessous–left posé de côté facing 5	
3	1	right coupé dessus	
	and	left coupé dessus–right posé de côté	
	2	left coupé dessous	
4	1	right assemblé dessous	
	2-and	left coupé dessous–right posé de côté	
5-8		repeat 1-4 to other side	
9-16		reverse 1-8	

No. 10 Grande Pirouette (Boys' Enchaînement) 3/4

Bar	Beat	Feet and Direction	Arms
Starting Position		5th right devant facing 5	bras bas
1	1	left fondu with right retiré devant	5th en avant
	2	left relevé with right développé à la seconde	2nd
	3	right into 2nd position demi-plié	right 4th en avant
2	1-2	pirouette à la seconde en dehors on left	2nd
	3	left fondu	

(continued)

No. 10 (continued)

Bar	Beat	Feet and Direction	Arms
3	1-2	pirouette en dehors on left with right retiré devant	5th en avant
	3	left fondu	through 2nd
4	1	right assemblé dessous	bras bas
	2, 3	hold	
5-16		repeat alternating sides	

No. 11 Batterie 2/4

Bar	Beat	Feet and Direction	Arms
Starting Position		5th right devant facing 5	bras bas
1	1	entrechat quatre	
	2	changement battu	
2	1	entrechat cinq onto left with right derrière	
	2	hold	
3	1	right petit jeté battu dessus	
	2	left petit jeté battu dessus	
4	1	right brisé dessus fermé 5th derrière	
	2	hold	
5-8		repeat 1-4 to other side	
9	1	right assemblé battu dessous	
	2	entrechat trois onto right with left derrière	
10	1	left coupé dessous	
	2	right ballonné battu dessous	
11	1	right petit jeté battu dessus	
	2	left glissade en arrière	
12	1	left assemblé battu dessus (from extension derrière)	
13-16		repeat 9-12 to other side	
Change to 3/4			
17		right brushes effacé devant into brisé avant, en fermé right 5th derrière facing 1	

No. 11 (continued)

Bar	Beat	Feet and Direction	Arms
18		hold	
19		right brushes en arrière to assemblé battu dessus	
20		temps levé onto left with right derrière	5th en avant
21		right glissade croisé en arrière	
22		cabriole onto left with right derrière	left 1st arabesque
23		brush right through 2nd to soutenu en dedans	2nd
24		lower heels in 5th left devant	bras bas
25-32		repeat 17-24 to other side	

No. 12 Girls' Enchaînement 2/4

Starting Position		5th right devant facing 5	1st
1	1	entrechat quatre	
	2	hold	
2	1	changement battu	
	and	changement	
	2	right relevé with left attitude derrière facing 1	through 5th to left 4th en haut
3	1	left coupé dessous	
	and	right posé de côté	
	2	left soutenu en dedans	through 2nd to bras bas
	and	demi-plié 5th right devant	
4	1	right relevé with left attitude derrière facing 5	through 5th to right 4th en haut
	2	left coupé dessous	
5	1	right posé de côté	
	2	left coupé dessous	
6	1	right assemblé porté dessous	2nd to
	and	échappé sauté to 2nd	demi-2nd
	2	right relevé with left retiré derrière	left 4th en avant
7	1	left coupé dessous	
	and-2	petit saut into 4th position with left devant	change to right 4th en avant

(continued)

No. 12 (continued)

Bar	Beat	Feet and Direction	Arms
8	1	temps levé turning to right onto left with right petit retiré devant	5th en avant
	2	right assemblé dessous	through 2nd to bras bas
9-16		repeat 1-8 to other side	

No. 13 Grand Allegro 3/4

Bar	Beat	Feet and Direction	Arms
Starting Position		5th right devant facing 5	bras bas
1		sissonne ouverte en avant onto left with right attitude derrière facing 2	through 5th to right 4th en haut
2		right assemblé dessous facing 5	bras bas
3		sissonne ouverte en avant onto right with left attitude derrière facing 1	through 5th to left 4th en haut
4		left jeté dessous facing 5	right 4th en avant
5		right posé de côté	2nd
6		left jeté en tournant dessous	5th en avant through 2nd
7		right assemblé dessous	bras bas
8		hold	
9-15		repeat 1-7 to other side	
16	1	hold	
	2-3	left fondu with right petit retiré devant facing 1	1st
17		right posé effacé en avant	
18		temps levé on right with left through passé into croisé devant	slowly through 5th en avant
19		left posé croisé en avant	to
20		temps levé on left with right développé effacé en avant	2nd
21		right jeté en avant dessus	bras bas
22		left glissade effacé en arrière	
23		left jeté battu dessus	
24		right petit jeté dessous facing 2	

No. 13 (continued)

Bar	Beat	Feet and Direction	Arms
25-31		repeat 17-23 to other side	
32		left assemblé dessous	
33		sissonne ouverte en avant onto right with left attitude derrière facing 1	through 5th to left 4th en haut
34		left assemblé dessous	through 2nd to bras bas
35		sissonne ouverte en avant onto left with right attitude croisé derrière	through 5th to 5th en haut
36	1	right jeté dessous with left dégagé croisé devant	slowly through
	2	hold	2nd
	3	left coupé dessus	to
37		right coupé dessous with left dégagé croisé devant	bras bas
38		left ballonné dessous	
39		left jeté battu dessus	
40		right assemblé dessous facing 2	
41-47		repeat 33-39 to other side	
48		left jeté dessus facing 2	bras bas
49		right glissade effacé en arrière	5th en avant
50		cabriole onto left with right derrière	left 1st arabesque
51-52		repeat 49-50	
	3	right coupé dessous into:	through 1st
53		left chassé contretemps effacé en avant	right 4th en avant
54	1-2	ending right 4th devant	
	3	left coupé dessous	
55	1	right posé de côté	
	2-3	left soutenu en dedans	through 5th to 5th en haut
56		lower right heel with left petit retiré derrière facing 1	through 2nd to bras bas
57-63		repeat 49-55 to other side	
64		lower heels in 5th right derrière	through 2nd to bras bas

No. 14 Girls' Enchaînement 3/4 Mazurka

Bar	Beat	Feet and Direction	Arms
Starting Position		5th left devant facing 5	1st
	3	right dégagé effacé devant facing 1	
1	1	right coupé dessus	
	and-2	left glissade en arrière	5th en avant
	3	cabriole onto right with left effacé derrière	right 1st arabesque
2	1	left jeté with right attitude derrière	5th en avant
	and-2	right glissade de côté 1/2 turning right to face 3	
	3	right jeté en attitude en avant facing 2	left 4th en haut
3	1	left jeté en avant with right dégagé devant	2nd
	and	right jeté en avant with left dégagé devant	
	2	left posé de côté	
	and	right fermé 5th derrière	
	3	left piqué effacé en avant with right dégagé croisé devant	left 4th en avant
4	1	right posé en avant	
	2	left assemblé battu dessous	bras bas
	3	left dégagé effacé devant	
5-8		repeat 1-4 to other side, but omit last beat in 4	

No. 14a Boys' Enchaînement

Bar	Beat	Feet and Direction	Arms
Starting Position		5th right devant facing 5	bras bas
	3	temps levé onto right with left petit retiré derrière	
1	1	echappé sauté into 2nd facing 6	right 4th en avant
	and	temps levé onto left with right retiré devant 1/2 turning right to face 8	5th en avant
	2	right posé en avant facing 7	through 2nd to right 4th en haut
	3	grand jeté en tournant landing on left with right attitude derrière	
2		repeat 1 to other side	

No. 14a (continued)

Bar	Beat	Feet and Direction	Arms
3	1	left coupé dessous	right 4th en avant
	and-2	right glissade en avant facing 2 travelling towards 5	
	3	right posé en avant facing 5	2nd
4	1	left assemblé dessous en tournant en dedans	5th en avant
	2, 3	tour en l'air landing on left with right 1st arabesque on demi-plié facing 5	left 1st arabesque
5-8		repeat 1-4 to other side	

No. 15 Pointe Enchaînement 2/4

Bar	Beat	Feet and Direction	Arms
Starting Position		5th right devant facing 5	1st
	and	left relevé with right retiré devant	right 4th en avant
1	1	right fermé 5th devant	1st
	2	hold	
	and	right relevé with left retiré derrière	left 4th en avant
2	1	left fermé 5th derrière	1st
	2	hold	
	and	left relevé with right retiré devant	
3	1	right fermé 5th devant	
	and	right relevé with left retiré derrière	
	2	left fermé 5th derrière	
	and	left relevé with right retiré devant	
4	1	right fermé 5th derrière	
	2	hold	
	and	right relevé with left retiré devant	left 4th en avant
5-15		repeat alternating sides	
16	1	left fermé 5th derrière	
	2	hold	
17	1	right relevé with left retiré derrière facing 2	through 2nd to right 4th en
	2	hold	haut
	and	left fermé 5th derrière	

(continued)

No. 15 (continued)

Bar	Beat	Feet and Direction	Arms
18	1	right relevé with left retiré derrière	left 4th en avant
	2	hold	
	and	left fermé 5th derrière	
19	1	right relevé with left retiré derrière facing 5	5th en haut
	2	left coupé dessous	
20	1	right assemblé dessous	through 2nd to
	2	hold	bras bas
21-24		repeat 17-20 to other side	

No. 16 Grand Allegro 3/4 (Girls)

Bar	Beat	Feet and Direction	Arms
Starting Position		on right with left tendu croisé derrière facing 2	right 4th en avant
Intro	2-3	left glissade de côté closing right devant facing 5	
1		left coupé dessous facing 8	5th en avant
2	1-2	right jeté en attitude en avant landing facing 2	5th en haut
	3	left coupé dessous	
3		right chasse contretemps en avant facing 1	2nd
4	1	ending left 4th devant	left 4th en avant
	2-3	right glissade de côté closing left devant facing 5	
5-8		repeat 1-4 to other side	
9		left piqué de côté with right dégagé à la seconde	through 5th to 2nd
10	1	left fondu with right petit retiré derrière	bras bas
	2-3	right glissade de côté closing left devant	through 5th
11		right piqué de côté with left à la seconde	to 2nd
12		right fondu with left retiré devant	left 4th en avant
13		left tombé effacé en avant facing 2	2nd
14		pirouette renversé on left	
15		right fermé 5th derrière facing 5	bras bas
16		right tendu croisé derrière facing 1	left 4th en avant

No. 16 (continued)

Bar	Beat	Feet and Direction	Arms
17-32		repeat 1-16 to other side	

No. 16a Grand Allegro 3/4 (Boys)

Bar	Beat	Feet and Direction	Arms
1-8		same as for girls	
9		left piqué de côté with right dégagé à la seconde	through 5th to 2nd
10		left fondu with right through passé into 2nd arabesque in demi-plié facing 1	right 2nd arabesque
11		right glissade de côté turning to face 7	
12		right grand jeté en attitude en tournant finishing with left derrière facing 2	through bras bas 5th to left 4th en haut
13		left soutenu en dedans	bras bas
14		lower heels in 5th right devant facing 5	right 4th en avant
15		tour en l'air landing 5th left devant	bras bas
16		temps levé onto left with right derrière facing 1	left 4th en avant
17-32		repeat 1-16 to other side	

No. 17 Girls' Enchaînement 3/4 Mazurka

Bar	Beat	Feet and Direction	Arms
Starting Position		5th right devant facing 5	bras bas
1	1	right posé de côté	through en avant to 2nd
	2	left jeté en tournant dessous	right 4th en avant
	3	remaining demi-plié, right rond de jambe à terre en dehors into soutenu en dehors—left coupé dessous facing 1	bras bas
2	1	right posé en avant	
	2	temps de flèche landing left with right attitude derrière	through 2nd to right 4th en haut
	3	right coupé dessous with left dégagé devant	right 4th en avant
	and	left coupé dessus	

(continued)

No. 17 (continued)

Bar	Beat	Feet and Direction	Arms
3	1	right coupé dessous with left dégagé devant (pas de valse)	
	2	left ballonné dessous	left 3rd
	3	left glissade effacé en arrière	5th en avant
4	1	cabriole onto right with left derrière	right 1st arabesque
	2	left jeté battu dessus	
	3	right petit jeté dessous facing 5	left 4th en avant
5-8		repeat 1-4 to other side	
9		repeat bar 1	
10	1	repeat 3rd beat in bar 1	
	2	right coupé dessus facing 1	
	3	temps de flèche landing left with right attitude derrière	through 2nd to right 4th en haut
11	1	right coupé dessous	right 4th en avant
	2	left ballonné dessous	3rd
	3	left glissade effacé en arrière	
12		repeat bar 4	
13-15		repeat bars 9-11 to other side	
16	1-2	repeat bar 4, beats 1-2	
	3	left assemblé dessous	bras bas

No. 18 Male Variation 3/4

Bar	Beat	Feet and Direction	Arms
Starting Position		on the left with right tendu effacé derrière facing 2	right 4th en avant
	2-3	right chassé en arrière	2nd
1		right posé en avant facing 4 with left dégagé en avant	1st
2	1-2	fouetté sauté landing right with left attitude derrière facing 2	through 5th to left 4th en haut
	3	left ballonné en avant	
3		left posé en avant	5th en avant
4	1	right jeté en avant	2nd
	2	left coupé dessous	
	3	right posé de côté	

No. 18 (continued)

Bar	Beat	Feet and Direction	Arms
5		left fermé 5th devant	bras bas
6	1	right sissonne ouverte en attitude with left derrière facing 1	through 5th to left 4th en haut
	2	left coupé dessous	
	3	right posé de côté	
7		left fermé 5th devant	bras bas
8	1	right sissonne into arabesque with left derrière	through 5th to left 2nd arabesque
	2-3	left chassé en arrière	
9-15		repeat 1-7 to other side	
16	1	temps levé onto right with left retiré derrière facing 2	
	2-3	left fermé 5th derrière demi-pointe, right posé de côté (pas de bourrée) facing 5	demi-2nd
17		left coupé dessous with right dégagé de côté	
18		right assemblé battu dessus	right 4th en avant
19		tour en l'air landing left 5th devant	
20		temps levé onto left with right derrière facing 1	bras bas
21		right glissade croisé en arrière	
22	1	cabriole onto left in 1st arabesque croisée	left 1st arabesque
	2-3	pas couru en avant (right-left)	through 5th to
23		right tendu effacé devant, left demi-plié	left 4th en haut
24	1	left fondu with right retiré derrière facing 5	
	2-3	pas de bourrée, derrière to the left facing 5 (right-left)	
25-32		repeat 17-24 to other side	
33		left coupé dessous with right dégagé à la seconde	2nd
34		right jeté battu dessus	left 4th en avant
35		left glissade en arrière turning to face 6 into:	
36	1-2	left grand jeté en attitude en avant landing facing 1 with right derrière	through 5th to right 4th en haut
	3	right coupé dessous	through 2nd
37		left chassé contretemps en avant ending	right 4th en avant
38	1-2	right 4th devant	
	3	left coupé dessous facing 1	demi-2nd

(continued)

No. 18 (continued)

Bar	Beat	Feet and Direction	Arms
39		right chassé contretemps en avant ending	left 4th en avant
40	1	left 4th devant	
	2-3	pas de bourrée derrière to the left (right-left) facing 5	
41-44		repeat 33-36 to other side	
45		right chassé contretemps en avant facing 1 ending	left 4th en avant
46		left 4th devant	
47	1-2	right glissade en avant	through 1st
	3	right grand jeté en attitude en avant	5th en avant
48		right relevé with left attitude derrière	left 4th en haut

No. 19 Girls' Enchaînement 3/4

Starting Position		on right with left tendu croisé derrière facing 2	1st
Intro	1	fondu right with left derrière	
	2-3	left coupé dessous—right posé de côté	
1		left fermé 5th devant facing 5 (pas de bourrée)	bras bas
2	1	right sissonne ouverte en avant en attitude with left derrière facing 1	through 5th to left 4th en haut
	2	left coupé dessous	
	3	right posé de côté	
3		left fermé 5th devant facing 8	bras bas
4	1	right sissonne ouverte turning to the right landing with left arabesque facing 6	right 1st arabesque
	2	left coupé dessous	
	3	right posé en avant facing 1	
5		left coupé dessous	
6	1	right jeté battu dessus	left 4th en avant
	2	hold	
	3	left posé de côté	2nd
7		right into soutenu en dedans to face 5	through bras bas to 5th en haut

No. 19 (continued)

Bar	Beat	Feet and Direction	Arms
8	1	left fondu with right petit retiré derrière facing 1	
	2	right coupé dessous	
	3	left posé de côté	bras bas
9-16		repeat 1-8 to other side	
17		left fermé 5th devant	
18	1	right sissonne ouverte en avant en attitude with left derrière facing 1	through 5th to left 4th en haut
	2	left coupé dessous	
	3	right posé de côté	
19	1	left tendu devant facing 5	5th en avant
	2	hold	
	3	left fermé 5th devant demi-plié	
20	1	left fondu with right dégagé derrière into 1st arabesque	left 1st arabesque
	2	hold	
	3	right fermé 5th derrière facing 1	bras bas
21		turn to the right into right tendu devant facing 6	through 5th to right 4th en haut
22	1	right coupé dessus	
	2-3	left into pas de bourrée en dedans en tournant	bras bas
23		(dessus-dessous)	
24		right ballonné dessous facing 5	
25-32		repeat 17-24 to other side	

No. 20 Girls' Allegro 6/8 (count 2)

Bar	Beat	Feet and Direction	Arms
Starting Position		on right with left tendu effacé derrière facing 1	left 4th en avant
1	and-1	left glissade en arrière	5th en avant
	2	cabriole onto right with left derrière	right 1st arabesque

(continued)

No. 20 (continued)

Bar	Beat	Feet and Direction	Arms
2	and-1	left glissade en arrière	bras bas
	2	left jeté battu dessus	
	and	right coupé dessous–left posé effacé en avant	1st
3	1	right posé en avant	
	and	left coupé dessous–right posé effacé en avant	
	2	left posé effacé en avant	
	and	right coupé dessous	
4	1	left glissade de côté fermé right derrière facing 5	
	2	left ballonné dessous	
	and	left glissade en arrière	through 5th
5	1	left piqué tour en dedans with right attitude derrière turning to left	to left 4th en haut
	2	left fondu facing 1	
	and	pas de bourrée right derrière to the left	
6	1	right coupé dessous facing 5	
	2	pas de chat landing right devant	through 2nd to bras bas
	and	left coupé dessous–right posé en avant–demi-pointé	
7	1	left coupé dessous with right dégagé en devant facing 1	right 4th en avant
	and	right coupé dessus–left posé en arrière–demi-pointe	
	2	right coupé dessus with left dégagé derrière	left 4th en avant
	and	left coupé dessous–right posé de côté	
8	1	left posé en avant with right dégagé devant	5th en avant
	2	fouetté sauté onto left ending 1st arabesque facing 6	left 1st arabesque
9-16		repeat 1-8 to other side	

No. 21 Male Variation 3/4

Bar	Beat	Feet and Direction	Arms
Intro:	5 bars	run forward to corner 2	
5	1	posé left en avant with right tendu derrière facing 2	right 4th en avant
	2-3	turn to face 4, right chassé en avant	2nd
1		right posé en avant with left dégagé devant	through bras bas
2		fouetté sauté landing right with left attitude derrière facing 2	right 4th en haut
3		left glissade en arrière	
4	1-2	left jeté dessus facing 5	bras bas
	3	temps levé on left facing 1	
5		right chassé contretemps en avant	through 5th en avant to
6		ending left 4th devant	
7		right glissade en avant through 4th	
8		right grand jeté en avant landing with left attitude derrière	left 2nd arabesque
	2-3	turn to face 3, left chassé en avant	2nd
9-12		repeat 1-4 to other side	
	3	left coupé dessous	
13		right posé en avant facing 4	left 4th en avant
14		right temps levé facing 7 with left passé through retiré into:	
15		left glissade en avant facing 2	bras bas
16	1-2	left grand jeté en attitude en avant with right derrière facing 5	through 5th to 2nd
	3	right dégagé devant	
17		right rond de jambe sauté en dehors ending right dégagé devant	through 1st, 5th to 2nd
18		right assemblé dessus	right 4th en avant
19		tour en l'air ending left 5th devant	bras bas
20	1	left temps levé with right petit retiré derrière facing 1	
	2-3	right glissade en avant	
21		right posé en avant	through 5th
22		left grand jeté en attitude en avant	2nd
23		right glissade en arrière	bras bas
24		right jeté dessous facing 5	

(continued)

No. 21 (continued)

Bar	Beat	Feet and Direction	Arms
25-27		repeat 17-19 to other side	
28		right temps levé with left derrière	
29		left glissade effacé en arrière facing 1	
30		jeté effacé en arrière	demi-2nd
31		right posé croisé en arrière into 4th position derrière, demi-plié	1st
32	1	left tendu croisé devant	right 4th en avant
	2	hold	
	3	left posé en avant	
33	1-2	right assemblé porté battu dessous facing 5	bras bas
	3	temps levé onto left with right effacé derrière facing 2	right 4th en avant
34		right posé croisé en avant	1st
35	1-2	left assemblé battu dessous effacé en avant facing 5	left 4th en avant
	3	temps levé onto right with left effacé derrière facing 1	
36		pas de bourrée couru to the right with 5th right devant facing 5	1st
37		right tombé de côté with left dégagé croisé devant	right 4th en avant
38		left coupé dessus facing 1	
39		right glissade en arrière	bras bas
40	1	right grand jeté en attitude en tournant turning to the right landing facing 2	through 5th to left 4th en haut
	2, 3	left coupé dessous, right posé en avant	
41-44		repeat 33-36 to other side	
45	1-2	left tombé de côté with right dégagé croisé devant facing 2	left 4th en avant
	3	right coupé dessus	
46		left into 2nd position demi-plié facing 5	right 4th en avant
47		pirouette en dehors on left	
48		right fermé 5th derrière	bras bas

No. 22 Girls' Allegro 2/4

Bar	Beat	Feet and Direction	Arms
Starting Position		on right with left tendu croisé devant facing 1	bras bas
	2	left posé en avant	
1	1	brisé dessus landing 5th right derrière	
	2	entrechat trois onto right with left derrière	
2	1	left coupé dessous	
	2	pas de chat landing 5th left devant	
3	1	right coupé dessous facing 2	through 5th en avant
	2	pas de valse (right dessous)	to left 4th en haut
4	1	left coupé dessus	
	2	right jeté battu dessus	bras bas
5-8		repeat 1-4 to other side	
9	1	right jeté en avant with left dégagé croisé devant	
	and	left jeté en avant with right dégagé effacé devant	
	2	right chassé de côté into left 5th derrière	
10	1	right posé de côté	
	2	left posé croisé devant	
	and	right dégagé de côté	2nd
11	1	right fermé 5th devant demi-pointe facing 5	
	and	left posé de côté	
	2	right fermé 5th derrière demi-pointe	1st
	and	left posé de côté	
12	1	right coupé dessus	
	2	left jeté battu dessus	right 4th en avant
13	1-and	pas de bourrée en avant (right-left) facing 1	
	2	right into 2nd position demi-plié	2nd
	and	left relevé with right petit retiré derrière	right 4th en avant
14	1	right coupé dessous–demi-pointe	
	and	left posé de côté–demi-pointe	
	2	right coupé dessus facing 2 (pas de bourrée piqué)	left 4th en avant
15	1	left coupé dessous–demi-pointe	
	and	right posé de côté–demi-pointe	
	2	left coupé dessus facing 1 (pas de bourrée piqué)	right 4th en avant

(continued)

No. 22 (continued)

Bar	Beat	Feet and Direction	Arms
16	1	right coupé dessous–demi-pointe	
	and	left posé de côté	
	2	right coupé dessus (pas de bourrée piqué en tournant to the right ending facing 2)	left 4th en avant
17-32		repeat 1-16 to other side	

Note: The pas de bourrées in bars 14-16 are on demi-pointe, working foot lifting to the knee (pas de bourrée piqué).

THURSDAY'S CLASS

Mydtskov

No. 1 Adagio 4/4

Bar	Beat	Feet and Direction	Arms
Starting Position		1st facing 5	bras bas
1		left fondu and right posé chassé en avant to 4th with left tendu derrière	
2		left fermé 1st	
3		grand plié and straighten	
4	1-2-3	left développé à la seconde	through 5th to 2nd
	4	left fermé 1st	1st
5-8		repeat 1-4 to other side	
9		left fondu and right posé chassé en arrière to 4th with left tendu devant	
10		left fermé 1st	
11		grand plié and straighten	
12	1-2-3	left développé à la seconde	through 5th to 2nd
	4	left fermé 1st	1st
13-16		repeat 9-12 to other side	
17		right through 5th devant–demi-plié and right posé chassé croisé en avant to 4th with left tendu derrière facing 2	through 5th to left 4th en haut
18		left fermé 5th derrière facing 5	through 2nd to bras bas
19-20		grand plié and straighten	
21		left retiré derrière and	
22		développé derrière	5th en avant
23		left grand rond de jambe en dedans to 2nd	2nd
24		left fermé 1st	1st
25-32		repeat 17-24 to other side	
33		right through 5th derrière–demi-plié and right posé chassé en arrière to 4th with left tendu croisé devant facing 1	through 5th to right 4th en haut
34		left fermé 5th devant facing 5	through 2nd to bras bas
35-36		grand plié and straighten	
37		left retiré devant and	

No. 1 (continued)

Bar	Beat	Feet and Direction	Arms
38		développé devant	5th en avant
39		left grand rond de jambe en dehors into 2nd	2nd
40		left fermé 1st	1st
41-47		repeat 33-39 to other side	
48		right fermé 5th devant	1st
49		right posé chassé effacé through left fondu into 4th with left tendu derrière facing 1	through 5th to left 4th en haut
50		left fermé 5th derrière facing 5	through 2nd to bras bas
51-52		grand plié and straighten	
53		left retiré derrière and	5th en avant
54		développé derrière	
55		left grand rond de jambe en dedans into 2nd	2nd
56		continue to effacé devant facing 2	right 4th en haut
	4	left fermé 5th devant facing 5	through 2nd to bras bas
57-64		repeat 49-56 to other side	
65		left posé chassé effacé through right fondu into 4th derrière with right tendu devant facing 1	through 5th to left 4th en haut
66		right fermé 5th devant facing 5	through 2nd to bras bas
67-68		grand plié and straighten	
69		right retiré devant and	5th en avant
70		développé devant	
71		right grand rond de jambe en dehors into 2nd	2nd
72	1-2	continue to attitude derrière facing 2	right 4th en haut
	3	extend derrière	through 2nd to
	4	right fermé 5th derrière facing 5	bras bas
73-80		repeat 65-72 to other side	

No. 2 Port de Bras

Bar	Beat	Feet and Direction	Arms
As Monday No. 2			

No. 3 Adagio with Pirouette 4/4

Bar	Beat	Feet and Direction	Arms
Starting Position		5th right devant facing 5	bras bas
1		left fondu with right développé devant into grand rond de jambe en dehors ending 2nd	through 5th en avant to 2nd
2	1	right posé de côté onto demi-pointe	left to 4th en haut
	2-3	left fermé 5th derrière demi-pointe	
	4	lower heels	through 2nd to bras bas
3-4		repeat bars 1-2 without lowering heels	
5-6		release left derrière and place in 4th derrière facing 2,—lowering heels and slightly bending right knee—grand port de bras into	left 4th en haut
7		pirouette en attitude en dedans on right	5th en avant
8	1-2-3	extend left derrière and grand rond de jambe en dedans into 2nd	2nd
	4	left fermé 5th devant facing 5	bras bas
9-16		repeat 1-8 to other side	
17-20		reverse 1-4	
21-23		repeat bars 5-7	
24	1-2-3	lower right heel with left attitude derrière facing 1	left 4th en haut
	4	extend left derrière and fermé 5th devant facing 5	through 2nd to bras bas
25-32		repeat 17-24 to other side	
33-34		repeat bars 1-2	
35		right fondu with left développé derrière and grand rond de jambe en dedans into 2nd	left through 5th en avant to 2nd

No. 3 (continued)

Bar	Beat	Feet and Direction	Arms
36		left posé de côté demi-pointe–right fermé 5th devant demi-pointe	right to 4th en haut
37-38		release right devant and rond de jambe en dehors demi-hauteur ending derrière facing 1; place right 4th derrière, lowering left heel and slightly bending left knee; grand port de bras into:	
39		pirouette en attitude en dedans on left	5th en avant
40	1-2-3	lower the left heel and extend right into 1st arabesque facing 6	left 1st arabesque
	4	right fermé 5th derrière facing 5	bras bas
41-48		repeat 33-40 to other side	
49-50		repeat 35-36	
51-52		repeat 3-4	
53-54		repeat 5-6	
55	1-2-3	pirouette renversé on right	
	4	right fondu	5th en avant
56	1-2	right relevé and left développé à la seconde	5th en haut
	3-4	left fermé 5th devant	bras bas
57-64		repeat 49-56 to other side	

No. 4 Posé Chassé, Assemblé 4/4 (count 2)

Bar	Beat	Feet and Direction	Arms
Starting Position		5th right devant facing 5	bras bas
1	1	right posé chassé en avant	5th en avant
	2	left fermé 5th derrière	2nd
2	1	right assemblé dessous	bras bas
	2	hold	
3-4		repeat 1-2 to other side	
5-8		reverse 1-4	

(continued)

No. 4 (continued)

Bar	Beat	Feet and Direction	Arms
9	1	right posé chassé de côté	5th en avant
	2	left fermé 5th derrière	2nd
10	1	right assemblé dessous	bras bas
	2	hold	
11-12		repeat 9-10 to other side	
13-16		reverse 9-12	
17	1	right posé chassé en avant	slowly through
	2	left fermé 5th derrière	5th en avant
18		repeat 17	to 2nd
19	1	right assemblé dessous	
	2	left assemblé dessous	slowly to
20	1	right assemblé dessous	bras bas
	2	hold	
21-24		repeat 17-20 to other side	
25-32		reverse 17-24	
33	1	right posé chassé effacé en avant facing 1	right 4th en avant
	2	left fermé 5th derrière demi-plié	change across to left 4th en avant
34	1	left posé chassé effacé en arrière	
	2	right fermé 5th devant demi-plié	right 4th en avant
35	1	right piqué effacé en avant in attitude with left derrière	left 4th en haut
	2	left coupé dessous	through 2nd
36	1	right assemblé dessous facing 5	bras bas
	2	hold	
37-40		repeat 33-36 to other side	
41-48		reverse 33-40	

No. 5 Tendu 2/4

Bar	Beat	Feet and Direction	Arms
Starting Position		5th right devant facing 1	bras bas
1	1	left tendu effacé derrière	through 5th to left 4th en haut
	2	left fermé 5th derrière	
2	1	right tendu effacé devant	
	2	right fermé 5th devant	left through 4th en avant to
3	1	left tendu à la seconde facing 5	2nd
	2	left fermé 5th derrière—demi-plié	
4	1	right assemblé dessous	bras bas
	2	hold	
5-8		repeat 1-4 to other side	
9-16		reverse 1-8 (same arm movements)	
17	1	left tendu croisé derrière facing 2	through 5th to right 4th en
	2	left fermé 5th derrière	haut
18	1	right tendu croisé devant	change across to left 4th en
	2	right fermé 5th devant	haut
19	1	left tendu à la seconde facing 5	left through
	2	left fermé 5th derrière	4th en avant to 2nd
20	1	right assemblé dessous	bras bas
21-24		repeat 17-24 to other side	
25-32		reverse 17-24	

No. 6 Pirouette 4/4 (count 2)

Bar	Beat	Feet and Direction	Arms
Starting Position		5th right devant facing 5	bras bas
1	1	right posé chassé de côté	through 5th to
	2	left fermé 5th derrière	2nd
	and	left relevé with right dévéloppé à la seconde into:	

(continued)

No. 6 (continued)

Bar	Beat	Feet and Direction	Arms
2	1	2nd position demi-plié	left 4th en avant
	2	left fermé 5th derrière	change across to
	and	demi-plié	right 4th en avant
3		pirouette en dehors on left	
4	1	right fermé 5th derrière	bras bas
	2	hold	
5-8		repeat 1-4 to other side	
9	1	left posé chassé de côté	through 5th to
	2	right fermé 5th devant	2nd
	and	right relevé with	
10	1	left petit développé effacé in arrière into: 4th position, demi-plié facing 1	left 4th en avant
	2	right fermé 5th devant facing 5	change to right 4th en avant
11		pirouette en dedans on right	
12	1	left fermé 5th devant	bras bas
	2	hold	
13-16		repeat 9-12 to other side	

No. 7 Pirouette 3/4

Starting Position	5th right devant facing 1	bras bas
1	right posé effacé en avant	through 5th to left 4th en haut
2	left fermé 5th derrière	2nd
3	right rond de jambe à terre into soutenu en dehors ending 5th devant	bras bas
4	demi-plié	
5	changement and straighten	

No. 7 (continued)

Bar	Beat	Feet and Direction	Arms
6		grand plié	
7		changement	
8		hold	
9		right posé croisé en avant facing 2	through 5th to left 4th en haut
10		left fermé 5th derrière, demi-plié	change to right 4th en avant
11		pirouette en dedans on right, end facing 5	
12		left fermé 5th devant	bras bas
13		right assemblé dessus	
14		hold	
15		left assemblé dessus	
16		hold	
17-32		repeat 1-16 to other side	
33		left posé effacé en arrière facing 1	through 5th to left 4th en haut
34		right fermé 5th devant, demi-plié	2nd
35		left rond de jambe à terre en dedans into soutenu ending right 5th devant	bras bas
36		demi-plié	
37		changement and straighten	
38		grand plié	
39		changement	
40		hold	
41		left posé croisé en arrière facing 2	through 5th to left 4th en haut
42		right fermé 5th devant, demi-plié	change to right 4th en avant
43		pirouette en dehors on left	
44		right fermé 5th devant facing 5	bras bas
45		sauté onto left with right tendu devant facing 1	left 3rd arabesque
46		right fermé 5th devant	
47		left assemblé dessus facing 5	bras bas
48		hold	
49-64		repeat 33-48 to other side	

No. 8 Rond de Jambe Sauté 4/4 (count 2)

Bar	Beat	Feet and Direction	Arms
Starting Position		5th right devant facing 5	bras bas
1	1	left fondu with right petit retiré devant	right 3rd
	2	hold	
2	1	right rond de jambe sauté en dehors	
	2	right jeté dessous	bras bas
3	1	left posé de côté	
	2	right fermé 5th derrière	
4	1	sissonne ouverte en attitude onto right with left derrière facing 1	through 5th to left 4th en haut
	and	left coupé dessous	
	2	right assemblé dessous facing 5	through 2nd to bras bas
5-8		repeat 1-4 to other side	
9-11		repeat 1-3	
12	1	sissonne ouverte en attitude onto right with left derrière facing 1	through 5th to left 4th en haut
	and	left coupé dessous—right posé de côté (pas de bourrée)	
	2	left fermé 5th devant facing 5	through 2nd to bras bas
13-16		repeat 9-12 to other side	

No. 9 Rond de Jambe Sauté 3/4

Bar	Beat	Feet and Direction	Arms
Starting Position		5th right devant facing 5	bras bas
1		rond de jambe sauté en dehors with right ending à la seconde, demi-hauteur	
2		hold	
3	1-2	repeat bar 1	
	3	right jeté dessus	
4	1-2	left posé effacé en arrière	
	3	left temps levé with right retiré derrière facing 1	

No. 9 (continued)

Bar	Beat	Feet and Direction	Arms
5	1-2	right posé croisé en arrière with left dégagé devant	right 4th en avant
	3	right temps levé	
6		left posé croisé en avant	
7		right assemblé battu dessous facing 5	bras bas
8		temps levé onto right with left retiré devant	
9-16		repeat 1-8 to other side	
17-32		repeat with 1/2 turn en dehors on each rond de jambe sauté (bar 1: land facing 7; bar 3: land facing 5, etc.)	

No. 10 Jeté 6/8 (count 2)

Bar	Beat	Feet and Direction	Arms
Starting Position		5th right devant facing 1	bras bas
1	1	right jeté en avant	left 4th en avant
	2	hold on demi-plié with left petit retiré derrière	
	and	extend left effacé derrière	
2	1	left posé effacé en arrière	2nd
	2	right jeté en tournant dessous landing left retiré devant facing 5	left 4th en avant
3	1	left tombé de côté	2nd
	2	pirouette renversé on left	
	and	left fondu	bras bas
4	1	left relevé with right développé à la seconde	through 5th to 5th en haut
	2	left fondu with right petit retiré devant facing 1	through 2nd to left 1st
5-7		repeat 1-3, but omit fondu	
8	1	right fermé 5th devant	bras bas
	2	temps levé onto right with left petit retiré devant facing 2	right 4th en avant
9-16		repeat 1-8 to other side	

No. 11 Ballotté 3/4

Bar	Beat	Feet and Direction	Arms
Starting Position		5th right devant facing 1	bras bas
Preparation		right développé effacé devant into:	
1		ballotté dessus landing on right with left derrière	5th en avant
2		ballotté dessous landing on left with right devant	to
3		temps levé onto left and rond de jambe right to attitude derrière facing 2	right 4th en haut
4		temps levé on left with right through retiré and développé devant facing 1	through 2nd bras bas
5		ballotté dessus landing on right with left derrière	
6		left coupé dessous	
7		rond de jambe sauté en dehors with right ending à la seconde facing 5	through 5th to 2nd
8		right jeté dessous, left développé effacé en devant facing 2 into:	bras bas
9-32		repeat 1-8 alternating sides	
33	polonaise		
	1	ballotté dessus landing on right with left derrière	
	2	ballotté dessous landing on left with right devant	through 5th to
	3	ballotté dessus landing on right with left derrière	2nd
34	1	left posé de côté facing 2	bras bas
	2	right dégagé devant facing 3, fouetté sauté landing on left with right attitude derrière facing 1	right 4th en haut
	3	right coupé sauté, left développé effacé devant facing 2 into:	2nd
35-40		repeat 33-34 alternating sides; (on last beat, left assemblé dessous facing 5)	through 2nd to bras bas

No. 12 Temps Levé with Grande Cabriole 3/4

Bar	Beat	Feet and Direction	Arms
Starting Position		5th right devant facing 5	bras bas
1		temps levé onto left with right petit retiré derrière facing 2	
2		right glissade effacé en arrière	5th en avant
3		grande cabriole onto left with right derrière	left 1st arabesque
4		right assemblé dessous facing 5	bras bas
5-8		repeat 1-4 to other side	
9		temps levé onto left with right petit retiré derrière facing 1	
10		right glissade croisé en arrière	5th en avant
11-12		repeat bar 3-4	
13-16		repeat 9-12 to other side	
17	1	temps levé onto right with left petit retiré devant facing 2	
	2-3	left chassé en avant	
18		left posé effacé en avant	5th en avant
19		grande cabriole onto left with right derrière	left 1st arabesque
20		right assemblé dessous facing 5	bras bas
21-24		repeat 17-20 to other side	
25-32		repeat 17-24 in croisé directions (begin facing 1)	

Note: All temps levés in the first bar of each four-bar phrase can be executed en tournant—en dehors during first sixteen bars, en dedans during last sixteen bars.

THURSDAY'S CLASS

No. 13 Girls' Allegro 2/4

Bar	Beat	Feet and Direction	Arms
Starting Position		on left with right tendu croisé devant facing 2	right 4th en avant
1	1	right posé de côté	2nd
	2	left jeté en tournant dessous	right 4th en avant
2		repeat bar 1	
3	1	right petit jeté dessus	1st
	2	left petit jeté dessus	
4		repeat bar 3	
5	1-and-2	pas de valse right dessous facing 2	left 3rd
6	1-and-2	pas de valse left dessous facing 1	right 3rd
7	1	right jeté dessous with left petit développé devant facing 5	1st
	2	left petit jeté dessus	
8	1	right glissade en arrière	bras bas
	2	right jeté dessous	left 4th en avant
9-16		repeat 1-8 to other side	

No. 14 Boys' Enchaînement 2/4

Bar	Beat	Feet and Direction	Arms
Starting Position		5th right devant facing 5	bras bas
1	1	relevé	
	2	demi-plié	
2	1	entrechat six	
	2	hold	
3		repeat bar 1 (other side)	
4	1	sissonne ouverte en attitude en avant onto right with left derrière facing 2	through 5th to 5th en haut
	2	left coupé dessous	
	and	right coupé dessus	2nd
5	1	left coupé dessous (pas de valse)	
	2	right ballonné dessous	bras bas
6	1	temps de flèche landing right with left derrière	open through 2nd to left 4th en haut
	2	left coupé dessous	
7	1	jeté fermé en avant onto right with left closing 5th derrière	through 2nd to bras bas
	2	entrechat quatre	right 4th en avant

No. 14 (continued)

Bar	Beat	Feet and Direction	Arms
8		tour en l'air landing 5th right derrière facing 5	bras bas
9-16		repeat 1-8 to other side	

No. 15 Girls' Enchaînement 2/4

Bar	Beat	Feet and Direction	Arms
Starting Position		on right with left tendu croisé derrière facing 2	right 4th en avant
	and	left dégagé à la seconde into soutenu en dedans ending	through 2nd and en avant to
1	1	facing 1 and développé right en avant, left demi-pointe	right 4th en haut
	2	right tombé effacé en avant	2nd
	and	left coupé dessous	
2		right chassé contretemps en avant ending	left 4th en avant
	2	4th croisé devant	
	and	right dégagé à la seconde into soutenu en dedans	
3-4		repeat 1-2 to other side, but omit last soutenu	
5	and	left glissade de côté facing 5	through 5th to
	1	left piqué de côté with right dégagé à la seconde facing 5	2nd
	2	left fondu with right retiré derrière	1st
6	1-2	repeat bar 5 to other side	
	and	left glissade en arrière facing 2	
7	1	left posé en avant turning left to face 8	
	2	cabriole onto left with right derrière facing 1	left 1st arabesque
8	and	right coupé dessous	1st
	1	left posé croisé en avant	
	2	left temps levé with right petit retiré derrière	left 4th en avant
9-16		repeat 1-8 to other side	

No. 16 Ballotté and Temps de Flèche 3/4 Mazurka

Bar	Beat	Feet and Direction	Arms
Starting Position		on left with right croisé tendu derrière facing 1	bras bas
1	1	right jeté en avant with left dégagé croisé devant	
	2	right temps levé with left through retiré to effacé derrière	5th en avant
	3	temps de flèche landing left with right attitude derrière	through 2nd to right 4th en haut
2	1	right posé en avant	1st
	2	ballotté dessous landing left with right effacé devant	through 5th to left 4th en haut
	3	right jeté dessus facing 2	bras bas
3-8		repeat 1-2 alternating sides	
9	1	right posé effacé en avant facing 1	
	2	ballotté dessous landing left with right effacé devant	through 5th to left 4th en haut
	3	right jeté dessus	though 2nd to bras bas
10	1	left glissade en arrière	through 2nd to
	2	left jeté dessus into right attitude croisé derrière	right 4th en haut
	3	right jeté dessous	left 4th en avant
11	1	left posé de côté facing 5	2nd
	2	right jeté en tournant dessous	
	3	left jeté en avant landing with right retiré derrière facing 2	right 4th en avant
12	1	right posé en avant facing 4	bras bas
	2	left grand jeté en attitude en tournant landing with right derrière facing 2	through 5th to 5th en haut
	3	right jeté dessus	through 2nd to bras bas
13-16		repeat 9-12 to other side	

No. 16a Temps de Flèche and Cabriole 3/4

Bar	Beat	Feet and Direction	Arms
Starting Position		5th right devant facing 1	bras bas
1	1	right posé effacé en avant	through 2nd to
	2	temps de flèche landing left with right attitude derrière	right 4th en haut
	3	right jeté dessous with left dégagé croisé devant	through 2nd to 1st
2	1	left jeté en avant, right in arabesque	5th en avant
	2	cabriole onto left in 2nd arabesque	left 2nd arabesque
	3	right jeté dessous facing 2	bras bas
3-8		repeat 1-2 alternating sides	
9	1	right posé de côté facing 5	2nd
	2	left jeté en tournant dessous	right 4th en avant
	and-3	pas de valse right devant, left dessous facing 1	right 4th en haut
10	1	right jeté dessus	through 2nd to
	2	left jeté dessus	
	3	right jeté dessus	bras bas
11	1	left posé de côté facing 2	demi 2nd
	2	right dégagé devant facing 3 and temps levé onto left turning 1/2 to left with right retiré derrière facing 1	left 4th en avant
	3	right jeté dessus	1st
12	1-2	repeat 11, beats 1-2	
	3	right jeté dessous facing 5	bras bas
13-15		repeat 9-11 to other side	
16	1	right tombé de côté	2nd
	2	pirouette renversé on right	
	3	left fermé 5th derrière	bras bas

No. 17 Girls' Allegro 2/4

Bar	Beat	Feet and Direction	Arms
Starting Position		on left with right tendu croisé derrière facing 1	1st
	and	pas couru effacé en avant	
1	1	left posé with right tendu effacé devant, left demi-plié	through 5th to left 4th en haut
	2	right coupé dessus	1st
2	1	left glissade en arrière	through 5th
	2	cabriole onto right with left derrière	to right 1st arabesque
3	1	left coupé dessous	bras bas
	2	right rond de jambe sauté en dehors ending 2nd, demi-hauteur	
4	1	right coupé dessus	
	2	left jeté dessus	
	and	pas couru en avant	
5	1	left posé en avant with right tendu devant, left demi-plié	through 5th to left 4th en haut
	2	right fermé 5th devant	
	and	left posé en arrière	bras bas
6	1	place right in 4th croisé derrière, left demi-plié	through 5th to right 2nd arabesque
	2	right fermé 5th derrière	left 4th en avant
7	1	temps levé onto right turning to left with left petit retiré devant to face 5	
	2	left petit jeté dessus	bras bas
8	1	right petit jeté dessus	
	and	left petit jeté dessus	
	2	right petit jeté dessus	
	and	pas couru en avant facing 2	
9-15		repeat 1-7 to other side	
16	1-and-2	repeat 8 to other side	
	and	right glissade effacé en arrière facing 2	
17	1	right coupé dessous facing 3	through 5th to 2nd
	and	right temps levé with left dégagé devant facing 1	
	2	left posé en avant	
18	1	brisé dessus landing 5th right derrière facing 5	bras bas
	2	temps levé onto right with left derrière	left 4th en avant
	and	left glissade de côté	

No. 17 (continued)

Bar	Beat	Feet and Direction	Arms
19	1	left piqué effacé en arrière with right retiré devant	right 4th en avant
	and	right coupé dessus	
	2	repeat beat 1	
20	1	right coupé dessus	
	2	left jeté dessus	left 4th en avant
	and	right glissade de côté	
21	1	right coupé dessous facing 3	
	and	right temps levé with left dégagé devant facing 1	2nd
	2	left posé en avant	
	and	right ballonné en avant	5th en avant
22	1	right piqué effacé en avant into 1st arabesque	right 1st arabesque
	2	hold	
	and	left coupé dessous–right posé de côté–demi-pointe into	
23	1	left tendu croisé devant	à la lyre (right up)
	2	right temps levé with left through retiré to effacé derrière	through 2nd to à la lyre (left up)
	and	left coupé dessous	
24	1	right glissade de côté, left fermé 5th derrière	
	2	right jeté dessus	bras bas
	and	left glissade effacé en arrière	
25-32		repeat 17-24 to other side but omit last glissade	

No. 18 Girls' Enchaînement 4/4

Bar	Beat	Feet and Direction	Arms
Starting Position		on left with right tendu croisé derrière facing 1	1st
1	1	right jeté en avant with left dégagé devant	
	2	left jeté en avant with right dégagé en avant	
	3	right assemblé dessus	
	4	temps levé onto right with left petit retiré devant	

(continued)

No. 18 (continued)

Bar	Beat	Feet and Direction	Arms
2	1	left posé croisé en avant	
	2	right ballonné en avant	
	3	right piqué effacé en avant into 1st arabesque	right 1st arabesque
	4	right fondu	
3	1-and-2	left pas de bourrée dessous-dessus facing 5	bras bas
	3-and-4	right pas de bourrée dessous-dessus	
4	1-2	left coupé dessous	
	3-4	right jeté battu dessus facing 2	1st
5-16		repeat 1-4 on alternating sides	

No. 19 Allegro Enchaînement

As Monday No. 20

No. 20 Girls' Allegro 2/4

Bar	Beat	Feet and Direction	Arms
Starting Position		on left with right tendu croisé derrière facing 1	1st
1	1	pas couru effacé en avant into 4th position, demi-plié right devant	
	2	entrechat trois landing on left with right derrière	
2	1	pas couru de côté into 4th position right derrière	
	2	entrechat trois landing right with left derrière	
3	1-and-2	3 petits jetés (left-right-left dessus) facing 5	
4	1-and-2	3 petits jetés (right-left-right dessus)	
5	and-1	pas de bourrée effacé en arrière left-right ending left with right dégagé effacé devant facing 1	right 4th en avant
	and-2	pas de bourrée effacé en arrière right-left ending right with left dégagé effacé derrière	left 4th en avant
	and	left coupé dessous	

No. 20 (continued)

Bar	Beat	Feet and Direction	Arms
6	1	right posé en avant	bras bas
	2	left grand jeté en attitude en avant with right derrière	through 5th to 2nd
7-8		repeat 5-6 to other side	
9-16		repeat 1-8 to other side	

No. 21 Grand Allegro 2/4

Bar	Beat	Feet and Direction	Arms
Starting Position		on right with left tendu croisé derrière facing 2	left 4th en avant
	2, 3	left chassé croisé en arrière	2nd
1	1	left posé en arrière	bras bas
	2, 3	turning to left to face 4, right dégagé devant and sauté into	through 5th en avant
2	1	grande cabriole fouettée sautée landing on left in 1st arabesque facing 2	left 1st arabesque
	2, 3	pas de bourrée dessus en tournant (right-left)	through 2nd
3		right coupé dessous	
4		left ballonné dessous	left 4th en avant
5-8		repeat 1-4	
	2-3	left glissade effacé en arrière facing 5	
9		left piqué effacé en arrière with right retiré devant	right 4th en avant
10	1	right coupé dessus	
	2-3	left glissade effacé en arrière	bras bas
11		left piqué effacé en arrière with right retiré devant	through 5th to 5th en haut
12	1	right coupé dessus facing 1	
	2	left coupé dessous	through 2nd
	3	right posé de côté (pas de bourrée)	bras bas
13		left posé croisé en avant	
14	1-2	cabriole onto left in arabesque croisée	left 1st arabesque
	3	right coupé dessous	

(continued)

No. 21 (continued)

Bar	Beat	Feet and Direction	Arms
15		left glissade en avant	through 2nd to bras bas
16		left grand jeté en attitude en avant with right derrière	through 5th to 2nd
17-32		repeat 1-16 to other side	
Change to 6/8 (count 2)		part 2 (for girls only)	
33	and	left glissade de côté	through 2nd to
	1	left piqué de côté with right dégagé à la seconde facing 2	à la lyre (left up)
	2	right fermé 5th devant	through 2nd to
34	1	entrechat quatre	bras bas
	2	temps levé onto left with right derrière facing 1	
35-40		repeat 33-34 alternating sides	
41	and	left glissade effacé en avant facing 2	
	1	left piqué effacé en avant with right derrière, demi-hauteur	demi-2nd
	2	right posé croisé en avant	
	and	left glissade en avant	bras bas
42	1	repeat bar 41, beat 1	
	2	right coupé dessous	
	and	left chassé en avant facing 3	right 4th en avant
43	1	left posé en avant facing 7	
	2	left temps levé	
44	1	right jeté dessus facing 1	bras bas
	2	left jeté dessous facing 2	right 4th en avant
45		tours chaînés déboulés (right-left-right-left) on the diagonal	
46	1	chaîné (right-left)	
	2	right coupé dessus	
47	and-1	left pas de bourrée dessus en tournant to the right to face 7	
	and-2	right pas de bourrée dessous en tournant to the right to face 5	
48	1	left coupé dessous	
	and-2	pas de basque right ending left 4th croisé devant and posé into right tendu croisé derrière facing 1	through 5th to 2nd

No. 22 Boys' Enchaînement 2/4

Bar	Beat	Feet and Direction	Arms
Starting Position		on left with right tendu croisé derrière facing 1	right 4th en avant
1	1	right piqué with left développé à la seconde facing 5	2nd
	2	left coupé dessus facing 1	bras bas
2	1	right glissade en arrière facing 1	through 5th
	2	right grand jeté en attitude en tournant turning 3/4 to the right landing with left derrière facing 2	to left 4th en haut
3	1	left coupé dessous facing 5	5th en avant
	and	right grand jeté en attitude en tournant turning 3/4 to the right landing with left derrière facing 2 (same as above)	left 4th en haut
	2-and	repeat 1-and	
4	1	repeat 1st beat in 3	
	2	repeat "and" beat in 3	
5	1	left coupé dessous facing 2	1st
	2	right jeté battu dessus	
6	1	left assemblé dessus	bras bas
	2	sissonne ouverte en attitude en avant onto left with right derrière	through 5th to right 4th en haut
	and	right coupé dessous	
7	1	left posé effacé en avant	2nd
	2	left temps levé with right passé through retiré to dégagé croisé devant	1st
8	and-1	right glissade en avant	through 5th to
	2	right grand jeté en attitude en avant with left derrière	2nd
9-16		repeat 1-8 to other side	

Kirsten Ralov teaching American students. (*Maria Finitzio*)

Kirsten Ralov teaching boys in the Royal Danish Ballet in 1969. (*Mogens von Haven*)

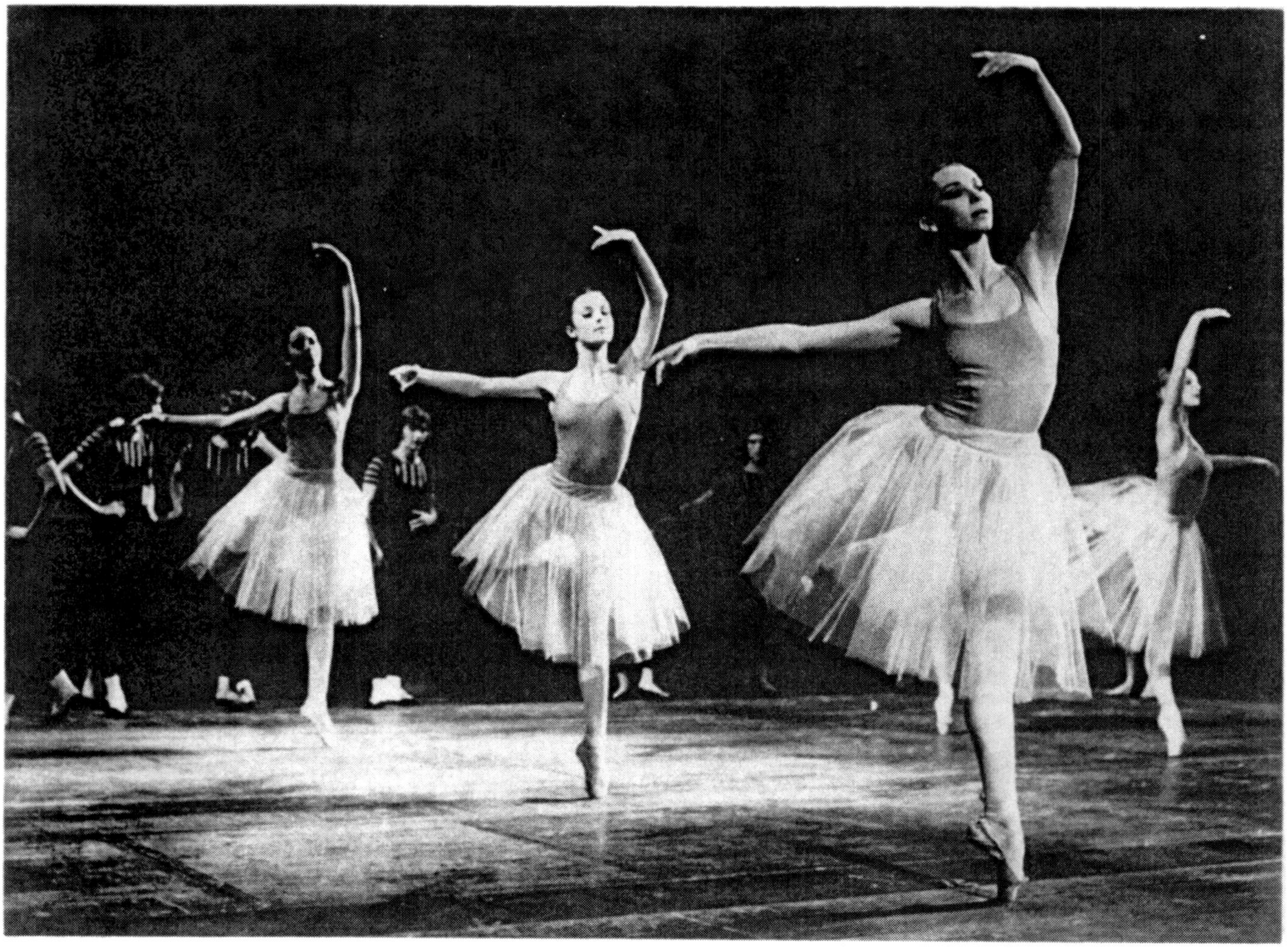

Annemari Vingaard, Ann Kristin Hauge, and Kirsten Wulff in *Wednesday's Class*. (*John R. Johnsen*)

Flemming Ryberg in *Wednesday's Class*. (*John R. Johnsen*)

Konservatoriet performed by the Royal Swedish Ballet in 1973. (*Enar Merkel Rydberg*)

John Lindquist

FRIDAY'S CLASS

No. 1 Adagio 4/4

Bar	Beat	Feet and Direction	Arms
Starting Position		1st facing 5	1st
Intro		right posé chassé en avant left fermé 1st	
1		grand plié	
2	1-2	straighten	
	3-4	left développé à la seconde	through 5th to 2nd
3		right fondu	
4	1-2	left into soutenu en dehors ending sur les pointes left 5th devant	through bras bas to 5th en haut
	3-4	with left, battements serrés and fermé 5th derrière	bras bas
5		grand plié and straighten	
6	1-2-3	right développé à la seconde	through 5th
	4	hold	to 2nd
	and	right retiré passé into	
7	1-2	développé devant facing 1	left 4th en haut
	3-4	rond de jambe en dehors	
8	1-2	right retiré passé into	through 2nd to
	3-4	attitude croisé derrière	right 4th en haut
9	1-2	right tendu croisé derrière, facing 1 and inclining body to the left	right through 2nd to 4th en avant
	3-4	turn to the right into right tendu croisé devant	2nd
10	1-2	fondu left and bend forward facing 2	bras bas
	3	straighten	through 5th to left 4th en haut
	4	facing 5 open right to tendu à la seconde	2nd
11		right through 5th devant and développé devant	through bras bas to 5th en avant
	and	right coupé dessus	
12		left développé derrière into grand rond de jambe en dedans ending à la seconde	through 2nd to 5th en haut
13-16		repeat 9-12 to other side	
17	1	right coupé dessous and left dégagé to à la seconde, demi-hauteur	2nd
	2	double rond de jambe en l'air en dehors with left ending à la seconde	
	3-4	left petits battements	

No. 1 (continued)

Bar	Beat	Feet and Direction	Arms
18	1	left coupé dessous and	
	2	right dégagé to à la seconde, demi-hauteur	
	3-4	right petits battements	
19	1	right développé effacé devant facing 1	left through 5th to left 4th en haut
	2	right through retiré passé into attitude derrière facing 2	through 5th to right 4th en haut
	3	right through retiré passé into à la seconde	through 5th to 2nd
	4	right coupé dessus with left	
20	1	dégagé à la seconde	
	2-and-3	3 single ronds de jambe en dedans turning to the right to face 7	
	and	hold	
	4-and	continue turning to right with 3 single ronds de jambe en dedans ending facing 5	
21		left grand rond de jambe en dedans through retiré passé into arabesque facing 8	through 5th to 3rd arabesque

No. 2 Port de Bras

As Tuesday No. 2

No. 3 Adagio with Pirouette 4/4

Starting Position		5th right devant facing 2	1st
Intro	1	relevé	
	2	demi-plié	through 5th to left 4th en haut
	3-4	right posé chassé croisé en avant into 4th	
1		sliding left toe slightly back place sole of left on the floor and demi-plié on right, begin	
2		grand port de bras into	
3		pirouette en attitude en dedans on right, finish facing 2	5th en avant
4		lower right heel extending left derrière and grand rond de jambe to à la seconde facing 5	2nd

(continued)

No. 3 (continued)

Bar	Beat	Feet and Direction	Arms
5-6	1-4	promenade en dedans	slowly to
	1-2-3	one whole turn	5th en haut
	4	turn 1/4 to right into 1st arabesque facing 8	right 1st arabesque
7		arabesque penchée, and straighten	
	and	right relevé with left through retiré,	bras bas
8		lower heel and left posé chassé croisé en avant into 4th facing 1	through 5th to right 4th en haut
9-16		repeat 1-8 to other side	

No. 4 Adagio 4/4

Bar	Beat	Feet and Direction	Arms
Starting Position		5th right devant facing 1	bras bas
1	1-2-3	left fondu with right développé devant	5th en avant
	4	right tendu devant on left demi-plié	2nd
2	1-2-3	right fermé in 5th devant sur les pointes	right to 4th en haut
	4	lower heels	
3	1-2-3	right fondu with left développé effacé derrière	right through en avant to 2nd
	4	left tendu effacé derrière on right demi-plié	
4	1-2-3	left fermé in 5th derrière sur les pointes	bras bas
	4	lower heels	
5	1-2-3	right développé effacé devant on left demi-plié	5th en avant to
	4	right fermé 5th devant and	left 4th en
6		left développé en attitude derrière	haut
7	1-2-3		left slowly through 2nd to
	4	right fondu	left 4th en avant
8	1-2	pirouette en dehors on right with left attitude derrière	2nd
	3	hold facing 2	
	4	left retiré passé	bras bas
9-16		repeat 1-8 to other side	

No. 4 (continued)

Bar	Beat	Feet and Direction	Arms
17		left fondu with right développé devant facing 1	through 5th to 2nd
18	1-2	right fermé in 5th devant sur les pointes	left 4th en haut, right right 4th en avant
	3-4	hold	5th en avant
19		right fondu with left développé derrière into arabesque facing 8	right 1st arabesque
20	1-2-3	left through tendu derrière to 5th derrière sur les pointes facing 1	
	4	lower heels	bras bas
21		left fondu with right développé devant	through 5th en avant
22		hold	to 2nd
23		right pirouette renversé en dedans on left ending attitude derrière facing 2	5th en avant to right 4th en haut
24		extend right to arabesque and fermé 5th derrière	through 2nd to bras bas
25-32		repeat 17-24 to other side	

No. 5 Relevé and Pirouette 3/4

Bar	Beat	Feet and Direction	Arms
Starting Position		5th right devant facing 5	bras bas
1	1	left relevé with right développé à la seconde	through 5th to 2nd
	2-3	hold	
2	1	left fondu with right sur le cou-de-pied facing 1	bras bas
	2-3	hold	
3	1	left relevé with right dégagé attitude croisé derrière facing 1	through 5th to right 4th en haut
	2	left fondu with right dégagé à la seconde, demi-hauteur	right opens to 2nd
	3	pirouette renversé en dedans on left	
4	1	ending à la seconde facing 5	5th en haut
	2	hold	
	3	right retiré facing 1	left opens to 2nd
5-6		grand port de bras into	

(continued)

No. 5 (continued)

Bar	Beat	Feet and Direction	Arms
7		pirouette en dedans en attitude on left with right derrière	5th en avant
8	1-2	lower heel in attitude position facing 2	right 4th en haut
	3	right fermé 5th derrière facing 5	through 2nd to bras bas
9-16		repeat 1-8 to other side	
17-22		repeat 1-6	
23	1-2	pirouette renversé on left	5th en avant
	3	left fondu	
24	1-2	left relevé with right développé à la seconde facing 5	5th en haut
	3	right fermé 5th derrière	through 2nd to bras bas
25-32		repeat 17-24 to other side	

No. 6 Petit Allegro 2/4

Bar	Beat	Feet and Direction	Arms
Starting Position		5th right devant facing 5	bras bas
1	1	right relevé with left attitude derrière facing 1	through 5th to left 4th en haut
	2	left fermé 5th derrière	through 2nd
2	1	changement	to bras bas
	2	échappé sauté into 2nd position—demi-plié facing 5	left 4th en avant
3		pirouette en dehors on right	
4		on demi-pointe, extend left dégagé devant facing 2 and place it 4th position devant, demi-plié	right 4th en avant
5		pirouette en dedans on right	
6	1	left coupé dessus facing 5	bras bas
	2	right assemblé dessus	
7	1	right tendu devant facing 1	through 5th to left 4th en haut
	2	right fermé 5th devant	2nd
8	1	left assemblé dessus facing 5	bras bas
	2	hold	

No. 6 (continued)

Bar	Beat	Feet and Direction	Arms
9-16		repeat 1-8 to other side	
17	1	right posé chassé de côté	through 5th to 2nd
	2	left fermé 5th derrière	
18	1	right assemblé dessous	bras bas
	2	échappé sauté into 2nd	left 4th en avant
19		pirouette en dehors on right	5th en avant
20		lower heel and dégagé left into attitude derrière facing 2	left 4th en haut
21	1	left coupé dessous facing 5	through 2nd to
	2	right assemblé dessous	bras bas
22	1	changement	
	2	échappé sauté into 4th position demi-plié, right devant facing 1	left 4th en avant
23		pirouette en dedans on left	
24	1	right fermé 5th derrière facing 5	bras bas
	2	hold	
25-32		repeat 17-24 to other side	
Change to 3/4			
32a: extra bar of music			
33		right posé chassé en avant	
34		left fermé 5th derrière	
35	1	right assemblé dessous	
	2	hold	
	3	right relevé with left développé à la seconde into	through 5th to 2nd
36		2nd position, demi-plié	left 4th en avant
37-38		pirouette en dehors on right	
39		place left tendu à la seconde while lowering right heel facing 5	2nd
40		left fermé 5th devant	bras bas
41	1	right jeté en avant facing 1	left 4th en avant
	2	hold	
	3	right fondu with left dégagé effacé derrière	
42		left tombé effacé en arrière	2nd
43-44		pirouette renversé en dedans on left	
45		right posé chassé croisé en avant facing 2	through 5th to 5th en haut

(continued)

No. 6 (continued)

Bar	Beat	Feet and Direction	Arms
46		left coupé dessous	
47		right assemblé dessous facing 5	through 2nd to bras bas
48		hold	
49-64		repeat 33-48 to other side	

No. 7 Female Variation 3/4

Bar	Beat	Feet and Direction	Arms
Starting Position		on left with right tendu croisé derrière facing 1	1st
Intro		left fondu	
1	1	right coupé 5th derrière demi-pointe, left posé de côté (pas de bourrée)	
	2	right posé piqué en avant facing 8 with left développé derrière	right through 5th
	3	right fondu with left derrière, demi-hauteur	to 4th en haut
2		repeat 1 to other side	
3		repeat 1 but face 5 on posé piqué	
4	1	left fermé 5th derrière	
	2	entrechat six	through 2nd to bras bas
	3	left relevé with right développé derrière, then lower left heel	through 5th to left 4th en haut
5	1	right posé en arrière with left tendu devant, left fermé 5th devant	bras bas
	2	right piqué en arrière with left retiré	through 5th en avant
	3	lower right heel into demi-plié and développé left derrière	right 4th en haut
6		repeat 5 to other side	
	and	right fermé 5th derrière	
7		left dégagé croisé devant facing 1, rond de jambe through 2nd to arabesque on right demi-plié	through 5th to right 3rd arabesque
8		penchée and straighten	

No. 7 (continued)

Bar	Beat	Feet and Direction	Arms
9	1	left through retiré passé to posé croisé en avant	bras bas
	2	right glissade en avant	
	3	right tendu effacé devant facing 1	left 4th en haut
10		repeat 9 to other side	
11		repeat 9	
	and	right petit jeté dessus	left 4th en avant
12	1	left tombé de côté facing 5	2nd
	2-3	pirouette renversé en dedans on left, when facing 2 lower heel and dégagé right croisé devant, open right through 2nd to arabesque on left demi-plié facing 6	5th en avant left 3rd arabesque
13		right coupé dessous demi-pointe, left posé de côté right into 4th position devant demi-plié facing 4 (pas de bourrée)	left 4th en avant
14		relevé in 4th turning 1/2 to the left to face 2, lower the heels in 4th position, demi-plié	right 4th en avant
15		pirouette en dehors on left ending facing 5 with right petit dégagé devant right assemblé en avant	2nd to bras bas
16	1	left dégagé à la seconde	through 1st to 2nd
	2	left rond de jambe en dedans into retiré passé facing 8	5th en avant
	3	right fondu with left développé derrière to arabesque	right 3rd arabesque
17	1	left fermé 5th derrière, sissonne ouverte en avant landing on right facing 1	bras bas
	2	left piqué croisé en avant with right petits battements sur le cou-de-pied ending petit dégagé devant	demi-2nd
	3	right posé effacé en avant	
18	1	left coupé dessous, right petit assemblé en avant	left 4th en avant
	2	right dégagé devant	
	3	right through 2nd while turning to face 2 into 2nd arabesque on left demi-plié	right 2nd arabesque

(continued)

No. 7 (continued)

Bar	Beat	Feet and Direction	Arms
19-20		repeat 17-18 to other side	
21	1-and	left coupé dessous demi-pointe, right posé de côté (pas de bourrée),	
	2	left piqué croisé en avant facing 1	right 4th en avant
	3	left fondu	
22	1-and	right coupé dessous demi-pointe, left posé de côté (pas de bourrée dessous en tournant to right)	
	2	right piqué en avant facing 5 with left attitude derrière	2nd
	3	right fondu	
	and	left coupé dessous	bras bas
23	1-2	left relevé with right développé à la seconde into 2nd position demi-plié	through 5th and 2nd to right 4th en avant
	3	pirouette en dehors on left opening right à la seconde when facing 5	demi-2nd
24		right fermé 5th derrière, demi-plié, soutenu to the right, sur les pointes ending right 5th devant facing 5	through bras bas 5th en avant to wide 5th en haut (palms facing out)

No. 8 Posé Chassé 4/4 (count 2)

Bar	Beat	Feet and Direction	Arms
Starting Position		5th right devant facing 5	bras bas
1	1	right posé chassé en avant	
	2	left fermé 5th derrière	5th en avant
2		repeat 1	2nd
3	1	right assemblé dessous	
	and	temps levé onto right with left derrière	bras bas
	2	left coupé dessous	
4	1	right assemblé dessous	
	2	hold	
5-8		repeat 1-4 to other side	
9-16		reverse 1-8 (same arm movements)	

No. 8 (continued)

Bar	Beat	Feet and Direction	Arms
17	1	right posé chassé en avant	
	2	left fermé 5th derrière	
18	1	right assemblé dessous	
	and	temps levé onto right with left derrière	
	2	left petit jeté dessous	5th en avant
19	1	right posé chassé de côté	2nd
	2	left fermé 5th derrière	
20	1	right assemblé dessous	bras bas
	2	hold	
21-24		repeat 17-20 to other side	
25-32		reverse 17-24 (same arm movements)	
33	1	right posé chassé en avant	
	2	left fermé 5th derrière	
	and	right dégagé de côté, coupé dessous demi-pointe, left posé de côté (pas de bourrée)	
34	1	right coupé dessus	
	2	left coupé dessus	
	and	right jeté dessus	
35	1	left posé chassé en arrière	
	2	right fermé 5th devant	
36	1	left assemblé dessus	
	2	hold	
37-40		repeat 33-36 to other side	
41-48		reverse 33-40	
49	1	right posé chassé en avant facing 1	through 5th to
	2	left fermé 5th derrière	left 4th en haut
	and	right dégagé à la seconde, coupé dessous, left posé de côté (pas de bourrée)	2nd
50	1	right coupé dessus	
	2	left ballonné dessus	bras bas
	and	left ballonné dessous	through 5th
51	1	left posé chassé effacé en arrière	left 4th en haut
	2	right fermé 5th devant	
52	1	left assemblé dessus facing 5	bras bas

(continued)

No. 8 (continued)

Bar	Beat	Feet and Direction	Arms
53-56		repeat 49-52 to other side	
57-64		reverse 49-56 (same arm movements)	

No. 9 Tendu 2/4

Bar	Beat	Feet and Direction	Arms
Starting Position		5th right devant facing 5	bras bas
1	1	right tendu à la seconde	
	2	left fondu with right sur le cou-de-pied	
2-3		repeat 1	
4	1	right tendu à la seconde	
	2	right fermé 5th derrière	
5-8		repeat 1-4 to other side	
9	and-1	right grand battement closing 5th devant	through 5th to 2nd
	2	hold	
10	and-1	right grand battement closing 5th derrière	
	2	hold	
11-12		repeat 9-10	
13-16		repeat 9-12 to other side	bras bas
17	1	right tendu devant facing 2	slowly to
	and-2	right rond de jambe à terre en dehors ending tendu devant	5th en haut
18-19		repeat rond de jambe 4 times	
20	and-1	rond de jambe as above onto left demi-plié	2nd
	and-2	rond de jambe à terre into 5th derrière while turning to face 1	bras bas
21-23		repeat 17-19 to other side	

No. 9 (continued)

Bar	Beat	Feet and Direction	Arms
24	and-1	left rond de jambe à terre on right demi-plié into:	
	and	left dégagé à la seconde facing 5	1st
	2	left fermé 5th derrière demi-pointe	
	and	right into 5th derrière demi-pointe	
25	1	left into 5th derrière demi-pointe	
	and	left demi-plié with right dégagé à la seconde	
	2	right into 5th derrière demi-pointe	
	and	left into 5th derrière demi-pointe	
26	1	right into 5th derrière demi-pointe	
	and	right demi-plié with left dégagé à la seconde	
	2	left into 5th derrière demi-pointe	slowly through 5th en avant
	and	right into 5th derrière demi-pointe	
27	1-and-2	left-right-left into 5th derrière finishing facing 2	to 5th en haut

No. 10 Male Variation 3/4

Starting Position		5th right devant facing 5	bras bas
1	1	changement	
	2	changement	
	3	échappé sauté into 2nd	right 4th en avant
2	1-2	pirouette en dehors on left	
	3	right fermé 5th derrière	bras bas
3-4		repeat 1-2 to other side	
5		repeat 1	
6	1-2	pirouette en dehors on left with right à la seconde	2nd
	3	left fondu with right à la seconde	
7	1-2	pirouette en dehors on left with right en attitude derrière	right 4th en haut
	3	left demi-plié with right attitude	

(continued)

No. 10 (continued)

Bar	Beat	Feet and Direction	Arms
8	1	left relevé with right attitude	
	2-and	right coupé dessous demi-pointe, left de côté (pas de bourrée) turning to the right	
	3	right fermé 5th devant facing 2	bras bas
9	1	left demi-plié with right dégagé croisé devant	through 5th to left 4th en haut
	2	straighten left and open right to à la seconde facing 5	2nd
	and	right retiré	
	3	right fermé 5th derrière facing 1	bras bas
10		repeat 9 to other side	slowly
11	1	right dégagé à la seconde	through 5th to 5th en haut
	2-3	promenade on left with right ronds de jambe en l'air (6 continuous) in one turn to the right	
12	1	finishing with right extended à la seconde	
	2	hold	slowly through
	3	right fermé 5th derrière	2nd to bras bas

No. 11 Petits Sauts 2/4

Bar	Beat	Feet and Direction	Arms
Starting Position		5th right devant facing 5	bras bas
1	1-and-2	3 changements	
2	1	temps levé onto left with right devant	
	2	right assemblé dessous	
3-8		repeat alternating sides	
9		2 entrechats quatre	
10	1-and-2	3 changements	
11-14		repeat alternating legs	
15		4 petits changements	slowly through
16		3 petits changements (these 7 changements taking one turn to the right)	5th to 5th en haut, 2nd, and bras bas

No. 11 (continued)

Bar	Beat	Feet and Direction	Arms
17	1	right glissade de côté closing left 5th derrière	
	2	repeat beat 1	
18	1	right jeté dessus	
	and	left assemblé dessus	
	2	hold	
19-20		repeat 17-18 to other side	
21		right posé de côté into a curtsey	

No. 12 Ballonné, Jeté 4/4

Starting Position		on right with left tendu croisé derrière facing 2	bras bas
	4	right fondu	1st
1	1	left coupé dessous	
	2	right ballonné devant	right 4th en avant
	3	right posé effacé en avant facing 1	5th en avant
	4	left grand jeté en attitude en avant with right derrière	2nd
2-3		repeat 1 on alternating sides	
4	1-and-2	3 petits jetés dessus (right-left-right) travelling forward facing 5	slowly to bras bas
	and	left posé de côté	
	3	right into soutenu en dedans ending 5th left devant facing 5	through 5th to 5th en haut
	4	left fondu facing 1, right retiré derrière	1st
5-8		repeat 1-4 to other side but omit last fondu	
Boys:			
1-3		same as for girls	
4	1	right coupé dessous facing 5	
	2	left assemblé en avant	left 4th en avant
	3	tour en l'air to the left landing 5th left devant facing 5	bras bas
	4	left fondu right extended derrière facing 1	
5-8		repeat 1-4 to other side but omit last fondu	

No. 12a Female Variation 4/4

Bar	Beat	Feet and Direction	Arms
Starting Position		5th right devant facing 2	bras bas
1	1-2	2 entrechats quatre	
	3	relevé sur les pointes in 5th with left devant facing 1	through 5th to demi-2nd
	4	lower heels	bras bas
2-3-4		repeat 1 on alternating sides but in bar 4 on beat 4 lower right heel onto demi-plié with left petit retiré derrière facing 2	right 3rd
5	1	left coupé dessous	
	2	right ballonné en avant facing 1	1st
	3	right posé effacé en avant	5th en avant
	4	left grand jeté en avant—right attitude derrière	2nd
6-7		repeat bar 5 on alternating sides	
8	1-and-2	3 petits jetés dessous (right-left-right) travelling slightly backwards facing 5	1st
	and	left dégagé à la seconde on right demi-plié into:	demi-2nd
	3	soutenu en dehors ending 5th left devant facing 5	through 2nd to 5th en haut
	4	hold (sur les pointes)	
9-16		repeat 1-8 to other side	

No. 13 Male Variation (Pirouette) 4/4

Bar	Beat	Feet and Direction	Arms
Starting Position		5th left devant facing 5	bras bas
1	1	entrechat six	
	2	hold	
	3	left relevé with right développé à la seconde	through 5th to 2nd
	4	right into 2nd position demi-plié	right 4th en avant
2	1-2-3	pirouette en dehors à la seconde on left	2nd
	4	lower left heel and rond de jambe en l'air en dehors ending à la seconde	
3	1	right fermé 5th derrière	bras bas
	2	hold	
	3	right relevé with left développé à la seconde	through 5th to 2nd
	4	left into 2nd position demi-plié	left 4th en avant

No. 13 (continued)

Bar	Beat	Feet and Direction	Arms
4-5		repeat bars 2-3 to other side	
6	1-2	pirouette en dehors à la seconde on left	2nd
	and	left fondu with right à la seconde	2nd
	3-4	pirouette en attitude with right derrière	right 4th en haut
7	1	left fondu with right through retiré to dégagé croisé devant facing 2	left 4th en avant
	2	right posé en avant	
	3	brisé dessous en avant with left fermé 5th derrière	bras bas

No. 13a Pas de Bourrée 4/4

Bar	Beat	Feet and Direction	Arms
Starting Position		5th right devant façing 5	bras bas
Intro: bar 7 from No. 13	4	left fondu with right dégagé à la seconde, right coupé dessous, left de côté (pas de bourrée)	
1	1	right dessus	
	and	left dessus, right de côté	
	2	left dessous	
	and	right dessous, left de côté	
	3	right dessus	
	and	left dessus, right de côté	
	4	left dessous	
	and	right dessous	
2	1-2-3	left petits battements sur le cou-de-pied	
	4	right fondu with left dégagé à la seconde	
	and	left dessous, right de côté	
3-4		repeat 1-2 to other side, but omit beat "and"	
5	1	right rond de jambe sauté en l'air en dehors	
	2	repeat beat 1	
	3-and-4	3 petits jetés dessous (right-left-right) travelling slightly backwards	

(continued)

No. 13 (continued)

Bar	Beat	Feet and Direction	Arms
6-7		repeat bar 5 alternating sides	
8	1	temps levé onto right with left through 2nd, demi-hauteur to derrière facing 1	left low 2nd arabesque
	2	left jeté en attitude with right derrière facing 5	5th en avant
	3	right jeté en attitude with left derrière	
	4	left jeté dessus	bras bas
9	1	right rond de jambe sauté en l'air en dedans	
	2	repeat beat 1	
	3-and-4	3 petits jetés dessus (right-left-right) travelling slightly forwards	slowly to demi-2nd
10-11		repeat bar 9 on alternating sides	
12	1	left jeté dessus	
	2	right assemblé dessus	bras bas
	3	hold	
	and-4	right glissade de côté fermé left 5th derrière	
13	1	right piqué effacé en avant with left attitude derrière facing 1	left 4th en avant
	2	hold	
	3	left fermé 5th devant	bras bas
	and-4	left glissade de côté fermé right 5th derrière facing 5	
14		repeat 13 to other side but omit last glissade	
15-16-17		hold (or walk off stage)	

No. 14 Male Variation 2/4

Starting Position		5th right devant facing 5	bras bas
1	1	entrechat cinq onto right with left derrière	
	and	right relevé with left dégagé à la seconde	
	2	left fermé 5th devant	
2		repeat 1 to other side	

No. 14 (continued)

Bar	Beat	Feet and Direction	Arms
3	1	entrechat cinq onto right with left derrière	
	2	left glissade effacé en arrière	
4	1	left jeté battu dessus	
	2	right assemblé battu dessus	
5	1	sissonne battue ouverte en arrière onto right with left devant facing 2	1st
	and	left coupé dessus	
	2	right assemblé battu dessus facing 5	
6	1	sissonne en attitude onto right turning 3/4 to the right ending with left derrière facing 2	through 5th to 5th en haut through 2nd
	2	left assemblé dessous	bras bas
7		repeat 5	
8	1	sissonne en attitude onto left turning 3/4 to the left ending with right derrière facing 1	through 5th to 5th en haut
	2	right jeté dessous	through 2nd to bras bas
9	1	left posé en avant facing 2	5th en avant
	2	cabriole derrière onto left	left slowly
10	1	cabriole derrière onto left	to 1st arabesque
	2	cabriole onto left	
11	1	right coupé dessous	2nd
	and	pas couru in 5th left devant to the left facing 5	
	2	left ballonné dessous	
12	1	left assemblé derrière	bras bas
	2	hold	
13-20		repeat 5-12	
21	1	entrechat six into échappé landing in 2nd	
	2	entrechat six landing 5th right devant	
22	1	entrechat six	
	2	entrechat trois onto right with left derrière	
	and	left coupé dessous	

(continued)

No. 14 (continued)

Bar	Beat	Feet and Direction	Arms
23	1	right glissade de côté fermé left 5th derrière	through 5th to
	and	left relevé with right développé à la seconde	2nd
	2	right into 2nd position demi-plié	right 4th en avant
24	1	pirouette en dehors on left	
	2	right fermé 5th derrière	bras bas
25		hold	

No. 15 Female Variation 2/4

Bar	Beat	Feet and Direction	Arms
Starting Position		5th right devant facing 5	bras bas
1	1	right piqué en avant with left attitude derrière	right 4th en avant
	2	left fermé 5th derrière	
2	1	right rond de jambe sauté en l'air en dehors landing left demi-plié with right dégagé à la seconde	2nd
	2	right posé de côté	bras bas
3		repeat 1 to other side	
4	1	repeat beat 1 in bar 2 to other side	
	2	left assemblé dessous	bras bas
5	1	sissonne ouverte en avant onto right facing 1	left 4th en avant
	and	pas de bourrée en avant (left 5th derrière)	
	2	left fermé 5th derrière	
6	1	sissonne ouverte en arrière onto left	right 4th en avant
	and	pas de bourrée en arrière (right 5th devant)	bras bas
	2	right fermé 5th devant	
7	1	sissonne ouverte en attitude en avant onto right with left derrière	through 5th to left 4th en haut
	2	hold	
	and	left coupé dessous	
8	1	right posé de côté into left soutenu en dedans ending right 5th devant	2nd bras bas
	2	demi-plié	
9	1-2	2 entrechats quatre	
10	1	pirouette en dehors	
	2	right fermé 5th derrière	

No. 15 (continued)

Bar	Beat	Feet and Direction	Arms
11-12		repeat 9-10 to other side	
13	1-2	2 entrechats quatre	
14	1	1 entrechat quatre	
	2	sissonne ouverte en attitude en avant onto right with left attitude derrière facing 1	through 5th to left 4th en haut
15	1	temps levé right with left through retiré to croisé devant facing 1	2nd
	and-2-and	3 jetés en avant with extended feet devant (left-right-left)	1st
16	1	right posé en avant	
	2	left grand jeté en attitude en avant with right derrière	2nd
17	1	right coupé dessous	
	and-2	left posé de côté into soutenu en dedans ending	through 1st to
18	1	5th sur les pointes left devant facing 1	right 3rd arabesque
	2	left fondu with right retiré derrière	
19-20		repeat 17-18	
	and	right coupé dessous onto demi-pointe with left développé à la seconde into 2nd position demi-plié facing 5	2nd left 4th en avant
21		pirouette en dehors à la seconde on right continuing turn in left attitude derrière	2nd through bras bas to 5th en avant to
22	1-2	ending in attitude on right demi-plié facing 2	2nd
	and	pas de bourrée (left dessous–right de côté)	
23	1	left posé en avant	bras bas
	2	left temps levé with right in arabesque	left 3rd arabesque
24	1	pas de bourrée (right dessous–left dessus–right dessous)	
	2	left jeté dessous facing 5	bras bas
	and	right chassé en avant facing 1	
25	1	right posé en avant	
	2	right temps levé with left arabesque	right 3rd arabesque
	and	left coupé dessous facing 5	
26	1	right glissade de côté fermé left dessous	
	2	right jeté dessous	bras bas
	and	left chassé en avant facing 2	

(continued)

No. 15 (continued)

Bar	Beat	Feet and Direction	Arms
27	1	left posé en avant	left 3rd arabesque
	and	left temps levé	
	2	right coupé dessous	
	and	left jeté dessus	
28	1	right tombé de côté into pirouette en dedans ending on right demi-plié	2nd 5th en avant
	2	right relevé with left développé à la seconde	5th en haut
	and	left coupé dessous	
29	1	right chassé contretemps facing 1	through 2nd to
	2	to left 4th devant	bras bas
	and	right jeté en avant with left retiré derrière	
30	1	right relevé with left attitude derrière	through 5th to left 4th en haut

No. 16 Cabriole 6/8 (count 2)

Bar	Beat	Feet and Direction	Arms
Starting Position Intro: 2 bars		5th right devant facing 1	bras bas
1	1	right posé effacé en avant, left in 1st arabesque	through 5th to right 1st arabesque
	2	cabriole derrière onto right	
2	1	left coupé dessous	
	2	right jeté dessous facing 2	bras bas
3-6		repeat bars 1-2 on alternating sides	
7		repeat bar 1 to other side	
8	1	right coupé dessous	
	2	left posé en avant with right tendu derrière facing 2	right 4th en avant
	and	right chassé effacé en arrière	
9	1	right posé en avant facing 4 and left grand battement devant into	through 2nd and 5th
	2	fouetté sauté onto right with left attitude derrière facing 2	into right 4th en haut
	and	pas de bourrée couru de côté facing 5	open to

No. 16 (continued)

Bar	Beat	Feet and Direction	Arms
10	1	left coupé dessous	2nd
	2	right jeté battu dessus facing 1	bras bas
11-24		repeat 9-10 on alternating sides	

No. 17 Female Variation 6/8 (count 2)

Bar	Beat	Feet and Direction	Arms
Starting Position		5th right devant facing 1	bras bas
Intro:		right petit retiré devant and posé en arrière into left tendu croisé devant	through 5th en avant to 2nd
1	1	left posé croisé en avant	
	and	brisé ouvert en avant onto right with left croisé devant	bras bas
	2	left posé croisé en avant	
2	1	right ballonné dessus facing 5	
	2	right ballonné dessous	
3		repeat bar 2	
4	and-1	right glissade en arrière–left fermé 5th devant	
	2	left piqué effacé en avant facing 2 with right développé croisé devant	through 5th to right 4th en haut
	and	left fondu	2nd
5-6		repeat bars 1-2 to other side	
7	1	left ballonné dessus	bras bas
	2	left glissade en avant through 4th facing 2	through 5th
	and	left jeté en avant landing with right retiré derrière	
8	1	left relevé with right attitude derrière	demi-2nd
9-16		repeat 1-8 to other side	

No. 18 Male Variation 6/8 (count 2)

Bar	Beat	Feet and Direction	Arms
Starting Position		5th right devant facing 5	bras bas
1	1	right assemblé en avant	
	2	right rond de jambe sauté en l'air en dehors	through 5th to 2nd
2	1	right piqué into pirouette en dedans en attitude ending facing 5	right 4th en avant
	2	left coupé dessous	bras bas
3-4		repeat bars 1-2	
	and	right coupé dessus	left 4th en avant
5	1	left coupé dessous	
	2	right ballonné dessous	5th en avant
6	1	cabriole derrière onto left in 1st arabesque facing 2	left 1st arabesque
	2	right jeté dessous with left dégagé croisé devant facing 1	right 4th en avant
	and	left coupé dessus	
7-10		repeat alternating sides but omit last coupé dessus	
11	1	left posé en avant facing 1	
	and	brisé ouvert onto right with left croisé devant	right 4th en avant
	2	left posé en avant	
	and	right jeté en avant landing with left retiré derrière	
12	1	right relevé with left attitude derrière facing 1	through 5th to left 4th en haut
	2	hold	

No. 19 Traversée (one dancer on either side) 6/8 (count 2)

Bar	Beat	Feet and Direction	Arms
Starting Position		5th right devant facing 5	bras bas
1	1	right jeté de côté with left in 2nd demi-hauteur	5th en avant
	2	left fermé 5th derrière into pas de bourrée couru de côté	slowly to 2nd
2		repeat bar 1	

No. 19 (continued)

Bar	Beat	Feet and Direction	Arms
3	1	right jeté de côté with left in 2nd demi-hauteur	
	2	left ballonné dessus facing 8	bras bas
4	1	left ballonné dessous facing 3	
	2	left jeté dessus facing 2	
5	1	right glissade en arrière facing 5	
	2	right jeté dessus	
6	1	left glissade en arrière	
	2	left jeté dessus	
7	1	right petit jeté dessus	
	2	left assemblé dessus	
	and	right relevé with left développé à la seconde into:	through 5th to 2nd
8	1	2nd position demi-plié	left 4th en avant
	2	pirouette en dehors on right	
9	1	left fermé 5th derrière	bras bas

This dancer travels from 6 towards 8. The other starts from 8 and travels towards 6 with the other leg.

No. 19a Brisé Volé 6/8 (count 2)

Bar	Beat	Feet and Direction	Arms
Starting Position		on right with left tendu croisé devant facing 1	bras bas
1	1	brisé onto right with left dégagé croisé devant	
	2	brisé onto left with right dégagé croisé derrière	
2-3		repeat bar 1	
4	1	repeat beat 1 in bar 1	
	2	temps levé on right with left ballonné battu dessous facing 2	
5-8		repeat 1-4 to other side	
	and	right coupé dessus, left coupé dessous	

(continued)

No. 19a (continued)

Bar	Beat	Feet and Direction	Arms
9	1	right pas de basque, left fermé 5th devant facing 5	
	2	entrechat cinq onto left with right derrière	
	and	right ballonné dessus	5th en avant
10	1	right piqué en avant facing 1, left développé devant	right 4th en haut
	2	left pas de bourrée dessus-dessous travelling to the right facing 5	through 2nd to bras bas
11-12		repeat 9-10	left 4th en haut
13		repeat 9, beats 1-2	
14	1	right piqué effacé en avant, left devant	right 4th en haut
	and	left coupé dessus facing 1	2nd
	2	right posé en avant turning to the right to face 3	bras bas
15	1	right temps levé with left derrière	
	2	left glissade en avant through 4th	
16	1	left jeté dessus turning to the right to face 1	
	2	finale starts	

No. 19b Finale from *Konservatoriet* 6/8 (count 2)

Bar	Beat	Feet and Direction	Arms
16	1	on left with right tendu croisé derrière facing 1	bras bas
	and	pas de bourrée en avant to:	
	2	4th position right effacé devant, demi-plié	
17	1	temps levé onto left with right derrière	
	and	pas de bourrée en avant to:	
	2	4th position right effacé devant, demi-plié	
18	1	temps levé onto left with right derrière	
	2	right jeté dessous with left dégagé devant facing 5	left 3rd to
19	1	left coupé dessus	bras bas
	2	right glissade en arrière fermé left 5th devant	
20	1	right jeté dessus facing 2	
	and	pas de bourrée en avant to:	
	2	4th position left effacé devant, demi-plié	

No. 19b (continued)

Bar	Beat	Feet and Direction	Arms
21-23		repeat 17-19 to other side	
24	1	left jeté dessus	
	and	right chassé effacé en avant facing 4	demi-2nd
	2	right posé en avant	
25	1	fouetté sauté on right landing with left en attitude derrière facing 2	right 4th en avant
	2	left coupé dessous	
26	and-1	right rond de jambe sauté en l'air en dehors with right ending 2nd demi-hauteur	demi-2nd
	and	right chassé en avant facing 4	
	2	right posé en avant	
27		repeat 25	
28	and-1	right rond de jambe sauté en l'air en dehors facing 5 ending 2nd, demi-hauteur	1st
	and-2	right pas de bourrée dessous-dessus en avant towards 2	
29	and-1	left pas de bourrée dessous-dessus en avant towards 2	
	and-2	right pas de bourrée dessous-dessus towards 2	
30	1	left assemblé battu porté dessous	
	2	hold	
31	and-1	right retiré and fermé 5th derrière	
	2	hold	
32	and-1	left grand battement à la seconde fermé 5th derrière	through 5th to 2nd
	2	hold	
33	and-1	right grand battement à la seconde fermé 5th derrière	
	and-2	left grand battement à la seconde fermé 5th derrière	
34	and-1	right grand battement à la seconde fermé 5th derrière	bras bas
	2	hold	
35		grand plié and straighten	

(continued)

No. 19b (continued)

Bar	Beat	Feet and Direction	Arms
36	1	right dégagé into attitude derrière facing 2	through 5th to right 4th en haut
	2	hold	

Nos. 1, 3, 7, 9-19 are all from the ballet *Konservatoriet.*

No. 19a is danced by a male dancer who joins the entire cast in 19b. The two principal girls dance on either side.

SATURDAY'S CLASS

Mydtskov

SATURDAY'S CLASS

No. 1 Adagio 4/4

Bar	**Beat**	**Feet and Direction**	**Arms**
Starting Position		5th right devant facing 5	bras bas
1		grand plié	
2	1-2	straighten	through 5th en
	3-4	left tendu à la seconde, lower in 2nd position	avant to 2nd
3		grand plié	bras bas
4	1-2	straighten	through 5th en
	3-4	left tendu à la seconde	avant to 2nd
5		hold	
6		left lifts to à la seconde	
7		hold	
8		left fermé 5th devant	bras bas
9		grand plié	
10		straighten	
11		right petit retiré derrière facing 2	
12		right développé into attitude derrière	through 5th en avant to right 4th en haut
13			left slowly to 5th en haut
14		change to 1st arabesque facing 6	left 1st arabesque
15	1-2-3		change to 2nd arabesque through 5th en avant
	4	left demi-plié	
16	1	left relevé in attitude with right derrière facing 5	right 4th en haut
	2-3	hold	
	4	extend right and fermé derrière	through 2nd to bras bas
17-32		repeat 1-16 to other side	
33		grand plié	
34	1-2	straighten	through 5th en
	3-4	right tendu à la seconde, lower heel in 2nd	avant to 2nd
35		grand plié in 2nd	bras bas
36		straighten	
37		left tendu à la seconde	through 5th en avant to 2nd

No. 1 (continued)

Bar	Beat	Feet and Direction	Arms
38		left lifts to à la seconde	
39		hold	
40		left fermé 5th devant	bras bas
41		right petit retiré derrière facing 2	5th en avant
42		right développé into attitude derrière facing 6	left 4th en haut
43		hold	
44			right to 4th en avant
45		lean forward turning torso towards 2	change through 2nd to right 4th en haut, left 4th en avant
46	1-2-3	1st arabesque facing 2	through 5th en avant to 1st arabesque
	4	left demi-plié	
47		left relevé in attitude with right derrière	left 4th en haut, right 4th en avant
48	1-2	lower heel and extend right derrière	through 2nd to
	3-4	right fermé 5th derrière facing 5	bras bas
49-64		repeat 33-48 to other side	

No. 2 Port de Bras

As Wednesday No. 2

No. 3 Adagio 4/4

Bar	Beat	Feet and Direction	Arms
Starting Position		5th right devant facing 1	bras bas
1		left fondu with right développé effacé devant	5th en avant
2	1-2	right posé en avant	
	3-4	left dégagé en attitude derrière	left 4th en haut
3		left through retiré passé to croisé devant	change to right en haut
4	1-2	left posé en avant	
	3-4	right dégagé en attitude derrière	

(continued)

No. 3 (continued)

Bar	**Beat**	**Feet and Direction**	**Arms**
5	1-2	left relevé	
	3-4	place right croisé derrière in 4th, heel lowered, left demi-plié	
6		grand port de bras into:	
7		pirouette en dedans en attitude on left, finishing facing 5	5th en avant
8	1-2	extend right derrière	
	3	right rond de jambe en dedans ending 2nd	2nd
	4	right fermé 5th derrière	bras bas
9-16		repeat 1-8 to other side	
17		right fondu with left développé derrière facing 1	5th en avant
18	1-2	left posé effacé en arrière with right tendu devant	
	3-4	right lifts devant	left 4th en haut
19		right through retiré passé to attitude derrière	change to right 4th en haut
20	1-2	right posé croisé en arrière	
	3-4	left lifts devant	
21	1-2	right relevé with left retiré facing 2	change to left 4th en haut
	3-4	left into 4th derrière, heel lowered, right demi-plié	
22		grand port de bras into:	
23		pirouette en dedans en attitude on right, left derrière, ending facing 1	5th en avant to left 4th en haut
24	1-2	extend left derrière	through 2nd to
	3-4	left fermé 5th devant	bras bas
25-32		repeat 17-24 to other side	
33		left fondu with right développé croisé devant	5th en avant
34	1-2	right posé en avant facing 2	
	3-4	left dégagé into attitude derrière	left 4th en haut
35		left through retiré passé to effacé devant	change to right 4th en haut
36	1-2	left posé en avant	
	3-4	right dégagé en attitude derrière	

No. 3 (continued)

Bar	Beat	Feet and Direction	Arms
37	1-2	left relevé turning 1/4 right to face 1	
	3-4	right into 4th croisé derrière, heel lowered, left demi-plié	
38		grand port de bras into:	
39		pirouette en attitude on left	5th en avant
40	1-2	ending 1st arabesque facing 6	1st arabesque
	3-4	right fermé 5th derrière facing 5	bras bas
41-48		repeat 33-40 to other side	
49		right fondu with left développé croisé derrière facing 2	5th en avant
50	1-2	left posé croisé en arrière	
	3-4	right lifts devant	left 4th en haut
51	1-2	right through retiré passé to	change to right
	3-4	attitude derrière	4th en haut
52	1-2	right posé effacé en arrière	
	3-4	left lifts devant	
53	1-2	right relevé with left retiré	change to left 4th en haut
	3-4	left into 4th croisé derrière, heel lowered, right demi-plié	
54		grand port de bras into:	
55	1-2-3	pirouette en dedans on right	5th en avant
	4	right demi-plié	bras bas
56	1-2	right relevé with left développé à la seconde	5th en haut
	3-4	left fermé 5th devant	through 2nd to bras bas
57-64		repeat 49-56 to other side	

No. 4 Tendu 2/4

Bar	Beat	Feet and Direction	Arms
Starting Position		5th right devant facing 5	bras bas
1	1	right tendu devant	
	and	right fermé 5th devant	
	2	right tendu à la seconde	
2	1	right fermé 5th derrière	
	2	left assemblé dessous	

(continued)

No. 4 (continued)

Bar	Beat	Feet and Direction	Arms
3	1	right tendu devant facing 1	
	and	right fermé 5th devant demi-plié	
	2	right relevé with left attitude derrière	through 5th to left 4th en haut
4	1	left coupé dessous	
	2	right assemblé dessous facing 5	through 2nd to bras bas
5-8		repeat 1-4 to other side	
9	1	left tendu derrière	
	and	left fermé 5th derrière	
	2	left tendu à la seconde	
10	1	left fermé 5th devant	
	2	right assemblé dessus	
11	1	left tendu derrière facing 1	
	and	left fermé derrière in demi-plié	
	2	left relevé with right développé devant	through 5th to left 4th en haut
12	1	right fermé devant	through 2nd to bras bas
	2	left assemblé dessus facing 5	
13-16		repeat 9-12 to other side	
17	1	right posé en avant	
	2	left fermé 5th derrière demi-plié	
18	1	left posé en arrière	
	2	right fermé 5th devant demi-plié	
	and	right glissade de côté with left fermé 5th derrière	
19	1	right posé de côté	
	2	left coupé dessous	through 5th en avant to right 4th en haut
20	1	right assemblé dessous	bras bas
	2	hold	
21-24		repeat 17-20 to other side	
25-32		reverse from 17-24, but move arms to 4th en haut sideways through 2nd	

No. 4 (continued)

Bar	Beat	Feet and Direction	Arms
33	1	right posé de côté	bras bas
	2	left fermé 5th derrière demi-plié	
34	1	left posé de côté	
	2	right fermé 5th devant demi-plié	
	and	right glissade en avant with left fermé 5th derrière	
35	1	right posé en avant	through 5th en avant to
	2	left fermé 5th derrière demi-plié	5th en haut
36	1	right assemblé dessous	through 2nd to
	2	hold	bras bas
37-40		repeat 33-36 to other side	
41-48		reverse bars 33-40, but move arms to 5th en haut through 2nd	

No. 5 Pirouette 2/4

Starting Position		5th right devant facing 5	bras bas
1		right dégagé diagonally forward	right 4th en avant
2	1	left relevé with right retiré	5th en avant
	2	right fermé 5th devant in demi-plié	right 4th en avant
3		pirouette en dehors on left	
4		right fermé 5th derrière	bras bas
5-8		repeat 1-4 to other side	
9		left dégagé slightly effacé devant	left 4th en avant
10	1	left retiré on right relevé	5th en avant
	2	left fermé 5th derrière in demi-plié	right 4th en avant
11		pirouette en dedans on right	
12		left fermé 5th devant	bras bas
13-16		repeat 9-12 to other side	

No. 6 Échappé Sauté with Pirouette 2/4

Bar	Beat	Feet and Direction	Arms
Starting Position		5th right devant facing 5	bras bas
1	1	échappe sauté to 2nd	
	2	sauté fermé 5th left devant	
	and	changement	
2	1	échappé sauté to 2nd	right 4th en
	2	hold in demi-plié	avant
3		pirouette en dehors on left	
4		right fermé 5th derrière	bras bas
5-8		repeat 1-4 to other side	
9	1	échappé sauté to 4th, right devant facing 1	
	2	sauté fermé 5th left devant	
	and	changement	
10	1	échappé sauté to 4th right devant	left 4th en
	2	hold in demi-plié	avant
11		pirouette en dedans on left	
12		right fermé 5th derrière facing 5	bras bas
13-16		repeat 9-12 to other side	
17	1	échappé sauté to 4th, right devant facing 1	
	2	sauté fermé 5th left devant	
	and	changement	
18	1	échappé sauté to 2nd facing 5	right 4th en
	2	hold in demi-plié	avant
19		pirouette en dehors on left	
20		right fermé derrière facing 5	bras bas
21-24		repeat 17-20 to other side	
25	1	échappé sauté to 2nd	
	2	sauté fermé 5th left devant	
	and	changement	
26	1	échappé sauté to 4th, right devant facing 1	left 4th en avant
	2	hold in demi-plié	

No. 6 (continued)

Bar	Beat	Feet and Direction	Arms
27		pirouette en dedans on left	
28		right fermé 5th derrière facing 5	bras bas
29-32		repeat 25-28 to other side	

No. 7 Heavy Échappé 2/4

Bar	Beat	Feet and Direction	Arms
Starting Position		5th right devant facing 5	bras bas
1	1	échappé sauté into 2nd	
	2	sauté fermé 5th right devant	
	and	changement	
2		repeat bar 1 to other side	
3	1	échappé sauté into 4th, right devant	
	2	sauté fermé 5th right devant	
	and	changement	
4		repeat bar 3 to other side	
5	1	sissonne ouverte en attitude en avant onto right with left attitude derrière facing 1	through en avant to left 4th en haut
	2	left coupé dessous	
	and	right assemblé dessous facing 5	open through 2nd to bras bas
6		repeat bar 5 to other side	
7	1	sissonne ouverte en attitude en avant onto right with left attitude derrière facing 2	through en avant to 5th en haut
	2	left coupé dessous	
	and	right assemblé dessous facing 5	open to bras bas
8	1	sissonne ouverte en attitude en avant onto left with right attitude derrière facing 1	through en avant to 5th en haut
	2	right assemblé dessous facing 5	open to bras bas
9-16		repeat 1-8 to other side	

No. 8 Allegro 3/4

Bar	Beat	Feet and Position	Arms
Starting Position		on right with left tendu croisé derrière facing 2	1st
1		sauté onto left with right tendu effacé devant facing 1	through en avant to right 4th en haut
2		right ballonné dessous	open to bras bas
3		sauté onto right with left tendu croisé devant	through en avant to left 4th en haut
4		left ballonné dessous facing 5	open to bras bas
5		left petit jeté dessous	
6-7		2 jetés dessous (right-left)	
8		right ballonné dessous	
9-16		repeat 1-8 to other side	
	3	left coupé dessous	
17		right glissade de côté, left fermé 5th devant	
18		right glissade de côté, left fermé 5th derrière	
19		right glissade effacé en avant through 4th facing 1	
20		right grand jeté en avant landing 2nd arabesque	through 5th to left 2nd arabesque
21		left glissade en arrière, right fermé 5th devant facing 5	
22		left jeté dessus	bras bas
23		right glissade en arrière fermé left 5th devant	
24		right jeté dessous	
25-32		repeat 17-24 to other side	
	and	right dégagé effacé en avant and sauté beating with right 5th devant into:	
33		deep plié on right with left tendu derrière facing 1	through 5th to right 4th en haut
34		temps levé on right with left dégagé croisé devant and sauté beating with left 5th devant into:	left 4th en avant
35		deep plié on left with right tendu croisé derrière	left 4th en haut
36		left temps levé with right retiré derrière facing 5	open to bras bas

No. 8 (continued)

Bar	Beat	Feet and Direction	Arms
37-38-39		3 jetés dessus with alternating legs (right-left-right)	
40		left ballonné dessus	
41-48		repeat 32-40 to other side	

No. 9 Ballonné 3/4

Bar	Beat	Feet and Direction	Arms
Starting Position		5th right devant facing 5	bras bas
1	and-1	right ballonné dessous	
2		hold	
3		right ballonné dessus	
4	1	right ballonné dessous	
	2-3	right ballonné dessus	
5		right posé en avant facing 1	through en avant to left 4th en haut
6		left coupé dessous	2nd
7		right assemblé dessous	bras bas
8		hold facing 5	
9-16		repeat 1-8 to other side	
17-32		reverse 1-16	
33		right rond de jambe sauté en dehors en l'air ending dégagé à la seconde	1st
34		hold	
35	1	rond de jambe sauté right en l'air en dehors	
	2	right coupé dessous	
	3	left posé de côté	
36		right coupé dessus facing 2	
37		left coupé dessous facing 5	
38		right glissade de côté, fermé left 5th devant facing 1	
39		right assemblé battu dessous facing 5	
40		right temps levé with left retiré devant	
41-64		repeat 33-40 on alternating sides	

No. 10 Jeté en Tournant 2/4

Bar	Beat	Feet and Direction	Arms
Starting Position		5th right devant facing 5	right 4th en avant
1	1	right posé de côté	2nd
	2	left jeté en tournant dessous	5th en avant
2	1	right posé de côté	2nd
	and	left jeté en tournant dessous	5th en avant
	2	right jeté en avant landing en attitude facing 1	left 4th en haut
3		hold in demi-plié	through 2nd
4	1	left assemblé dessous	to bras bas
	2	temps levé onto right with left devant facing 5	left 4th en avant
5-16		repeat 1-4 alternating sides	
17	1	right posé de côté	2nd
	2	left jeté en tournant dessous	5th en avant
18	1	jeté en avant landing in 2nd arabesque on demi-plié facing 1	left 2nd arabesque
	2	hold	
19	1	échappé sauté into 2nd facing 5	right 4th en avant
	and	left temps levé with right retiré devant facing 7 (1/2 turn to right)	5th en avant
	2	right coupé dessus facing 2	2nd
20	1	left assemblé battu dessous	bras bas
	2	temps levé onto right with left retiré devant facing 5	left 4th en avant
21-32		repeat 17-20 on alternating sides	

No. 11 Grand Allegro 3/4

Bar	Beat	Feet and Direction	Arms
Starting Position		on right with left tendu croisé devant facing 1	bras bas
	2-3	left posé croisé en avant and brisé onto right	
1	1	finishing left dégagé devant	
	2-3	left posé en avant and right dégagé devant into:	
2		right assemblé dessus	5th en avant
3	1	left temps levé with right développé effacé devant	right 4th en haut
	2	right coupé dessous	
	3	left posé de côté facing 2	through 2nd to
4		right coupé dessus	bras bas
5		left coupé dessous	
6		left temps levé with right grand rond de jambe en l'air en dehors, ending attitude croisé derrière facing 1	through 2nd to right 4th en haut
7		right fermé 5th derrière, left posé de côté facing 7 and bring right through retiré to croisé devant on left demi-plié facing 2	through 5th to left 4th en avant
8		right posé en avant, brisé onto left	bras bas
9-16		repeat 1-8 to other side	
17-18		repeat bar 1-2	
19	1	sissonne ouverte onto left en attitude, right derrière, facing 2	right 4th en haut
	2	right coupé dessous	
	3	left posé de côté	through 2nd
20	1-2	right coupé dessus	
	3	left dégagé à la seconde into:	
21		soutenu en dedans ending right 5th devant facing 5	
22		demi-plié	bras bas
23	1-2	changement	
	3	failli onto left with right effacé derrière facing 2 into:	demi-2nd
24		right 4th croisé devant, brisé onto left	left 4th en avant
25-32		repeat 17-24 to other side ending 4th right devant	

No. 12 Pointe Enchaînement 3/4

Bar	Beat	Feet and Direction	Arms
Starting Position		on left with right tendu derrière facing 1	1st
1		right piqué en avant with left arabesque, demi-hauteur	through 5th en avant to 2nd
2		right fondu with left retiré derrière	bras bas
3		right relevé with left développé croisé devant	through 5th to right 4th en haut
4		right fondu with left retiré	through 2nd to bras bas
5	1-2	right relevé with left développé à la seconde facing 5	2nd
	3	right fondu with left retiré derrière	
6-7		pas de bourrée couru sur les pointes in 5th with left derrière travelling to the right	slowly to
8		right posé de côté with left retiré devant facing 2	bras bas
9-32		repeat 1-8 on alternating sides	

No. 13 March 4/4

Bar	Beat	Feet and Direction	Arms
Starting Position		5th right devant facing 5	bras bas
Intro 1		relevé	
2	1-2	lower heels	
	3-4	right glissade de côté fermé left 5th derrière	right 4th en avant
1	1-2	right posé de côté	2nd
	3-4	left jeté en tournant dessous	5th en avant
2	1	right jeté en avant landing in 2nd arabesque, demi-plié	left 2nd arabesque
	2-3-4	hold facing 1	
3	1-2	left posé croisé en avant	2nd
	3-4	right assemblé battu dessous	bras bas
4	1-2	temps levé onto right with left retiré devant facing 5	left 4th en avant
	3-4	left glissade en avant fermé right 5th derrière facing 2	

No. 13 (continued)

Bar	Beat	Feet and Direction	Arms
5	1-2	left posé en avant in 1st arabesque facing 6	left 1st arabesque
	3-4	petit sauté in arabesque turning 3/4 to the left, to face 1	
6	1-2	right coupé dessous facing 5	
	3-4	left ballonné dessous	bras bas
7	1-2	left coupé dessous	
	3-4	right glissade de côté, fermé left 5th devant	
8	1-2	right coupé dessous	
	3-4	left glissade de côté fermé right 5th derrière	left 4th en avant
9-15		repeat 1-7 to other side	
16	1-2	left coupé dessous	
	3-4	right posé effacé en avant facing 1	demi-2nd
17	1-2	left jeté fermé croisé en avant with right 5th derrière	right 4th en avant
	3-4	entrechat cinq onto left with right derrière	1st
18	1-2	right coupé dessous	
	3-4	left jeté battu dessus	
19	1-2	échappé sauté into 2nd	
	3-4	right temps levé with left petit retiré derrière facing 2	through 5th
20	1-2	cabriole onto right with left derrière	to right 1st arabesque
	3-4	left coupé dessous	bras bas
21-24		repeat 17-20 to other side	
Girls			
25	1-2	left glissade de côté into 4th with right derrière facing 2	right 4th en avant
	3-4	right coupé dessous	
26	1-2	left piqué de côté with right retiré devant	left 3rd arabesque
	3-4	right coupé dessus	
27-28		repeat 25-26	
29	1-2	left coupé dessous	
	3-4	right posé de côté facing 5	2nd
30	1-2	left soutenu en dedans	bras bas
	3-4	ending left 5th derrière	
31	1-2	right relevé with left attitude derrière	through en avant to 5th en haut
	3-4	left coupé dessous	(palms facing out)

(continued)

No. 13 (continued)

Bar	Beat	Feet and Direction	Arms
32	1	right assemblé dessous	bras bas
	2-3	hold	
	4	left dégagé à la seconde on right demi-plié	
33	1-2	left coupé dessous	
	3-4	right petits battements sur le cou-de-pied	
34	1-2	right posé effacé en avant with left tendu croisé devant facing 1	left 4th en haut
	3-4	left coupé dessus	bras bas
35		repeat bar 33 to other side	
36	1-2	left posé effacé en avant with right tendu croisé devant facing 2	right 4th en avant
	3-4	right fermé 5th devant	
37	1-2	posé left, place right in 4th position devant	left 4th en avant
	3-4	temps levé onto right turning to left with left retiré devant	5th en avant
38		repeat bar 37	
39	1-2	left petit jeté dessus	
	3-4	right petit jeté dessus	
40	1-2	left assemblé dessous facing 5	bras bas
	3-4	right dégagé à la seconde on left demi-plié	
41-44		repeat 33-36 to other side	
45-46-47		repeat bar 37 to other side	
48		pas de basque onto right and left posé en avant into 4th croisé devant	demi-2nd
Boys			
1-23		same as for girls	
24	1-2	cabriole on left with right derrière	left 1st arabesque
	3-4	right assemblé dessous facing 5	left 4th en avant
25	1-2	tour en l'air to the left landing 5th left devant	
	3-4	repeats beats 1-2	
26	1-2	repeat beats 1-2 in bar 25	
	3-4	right temps levé with left retiré derrière facing 2	
27	1-2	left coupé dessous	
	3-4	right rond de jambe sauté en l'air en dehors ending demi-2nd facing 5	demi-2nd

No. 13 (continued)

Bar	Beat	Feet and Direction	Arms
28	1-2	right coupé dessus	
	3-4	left assemblé dessous	bras bas
29		repeat bar 25 to other side	
30	1-2	repeat beats 1-2 from bar 25 to other side	
	3-4	échappé sauté to 2nd	right 4th en avant
31		pirouette en dehors on left	
32		right fermé 5th derrière	bras bas
33-48			

No. 14 Grand Allegro 3/4

Bar	Beat	Feet and Direction	Arms
Starting Position		5th right devant facing 5	bras bas
1		sissonne ouverte en attitude en avant onto left with right derrière facing 2	right 4th en haut
2		sauté fermé 5th right derrière facing 5	through 2nd to bras bas
3		sissonne ouverte en attitude en avant onto right with left derrière facing 1	left 4th en haut
4		left coupé sauté dessous	
5		glissade en avant through 4th	through 2nd to bras bas
6		right grand jeté en avant into attitude with left derrière	through 5th en avant to left 4th en haut
7		left glissade en arrière fermé right 5th devant	through 2nd to bras bas
8		left jeté dessous facing 1	right 4th en avant
9		right posé de côté facing 5	2nd
10	1	left jeté en tournant dessous	5th en avant
	2-3	right glissade de côté fermé left 5th derrière	
11		right posé de côté	2nd
12		left jeté en tournant dessous	5th en avant
13	1	right ballonné dessous	demi-2nd
	2-3	right glissade en arrière	
14		right posé en arrière leaving left dégagé devant	bras bas
15		left fermé devant	
16		entrechat quatre	
17-32		repeat 1-16 to other side	

No. 15 Girls' Enchaînement 2/4

Bar	Beat	Feet and Direction	Arms
Starting Position		on left with right tendu croisé derrière facing 1	1st
1	1	right jeté en avant with left dégagé croisé devant	
	and	left jeté en avant with right dégagé effacé devant	
	2-and	right chassé de côté into left fermé 5th derrière	
2	1	right posé éffacé en avant	through 5th
	2	left jeté en avant	to 2nd
3	1	right coupé dessous	
	2	left ballonné dessous	demi-bras
4	1	left glissade en arrière	
	2	left jeté dessus	bras bas
5-6		repeat 1-2	
7	1	right jeté dessous with left petit développé devant	left 3rd
	2	left petit jeté dessus	
8	1	right glissade en arrière facing 5	
	2	right jeté dessus facing 2	1st
9-16		repeat 1-8 to other side	
17		repeat bar 1	
18	1	right piqué with left dégagé croisé devant and fouetté body	through 5th en avant to
	2	to face 8 with left rond de jambe ending derrière	right 3rd arabesque
19	1	left coupé dessous	
	2	right jeté dessus facing 5	bras bas
20	1	left glissade en arrière	
	2	left jeté battu dessus	
21		repeat bar 1	
22	1	right piqué with left dégagé croisé devant and fouetté	through 5th
	2	3/4 to the right so the left becomes attitude derrière, now facing 5	to right 4th en haut
23	1	left coupé dessous	
	2	right ballonné dessous	through 2nd

No. 15 (continued)

Bar	Beat	Feet and Direction	Arms
24	1	right glissade en arrière	
	2	right jeté battu dessus facing 2	to 1st
25-32		repeat 17-24 to other side	

No. 16 Female Variation 2/4

Starting Position		5th right devant facing 5	bras bas
	and	temps levé on right with left retiré derrière	
1	1	left posé into 2nd position facing 2	demi-2nd
	and	brush right through 5th to retiré devant and temps levé on left travelling backwards	right 4th en avant
	2	right coupé dessus	
	and	left coupé dessus	
2		repeat bar 1 to other side	
3	1	left piqué en arrière with right retiré devant facing 1	right 4th en avant
	and	right coupé dessus	
	2-and	repeat 1-and	
4	1	left tendu effacé derrière on right demi-plié facing 1	left 4th en avant
	and	left coupé dessous	
	2	right assemblé dessous facing 5	bras bas
5-8		repeat 1-4 to other side	
9	1	right posé effacé en avant into arabesque facing 1	left 4th en avant
	and	temps levé on right	
	2-and	left coupé dessous, right posé de côté	2nd
10		repeat bar 9 with other leg, but still facing 1	right 4th en avant
11	1	right posé effacé en avant with left dégagé à la seconde	through 2nd to
	and-2-and	3 petits sauts on right while turning to the right to face 2	5th en haut
12	1	left piqué with right retiré derrière	slowly through 2nd
	and	right piqué with left retiré devant	
	2	left fermé 5th devant sur les pointes facing 5	to bras bas

(continued)

No. 16 (continued)

Bar	**Beat**	**Feet and Direction**	**Arms**
13-16		repeat 9-12 to other side	
17	1	right jeté en avant facing 1	
	and	left jeté en avant	
	2	right jeté en avant with left demi-hauteur derrière in arabesque	
	and	brush left forward through 1st	left 4th en avant
18	1	right relevé with left retiré devant	
	2	left coupé dessus facing 5	
19	1-and-2	right pas de valse dessous with left effacé devant turning to the left, ending facing 2	left 4th en haut
20	1	left coupé dessus	through 2nd to
	2	right petit jeté battu dessus facing 5	bras bas
21-24		repeat 17-20 to other side	
25	1	right piqué effacé en avant facing 5 with left retiré derrière	
	and	left beat devant and open dégagé effacé devant, right demi-plié	
	2-and	repeat 1-and with other leg	
26	1-and-2	3 petits jetés dessus en avant	slowly to 5th en haut
27	1	posé into 2nd position facing 2	through 2nd to right 4th en avant
	and	left relevé with right retiré devant facing 1	bras bas
	2	posé into 2nd position	
	and	release left	
28	1	posé to 2nd facing 2	right 4th en avant
	and	left relevé with right retiré devant facing 5	
	2	right jeté dessous	bras bas
29-31		repeat 25-27 to other side	
32		left fermé 5th derrière	bras bas

No. 17 Male Variation 3/4

Bar	Beat	Feet and Direction	Arms
Starting Position		5th right devant facing 5	bras bas
1		right assemblé devant	
2	1-2	entrechat six	
	3	entrechat sept onto left with right devant	
3		right posé croisé en avant	
4	1-2	assemblé battu en avant (beat left-right-left in front) landing right 5th devant facing 2	
	3	temps levé with left retiré derrière	
5	1-2	left coupé dessous facing 5	
	3	right ballonné dessous	
6	1	right jeté dessus	
	2-3	left glissade en arrière, fermé right 5th devant	
7	1	left coupé dessous	
	2-3	right ballonné dessous	
8		right coupé dessous	
9-14		repeat 1-6 to other side	
15	1	right coupé dessous	
	2-3	left glissade de côté, fermé right devant	
16		left posé effacé en avant into right tendu derrière facing 2	right 2nd arabesque
17	1	right posé de côté	
	2-3	left rond de jambe sauté en l'air en dedans ending dégagé demi-2nd turning 1/2 right to right to face 7	2nd
18	1	left posé de côté	
	2-3	right rond de jambe sauté en l'air en dehors ending dégagé demi-2nd turning 1/2 right to face 5	
19	1-2	right posé effacé en avant facing 1	bras bas
	3	left ballonné en avant	through 5th en avant
20		left piqué croisé en avant with right attitude derrière	to right 4th en haut
21	1	right coupé dessous facing 5	
	2-3	left glissade de côté, fermé right 5th derrière	2nd
22		left piqué turning en dedans with right attitude derrière ending facing 1	left 4th en avant

(continued)

No. 17 (continued)

Bar	Beat	Feet and Direction	Arms
23	1	right coupé dessous	
	2	pas de chat ending right 5th devant facing 5	right 4th en avant
	3	left coupé dessous	
24		right posé effacé en avant into left tendu derrière facing 1	left 2nd arabesque
25-32		repeat 17-24 to other side	
33	1-2	right posé en avant facing 4 with left dégagé devant	2nd
	3	right temps levé turning 1/2 right landing left retiré derrière facing 2	right 4th en avant
34	1	left posé en avant	through 5th en avant
	2-3	right grand jeté en avant with left attitude derrière	to 2nd
35	1	left coupé dessous	through bras bas
	2-3	cabriole on left with right croisé devant	and 5th en avant
36	1	right coupé dessus	
	2	left into 5th derrière and pas de bourrée couru to the right facing 5	right gradually opens to 2nd
	3	right posé de côté into:	
37	1-2	soutenu en dedans ending 5th left derrière	5th en avant
	3	échappé into 2nd	right 4th en avant
38		pirouette en dehors on left	
39	1	right coupé dessus	5th en avant
	2	left coupé dessous	
	3	right glissade en avant with left fermé 5th derrière facing 1	
40	1	right posé en avant into left tendu derrière	left 2nd arabesque
41-48		repeat 33-40 to other side	

No. 18 Girls' Enchaînement 3/4

Starting Position		on left with right tendu croisé derrière facing 1	1st
1	1-2	right piqué effacé en avant	left 4th en avant
	3	right fondu with left retiré derrière	
2		left piqué croisé en avant	right 4th en avant

No. 18 (continued)

Bar	Beat	Feet and Direction	Arms
3	1-2	pas de bourrée sur place sur les pointes ending:	
	3	right 5th derrière demi-plié	bras bas
4	1	right relevé with left attitude derrière	through 5th to left 4th en haut
	2	hold	
	3	right fondu with left retiré devant facing 2	1st
5-8		repeat 1-4 to other side	
9	1	right piqué effacé en avant	left 4th en avant
	2	hold	
	3	right fondu with left retiré derrière	
10		left piqué into pirouette en dehors, right through retiré ending dégagé devant facing 1	through 5th to 2nd
11		3 petits jetés dessus (right-left-right) facing 5	bras bas
12	1	left assemblé dessus	
	2-3	hold	
13-16		repeat 9-12 to other side	

No. 19 Male Variation from *Flower Festival in Genzano* 6/8 (count 2)

Bar	Beat	Feet and Direction	Arms
Starting Position		on right with left tendu croisé derrière facing 2	bras bas
	and	left coupé dessous	
1	1	right petit jeté battu dessus	
	2	left ballonné dessus	
2	1	left ballonné dessous	
	2	left ballonné dessus	
3	1	left jeté fermé en avant closing right derrière	
	2	right sissonne fermée en arrière into left 5th devant	
4	1	temps levé on left with right petit retiré derrière facing 5	
	2	pas de bourrée couru to the left with right 5th derrière	
	and	right coupé dessous	

(continued)

No. 19 (continued)

Bar	Beat	Feet and Direction	Arms
5-8		repeat 1-4 to other side	
9	1	right assemblé dessous facing 1	
	2	sauté onto left in arabesque	left 1st arabesque
	and	right posé en arrière, left coupé dessous turning 1/2 right	
10	1	right posé en avant facing 3	bras bas
	2	left through dégagé devant into fouetté sauté landing right with left attitude derrière facing 1	through 5th en avant to left 4th en haut
11-12		repeat 9-10 to other side	
13		repeat bar 9	
14	1	right posé en avant facing 2	bras bas
	2	left jeté with right dégagé croisé devant, demi-hauteur	right 4th en avant
15	1	right assemblé dessus	bras bas
	2	right rond de jambe sauté en l'air en dehors ending demi-2nd	2nd
16	1	pas de basque onto right	
	and-2	pas de bourrée dessus en tournant ending with right petit dégagé devant facing 2	bras bas
17		repeat bar 15	
18		repeat bar 16	
19		repeat bar 16	
20	1	right jeté dessus	
	2	left jeté dessus facing 5	
21	1	right ballonné dessus	right 4th en avant
	2	right tombé effacé en avant into pirouette renversé en dedans	2nd to 5th en avant
22		left fermé 5th derrière	bras bas

No. 20 Female Variation 4/4 (count 2)

Bar	Beat	Feet and Direction	Arms
Starting Position		5th right devant facing 5	bras bas
1	1	left relevé with right high dégagé à la seconde	through 5th to right 4th en haut
	2	left fondu with right retiré derrière	through 2nd to bras bas
2	1	right coupé dessous facing 1	through 5th en avant to
	and-2	left 2 glissades en avant	left 4th en haut
3	1	left ballonné dessous	2nd
	and-2-and	pas de bourrée couru de côté in 5th with left derrière	
4	1	right assemblé dessous facing 5	bras bas
	2	hold	
5-7		repeat 1-3 to other side	
8	1	left assemblé dessous	
	2	entrechat trois with right derrière facing 1	
9	1	right assemblé battu dessous	
	and	left fondu with right retiré derrière, right coupé dessous, left coupé dessus	
	2	right posé effacé en avant	left 4th en avant
	and	left coupé dessous	
10	1	right posé effacé en avant with left développé croisé devant	right 4th en avant
	2	temps levé on right with left développé into derrière	left 4th en avant
11	1	left glissade en arrière	
	2	left dégagé à la seconde into soutenu en dedans, ending facing 5	2nd
12	1	lower heels in 5th right devant	bras bas
	2	entrechat cinq onto right with left derrière facing 2	
13-16		repeat 9-16 to other side	

No. 21 Galop Variation 2/4

Bar	Beat	Feet and Direction	Arms
Starting Position		5th left devant facing 5	bras bas
Intro: 4 bars			
1-2		relevé	left 4th en
3-4		lower heels	avant
1	1	right piqué de côté with left retiré devant	change slowly to right 4th
	2	left coupé dessus	en avant
2		repeat bar 1	
3		piqué pirouette en dedans on right	5th en avant
4	1	left coupé dessus	bras bas
	2	right petit jeté dessus	
5		left petit jeté dessus	
6		right jeté dessus	
7		left coupé dessous, right glissade de côté, left fermé 5th devant	
8	1	right coupé dessous	
	2	left ballonné dessous	left 4th en avant
9-15		repeat 1-7 to other side	
16	1	left coupé dessous	
	2	right chassé de côté	2nd
17	1	right posé de côté	2nd
	2	left jeté en tournant dessous	through 5th to right 4th en avant
18	1	right posé en avant facing 1	5th en avant
	2	left grand jeté en attitude, croisé en avant	2nd
19	1	right coupé dessous	
	2	left ballonné devant facing 2	left 4th en avant
20	1	left piqué in pirouette en attitude en dedans	left 4th en haut
	2	left fondu facing 5	
21	1	right coupé dessous	slowly to
	2	left petit jeté dessus	bras bas
22	1	right glissade en arrière	
	2	right petit jeté dessus	
23	1	left coupé dessous	
	2	right ballonné dessous	
24	1	right coupé dessous	
	2	left chassé de côté	

No. 21 (continued)

Bar	Beat	Feet and Direction	Arms
25-30		repeat 17-22 to other side	
31	1	right coupé dessous	
	2	left glissade de côté, right fermé 5th devant	
32	1	left assemblé dessous	
	2	hold	
33	1	right chassé de côté	through 5th to
	2	right posé de côté	2nd
34	1	left posé croisé en avant	
	2	left temps levé with right développé effacé devant	
35	1	right coupé dessus	bras bas
	2	left glissade en arrière	
36	1	left coupé dessous	
	2	right assemblé en avant	right 4th en avant
37	1	pirouette en dehors on left	
	2	right fermé 5th devant	right 4th en avant
38		repeat bar 37	
39		double pirouette en dehors on left	
40		right fermé 5th derrière	bras bas
41-48		repeat 33-40 to other side	

No. 22 Girls' Enchaînement 4/4

Bar	Beat	Feet and Direction	Arms
Starting Position		on left with right tendu croisé derrière facing 1	1st
1	1	jeté en avant onto right with left dégagé devant	
	and	jeté en avant onto left with right dégagé devant	
	2	right chassé de côté, left fermé 5th derrière	
	3	right posé effacé en avant	
	4	left posé croisé en avant	right through
	and	right rond de jambe en l'air, demi-hauteur en dedans	2nd to 4th en avant

(continued)

No. 22 (continued)

Bar	Beat	Feet and Direction	Arms
2	1	right coupé dessus facing 5	1st
	and-2	left glissade diagonally en arrière with right closing dessous	
	and-3	left glissade diagonally en arrière with right closing dessus	
	and-4	left glissade diagonally en arrière with right coupé dessous	
3-4		repeat bar 1-2 to other side	
5	1	right piqué en arrière with left retiré devant facing 2	left 4th en avant
	and	left coupé dessus	
	2-and	repeat 1-and	
	3-and	repeat 1-and	
	4	right piqué with left retiré devant	
6	1	left coupé dessus	
	2	right glissade en arrière	demi-2nd
	3	right assemblé dessous	
	4	temps levé onto right with left derrière	bras bas
7-8		repeat 5-6 to other side	
9		repeat bar 1	
10	1-and-2	repeat bar 2, beats 1-and-2	
	3	left glissade diagonally en arrière with right coupé dessus	
	4	left jeté battu dessus facing 1	
11	1-2	repeat bar 1, beats 1-2	
	3	right posé effacé en avant	through 5th to
	4	left grand jeté en avant with right attitude derrière	2nd
12	1-2	pas de bourrée dessous-dessus en tournant to right to face 5	1st
	3	left coupé dessous	
	4	right jeté battu dessus facing 2	bras bas
13-14		repeat 9-10 to other side	

No. 22 (continued)

Bar	Beat	Feet and Direction	Arms
15	1	left coupé dessous facing 5	
	and-2	right glissade de côté with left fermé 5th devant	
	and-3	right glissade de côté with left fermé 5th derrière, demi-plié	
	and	left relevé with right développé à la seconde into:	through 5th en avant to 2nd
	4	2nd position demi-plié	right 4th en avant
16	1-2	pirouette en dehors on left	
	3	right fermé 5th derrière	bras bas
	4	hold	

No. 23 Grand Allegro 4/4

Bar	Beat	Feet and Direction	Arms
Starting Position		on left with right tendu croisé derrière facing 1, upstage left corner	bras bas
	and	right posé en avant	
1	1	left posé croisé en avant into temps levé en attitude with right derrière	through 5th en avant to right 4th en haut
	2	right posé en avant	
	and-3	left glissade en avant through 4th	through 2nd to bras bas
	4	left grand jeté en avant landing attitude right derrière	through 5th to 2nd
	and	right glissade en avant, left through 4th	
2	1	right posé en avant	bras bas
	2	left grand jeté en avant landing attitude right derrière	through 5th to 2nd
	3	right glissade en arrière, left 5th devant	
	4	right jeté dessus turning to the right to face 7	bras bas
3		repeat bar 1 to other side, travelling to upstage right corner	
4	1	left posé en avant	bras bas
	2	right grand jeté en avant landing attitude with left derrière	through 5th to 2nd
	3	left jeté dessus turning to the right	
	4	right jeté dessus to face 2	bras bas
5-16		repeat 1-4 alternating sides	

Kirsten Ralov entered the Royal Danish Ballet School in 1929, at the age of seven. She also studied separately with Alexander Volinine, Vera Nemtchinova, Anna Severskaya, Vera Volkova, and Antony Tudor in Paris, London, and New York. She danced with the Royal Danish Ballet from 1940 to 1962, as a principal dancer from 1942 on. She danced in almost all the Bournonville ballets, and had leading roles in the international repertoire, including *Petrushka*, *Les Sylphides*, *Swan Lake*, *Symphony in C*, *Concerto Barocco*, *Widow in the Mirror*, *Aurora's Wedding*, *Le Beau Danube*, and others. She has toured extensively in North America, both with a group of soloists and with the Royal Danish Ballet, and has toured South America with the solo company. She has staged and directed ballets in Canada, New Zealand, Germany, Sweden, Switzerland, and Denmark. Ballets choreographed by her have been presented by the Royal Danish Ballet and by Danish television. Ms. Ralov is a teacher with the Royal Danish Ballet and is frequently a guest teacher abroad. She is president of the Bournonville Council in Copenhagen. She was made Knight of Dannebrog in 1953. In July 1978 she will assume her duties as Associate Director of the Royal Danish Ballet. (*Photo by Mydtskov*)

CPSIA information can be obtained at www.ICGtesting.com
Printed in the USA
LVOW09*1521130315

430459LV00011B/94/P

9 781906 830533

The Vision Within

A Practical Introduction to Creative Visualization for use in the Primary Classroom

Catherine Caldwell

Publisher's information

Published by Brilliant Publications
Unit 10,
Sparrow Hall Farm,
Edlesborough,
Dunstable,
Bedfordshire,
LU6 2ES

Website: www.brilliantpublications.co.uk
General information enquiries:
Tel: 01525 222292
Fax: 01525 222720
Email: info@brilliantpublications.co.uk

Written by Catherine Caldwell
Illustrated by Brilliant Publications
Cover illustration by Caroline Ewen
Printed in the UK

Printed ISBN: 978-1-905780-73-0
ebook ISBN: 978-0-85747-128-4
First published 2010
10 9 8 7 6 5 4 3 2 1

Related books by Brilliant Publications:

Into the Garden of Dreams	ISBN	978-1-897675-76-2
Positively Me!		978-1-903853-13-9
Smiling Inside, Smiling Outside		978-1-903853-73-3
100+ Fun Ideas for Creating a Happier Classroom		978-1-905780-76-1

Contents

Preface

I am passionate about the value of visualization techniques in calming and expanding the mind. My work with primary-aged children over the past decade has taught me that, whilst it is important to equip children with academia, life skills are the lasting impression we should and will impart. The stressful society in which most of us now live and work confronts our future adults with the challenge of balancing mind, home and work. My hope is that teachers can support this task and journey by providing the art of meditation into their pupils repertoire of life skills.

I would like to thank Brenda Golding; holistic therapist and creative meditation specialist, for giving me the inspiration and self-belief to write this book.

Introduction

Reasons for incorporating 'visualizations' into classroom teaching

There has been much research and development within education in recent years, on the importance of stimulating and motivating the brain and the body to achieve optimum learning. Whether this be through widespread daily classroom brain exercises, drinking more water, employing accelerated learning techniques or physical aerobic activities to balance and coordinate the senses. However, I purport that meditation-based activities are equally important. Calming meditative activities that relax the body and, in turn, stimulate the imaginative aspects of the brain can wake up the creative potential of our brains. The visualization activities in this book provide ideas for such relaxation and meditation work within the classroom environment.

Visualization can be used on many different levels to develop the individual child and enhance the curriculum. Visualization techniques and journeys of the mind allow children to expand and explore their creative minds and therefore extend imaginative and creative thinking processes; as now identified by the DfE as a key aspect of learning within education. Visualization affords the opportunities to teach children how to relax and reflect on their own thoughts rather than simply relying on external stimuli to relax. This, in turn, will undoubtedly provide a valuable long term life skill of being able to individually relax when required, reflect and self regulate, as children develop into adults in our ever increasingly stressful world.

Exploring visualizations and understanding how to relax the body and mind can be extremely powerful. We all have the ability to explore journeys in our minds. Some adults and children can immediately see and experience what is heard during a guided visualization whilst others may take longer to be able to fully engage with the experience. The art of visualization allows us to enter our own 'virtual realities' where our subconscious minds extend our creative thoughts. Having worked through visualizations as an adult, I have used a simplified version and techniques to guide children through familiar settings but with freedom to allow their creative minds to wander. It is important that visualizations for children are within the realms of their current knowledge of the world around them and that the children have an understanding of the vocabulary used; both for real and fantasy journeys.

Some of the visualizations within the book are short stand-alone sessions that can be used repeatedly, whilst others build upon each other over several sessions with a similar theme and structure. Use this book as a recipe book of visualizations and, as with all good recipe books, the reader will be able to follow the visualizations word for word. However, in time the reader will hopefully begin to experiment and change the contents depending on the needs in their class and with whom they are working. Also, with experience, the reader will begin to feel more confident and flexible with timings. For these reasons I have included the section 'Creating your own visual journeys' (page 58) at the end of the book. This section provides guidance on how to structure and develop your own visualization sequences.

When to incorporate visualization into the timetable

Visualization and relaxation techniques can be addressed as frequently as the timetable allows! The visualizations within this book are of varying lengths and therefore can be incorporated into a timetable in a highly flexible way. It may be most appropriate to develop relaxation within the curriculum during a specific theme or allocated term. Alternatively, visualizations may be explored at the start or end of a day for short periods of time. Visual journeys typically last for approximately 10 minutes and therefore provide an ideal teaching aid as a mental warm-up to a lesson or a plenary to reinforce or develop a session further. Many teachers already use a form of relaxation as part of the classic physical education cool down. This is an ideal time to begin exploring and investigating the art of relaxation and breathing techniques with children; although possibly not the visualization activities. Those teachers amongst us who are well versed in the art of yoga will know the value and positive experience of cool down and meditation activities at the end of a yoga session.

Creative visualizations do not necessarily need follow-up activities to complete the experience. The long-term benefits of exploring the art of creative visualization techniques may be the focus of the work. You may decide that the activity and process of visualizing is enough. The children have relaxed and experienced a quiet thoughtful journey in their mind and this alone is the learning experience. However, activities may be usefully utilized before and after each visualization in order for the children to explore their experiences further and express what they have seen whilst in a meditative state. Many children will want to share their thoughts and will find it beneficial to do so. Therefore, each visualization sequence is accompanied by a selection of possible follow-up activities. Many of the activities are generic and can easily be adapted for use with different visualizations within this book.

The creative visualizations sequences developed within this resource book are designed to be used with children aged 6–10, however, visualizations can be accessed throughout the primary years.

Linking visualization and the Key Aspects of Learning

The drive to improve standards in education has resulted in several important and wide reaching documents being created during recent years. A whole school or class focus on visualization fits comfortably within the agendas of Every Child Matters (DfES 2003) and Excellence and Enjoyment: learning and teaching in the primary years (DfES 2004); which includes a focus on the twelve Key Aspects of Learning. In approaching and integrating the Key Aspects of Learning the most obvious aspect addressed by visualization work is 'Creative Thinking'. However, of the twelve key aspects, most can be developed through meditative style work. Furthermore, the widely used Social and Emotional Aspects of Learning (SEAL)(DfES 2005) resource advocates the use of visualizations within some of the specific modules of work.

Creative thinking

Creative thinking involves using our imagination and developing our own original thoughts and ideas. Whilst children are guided through each visualization, they must imagine and develop each scene for themselves since each visualization is led by words without pictures. The words therefore act as a guide for images which will be as unique as the individual mind in which they are constructed. The visualization presents a stimulus for children to develop their own thinking.

Information processing

Information processing involves collecting and comparing a range of information from a variety of sources. During a visualization pupils are required to mentally sort and process familiar and abstract information that is provided in an oral form. Information is added from the listener by drawing upon first-hand experiences which are then processed for that individual listener to comprehend and to make sense of the happenings within the visualization.

Enquiry and problem solving

Enquiry and problem solving involves questioning and answering in relation to our surroundings and the wealth of everyday scenarios with which we are presented. Visualizations afford an occasion for children to explore their own imagination. This is achieved through the inclusion of questions during the visualizations, for example in Colours (pages 52–56); and after visualization through the utilization of open questioning in the follow-up activities, for example The beach (pages 13–16).

Reasoning

Reasoning involves supplying opinions and making informed choices. During the visual sequences, scenarios are posed and each child will create their own solutions. The children must make reasoned decisions based on limited information, for example the clothes they choose to wear during The seasons (pages 31–38).

Evaluation

Evaluation involves making judgements and unravelling experiences. After completing a visualization journey the children are encouraged to evaluate their own thoughts and share their views. Furthermore, through this sharing process they support one another in the interpretation of each other's ideas.

Communication

Communication involves all the skills related to spoken and written language. Visualizations can be viewed as individual 'role play' in the mind where children act out scenes and images that involve all of the senses. By listening intently to the reader (usually an adult) children are developing their auditory processing skills. Whilst some children will comprehend every word and be able to follow precisely what is heard during the first reading, others will hear and perceive just a few limited elements on a first reading and they will begin to strengthen familiar images and successfully start to incorporate other images upon further readings.

Social skills and empathy

Social skills and empathy involves developing relationships and an understanding of others. The development of social skills through visualization largely takes place after the visualization as children verbally share in a common experience. Children can be encouraged to listen, value the ideas of others and recognize similarities and differences between their journeys.

Self-awareness and managing feelings

Self-awareness and managing feelings involves having an awareness and appreciation of our own thoughts and emotions.

Through visualizations children are required to individually reflect on their own feelings, favourite objects, favourite colours, etc. These individual and largely independent reflections allow opportunities for children to gain a better understanding of the self.

Introduction

The feelings and emotions addressed through this book are of a positive nature and therefore afford occasions for children to identify their feelings in response to positive language. Children are also required to identify reasons linked to particular feelings which can then be further developed into strategies for positive management of emotions.

Motivation

Motivation involves positive engagement and persistence with an activity. The process of following a visualization sequence intrinsically involves zero failure learning if presented within a framework where the expectation requires that children listen to and possibly remember some aspects of the journey. Initially the listeners do not need to actually see the objects and scenes presented but merely to hear the words and, as with hearing a story from a book, begin to understand some elements of the story. This approach means that children are motivated to remember their own thoughts and their own responses to different stories and all pupils can therefore have some degree of success with the process of visualization.

Each visualization sequence is accompanied by a series of suggested follow-up activities. Each activity has been cross-referenced to the key aspects of learning to demonstrate how integral they are to the art of visualization.

Breathing to relax

Preparation for visualization

Read the following relaxation exercise using a slow and low tone of voice. Depending on the dynamics of your classroom, children may either be lying on the floor or sat at tables, hence the alternatives at the start of the relaxation exercise.

Lie on your back or rest your head on your arms and the table in front of you. Make sure you feel comfortable ... wriggle your body around until you feel comfortable.

Now that you are lying or sitting still, close your eyes and let your body become nice and floppy.

You are beginning to relax. Now let's make our bodies nice and calm. Focus on your breathing ... think about your breathing ... about the air going in (*pause and hold own breath*) and out (*pause as you breathe out*) ... in (*pause and hold own breath*) and out (*pause as you breathe out*).

Take a nice big breath and hold it (*breathe in loudly so that the children can hear it*) ... and breathe out (*blow out so that the children can hear it*).

Let's do that again ... a nice deep breath in (*breathe in loudly and slowly to model the breathing*) ... and breathe out, nice and slowly (*breathe out loudly and slowly to model the breathing*). Think about the air coming in through your nose and travelling all the way down into your lungs ... breath in ... and going out through your mouth ... travelling all the way back up from your chest to your mouth ... breathe out ... and again ... coming in through your nose ... breath in ... and going out through your mouth ... breathe out.

(Now pause before beginning to read chosen visualization sequence.)

Waking up

Ending visualization

Pause for at least 10 seconds to mark the end of the chosen visualization sequence before reading the following wake up exercise.

Now begin to focus your mind on your breathing again ... air coming in *(pause)* ... and out *(pause)* ... air coming in *(pause)* ... and out *(pause)*.

On your next breath in take a deep breath (*model a loud breath*) ... and breathe out (*model loudly*) ... and again ... breath in *(pause)* ... and out *(pause)*.

Keeping your eyes closed we are going to slowly start to wake ourselves up. Begin to move your toes a little bit ... and your ankles *(pause)*.

Begin to stretch and wriggle your fingers ... and wrists.
Now move and stretch your legs ... and now your arms as if you have just woken up *(pause)*.

Keeping your eyes closed ... sit up when you are ready *(pause)*.

Now gently rub your face with the palms of your hands to wake up your face ... and open your eyes when you are ready.

The beach

Start with 'Breathing to relax' sequence (page 11) followed by:

You are standing on a beach ... a quiet, peaceful beach. All you can hear are the waves lapping gently on the sand ... swoosh, swoosh, swoosh ... slowly forwards ... and slowly backwards ... slowly forwards ... and slowly backwards.

(pause)

You can feel the sand between your toes. Screw your toes up and see the sand push up between them. The sunlight feels warm on your face. You feel happy inside ... you are smiling with happiness.

The sea looks lovely and cool. You walk into the water and let the gentle waves wash over your toes ... that feels really nice. The water looks so clear and cold ... go on bend down and let the cold water run through your fingertips.

(pause)

You spot something moving in the sand ... take a closer look ... oops, there it goes scuttling off into the sea.

(pause)

What's that noise behind you?

(pause)

Turn around and see if you can work out what it is ... is it an animal ... or a person ... or maybe something else?

(pause)

It feels lovely being so close to the sea ... standing on the sand. Breathe in deeply and smell the salty sea air. There are two seagulls above you ... their wings look so graceful as they move slowly through the clear blue sky. They beat their wings and fly gracefully over the water.

(pause)

Look far out onto the horizon where the sky meets the sea. There's a ship way out at sea moving slowly across the horizon. I wonder where it is going ... I wonder where it has been. You can't hear it ... it's too far away ... but you can clearly see it as small as a toy boat on the waves.

(pause)

Pause for a moment and look around you so that you can remember what you have seen.

(pause)

It's time to leave the beach now ...

End with 'Waking up' sequence (page 12).

Extending the activity

Preparation

'The beach' provides a wonderful visualization to be used during a topic or theme based on the seaside or after the summer holidays at the start of a new academic year. Before reading the sequence initiate a discussion about the seaside to check which children have first-hand experience of going to a beach. It is very likely that most children will have been to a seaside resort, but for those who have not had this experience, it is important to provide some knowledge either through role play, displayed images, etc. Explore the textures related to a beach before reading this visualization sequence. This will be particularly useful in familiarizing younger children and could be conducted through child-initiated play in sand and water.

Follow-up

- **Creating images**
  (creative thinking, motivation)
  Children could draw images of what they have visualized with pencils or pastels, or collage. Create watercolour washes and collages with textured materials related to the beach using sand and PVA glue. Once the basic scene has been constructed the children can then add their additional character or object that they met towards the end of the sequence. This can be a separate moveable image which is detachable and can be altered in response to any reflections after each reading of the visualization.

- **Introducing perspective**
  (information processing, problem solving)
  The ship on the horizon is an opportunity to teach perspective. Make comparisons between the actual size of a beach creature such as a crab and the size of a ship when placed next to each other (see resource sheets A & B, pages 17–18). Look at their relative sizes when shown in photographic or drawn images with a foreground and background. Discuss how 'perspective' reduces the size of the ship to the same size, or smaller, than the crab. Ask the children to work individually or in pairs to construct a beach scene with a foreground and a background. Draw or collage different sized objects that can be placed in the scene to depict their relative sizes and distances from one another.

'The beach' visualization

★ **What did you see?**
(empathy, communication, information processing)
Engage in speaking and listening activities after the visualization so that children can converse about one another's interpretation of what they have seen. Many children will see additional objects and animals to the ones they have heard in the visualization reading and will be keen to share their experiences and encounters with the class. Provide time for children to work with talk partners and feedback ideas to the rest of the class.

★ **Questioning the scene**
(information processing, creative thinking, evaluation, reasoning, self awareness)
Stimulate further thinking through higher order questioning linked to the creative thinking of the sequence:

What did the sand feel like when you screwed up your toes?
What did you see moving in the sand and where did it go to when it scuttled off?
What was the noise behind you?
How do you know what it was – did you see it?
If you could have stayed on the beach, what would you have done next?

★ **The noise behind me**
(communication, information processing, evaluation, creative thinking)
The beach sequence can be used as a stimulus for creative writing. This could simply be descriptive, writing about the individual beach that each child visited during the visualization, or could be extended to describe the senses that are aroused and touched on during the visualization; sight, smell, sound, touch. This can be linked to literacy-based work on adjectives, similes and metaphors. Older children could develop poetry and story writing linked to 'The noise behind me' and explore questions in order to create an opening or ending for a narrative text (see resource sheet C, page 19).

★ **View from above**
(enquiry, creative thinking, information processing)
Ask the children to work in pairs and imagine that they are the two seagulls. Describe the beach scene from the sky as an aerial view and focus on the child stood on the shoreline. Extend the scene to include objects and events in all directions; what is happening to the north, east, south and west? Who else is on the beach? Why are they there?

Resource A

Comparing foreground images

Resource B

Comparing background images

Resource C

Beach question frame

Name: ____________________

Date: ____________________

The noise behind me
What could the noise be?
Who is making the noise?
Where is the noise coming from? Which direction?
Why is it at this beach?
How does the noise make me feel?
What should I do next?

The magic butterfly garden

Start with 'Breathing to relax' sequence (page 11) followed by:

You are standing in a garden ... a quiet, peaceful garden ... and at your side is an animal ... a friendly animal ... it might be your favourite animal ... it might be your pet ... a dog or a cat ... or an imaginary creature.

(pause)

Begin to walk through your garden and look around. You pass a willow tree. The long leaves of the willow tree move gently in the breeze ... and the silvery undersides of the leaves catch the sunlight and shine.

(pause)

You can smell the sweet scent of flowers growing in the flowerbeds either side of you. Your animal friend begins to walk around the garden ... go on follow it ... it's safe here in your garden.

(pause)

Find a nice place to lie down on the ground and stretch your legs out in front of you. It's really relaxing here in the garden ... your own special peaceful place.

(pause)

You feel something land on your nose ... look, it's a beautiful butterfly with purple and yellow wings.

(pause)

Look, there's another butterfly landing on your toes ... with red and green coloured wings. The two butterflies begin to flutter around your head. Watch as they move back and forth in front of your eyes.

(pause)

A third butterfly joins them ... and lands on your elbow. It's wings are shades of blue and orange.

(pause)

They are magic butterflies and they tell you that it's really lovely that you have visited their garden.

Take time to just lie and listen to the sounds in this magical garden where the butterflies live and play.

(pause)

It's time to leave the garden now ... so you sit up and your animal friend comes to join you. You slowly stand up and walk back to the place where you were standing at the start. Take a final look around this peaceful, quiet garden before you leave.

End with 'Waking up' sequence (page 12).

Extending the activity

Preparation

'The magic butterfly garden' has obvious links to nature and minibeast-based science themes. Before reading the visualization it may be useful to explore different types of leaves and the differences between the top and underside as seen when looking at the willow leaves. During the visualization journey the children smell the scent of flowers and need to be familiar with the appearance of a range of flowers. Take a nature walk around the school grounds, encourage the children to identify different flowers and to study their shapes, colours and scents. Get the children to make comparisons between wild native flowers in the local area and flowers which have been planted or sown in these natural surroundings, in preparation for this sequence.

Follow-up

- **Mathematical patterns**
  (creative thinking, information processing)
  Display a variety of enlarged photographs of butterflies and identify the symmetrical patterns on their wings. Expand the children's use of mathematical shape language by describing the patterns seen. Children can then apply this information whilst developing their own butterfly patterns and describe the details using identified shapes or geometry terminology (see resource sheets D and E, pages 24–25).

- **Contrasting colours**
  (creative thinking, information processing)
  Each butterfly is described using two colours. These are the complementary colours as seen on a colour wheel; yellow and purple, red and green, blue and orange. The butterflies provide a starting point for learning complementary colours and how each primary colour is paired with the opposite secondary colour on the colour wheel. The children could imagine and describe a fourth and a fifth butterfly with different colour combinations depending on the type of garden they create in their minds; eg hot colours, cold colours, shades of one specific colour that is dominant in their garden.

* **Organizing the journey**
(information processing, creative thinking, reasoning, evaluation)
Utilize a range of visual organizers (such as spider or venn diagrams) to help children interpret their observations whilst in the butterfly garden. Ask the children to recall and discuss their journey into the butterfly garden with talk partners. Use a spider diagram, or similar visual organizer, to record ideas of what was seen in each child's garden. The children could sequence the events and experiences along a simple recount timeline and use this information to compare and contrast their individual experiences with one another using comparison organizers; for example a Venn diagram.

* **Animal character portraits**
(evaluation, reasoning, managing feelings, creative thinking)
Question the children about the animal friend that they chose to accompany themselves into their gardens. The children are asked to make a relatively quick and spontaneous decision regarding the animal and during the visualization the creature features as a secondary and largely insignificant character. However, the animal is important from an emotional perspective since it provides security for children when they are in the garden, thus making this visualization feel safe, non-threatening and not lonely. After visualization, without discussion, get the children to sketch their animal friend and briefly write a character description. Ask the children to evaluate their feelings towards the creature; How did you feel having a companion? Why do you think you chose this particular animal? Did it go anywhere whilst you were lying down? Where do you think it might have gone? etc.

Resource D

Bufferfly outlines

Resource E

Bufferfly outlines

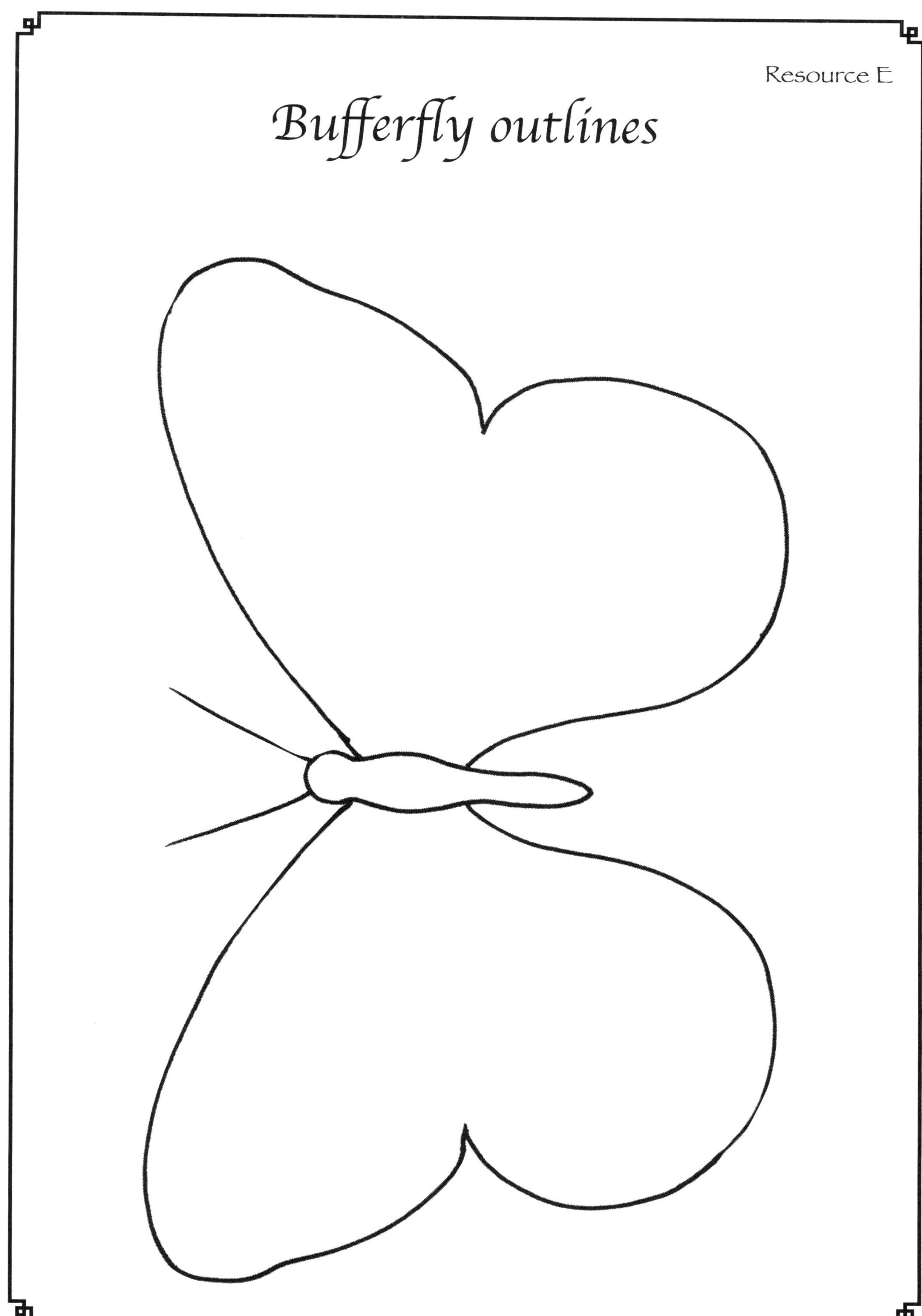

The forest of sounds

Start with 'Breathing to relax' sequence (page 11) followed by:

Take a step forward, you are now inside a forest. Look up at the trees and see the canopy of leaves hanging over, high above your head. Take a walk forward into the dappled light ... leaves cover the forest floor beneath your feet like a soft carpet.

(pause)

A squirrel runs out across in front of you. He stops frozen ... looks at you ... and quickly scurries up a tree. Breath in deeply (*model a deep breath*) and smell the cool air all around you. The air smells damp ... smells of rotting leaves.

(pause)

There are large trees either side of you. Stretch out one of your hands and touch the bark with your fingertips. Feel the bumpy and uneven texture as you run your hands across it. Listen carefully ... there are birds tweeting at each other across the trees.

(pause)

Walk on a little until you can hear a stream ahead of you ... and then suddenly it comes into view. As you get closer to the stream you see the light bouncing off the water as it races quickly over the rocks and pebbles in the bottom of the stream.

(pause)

Kneel down by the stream and breath in deeply (*model a deep breath again*). Feel refreshed by the cleaner and fresher air near to the water. Dip your hand into the stream ... and let the cool water move through your fingertips ... pushing against your palm.

(pause)

Look into the clear water ... can you see your reflection?
How do you feel right now?

(pause)

It's time to walk back now ... back to the edge of the forest. So stand up and gently shake the water off your hand. As you begin to walk back through the forest the sound of the stream becomes fainter ... and fainter ... and fainter ... until you no longer hear it. Listen instead to the sound of the leaves crunching beneath your feet and the birds tweeting to one another across the trees.

(pause)

You are nearly back to the edge of the forest ... back to where you started your walk. Turn around and glance back at the forest one more time before you leave.

End with 'Waking up' sequence (page 12).

Extending the activity

Preparation

'The forest of sounds' has been developed to focus on a range of senses but is primarily aimed at exploring children's auditory memory in relation to visualization techniques. Conduct a sounds walk of the school grounds in preparation for the visualization. Sounds are often a neglected sense when focusing on different aspects of descriptive writing. Take the children around the school grounds to specifically listen to the environment. What sounds would they expect to hear? – Make predictions before the walk. Use ICT to record sounds from different locations around school; can other children identify the sounds and locations? Discuss what sounds were heard that they did not expect and sounds which were not identifiable. Encourage the children to use the language of 'sounds' during descriptive story writing and brainstorm familiar sounds that relate to different types of settings.

Follow-up

- **Fantasy forest**
  (communication, creative thinking)
  As a class, read through the 'fantasy' version of the forest visualization: (Resource sheet F, page 30). Identify which aspects of the sequence have been changed and altered. Discuss what other creatures could appear in an imaginary forest; for example unicorns, elves, own fictional creatures. Provide opportunities for the children to create their own story setting based on the forest visualization. Talk about possible characters and fantasy experiences, as modelled in the fantasy version of the sequence, before writing their own settings. Share the new fantasy forests during subsequent visualizations.

★ **Reflections in water**
(enquiry, information processing)
Focus on the reflection in water element of the visualization. Explore different materials in which to see a reflection – metal, water, mirror – link to materials-based topic work in science. Develop reflections art work by sketching and using watercolours to demonstrate blurred and rippled lines as might occur in a reflection seen in water.

★ **Wildlife research**
(*enquiry, information processing, empathy*)
Research wildlife native to forests in the British Isles. What else could we possibly encounter, other than the squirrel? Use library books and the Internet to explore what the children already know and what they would like to know about British woodlands. Repeat the visualization and include some of the fauna and flora discovered during research.

Resource F

Story setting based on 'The forest of sounds'

As she entered the forest, she looked ahead of herself through a tunnel of bowing branches. Although the forest was full of trees it did not seem dark or frightening. And then, quite suddenly, she noticed something rather surprising and unexpected. The leaves which hung heavy as a canopy above her head were painted in all the colours of the rainbow. The leaves beneath her feet were faded shades of their former selves.

Suddenly, an elf peered out from behind the trunk of a tree. The girl ran over to greet him, but he had gone – disappeared into this mysterious forest. There was a freshness in the air, but a freshness that was tinged with sweetness. The girl walked on excitedly wondering where this fantasy forest would lead her. She then realized that she was not alone. One of the trees to her left appeared to be watching her. She spun around suddenly and within the gnarled twisted shapes of the bark she noticed that the tree was grinning at her. She smiled back and continued happily on her journey.

Ahead was the sound of a stream. But this was no ordinary stream. Just like the rest of the forest, the stream was truly magical in nature. Over the rocks and pebbles ran golden water. The sunlight which broke through the trees bounced in brilliant rays off the surface of the water ...

Winter

Start with 'Breathing to relax' sequence (page 11) followed by:

There's a garden in front of you with a swing in the middle ... a large horse chestnut tree stands in the corner. Walk over to the swing and sit on it ...

You are sitting on the swing ... push yourself backwards and begin to make the swing move ... swaying forwards and backwards and (*pause*) ... forwards and backwards (*pause*).

It's winter time. Feel the cold air on your face. Look at and feel the clothes you are wearing ... , you're wearing a thick hat, a warm scarf and cosy gloves. What else are you wearing to keep you warm on this wintry day?

(pause)

Look down at the snow on the ground. It is pure white. The horse chestnut tree in the corner of the garden is bare ... there are no leaves on it today but you can clearly see the thick rough bark on its trunk.

(pause)

The snow looks too inviting to just leave it untouched. You're desperate to play in it. Go on ... jump off the swing ... and scoop up some of the snow into your hands. Press it together ... really firmly ... and start to make a snowman. Roll the snow to make the body.

(pause)

Next make the head.

(pause)

And now add any other parts or features that you would like your snowman to have ... arms ... eyes ... nose ... mouth.

(pause)

Finish making your snowman and then stand back and have a really good look at him. He looks fantastic ... you've done a really good job and you should feel really proud of yourself.

(pause)

It's time now to leave this winter garden. So go and sit back on your swing ... and take one final look around.

End with 'Waking up' sequence (page 12).

Spring

Start with 'Breathing to relax' sequence (page 11) followed by:

There's a garden in front of you with a swing in the middle ... a large horse chestnut tree stands in the corner. Walk over to the swing and sit on it ...

You are sitting on the swing ... push yourself backwards and begin to make the swing move ... swaying forwards and backwards and (*pause*) ... forwards and backwards (*pause*).

It's spring time. Feel the warm sun on your face and feel a light cool breeze through your hair. You're wearing a jacket ... and your favourite clothes. Take a look at yourself ... these are the clothes you always feel really comfortable in.

(pause)

Push your feet into the air to make the swing go a bit higher. Notice the fresh green grass on the ground beneath you ... and the yellow trumpets of the daffodils bobbing in the breeze. The horse chestnut tree in the corner of the garden is covered in large green leaves and they move in the wind like large hands waving at you (*pause*) ... this makes you giggle inside.

(pause)

Put your head back a little bit and look up at the fluffy white clouds in the pale blue sky. It has been raining but has stopped now and the rain and the sunshine have left a beautiful rainbow arching through the sky ... past the clouds and trailing off down to the ground in the distance.

(pause)

Breathe in deeply and smell the beautiful flower perfume that's filling the air in the garden. You can see something moving by the tree ... it looks like a rabbit ... yes, it's a rabbit ... its body is curved over with a smooth dome of fur across its back. It looks up at you ... twitches its nose and then carries on nibbling the grass.

(pause)

It's time now to leave this spring garden. As you sit on your swing ... take one final look around.

End with 'Waking up' sequence (page 12).

Summer

Start with 'Breathing to relax' sequence (page 11) followed by:

There's a garden in front of you with a swing in the middle ... a large horse chestnut tree stands in the corner. Walk over to the swing and sit on it ...

You are sitting on the swing ... push yourself backward and begin to make the swing move ... swaying forwards and backwards and (*pause*) ... forwards and backwards (*pause*).

It's summer time. Feel the hot sunshine on your skin. What are you wearing today? Summery clothes to keep you cool in the heat?

(pause)

A butterfly flutters past you and gently lands on a flower near to the swing. There's luscious green grass and clover covering the ground ... you can smell the clover ... and almost taste that sweet nectar. You notice more butterflies and some bumble bees busying themselves in the clover, bright yellow buttercups and red poppies that lie ahead.

(pause)

What's that gentle noise in the tree? There's a bird singing softly. Other birds begin to join in. Watch the birds as they hop between the branches and chatter to one another. The horse chestnut tree in the corner of the garden is heavy with leaves and bright green prickly husks. It feels really peaceful in the garden ... you feel happy and content. Go on – swing a bit higher. The higher you go the happier you feel ... forwards and backwards (*pause*) ... forwards and backwards ... feel the warm air brushing passed your cheeks and moving through your hair.

(pause))

It's time to leave this summer garden now ... so begin to slow the swing down ... slower ... slower ... slower ... until it stops ... and take one final look around.

End with 'Waking up' sequence (page 12).

Autumn

Start with 'Breathing to relax' sequence (page 11) followed by:

There's a garden in front of you with a swing in the middle ... a large horse chestnut tree stands in the corner. Walk over to the swing and sit on it ...

You are sitting on the swing ... push yourself backward and begin to make the swing move ... swaying forwards and backwards and (*pause*) ... forwards and backwards (*pause*).

It's autumn. Feel the air ... breathe the air ... crisp and cool against the back of your throat. What are you wearing today? Maybe something to stop you from feeling chilly?

(pause)

Take a nice deep breathe of the air ... it fills you with energy to keep you swinging ... forwards and backwards (*pause*)... forwards and backwards. Listen ... there's a dog barking in the distance and then suddenly ... quiet. All you can hear is the rustling of leaves and the wind whistling through the garden.

(pause)

The sun is low in the sky and the clouds are tinged with grey. The leaves on the horse chestnut tree are beginning to fall in shades of red and yellow. Beneath the tree you can see shiny brown conkers breaking out of the shells they have grown inside. One of the conkers is very large ... you really want it. Slow the swing down and jump off ... run over to the horse chestnut tree and carefully pick up the husk which has the large conker in. Ooh ... be careful ... it's very prickly. Gently ease back the husk that surrounds the conker and take it out. Wow ... it's so smooth and shiny ... it will be perfect for playing with later.

(pause)

It's time now to leave this autumn garden. So go and sit back on your swing ... and take one final look around.

End with 'Waking up' sequence (page 12).

Extending the activity

Preparation

The four seasons are frequently utilized by teachers in a variety of contexts throughout the academic year; aspects of autumn are often used for harvest festivals and aspects of summer are used during holiday and seaside topics. 'The seasons' visualizations can be used individually throughout the year to fit in with such topics or as a block of creative work linking to themes, such as time in mathematics or weather in geography. In preparation for this set of visualizations, explain to the children that they will be entering a season and depending on the time of year, it may or may not be the current season.

Follow-up

- **Seasonal poetry**
  (creative thinking, communication)
  'The seasons' visualizations present an opportunity to engage the children in poetry writing. Traditionally the seasons have often been used as the basis of poetry writing to explore the differences seen in the outdoor environment throughout the year or as a traditional acrostic poem using the letters of the words Autumn, Winter, Spring, Summer. These visualizations allow a different approach with the children using the senses they experience in their minds, which in turn, will draw on their real first-hand experiences of each season. The poem on Resource sheet G (page 39) has been written using a repetitive structure and is based on the Autumn visualization sequence. Read through the poem as a whole class and identify which sense is the focus for each verse. Point out the last line of each verse uses a question to gain a response from the reader. Use the writing frame Resource sheet H (page 40) for the children to develop their own individual or group poems linked to one of the season visualizations.

- **Instructional writing**
  (communication, reasoning, information processing)
  The 'Winter' visualization can be linked to instruction-based literacy work. As the children slowly construct a snowman in their mind they are thinking through a sequence of events and the order needed to create the snowman. Children can use the instruction writing frame on Resource sheet I (page 41) to sketch or draw the order for creating their snowman.

★ **Seasonal comparisons**
(information processing, reasoning)
In looking at each season children can compare and contrast the differences between the seasons as viewed from the swing in their own visual gardens. Venn diagrams offer a quick and accessible way for children to jot down ideas and use higher order thinking skills to compare the similarities and differences between the two seasons selected. Enlarge the Venn diagrams from Resource sheet J (page 42) and complete in small groups after a visualization.

★ **Weather investigations**
(reasoning, enquiry, information processing)
The sun and rain elements seen during the Spring sequence can be investigated further with older children through the water cycle.

★ **Get dressed for the season**
(creative thinking, self awareness, reasoning)
During each visualization the children are asked to choose appropriate clothing for the season. After visualization, with talk partners, children should discuss their choices and provide reasons for wearing particular items of clothing. Use Resource sheet K (page 43) to make a list of the clothes and give reasons, ie gloves to keep my hands warm during winter, and Resource sheet L (page 44) to draw the appropriate clothes onto the body, add on hair and face details.

★ **Tree and leaf study**
(information processing, enquiry)
As a class, choose a tree in the school grounds to study throughout the year; preferably deciduous. Periodically discuss and record changes that occur in each season and draw conclusions as to why these changes have taken place. Make a collection of leaves during each study period to compare over time in relation to colour, shape and size. A large scale tree could be displayed with four branches to represent the four seasons. Changes that are observed throughout the year can then be displayed on the respective branches – changes in leaves, fruits, etc.

★ **Musical inspiration**
(motivation, evaluation)
Visualizations are often enhanced when accompanied by low-volume instrumental background music. Use each of the 'Four Seasons' compositions by Vivaldi and play either whilst reading each visualization or after visualization when reflecting and evaluating what has been seen.

★ **Garden planning**

(creative thinking, reasoning, information processing, self awareness)

Children will have visited and journeyed through the same garden setting four times after experiencing all of the season visualizations. Ask the children to draw a map of their garden. Discuss the common features that will appear in everyone's garden, eg the horse chestnut/conker tree, the swing, a flower bed. Encourage the children to add extra features that appeared in their mind each time but that are not part of the original visualization text.

★ **How does it feel to be there?**

(managing feelings, self awareness, information processing)

Explore different aspects of each season through mime work. This can be done prior to listening to each visualization or after the children have experienced being in the garden. Sit in a circle and use mime to act how it feels to pick up a prickly horse chestnut/conker husk. Demonstrate how to carefully peel back the husk and edge out the new conker from its skin. Let the children slowly mime this same action. Get the children to exaggerate each action and ask them to evaluate how they feel. Repeat by miming other situations from the visualizations: for example, building the snowman or approaching and stroking the rabbit.

'From my swing' poem

Autumn swing

From my swing my eyes catch
The polished wood of conker fruits
Earthy colours – golden and orangey brown
Will your eyes catch these too?

Swaying forwards, backwards
Forwards, backwards.

From my swing my ears find
The crunching of dry leaves
The cry of a far off creature
Will your ears find these tunes?

Swaying forwards, backwards
Forwards, backwards.

From my swing my tongue savours
The ripe blackberries, succulent yet piercing
The crisp apple, sweet yet sharp
Will your tongue envelop these flavours?

Swaying forwards, backwards
Forwards, backwards.

Silence.

Still.

Resource H

'From my swing' poetry writing frame

Name:

Date:

________________________swing

From my swing my eyes________________________

____

____

Swaying forwards, backwards
Forwards, backwards.

From my swing my ears________________________

____

____

Swaying forwards, backwards
Forwards, backwards.

From my swing my tongue ________________________

____

____

Swaying forwards, backwards
Forwards, backwards.

From my swing my fingers ________________________

____

____

Swaying forwards, backwards
Forwards, backwards.

From my swing my nose ________________________

____

____

Resource 1

Instructions for a snowman

Name:

Date:

1. Roll the snow to make the body ...	2. Next make the head ...
3. After that add other parts ...	4. ... or features ....
5. Finish making your snowman	6. Stand back and have a really good look at him ....

Resource J

Season Venn diagrams

Name:

Date:

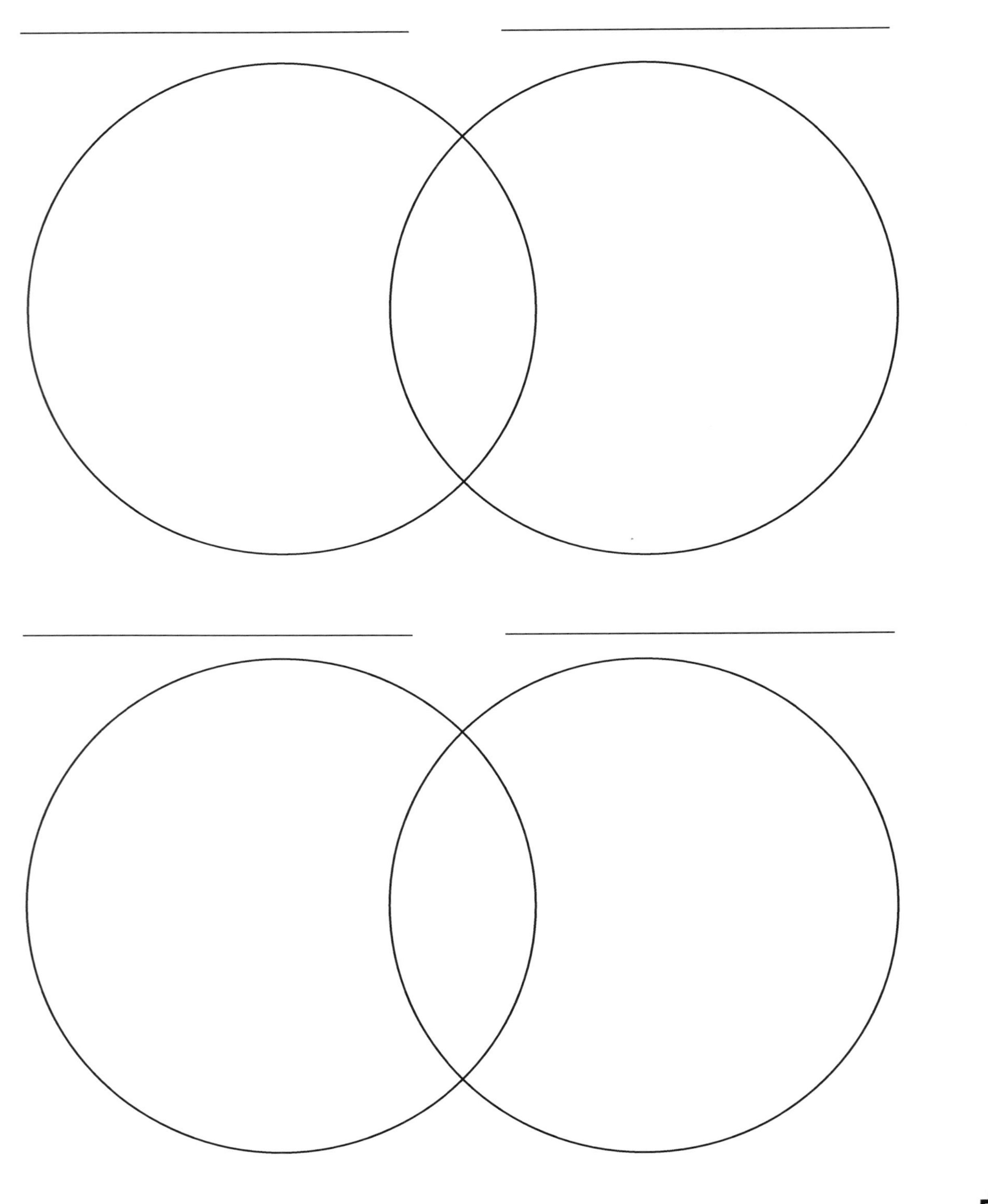

Seasonal clothes

Name:

Date:

Winter	Spring
Summer	Autumn

Resource L

Seasonal clothes

Name:

Date:

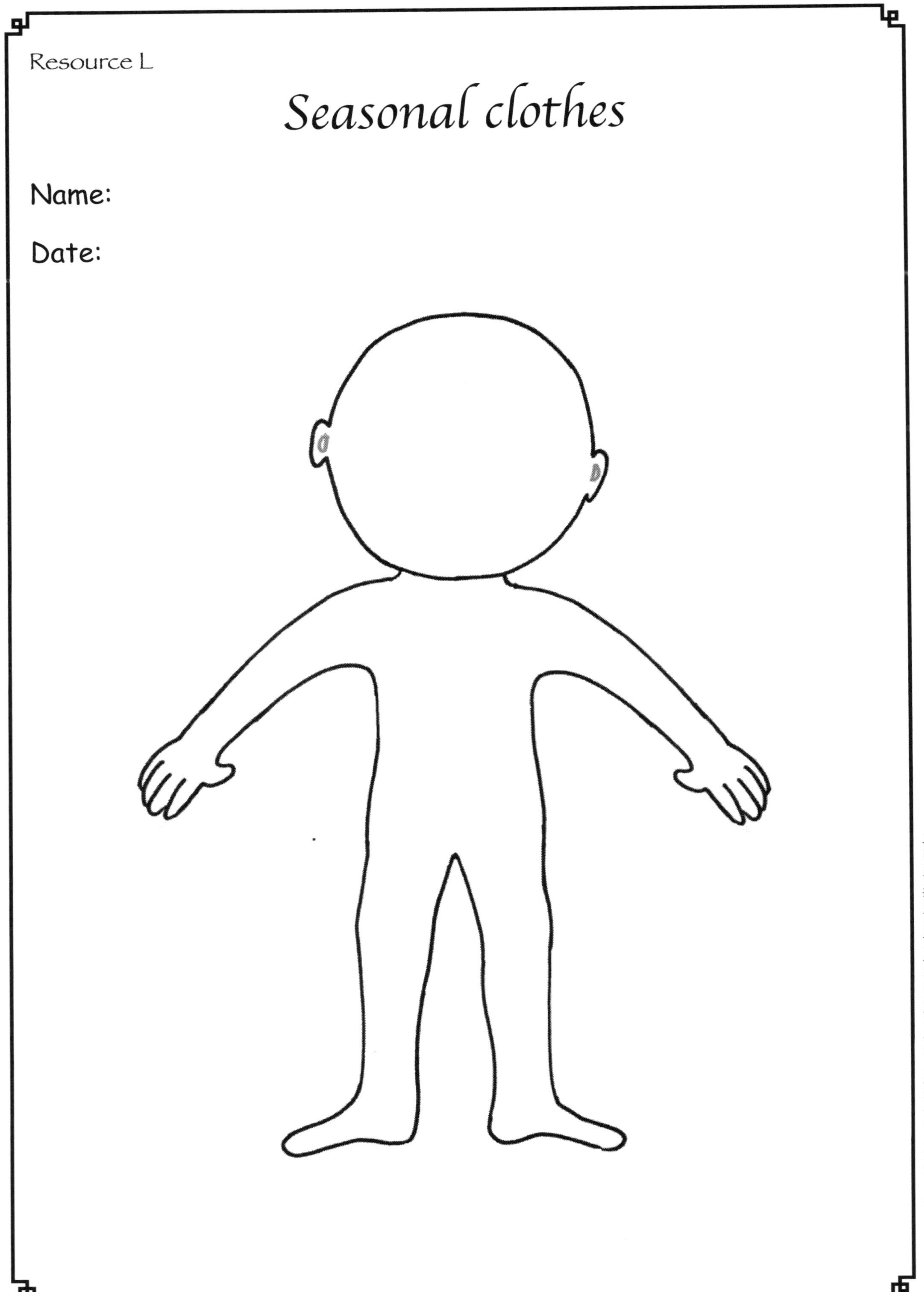

Changing shapes

Start with 'Breathing to relax' sequence (page 11) followed by:

Imagine you are holding a ball shape in your hands ... in front of you ... a sphere.
It might be still or maybe it is slowly spinning around. It is a soft pale purple colour. Notice that there are no corners or edges ... it is completely smooth and one continuous curved surface.

(pause)

Watch carefully as the sphere changes into a cube shape and the colour changes from purple to blue. Move the cube shape ... a box shape, around in your hands. Run the palms of your hands over the flat faces ... six faces. Count them in your mind. Run your fingers along the edges and pause each time your finger reaches a corner.

(pause)

Watch carefully as the cube changes into a triangular-based pyramid and the colour changes from blue to yellow. It's a tetrahedron ... four triangular faces. Move the pyramid around in your hands. Touch the sharp pointy corners and neat edges ... run your fingers along the edges where two faces meet.

(pause)

The pyramid is going to change into a different 3D shape now ... a shape that you choose. The colour is changing as well ... into your favourite colour.

(pause)

Look, your shape is starting to grow in your hands. Carefully place your 3D solid shape on the ground in front of you. Watch as it continues to grow ... getting larger ... and larger ... and larger ... until it is big enough for you to step inside.

(pause)

Step inside your shape and sit down on the floor. All the colour from your shape is going to gently shower down onto your body like fine rain ... it feels wonderful being covered in your favourite colour.

(pause)

It's time to leave your shape now ... so stand up and carefully step outside of your 3D shape. Watch as your shape slowly gets smaller ... and smaller ... and smaller ... until it is small enough to fit into your hands again.

End with 'Waking up' sequence (page 12).

Sparkle

Start with 'Breathing to relax' sequence (page 11) followed by:

Look in front of you. You can see something sparkling in front of your eyes. It looks like twinkling glitter ... colours of gold and silver ... purple and red ... against a dark, dark, black background.

(pause)

It's a firework display with colour streaming across the night sky. With the next bang, a burst of green sparkle fans out like a flower from a single point ... and then it... disappears. Watch ... another one ... bang ... burst of blue sparkle ... then it disappears.

(pause)

Next bright golden lights whizz up quickly in front of your eyes in straight parallel lines. Watch ... there they go again ... high, high into the sky.

(pause)

Look ... as pink and green lights flash around in a circle ... getting faster and faster and faster.

(pause)

And now the bursts of colour are happening again ... but this time much larger and brighter than before. Bang ... burst of colour ... then it disappears (*pause*). Bang ... burst of colour ... then it disappears (*pause*) ... and one final time now ... bang ... WOW! A huge and spectacular burst of sparkly colour fills the sky ... and then trails off and disappears.

End with 'Waking up' sequence (page 12).

Extending the activity

Preparation

The 'Changing shapes' and 'Sparkle' visualization sequences particularly lend themselves to mathematics activities. They are based around children's ability to visualize 3D and 2D shapes and patterns in their mind in relation to the names of the shapes and associated mathematical language. These form visualizations which will strengthen knowledge and reinforce understanding of the actual shapes. It is worth familiarizing children with 3D shapes in preparation for the 'Changing shapes' visualization. This sequence can be productively used after an initial introduction or revision session of seeing and holding 3D shapes and rehearsing shape names. It could also be used as a plenary to a shapes session or a mental starter for a revision lesson. Display pictures and models of the shapes to be used with their names attached. Some children require more support with recalling the structure of specific shapes when hearing shape names. During visualization offer the names of actual objects in addition to saying the names of the shapes to support instant recall of 3D shapes. For example, when introducing the purple sphere, simplified information is included by describing it as a ball.

Follow-up

- **Interpretations of shape**
  (information processing, creative thinking)
  Both visualizations support spatial awareness and work linked to geometry and transitions. This can be developed with the terminology of enlargement and translation of shapes. Drawing both 2D and 3D shapes can reveal not only what has been seen but also the angle and perspective from which it has been observed.

★ **Constructing shapes**
(information processing)
Make 3D shapes from nets using Resource sheets M and N (pages 50–51) Children should colour each net an appropriate colour corresponding to the colours seen in their own visualization. Older children could try to draw and colour the net for their own 3D shape as seen towards the end of the visualization. These net shapes can be swapped amongst the children and cut out and constructed by others.

★ **Splatter paintings**
(creative thinking)
Younger children can create splatter pictures to recreate the firework effects in the 'Sparkle' visualization. Apply small amounts of thick paint to black sugar paper and use a drinking straw to blow the paint in a specific direction. Alternatively use thinner paint on paintbrushes and throw and splatter the paint across the page or thumb through the paintbrush bristles to create a similar effect. Whilst the overall images created will not match the images seen they will resemble the abstract nature of the visualization.

Resource M

Net template for a cube

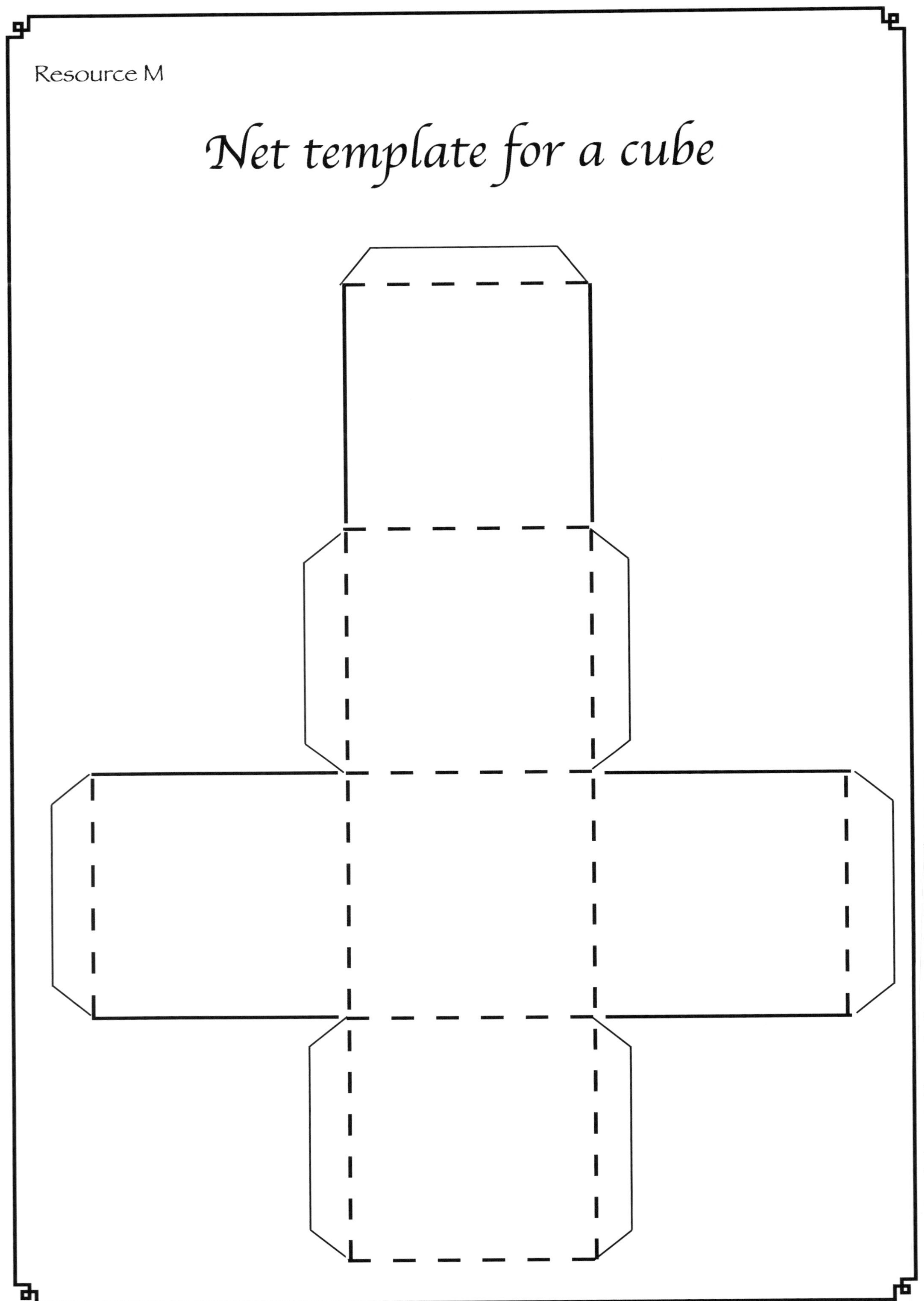

Net template for a tetrahedron

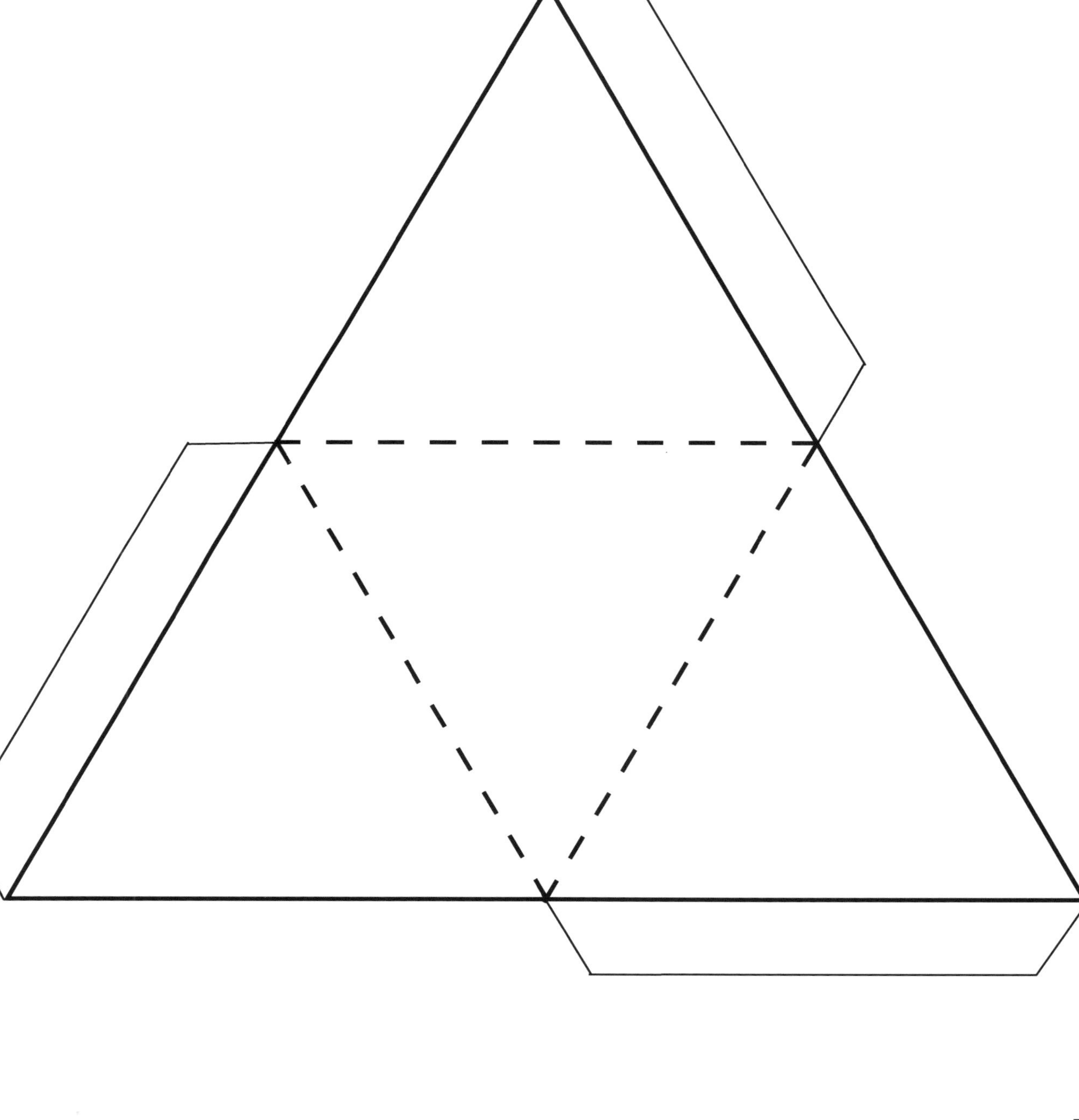

Peaceful green

Start with 'Breathing to relax' sequence (page 11) followed by:

Imagine you are sitting on a comfortable chair in a room. Today the room is a peaceful green colour. Most of the objects in your room are shades of green.

(pause)

Look around the room ... notice the pale green walls ... and the emerald green carpet beneath you. All the greens begin to remind you of natural things ... the greens of leaves on trees ... the greens of fresh green grass in the spring ... the greens of fruits ... apples, pears and kiwis. Look down under your chair ... and around the chair ... look as tiny shoots of grass grow up through the carpet.

(pause)

What objects are in your room?
Are these objects green or are they different colours?
What other shades of green can you see in your room?
Try to remember what your room looks like.

(pause)

Green is a positive colour ... it makes you feel balanced. Feel strong and happy and have a fun time with your friends today!

End with 'Waking up' sequence (page 12).

Calming blue

Start with 'Breathing to relax' sequence (page 11) followed by:

Imagine you are sitting on a comfortable chair in a room. Today the room is a calming blue colour. Most of the objects in your room are shades of blue.

(pause)

Look around the room ... notice the pastel blue colour of the walls ... and the turquoise blue carpet beneath you ... like a cool sea. All the blues reminds you of being outdoors ... like gazing up at a summer blue sky with wisps of white clouds floating across it.

(pause)

What objects are in your room?
Are these objects blue or are they different colours?
What other shades of blue can you see in your room?
Try to remember what your room looks like.

(pause)

Listen to the sound of the soft breeze moving around the room. Let your mind wander into a tranquil daydream of happy thoughts ... peaceful thoughts.

(pause)

As you begin to drift off with your thoughts, let a song or piece of music enter your mind with your daydream ... hopefully your tune will be as calm as your thoughts.

(pause)

Blue is a calming colour ... it makes you feel relaxed and able to get rid of fear. Feel calm and know that you can peacefully resolve conflicts and patiently attempt new challenges today!

End with 'Waking up' sequence (page 12).

Exciting red

Start with 'Breathing to relax' sequence (page 11) followed by:

Imagine you are sitting on a comfortable chair in a room. Today the room is an exciting red colour. Most of the objects in your room are shades of red.

(pause)

Look around the room ... notice the bright red colour of the walls ... and the burgundy red carpet beneath you. All the reds make you feel excited and adventurous. You feel like dancing or having a go at something you are normally frightened of. You don't have to stay sitting in your chair ... get up and move around the room.

(pause)

Look at your clothes ... are you wearing something with the colour red? ... perhaps you're wearing a red T-shirt, or red socks, or red shoes. If you're not wearing any red then put on something red now, I'll give you a few seconds to choose something and put it on. Maybe you would like to wear a red jumper or pin on a red badge ... you choose.

(pause)

What objects are in your room?
Are these objects red or are they a different colour?
What other shades of red can you see in your room?
Try to remember what your room looks like.

(pause)

Red is an exciting colour ... it makes you feel confident. Feel brave and know that you can succeed today in everything you do!

End with 'Waking up' sequence (page 12).

Extending the activity

Preparation

It is advisable to outline the format and discuss the different style before reading the 'Colour' visualizations. Individual colours evoke specific characteristics. Colour specialists work with the theory that each individual colour represents and communicates particular qualities. These qualities can be used in different aspects of our lives such as colour healing, the clothes that we choose to wear and the life paths we choose to follow. Individually display each colour to be looked at and initiate a discussion about the feelings that the colour evokes. Children will have preferences for specific colours so encourage analysis of those preferences: Why do you like pink so much? Is the preference linked to a favourite item in that colour? Does the colour make you feel a particular way: calm or excited?

Follow-up

★ **Colour blending**
(enquiry, creative thinking)
Individually mix colours to demonstrate the colours viewed in the child's mind. This is particularly successful when using powder paints to experiment with creating a range of shades. Cut a sheet of A4 paper into an 210mm square and rectangular strip. Use the strip to compile a sample card of shades using just one colour of powder paint and water. Children should mix a small amount of powder and water to create the colour. By adding more water the colour will begin to subtly change and become progressively lighter. Repeat until the paint is very thin and has a pale wash-like consistency. Using the paintbrush like a pencil, apply the different shades in free shaped patches over the square piece of paper. Allow each patch to touch until the paper is completely full. Extend this activity by introducing black and white powder paint to provide a wider range of colours.

Visualization sequences

★ **Imagine the image**
(information processing, creative thinking, communication)
Use Resource sheet O (page 57) to build up an image of each room from visual memory. Feedback individual responses and identify differences and similarities between the rooms. Ask the children to imagine that a still photograph has been taken of each room. What would the photographs look like? Repeat each visualization several times so that children can investigate the space further. These activities could be extended by making 3D models of the rooms with additional features added and removed depending on the colour displayed.

★ **ICT collage**
(information processing, creative thinking)
Use an ICT art programme and the Internet to cut, copy and paste images seen in each coloured room. Children can then recolour the images to the specific colour of each room visited during visualization.

★ **Word play**
(information processing, creative thinking, communication)
Play a word association game using colours as the initial word. Children take it in turns to say words associated with a specific colour. Play as a whole class or in pairs by quick firing words back and forth for a limited amount of time. The game can be extended to use words which belong to certain word categories; eg abstract nouns, verbs, etc. Words can be recorded on corresponding coloured paper and displayed for future additions. This game can be completed before visualization to give children a bank of ideas of what they might see in their room or after visualization as a means of collecting ideas and images already seen in their rooms.

★ **Musical association**
(creative thinking, reasoning, evaluation)
Discuss the songs and tunes that the children heard during the 'Calming blue' visualization. Display bands or blobs of colour on the interactive whiteboard and play a prepared selection of musical compositions from different styles and genre. Ask the children to close their eyes and listen to each piece of music. Link each excerpt of music to the displayed colours by thinking about the qualities of specific colours. Get the children to provide reasons for their choices and evaluate the choices of one another.

Resource O

Colours writing frame

Name ______________________ Date ______________

Peaceful green room

Calming blue room

Exciting red room

Creating your own visual journeys

Creating your own visualizations linked to a particular whole class theme can be an interesting way of introducing a new topic or supporting the progression of a topic. Visualization supports and develops all learning styles and thereby helps to develop the whole child in their learning.

The visualizations must always begin with a breathing exercise to calm the body and begin to focus the mind. This is an important aspect of a visualization and allows the individual to contemplate a few moments with their own thoughts and to leave behind stresses and conflicts from a previous session or activity.

Introduce the listeners to your planned scenario based upon their level of experiences associated with the topic to be covered. When working with younger children it is wise to introduce experiences with which they have some prior knowledge before widening and developing a visual journey. Older children will be able to more readily develop abstract visual journeys in their mind and develop their own images in connection with the journey you are taking them on.

Finally, visualizations must always end with a breathing exercise to refocus the mind and gently awaken the body. The importance of this aspect of the process should not be underestimated since a gradual awakening will allow the individual to more readily recall events whilst remaining in a calm state. A sudden awakening can result in children either feeling disorientated or excessively lively.

When planning your own visual journey use aspects of a topic that you are comfortable with and have enough knowledge of to develop into approximately 5–10 minutes of visualization. Always read and share the journey with children more than once. This reinforces the visual images in the children's minds and allows them to develop additional details and scenarios of their own within a safe and increasing familiar environment. As a topic progresses it may be appropriate to use an expanding vocabulary that reflects and utilizes words specific to the area being studied and explored.

Experiment and be creative as you start to journey into creative visualization. Begin to visualize and see the vision within both yourself and your pupils!

Lightning Source UK Ltd.
Milton Keynes UK
21 January 2011

166108UK00001B/2/P

9 781905 780730